JUNE FRANCIS

A Daughter's Choice

EBURY
PRESS

1 3 5 7 9 10 8 6 4 2

Ebury Press, an imprint of Ebury Publishing
20 Vauxhall Bridge Road,
London SW1V 2SA

Penguin
Random House
UK

Ebury Press is part of the Penguin Random House group of companies
whose addresses can be found at global.penguinrandomhouse.com

First published in 1997 as *Somebody's Girl* by Judy Piatkus (Publishers) Ltd
This edition published in 2015 by Ebury Press

www.eburypublishing.co.uk

A CIP catalogue record for this book
is available from the British Library

ISBN 9780091956387

Typeset in Times LT Std by Palimpsest Book Production Limited,
Falkirk, Stirlingshire

Printed and bound by
CPI Group (UK) Ltd, Croydon, CR0 4YY

Penguin Random House is committed to a sustainable future for
our business, our readers and our planet. This book is made from
Forest Stewardship Council® certified paper.

MIX
Paper from
responsible sources
FSC® C018179
www.fsc.org

'What are little girls made of?
Sugar and spice and all things nice,
That's what little girls are made of.'

Chapter One

Katie Mcleod was aware of eyes watching her: almond-shaped ones and liquid brown in dark faces, as well as blue and grey in pale faces. This part of the city had long been multi-racial even before the cry had gone out to the Commonwealth that Britain needed more workers. Katie tried to hurry but could only take tiny steps, her hips swaying seductively, as she crossed the street which had once been the boundary between old Liverpool and the hunting park of Toxteth.

She reached the comparative safety of the pavement in Hope Street, on one side of which lay the old cemetery of St James's. Her heartbeat slowed but she opted to walk on the other side where the four-storey houses of Gambier Terrace showed lights. At the far end of the terrace were the buildings of the Merchant Navy Welfare Board and clubs for seamen.

A car glided to a halt a few yards in front of her, and a woman who had been standing against a wall applying lipstick, clicked her compact shut and walked over to it. There was a murmur of voices then she slid into the car and it drove off.

Katie swayed on. She felt very alone now the woman

had gone and tried to put on a spurt – only to collide with a man who stepped out of the shadows. Her heart jumped as he steadied her and said in a foreign accent, 'I come with you and we have a good time?'

'No, thanks!' said Katie in alarm, freeing herself and smoothing the sleeve of her jumper.

'I have money.' He touched her hair. 'Preety colour.'

'Nice of you to say so but I've got to get home.' She walked on but he fell into step beside her. She eyed him warily. A sickly scent clung to him, and when he smiled he reminded her of a minor villain in a black and white film. She turned the corner into Sandon Terrace but he was still sticking with her. 'Will you go away?' she repeated, turning on him. 'You're not my type.'

He frowned. 'What do you mean? You play games with me?' He grabbed her arm and she stamped on his foot. His expression turned ugly and he kicked her in the shins.

'You pig!' she gasped, incensed, and began struggling like a wild thing as he seized her other arm.

The roar of a car coming up the steep hill shattered the evening calm. It came to a halt with a squeal of brakes. The next moment the man was being dragged away from her and there was a flurry of fists as blows were exchanged before her attacker tore free and ran down the hill.

Her rescuer turned and said in a slightly breathless voice, 'You're forrit, Katie! Ma's going to kill you!'

'No, she won't,' drawled a woman's voice from the car. 'You all ruin that girl.'

Katie ignored this and took hold of her half-brother's

arm. 'I think he thought I was one of them women . . . you know.'

'Serves you right,' said Ben Ryan, gazing down at her. 'Look at the muck on your face, and that skirt's too tight.'

'You're an old square, Ben.' She scowled at him as she fingered her shin gingerly.

'When you two are finished,' interrupted that cool female voice again, 'we're supposed to be going for a drink.'

'Coming, Sarah.' Ben turned towards the car where she sat in the driving seat, tapping scarlet-tipped fingers on the steering wheel.

Katie pulled a face but allowed him to hustle her over to the car. She would rather walk than accept a lift from Ben's girlfriend but knew he would yell blue murder if she even suggested it. Besides, her leg was hurting and Ma was going to have something to say about that!

Ben lifted her over the low door of the open-topped pre-war sports car and climbed in after her. Sarah nudged Katie in the ribs as she gave the car its head and it roared along Hope Street as if it had all the Keystone Cops after it. Katie looked at Ben and he winked.

She returned the wink and thought how nice-looking he was, with eyelashes she envied. His hair was dark gold and curled about his ears. He had Ma's blue eyes and determined chin, was stocky in build but all muscle. He was thirty-two and could have married years ago but it seemed he had never met anyone who could quite match up to the wayward, quick-tempered, vivacious but lovely

Sarah O'Neill, as the family still called her, despite her having married a Yank and been widowed.

The car screeched to a halt as it reached the crossroads by the Philharmonic Hall. Ben and Katie winced and exchanged looks. 'Mick phoned after you went out,' she said as they crossed Hardman Street.

'He did?' Ben frowned at the mention of his eldest brother who had been in the Royal Navy since the onset of the Second World War. Now, eighteen years on, he was coming home for good.

Sarah's head turned. 'When's he arriving?'

'Look where you're going!' yelled Ben as they narrowly missed hitting the pavement outside the Hope Hall cinema.

The car turned into Mount Pleasant where the Arcadia Hotel was situated and Sarah repeated her question.

'Tomorrow,' said Katie. 'He's quite old really is our Mick.'

'Seven years older than me,' said Ben.

'Why d'you think he never got married?'

Ben paused and lit a cigarette. 'Don't ask me,' he murmured. 'He's had enough girlfriends in his time.'

'Never found the right one,' said Sarah with an odd note in her voice, bringing the car abruptly to a halt. 'Out, kid,' she addressed Katie. 'We've wasted enough time chasing after you.'

Katie stuck out her tongue at her, climbed over Ben and out of the car. She blew a kiss at him before limping across the pavement and into the hotel.

Kitty Mcleod, past sixty and starting to feel her years, flung the offending tight skirt into a corner of Katie's bedroom and said, 'You'll unpick all those stitches, my girl! And I'll think twice before letting you go out to that so-called friend of yours again!'

'It's not her fault!' Katie sat on the bed with her bare legs stretched out in front of her. 'It was me who wanted to do it, and I knew if I did it here you'd kick up a fuss.'

'Too right I would!'

'See what I mean? I'm going to be seventeen soon and it's time you allowed me more freedom.'

'I gave you your freedom this evening and look what happened – you got molested!' Kitty shook her head and pressed the plaster down hard over the cut on the girl's leg, not wanting to think what might have happened if Ben had not gone looking for her. All her dreams were wrapped up in this girl whom she loved passionately. She remembered Katie entering her life as if it were yesterday . . .

It had been May 1941 and the Luftwaffe had been hellbent on wiping Merseyside from the face of the earth. For seven nights running they had rained down destruction and on the last night Celia Mcdonald had turned up, heavily pregnant and in need of shelter. She had laboured through the night, convinced she was going to die, and begged Kitty to bring up her baby if it survived. But Celia had not died. Instead she named her daughter Katherine, after Kitty, and then disappeared.

After four sons it had seemed like a gift from heaven and Kitty had brought the girl up to believe she was Kitty's own daughter. It had not always been easy, though only a few people knew the truth but Kitty still lived with the fear that one day Celia might return and claim her beloved girl.

She smiled down at Katie and slapped her leg lightly. 'Into bed with you now.'

Katie pulled down the skirt of her nightgown and yawned. She really was very tired and her stomach still quivered when she thought about what might have happened if Ben had not come along. He had always been there to protect her for as long as she could remember. She snuggled beneath the bedcovers, thinking of the others. She imagined Mick coming up the Mount tomorrow; she remembered his previous homecomings had always been something to look forward to because he'd always brought her presents. There had been dolls in foreign costume, embroidered fans, a fringed shawl, a music box which tinkled a lullaby or a waltz with a ballerina figure turning on tiptoe. His last voyage had taken in all the far-flung corners of the Commonwealth and she was hoping for a boomerang but guessed she was in for a disappointment because this family never forgot she was a girl.

In fact, it was her being a girl that her brother Jack seemed to hate most. Her senior by seven years, when she was born he was in Ireland staying with the O'Neill family on their farm where his parents had sent him at the beginning of the war, so they had not set eyes on each other until the war ended. They shared the same birthday and she had been prepared to adore him. *He was her full brother after all!* They were Mcleods! Mick, Teddy and Ben were the sons of Kitty's first husband Michael Ryan, who had died way back in the early thirties. She had not been able to understand it when Jack tore off her ribbons and hung her teddy bear by the neck from the light fitting in her room. He had taunted her, saying she was a spoilt baby and a rotten girl, and had nearly drowned her in Cornwallis Street baths. She had not split on him because she felt that would be sneaking, but one day she had come home barefoot because he had buried her shoes in the sand at New Brighton and she had been unable to find them. Ma and Pops had come down on him like a ton of bricks then and afterwards he seemed to hate her even more. When he was eighteen he left home for Edinburgh to study medicine. Since then she had seen little of him, but it still hurt that they had never been friends.

Teddy was the middle one of the Ryan brothers but she had never seen much of him because he had married before she was born and now lived in Oxford with his wife Jeannie, who was Pops' daughter from his first marriage and so was Katie's half-sister, and their two children. Relationships in the family could sound kind of complicated when trying to explain them to outsiders.

It was Ben who was her favourite and she hated the thought that one day Sarah might completely supplant her in his affections. For a moment she thought what she would like to do to Sarah, then drifted into sleep.

She was roused by the roar of a car engine and then a sudden stillness which was broken by Ben's angry voice. 'I tell you you're kidding yourself if you think you can get our Mick to marry you!'

'Will you keep your voice down?' hissed Sarah. 'I only said I was glad he was home.'

'Among other things – like his having sailed round the world while I stayed in my own back yard. That he's exciting while I'm a stick-in-the-mud.'

'It's true! I don't know why you're so offended by it. But it's not as if I'm not fond of you. I want us still to be friends.' Sarah's whisper carried straight up through Katie's open window.

'Friends?' sneered Ben. 'Thanks a lot! I want to get married. It's time I was married. I want me own place – and you're the only girl I've ever loved.'

'Shhh! That's because I'm the only girl you've ever asked out.'

'How do you know? You were missing for years. Anyway, it shows I'm faithful if that was true.' Ben had lowered his voice now and Katie scrambled from beneath the bedcovers and knelt up at the window with her elbows on the sill to listen closely.

'Oh, you don't understand women at all,' said Sarah in an exasperated voice.

'I understand you! You need to be the centre of attraction because you're the piggy in the middle in your family. Always jealous of Davy because he was a boy and resenting Siobhan because she was the baby and your dad fussed over her. Now you're jealous of Katie.'

'I am not!' Sarah's voice had risen again. 'But you *do* spoil her.'

'Well, that's only natural in a family like ours.'

'So you say. Anyway I don't want to talk about her. We were talking about us and staying friends.'

There was a silence which Ben broke. 'I suppose I'm

not rich enough? But I've worked hard, Sal! I've got money.' He sounded desperate.

'It's got nothing to do with money!' Sarah's voice was incensed. 'I married Max, didn't I, and we were broke half the time?'

'You married him because you didn't want your Siobhan beating you to the altar.'

Sarah gasped. 'That's a mean thing to say, Ben Ryan, and it's not true! I don't know why I go out with you when all you do is insult me. Just because I told you I'd written a few letters to your Mick and said I liked him, there's no need . . .'

'Letters is it now? I thought it was postcards?' he said in a furious voice.

'Well, it was letters. It was him who sent the postcards after Max was killed. Lovely ones with beaches and palm trees and sunshine. He wanted to cheer me up. He's always taken notice of me. Even when I was a kid, he never ignored me but always said nice things. I think he fancied me.'

'You're mad,' said Ben scornfully. 'Celia was on the scene then.'

'Well, she's not now!'

'It doesn't mean she won't turn up again one day.' A scornful laugh escaped him. 'Now *that* would put your nose out of joint!'

There was a brief silence before Sarah said in a muted voice, 'Saying that shows how much you care about me. Once you wouldn't have wanted me hurt. Once you were exciting and fun. We'd have a laugh and do mad things.

You made a girl feel – feel – oh, you've never even made proper love to me! I'm going home, I've got a headache.'

'But, Sarah, we did mad things because we were kids! We're in our thirties now. We're not young any more.' There was that note of desperation in Ben's voice again. 'As for making proper love –'

'We're not ninety either!' she interrupted. 'Goodnight, Ben.' There was the sound of a car door slamming and Katie dived back into bed again as the car roared down the Mount. She knew she should not have been listening, but then they should not have been arguing in the street. She expected to hear Ben's footsteps on the stairs but heard nothing, not even his bedroom door opening and closing before she fell asleep again.

Katie was sitting on the area steps eating an ice cream. She wore a green gingham blouse tucked into a pair of blue dungarees, which had been shortened with giant tacking stitches to reveal fluorescent green socks and black ballerina slippers. Her shining reddish-brown hair had lost its green plastic slides so that now it hung like a rippling curtain, almost concealing her face from passers-by. In between bites of her ice cream she sang: 'Not all the nice girls love a sailor. Not all the nice girls love a tar!'

'Yes, they do,' boomed a male voice. 'And where did you get that thing you're wearing? Does Ma know about it?'

Katie sprang to her feet. 'Mick, Mick, Mick!' She flung herself at him, causing him to drop his kitbag so he could catch her in mid-air. He was tall, dark-haired, bronzed, and despite being quite old in her estimation, still handsome. He also looked gratified by her welcome.

'Hell, Katie girl, what's Ma been feeding you on? There seems more of you.'

'I'm older and taller!' she said, sliding between his hands to the ground. 'And I'm not a kid any more so don't you forget it. I suppose I shouldn't have flung myself at you like that,' she added with a doubtful air.

'Think nothing of it.' He took up his kitbag again and there was a puzzled expression in his eyes as he gazed down at her. 'You're right! You're a young lady and I'm trying to think who you remind me of.' He slid an arm around her shoulders and continued to stare at her. Then he smiled. 'I can hardly believe I'm home for good. No more having my day ruled by eight bells. No more dog watches or middle watches, or me fancying I can see a floating mine. No more flying fish or hot springs!'

'No more white sands or blue lagoons,' she interrupted in lyrical tones, recalling postcards received.

'Aye,' he sighed because it had been a grey day in England so far. 'I'm home safe, just like that Spanish gypsy said I would be, years ago before the war. Now I've got to find meself a wife.'

Katie stared at him, thinking of what Ben had said, and muttered, 'Not you, too! And what Spanish fortune teller?'

Mick's brown eyes twinkled. 'I've never told you that tale? The one I met at the Pierhead when I was but a youth. She promised there'd be four women in my life but the one I would marry would choose me. I take that to mean I won't have any say in the matter. When it happens it'll be – POW! Anyway, who else is getting married? Not you, I bet.'

'Don't be silly! Ma's got my life mapped out for me. I'm to be mistress of all I survey!' she said in mocking tones.

'Ah, yes, the Arcadia. Us boys really were a disappointment to Ma there. I felt a bit guilty sometimes but your arrival made everything OK. She was in her element then. You were the answer to all her dreams: pink ribbons, pink frilly frocks and pink bonnets! Did anyone ever tell you she put Jack in a pink bonnet once? Pops wasn't pleased about that, I can tell you, but he was more worried about Ma than anything because it was down to her having lost a baby girl that she acted that way.'

'I never knew she lost a baby girl?' Katie was astonished that Kitty had never told her. 'How sad.'

'She probably doesn't like talking about it. Anyway she lavished a lot of love on us lot and the Arcadia.'

They both gazed up at the pink brick building with its tall windows and window-boxes filled with tulips and wallflowers.

'I remember helping make them boxes,' said Mick. 'It was round about the time Ma got married, and Celia . . .' He paused and his dark brows drew together. 'Lord, where have all the years gone? There's been a war, and people and places seem to have vanished off the face of the earth.'

'They have,' said Katie, adding, 'Who's Celia?'

'No one you know, kid. Let's go in.'

She led the way through the gate in the wrought-iron

railings and down the area steps to the family living quarters in the basement, and as she did – wondered what changes Mick's return would bring to their lives.

'So what are you going to do with yourself now you've finished?' said Pops, glancing up from polishing a boot.

'Don't be rushing him,' said Kitty, smiling at her eldest son. 'Give him time to take his bearings. I'm not getting any younger and I'd like him around for a while.'

'You're looking good,' said Mick in mild tones. 'Stuck at thirty-nine, like Bebe Daniels.'

'Don't give me that flannel. *You're* thirty-nine!' Kitty shook her head at him. 'John and I would like to retire and hand over to Katie as soon as we can, but she'll need someone older around who knows the ropes.'

Mick's eyes went from the girl's face to his mother. 'I see you're still trying to run our lives for us, Ma. You know I never wanted to be in the hotel business. As soon as I can I'm going to get my own place. I want to live a normal life, not one which has strangers coming and going all the time. Besides, I've another job in mind and I've already applied for it.'

'I was relying on you,' said his mother, looking hurt.

'Well, you shouldn't have. Anyway, what about Ben? It looks like he's here for life.'

'He's thinking of getting married,' said Pops, and winked at Katie.

She frowned. 'I don't need anyone to look after me. With decent staff, I'll cope. You've taught me so much already and the business is in my blood. It was your mother's before you and it'll be mine after you, so stop worrying about me needing someone to look after me.'

'OK, OK! Keep your hair on,' said Kitty, half-laughing at the girl's vehemence but wondering how it was that Mick could not look at Katie and see Celia and himself in her. How she loved the child, yet she wished she had some proof of Mick's being her father so she could make him take responsibility for her. Mick and Celia had been childhood sweethearts but had fallen out only to meet up again during the war when he had been on leave. Unfortunately she had never said that Mick was Katie's father but Celia *had* wanted her baby named Katherine and *begged* for Kitty to look after her child before she had disappeared, believing Mick's ship had sunk without a trace in the Atlantic.

Whatever had happened to Celia? With Katie's birthday looming Kitty always got herself into a tizz. She had intended telling Mick the truth in the beginning but what with the disruptions the blitz had caused and them spending a year in the house that had once belonged to John's grandfather in Scotland, somehow he and Jack had remained ignorant. Ben knew because he had been too young to join the forces and had been living at home serving his apprenticeship as a bricklayer by building air raid shelters.

'Who is it Ben's thinking of marrying?' asked Mick, rousing Kitty from her thoughts.

'Sarah O'Neill! She's been free the last few years. Remember I wrote and told you her husband was killed in Korea?'

Mick said abruptly, 'I'm tired myself. I think I'll have an early night.'

Kitty, who was still looking at John, turned and smiled at him. 'You do that, son. And you can tell us everything that's been happening to you and your plans in the morning. Perhaps after you've been home for a bit, you'll feel different about the ol' Arcadia?'

'Don't depend on it, Ma,' he drawled and left the kitchen.

Kitty sighed as she gazed at Katie. 'Time you were in bed, too, love. Early start in the morning. There's several new guests who'll be signing in and Eileen's expected.'

Eileen was her mother's cousin's daughter and lived in Kinsale on the west coast of Ireland where her parents, who had learnt the business at the Arcadia, now ran a hotel. The two girls had never met and Katie was looking forward to having her around, hoping that in the new-comer's company she would be allowed more freedom than she was now.

She went upstairs and for a moment stood on the landing up in the attics, which were well away from the guests' accommodation, with her ear pressed against the door of the room Ben shared with his brothers whenever they were home. She could hear movement but no voices. Perhaps one of them was in the bathroom? She knocked gently on the bathroom door but when there was no response, opened it and went inside, relieved that all was quiet on the bedroom front.

The room was tiny and had been wedged between hers and that occupied by Kitty and John when this part

of the hotel had been rebuilt during the war. She looked
at herself in the mirror and wished she looked more like
her handsome half-brothers. How could Sarah possibly
choose between them? Still, she was not going to think
about *her*.

She gazed at her reflection and into eyes which were
grey with just a hint of mauve ringed with a dark circle.
She would have preferred them to be blue. Her face was
a nice shape, though, being perfectly oval, but she hated
her freckles. 'The sun's kisses' were what Kitty called
them when Katie moaned about nobody else in the family's having them, but that didn't make her feel any better.
She wrinkled her nose, dabbed soap suds on her forehead,
cheeks and chin, and wished for a peaches-and-cream
complexion like the Lux toilet soap film stars.

Afterwards Katie went and stood on the landing again,
listening for any sound of a quarrel, but all was quiet so
she went into her bedroom.

She sat on the bed and began to give her hair a hundred
strokes with the hairbrush, gazing out of the window as
she did so at a couple of girls coming out of the YMCA
building opposite. She remembered Ben telling her the
Americans had taken it over during the war for their Red
Cross headquarters. Pops had worked for the British
branch and had often come home with doughnuts. Ma had
filled them with apple and custard and apparently,
according to Ben, Katie had loved them.

A couple came out of the building and she thought
there must be a dance on. For a moment she wished she
could have been one of those dancing away the evening

to the latest rock and roll records: Elvis, Cliff or the Everly Brothers. Photographs of all four plastered her walls but it was Cliff she kissed every night before going to sleep because Katie had never had a boyfriend.

It was as she slipped between the sheets that she heard men's voices. Immediately she was across the room and had the door ajar. 'I'm not having it,' she heard Ben say. 'She's *my* woman so you keep your smarmy face away from her!'

'I haven't been near her!' laughed Mick. 'I've been away for eighteen months, for God's sake! If you haven't been able to fix her interest in that time then you haven't got it, kid!'

'Don't call me kid, *old man*!' Ben's voice was vehement. 'You think you've only got to turn on the charm and the women'll fall for you like nine pins.'

'It has been known to happen – but you've got this all wrong, laddie.'

'Don't call me laddie either. You're not Pops! Although you might think you can rule the roost now you're home.'

'Again you've got me wrong,' said Mick, sounding weary. 'I want to get away from this place as soon as I can. Find meself a little house and a nice little wife and settle down for life.'

'As long as you don't pick Sarah for the role. There'll be trouble if you start making a play for her. I could tell her things about you . . .'

'Is that a threat?'

'Take it any which way you like, but keep away from her.'

'It *is* a threat! Big mistake, Ben. I don't like being told what to do. Especially by a kid brother whose nose I used to wipe.'

'I suppose *that's* a threat?'

'Too right it is! If Sarah wants to play games, then, dear brother, I'm ready to play,' said Mick softly. 'Now shut your mouth or you'll wake Katie and we don't want her upset, do we?'

Katie crept back to bed and it was a while before she slept, she was so upset her brothers had fallen out – and all because of Sarah O'Neill.

Chapter Two

But Katie had little time to be upset the next morning as she was rushed off her feet cooking and serving breakfast to the guests, with the help of Ruth and Jennifer, the part-time all-purpose maids. John attended to Reception while Kitty was down at the Pierhead meeting the Irish boat bringing Eileen on her first visit to Liverpool.

It was several hours before Katie had a chance to grab some breakfast herself and she was just wiping round her plate with a piece of fried bread when Mick sauntered in with a towel round his shoulders, naked except for a pair of pyjama bottoms. His hair was wet and he needed a shave. She stared at him open-mouthed, thinking she had been determined to be annoyed with him but now found it impossible. 'Ma'll have a fit if she sees you like that!'

'I know.' He yawned and scratched his head. 'Any coffee going?'

'Mick!' She swallowed a laugh. 'What about the guests? I don't know how you dare . . .'

'Don't you, little sister? He who dares wins.' Mick grinned. 'Have you seen any sign of our Ben? He got up awfully early this morning.'

'Good golly! I hope he hasn't done anything stupid.' Katie got up and spooned Nescafe into a cup.

Mick stared at her from narrowed eyes. 'What do you know?'

'Don't ask.' Katie bit her lip and added milk to the Nescafe. 'Sarah turned him down the other night,' she muttered. 'And then I heard you arguing . . .'

'Oh.' Mick gazed up at the ceiling and the sticky flypaper that hung there. 'It's more likely he's gone to work than thrown himself in the Mersey even on a Saturday, you know. Our Ben's not one to give up.'

'True.' There was a relieved expression on her face. 'Even so, if he was out that early, what's he been doing?'

'Probably walked the streets or went to the baths and had a swim. He'll be back. Now how about cooking me some breakfast?'

'The works?' she asked, relieved that he could take Ben's being missing so casually.

'Aye! Black pudding, too, if you've got it. The lot!' He'd picked up a morning paper and begun to read when the door opened and Sarah stood there.

Her face was pale and there were mauve shadows beneath her eyes. 'Is Ben in?'

'No, he's not,' said Katie coolly. 'So if you don't mind getting out of the way? We've work to do in this kitchen.'

'Temper, temper,' said Mick. 'Hello, Sarah. You're looking gorgeous.'

'I'm glad to see you home, Mick.' She sat down at the table. 'Although you're looking a bit like something the cat brought in this morning, if you don't mind my saying so?'

'Sarah, love, I've aged a hundred years since you last saw me.'

'I didn't mean you looked old,' she stammered. 'You're only seven years older than me. I just meant –'

'I know what you meant. I need a shave and to get dressed.' He took one of her hands that rested on the table and lifted it to his lips. 'Just let me drink my coffee in peace, have some breakfast, then give me an hour and I'll be a new man.'

'And then what?' she said, her cheeks pink.

'How about a spin in that motor of yours? That's if it's not going to fall apart on us.'

She hesitated. 'That would be nice.'

'Great!' said Mick. 'Katie girl, make Sarah a coffee and then leave us alone to talk.'

Katie was not going to do anything of the sort and was about to make cooking his breakfast her excuse when there were voices in the hall. The next moment Kitty entered the kitchen accompanied by a girl wearing a blue coat, navy tammy and flat black lace ups. The older woman stopped abruptly and her eyes went to Mick and Sarah, widening in an expression of pure horror. 'You're indecent! Go and get some clothes on, son, before the new guests arrive. I don't know what Sarah and Eileen must think . . .'

'I have been married,' countered Sarah with a laugh.

'That's beside the point,' said Kitty firmly, resting her hands on the back of a kitchen chair. 'Upstairs with –'

'I'm going.' Mick had risen. He kissed his mother's cheek and sauntered out, telling Katie over his shoulder to get on with cooking his breakfast.

There was silence and she was aware of a certain tension in the air, which wasn't surprising considering Mick and Sarah had been holding hands when Kitty entered the kitchen. Katie glanced at Sarah who flashed her a saccharine-sweet smile. 'Still making me that coffee, Katie, my sugar plum?'

'If I were a sugar plum, I'd hope you'd choke on me,' she retorted before turning her back. 'Ma, are you having coffee? And does –?'

'Eileen will. And, Katie, don't speak to Sarah like that!' Kitty softened the words with a smile, and putting an arm round the Irish girl, gently forced her further into the kitchen. 'Say hello to each other.'

'Hello,' said Eileen in an expressionless voice.

'Hello back!' Katie thought the girl looked like she wouldn't say boo to a goose. She had extremely pale skin, a thin nose, limpid blue eyes and very dark hair – a strand of which was wrapped round one finger which she promptly stuck in her mouth. GREAT! thought Katie. It doesn't look like *she*'s going to be much fun. Even so she leaned forward and planted a featherlight kiss on the girl's cheek. 'It's nice having you here. I'll soon show you the ropes and we'll have fun. Have you had anything to eat? Do you want some breakfast?'

'Sure, and wouldn't I like that! May I sit down, Aunt Kitty? My legs are threatening to go on me.'

'Of course you can sit down. You must be tired after

the overnight journey.' Kitty bustled round Eileen and soon had her sitting in a chair. 'You'll have to excuse me, though, love. There's guests due and I must get my coat off and relieve Mr Mcleod and see what the maids are doing. Katie'll look after you.'

Kitty hurried out, remembering how Eileen's grandmother had been the one to deliver Katie, and how her daughter Annie had worked with Celia here at the Arcadia; she hoped the two women had kept quiet about that. When women got together they talked about all sorts but she would just have to take a chance that Eileen's grandmother had kept her mouth shut about Katie's birth, and hope Eileen knew nothing about it.

Katie glanced at Sarah, whose cheekbones had a line of high colour running along them, and hoped she was feeling really guilt-ridden for having been caught holding the wrong brother's hand. Sarah's parents and Kitty and John had known each other for years and Katie had heard all about Sarah having treated the Arcadia like a second home as a child, but realised she didn't want her treating it like that now or ever again. That she didn't want her having Mick, never mind Ben. Katie wanted to get to know him better, not have Sarah waltzing off with him and breaking Ben's heart. They were her menfolk, not Sarah's, and she liked them making a fuss of her. She gave Sarah a hard stare and abruptly the older woman stood up.

'Tell Mick I've gone to do some shopping. I'll be back in an hour.' She strolled out without another word.

Katie thought, Like hell I will! And turning to the

range, put on the frying pan and reached for the bacon. She placed a few strips in the pan, forgetting Eileen was there. Instead she wondered whether to tell Ben about Sarah when he arrived home. Although come to think of it, maybe it would be best to say nothing and wait to see what happened when he discovered she had been out with Mick in that smoky chariot of hers. "'Oh, what a tangled web –'" she murmured, only to be recalled to her surroundings when Eileen cleared her throat and asked did she plan on burning the bacon as the pan was smoking?

Mick came in and asked after Sarah, and with Eileen there Katie felt she had to tell him the truth. He went out saying a mate of his had telephoned. He worked for the Salvage Corps patrolling bonded warehouses where goods were stored before duty was paid on them. Hopefully Mick too would soon have a job with Her Majesty's Customs and Excise.

Kitty was not pleased by the news when Katie told her but murmured that she supposed she had to accept that he had lived away too long not to make his own decisions. As for Ben . . . she decided, like Katie, that the least said to him about Sarah and Mick the better.

The days soon fell into their normal routine: of cooking, cleaning, shopping and informing the guests where to find bargains and what was going on in Liverpool. The Queen Mother was visiting the city soon and that pleased two American guests.

Eileen was placed in Katie's charge and proved to be

her constant shadow – something Katie was not too happy about. Eileen did not say much but somehow made her presence felt, and it was a gloomy presence. Katie was determined to escape the day before her birthday, as Ben and Mick had given her some money, and to leave the Irish girl in Ma's capable hands.

Kitty finished putting the shopping away and glanced at the clock on the kitchen wall. She had half an hour to find a place for herself and Eileen where they could see the Queen Mother. Her American guests had left half an hour ago to find a good spot to view the royal opening of the University's new School of Medicine. Not for the first time Kitty wished Jack could have studied here in Liverpool. The Royal Institute of Medicine had been opened early in the last century but had possessed scant facilities for medical education and so the school had been transferred to the Royal Infirmary earlier this century, and there thousands of lives had been saved by a doctor called Ross who discovered it was the mosquito that transmitted malaria. The curing of tropical diseases was important in a port which sent ships and men all over the globe. In those days, money for research had come from the great families and merchant princes of the city; now it came from the state.

'Have you finished there, Eileen?' Kitty turned to the girl who had soda bread baking in the oven, made from her Irish aunt's own special recipe.

'Just a minute more.' Eileen gazed at her from expressionless blue eyes. 'Where is it now we're going?' she asked in her soft Irish brogue. 'And why isn't Katie coming with us?'

Why indeed? thought Kitty, but Katie had vanished half an hour ago and she had no idea where. 'We're going to see the Queen Mother. It'll be something for you to write to your parents about.' She smiled at the girl.

'She's not my Queen Mother,' said Eileen firmly. 'We're a republic.'

'I know that,' said Kitty, realising not for the first time that the girl could speak up for herself when she felt strongly about something.

'Will Mam want to know what she's wearing?' she asked, taking the bread from the oven.

'It'll help fill a page.' Kitty went over and switched off the oven. 'Come on now or we won't see anything.'

But she could not hurry Eileen and it was ten minutes before they left the hotel. It was Wednesday but even so school children lined the pavements, despite the rain, and there were plenty of mothers with tots, and middle-aged men and women. Union Jacks fluttered in gnarled hands as well as small dimpled ones and there was a ripple of excited chatter as the news was passed along that the royal visitor was coming.

Kitty forced Eileen on until they reached a spot not far from the front of the new building and managed to drag her reluctant figure through a narrow gap in the waiting crowd, saying to those who protested that the girl had never seen royalty before and she was a visitor to the city. They were just in time. Hundreds of flags fluttered and a cheer went up as a black shiny limousine came into view. The matronly figure in cornflower blue waved graciously as she stepped out of the car and a dignitary held a large umbrella over her.

Kitty's heart swelled with affection as the Queen Mother waved to the crowd again before going inside the building.

'Is that it now?' said Eileen, twitching her shoulders with a restless movement.

Kitty glanced down at her and thought she looked pale. 'Are you OK?'

'Don't like crowds,' she said, twisting a length of hair round one finger. 'Can we go?'

Kitty took her arm and forced a way through but they had not gone far when the girl let out a shriek and collapsed on to the pavement. She went rigid, her eyes staring unseeing up at the sky. Kitty froze with shock. Then the girl began to thrash about, eyes rolling in her white face. Her breathing sounded terrible and for a moment Kitty thought she was going to die. She guessed the girl was having some kind of fit and remembered hearing there was a danger of the tongue being swallowed and the sufferer choking to death.

Trembling, she crouched on the pavement, aware that people were skirting round them. What to do? What to do? she thought frantically. What was it she had heard about spoons and them helping people to stop choking? But she didn't have a spoon. What was she thinking about?

'Can I help?' said a voice.

Kitty glanced up with a relieved expression. 'Please!'

The woman crouched beside her and turned Eileen on

to her side. She dragged off a scarf and eased it under the girl's head. 'Hopefully she'll be out of this in a minute.' She glanced at Kitty. 'Is this her first?'

'I don't know. Thanks for stopping.'

'That's OK.' The woman's clear grey eyes gazed into hers. 'I've seen this happen before. It's always frightening the first time.'

'I was thinking I'd need a spoon to put under her tongue?'

The woman's mouth curled into a smile. 'Have you ever tried to do it?'

'No.'

'You could have your fingers bitten off.' She glanced down at Eileen. 'She's coming out of it now. Give her some room.'

Kitty stood back as Eileen rolled over. Her face was ashen and her eyes dazed. Kitty hastened to reassure her: 'You're OK, love. You just had a funny turn. Can you sit up?'

Eileen did not move or speak.

'It'll take a bit,' said the woman.

'How long?' said Kitty in a worried voice. 'She'll be soaked with this rain and could end up with pneumonia.'

The woman hesitated and then said, 'Do you live far?'

'Not very. On Mount Pleasant.'

'I'll give you a hand to get her home.'

'Thanks!' Kitty could not conceal her relief.

The woman, who looked to be somewhere in her thirties, helped hoist Eileen to her feet and they proceeded to half-carry her to the Arcadia.

John was in Reception reading a newspaper. He looked up as soon as they entered and hurried towards them. 'What's happened?'

'Eileen's had some kind of fit,' gasped Kitty. 'She's wet, but if you carry her to her room, love, I'll be up soon.'

'Don't you worry, I'll see to her.' He lifted Eileen in his strong arms and left the two women staring after him.

'Poor kid,' said the woman, easing her left arm. 'But what a weight!'

Kitty's expression was concerned. 'I'm really grateful to you. You'll have a cup of tea, won't you? It's the least I can do after all your help.'

The woman smiled. 'I didn't do much. Is she your granddaughter?'

Kitty shook her head. 'My cousin's girl. I was lucky you came along. I didn't even know she took fits!'

'That's the way it goes sometimes. Some families are ashamed to talk about it.'

'But Annie and I used to be so close . . . Anyway, let me take your coat.'

'I can't stay long,' said the woman. 'I've a train to catch.'

'D'you live far?'

'Southport. I'm Rita. Rita Turner.'

'Kitty Mcleod, the owner of this establishment.' She held out her hand and they shook firmly.

'Lucky you,' said Rita, smiling.

At the sight Kitty felt something similar to an electric shock. For some reason she was reminded of Celia but before she could reason why, Rita had walked over to study a picture. 'That's a nice flower print. Victorian, I should say.'

'You're right. It originally belonged to an employer of my mother's.' Kitty hurried after her guest. 'Shall we go into the kitchen or would you rather the Smoking Room?' Kitty's voice sounded strained even in her own ears.

'The kitchen's fine,' said Rita, facing her. 'It's *the* important place in a hotel, in my opinion. People love their stomachs.'

Kitty thought Rita looked quite different now but as she led the way into the kitchen her own heart was beating painfully against her ribs and she was hoping that Katie would not be there. To her relief the kitchen was empty. 'Have a seat,' she said.

'Thanks.' Rita sat at the table and her eyes ranged the room as Kitty put the kettle on and fiddled with cups and teaspoons.

'Where did you learn how to cope in the street back there?' she asked.

'In a nursing home during the war. One of the patients used to take epileptic fits.' Rita smiled at Kitty. 'She used to shout "Flukes alivo!" and then thrash about. It was funny, frightening and pitiful all at the same time.'

'I wonder why *Flukes*?' Almost without realising she was doing it, Kitty was searching the woman's features for a reason why she should have been reminded of Celia. She tried to bring to mind the girl's thin freckled face and slender body as she had seen her before her committal to the sanatorium in Cheshire, suffering from TB, but it was difficult because that was more than Katie's lifetime away.

'That's what I wondered.'

The two women stared at each other and Kitty noticed Rita's eyes were that same clear grey touching on mauve as Katie's, and almost stopped breathing. 'It's peculiar, isn't it?' said Rita.

'What?' Kitty collected her thoughts. 'I mean, were you a nurse?'

'No, a patient. I had a fall on a train and knocked myself out. When I woke up, I didn't know who I was.'

'What!' Kitty's heart began to thump all over again. 'But you'd have had identification on you?' she said with a hint of breathlessness. 'They'd have known who you were, surely?'

'Oh, yes!' She accepted a steaming cup from Kitty. 'But for a long time, *I* didn't know who I was.'

Swiftly Kitty assimilated that information. It would explain so much about Celia's absence all these years, and yet . . . 'Do you know who you are now?' she asked earnestly. 'I mean, really know inside yourself who you are, or are there parts of your life that are missing?'

Rita took a sip of tea. 'There's still things I don't want to think about. It was painful when the memories started flooding back. Nobody came forward to claim me and I had to accept that I was all alone in the world. That fall changed me.'

Kitty did not know what to say. She could not tell simply by looking at this woman if she was the Celia she had once known. There were curves beneath the bright green and white spotted frock Rita wore and her hair was a different shade altogether, being a vibrant auburn. Her face was a perfect oval and there was hardly a freckle in sight. Of course, hair could be dyed, powder hides freckles, and weight could be gained. Could this woman really be Celia? What should Kitty do? What should she say? All she had to go on were those grey eyes so like Katie's, but Kitty had the strangest feeling that this woman was important to her. Was it her female intuition telling her this was Celia?

Suddenly Kitty was overwhelmed by a surge of conflicting emotions but the strongest of all was the instinct to hold on to what she had fought for all these years in bringing up Katie as her own daughter. 'Did you get your memory back completely?' Her voice was harsh. She barely recognised it as her own.

'You sound as if it matters to you. That's nice.' Rita smiled before glancing towards the table. 'Is that soda bread? I love soda bread. My gran used to make it. She lived off Scottie Road before she moved in with me and Mam.'

Kitty thought: Celia lived off Scottie Road *and* she had a grandmother. At that moment Kitty could have hit the woman in front of her because she was convinced she was playing games. She took a deep steadying breath. 'Please have some bread. Eileen made it.' She picked up a knife and sawed at the loaf. Unexpectedly her conscience smote her. 'I suppose I should have checked on her.'

'She'll be OK,' said Rita. 'Your husband looks like a man who can cope.'

'He is but –' How could she tell that without knowing

anything about him? thought Kitty, and forced a smile. 'He's a man and there's some things that they can't do as well as us women.'

'I wouldn't argue with that!' Rita's expression was suddenly grim. 'They're not trustworthy, some of them.'

There was a silence and Kitty wondered if she could be referring to Mick but before she could question her, Rita said, 'Does Eileen work for you? And do you have any other girls?'

Kitty's mouth went dry as she thought, What a leading question! 'Why do you ask?' she croaked.

Rita's eyes gleamed. 'I'm interested. How many rooms d'you have here? And do you have men other than your husband working for you?'

Kitty thought, If this woman is Celia, playing games with me, she might think Ben or Jack's still here. She won't know Mick is still alive because he was missing presumed dead when Katie was born. She thought how the old Celia wouldn't have played such games because she'd lacked confidence, but this woman said she had changed since her accident . . .

Kitty cleared her throat. 'What's your interest?'

Rita smiled. 'No big mystery – I work in an hotel. Southport has quite a few of them, you know. Come the season we're always looking for extra staff and Liverpool's not a bad place to snaffle them from.'

It sounded reasonable, but what a coincidence! Kitty's heart rate began to slow down. She was getting neurotic just because it was that time of year. 'Is that why you're in Liverpool today? Looking for staff?'

Rita laughed. 'Hell, no! I came to see the Queen Mother and to visit an old friend.' She rested her elbows on the table. 'Plenty of butter on my soda bread, please, if I may?'

'You may.' Kitty was feeling calmer now and spread the butter thick. 'Jam?'

'Do you have plum?'

Kitty darted her a swift glance. 'My daughter loves plum. It's her birthday tomorrow. She hasn't asked directly but has given out enough hints about wanting a record player. She loves music.'

'She's a lucky girl. How old will she be?'

'Seventeen.'

'A nice age. Does she work for you?'

Kitty nodded.

Rita bit into the bread with strong even teeth and there was silence. Kitty hoped Katie would continue to stay missing for the moment but was on pins and could contain herself no longer. 'What time's your train? You said you couldn't stop long. It's not that I want you to go but . . .'

Rita glanced at the kitchen clock. 'Hell, is that the time? I'd best get the next one.' She smiled at Kitty and said, 'You'll be wanting to have a look at Eileen. I'll tell you something, though, you're a hero taking her on. She could drop pans, anything, if she has a fit. It's real nice of you to care for her.'

Kitty sighed. 'What else could I do? She's family. I have to give her a chance.'

'Family? A good enough reason for her to stay then,' said Rita with a catch in her voice. She drained her cup and picked up her shopping bag, gazing at Kitty with a warm expression in her eyes. 'Thanks for the tea and soda bread. They've filled me up nicely.'

Kitty felt better now she was going and said cheerfully, 'Thanks for your help. I'll see you out.'

They walked to the front door and Rita paused in the hotel doorway and gazed out at the rain. 'I hope this isn't set for the summer.'

'Me too. But I should think the weather's more important to you in the seaside trade.'

'You're right there.' Rita held out a hand. 'It's been nice meeting you, Mrs Mcleod.'

'And you too. Goodbye, and thanks again.'

Kitty watched until the other woman had walked halfway down the Mount before turning and going inside. She found John in Reception. 'You're going to think me quite mad,' she blurted out, 'but that woman – I thought she was Celia for a minute.'

'You're going crazy, woman! She doesn't look a bit like Celia.'

'I know,' said Kitty ruefully. 'And her name isn't Celia, but she had the same colour eyes as Katie and there was something about her . . .' She paused before adding, 'She works in a hotel in Southport and used to live near Scottie Road.'

'Who works in a hotel in Southport and lived near Scottie Road?' asked a cheerful young voice.

Kitty jumped out of her skin and turned to look at Katie. 'Where've you been?' she said in a vexed voice. 'I could have cooked dinner the time you've been.'

'Exaggeration,' said Katie, her hands full of bags. 'I've been for my birthday presents and to see the Queen Mother.'

'So have Eileen and I!' Kitty's flaxen brows furrowed. 'Why didn't you wait? You could have been a help to me. Eileen had a fit.' She stared at Katie and was happy with what she saw. Her cheeks were flushed a becoming rose colour and her eyes sparkled with health. She hadn't done a bad job of bringing her up.

'Poor Eileen,' said Katie. 'That explains a lot. Does it mean she's not quite there?'

'I don't know!' replied Kitty with a sudden anxious quiver to her voice. 'I know next to nothing about epilepsy. Now go into the kitchen and peel the potatoes.'

'OK.' Katie gave her a thoughtful look and did as she was told.

Kitty turned to John who said, 'Stop worrying. That woman wasn't Celia. Why call herself by a different name if she was?'

'She said she'd lost her memory.'

'Then what are you worrying about? She's probably forgotten all about Katie in that case!'

'Can a mother forget her own daughter?' There was anguish in Kitty's voice.

John pulled her into his arms and rubbed his chin against her hair. 'You should have told her the truth years ago, Kit.'

'It's too late now,' she said in a dull voice.

He was silent and she lifted her head and looked at him. 'How's Eileen?'

'OK, I think. Like you, I know very little about epilepsy.'

'I could kill Annie for not telling me what to expect there,' muttered Kitty. 'What are we going to do?'

'About what exactly?' John's tone was cautious.

'At the moment – Eileen. If she has a fit in front of the guests, she'll frighten them. I'm going to have to keep her in the background and see what Annie has to say when I write to her. And what if she knows about Celia and blurts it out?'

'Poor kid.'

'That's what *she* said, that Miss Turner!'

'Forget her,' said John firmly, his arm slipping from her shoulders as the door opened and a man with a suitcase entered. John switched on his smile. 'Good afternoon. May I help you?'

Still upset, Kitty left him and went in search of Eileen but her mind was still on the mystery of Miss Turner who so strongly reminded her of Celia.

'You're looking down in the dumps, Ma,' said Mick, taking his dinner out of the oven and sitting down at the table later that day.

'I'm perfectly all right,' said Kitty, wondering how she could begin to tell him the truth about Katie. But she couldn't, so instead told him about Eileen.

The kitchen door opened and an angry-faced Ben stood there. 'Sarah's outside. She told me to tell Mick she's bloody waiting for him! What have you to say for yourself, brother?'

Mick's expression was inscrutable as he hit a bottle of H.P. sauce with the heel of one hand. 'I haven't made any arrangements. Ask her what she wants.'

'I did, and all she said was she wants you!' He dropped his rucksack on the floor by the door with a heavy thud. 'Hadn't you better go and speak to her?' he snarled.

Mick placed the bottle on the table and licked sauce from one thumb. 'Go and ask her again what she wants.'

'Will I hell! I'm not your lackey.' Ben slumped on to a chair and took out a packet of cigarettes. 'I'm bloody fed up.'

'You can put them away and have your dinner and stop swearing,' murmured Kitty. Picking up Mick's plate, she addressed him. 'And *you* can go outside and speak to that young madam. I don't know what the pair of you are playing at.'

'I'm not playing at anything,' said her eldest son, and blew her a kiss as he left the room.

Kitty put one plate in the oven and took out another to place in front of Ben. 'You tuck into that and forget women,' she said emphatically. 'Not everyone's meant to get married.'

He stared at her from tragic eyes and could only toy with his food. His heart ached with love but he was also seized by a sense of outrage. How could his brother do this to him? How could Sarah? He wished he could do something to make her sit up and see that he was worth ten of Mick. His brother would never be faithful. He'd had loads of women whilst Ben had been true blue to Sarah even after she had married.

'You're not eating,' said his mother.

He pushed the plate away. 'I'm not hungry.'

'"Faint heart never won fair lady",' she said roughly. 'Forget what I said before and think of how you can get her back.'

'I'm trying,' he said grimly.

Kitty sat down opposite him and filled two cups from the teapot. 'Eat up, son,' she said in a coaxing voice, 'and I'll tell you something that'll make you laugh. I had a visitor today and almost convinced myself she was Celia.'

He dropped his fork. 'You're joking! I mean – what d'you mean, you *think* she was Celia? She either was or wasn't.'

Kitty rested her chin in her hands. 'John thinks I'm neurotic,' she said dolefully.

'You probably are,' said Ben, taking up his fork and picking at his food. 'You always have been where Katie's concerned. You should have told her years ago who she is.'

'Don't say that!' protested his mother, through gritted teeth. 'It's what John says and it doesn't help at all.'

'OK,' he murmured. 'This Celia?'

'She called herself Miss Turner. Rita Turner. And works in a hotel in Southport. I never thought to ask the name of it.'

Ben forced himself to concentrate on what his mother was saying. 'You should tell our Mick.'

'I can't! I don't feel up to explaining the whys and the wherefores, why I did what I did and why I've never told him.'

'There's always been the chance it would come out.'

'So why didn't *you* tell him?' parried Kitty.

Ben shrugged. 'It wasn't my secret, and it was what you wanted.'

'And you know why!' She leaned closer towards him. 'There's still a stigma to illegitimacy. I don't want her being ashamed of who she was *and* I still think I was right to do what I did. She's turned out well, hasn't she?'

'Yes, but . . .' Ben hesitated. 'If you'd told Mick, he might have gone looking for Celia, they could have got married and then Katie would have been legal.'

'It's too late to think like that,' said Kitty crossly.

Ben did not think so. If Mick and Celia got together again it would leave the way clear for him and Sarah. What a thought! Suddenly he found his appetite and the discontented droop to his mouth lifted. 'What if you're right, though, Ma? And this Miss—'

'Turner.'

'– Miss Turner *is* Celia? What if she comes back?'

'Don't even think it!' There was utter dismay in Kitty's eyes.

Ben was about to say sorry when the door opened and Mick entered. 'I told her to come back later,' he said.

Immediately Ben forgot about Miss Turner. 'I hope you're not playing Sarah along?' he snapped.

'Why should you care?' Mick's eyes fixed on his brother's face and his gaze was intent. 'She hasn't exactly treated you like the bee's knees.'

Ben's hands curled into fists and he leant across the table, growling, 'Has she said anything to you about me?'

Mick said mildly, 'Keep your hair on. Do you think I'd be spending my time with a woman listening to her talk about *you*? Grow up! Where's my dinner, Ma? I'm starving.'

Ben wanted to punch him in the face but knew that wouldn't do. They weren't kids any more. Then he thought of Miss Turner and whether she and Celia were one and the same and had a brainwave. He was going to search for the mysterious Miss Turner, and when he found her and proved her to be Celia, he would bring her back here.

The difficulty was he did not know the name of the hotel where she worked, but that shouldn't prove impossible to find if he used his nous. For a moment he considered the upset it would cause and almost changed his mind, but then he thought about Sarah and the constant heartache he lived with and of the fury he felt towards his brother. It would be one in the eye for Mick! As for his mother, she had lied from the best of motives and surely Katie would realise that? And if it proved to be that Miss Turner was not Celia, then no harm was done and Ben would have lost nothing by searching for her but his time.

Chapter Three

Celia Mcdonald hurried in the direction of the level crossing which divided the working-class Upper Aughton Road, where she lived, from the more affluent Lower Aughton Road. The barriers were down and she waited patiently for the Southport-Liverpool train to pass, watching as it rattled over the crossing in the direction of Birkdale Station. In her mind's eye she imagined it passing the golf course and sandhills towards Ainsdale, Formby, Crosby and Waterloo. She visualised passengers alighting at Litherland and Seaforth, and remembered the overhead railway, or Dockers' Umbrella as Liverpudlians had nicknamed it. She pictured the line of docks as the train approached the city, the tobacco warehouse and Bibby's factory, and could almost smell the oily odour of seeds and nuts being crushed as well as the hops and yeast from the breweries. She could imagine the Wirral coastline on the other side of the water and the ferries which crossed the Mersey. She thought of liners, tugs, dredgers, and the oil tankers going to Eastham. It was in Eastham Woods that she had walked hand in hand with Mick when they were little more than children. Today was their daughter's seventeenth birthday.

She gazed unseeingly at the barrier, her throat aching with unshed tears, remembering that day in Cheshire when they had made love in a field. She had believed he felt the same as she did but the next morning he had gone and there had been no note, nothing. She had been deeply hurt and had almost hated him then.

When she'd realised a baby was coming, she had been devastated. She had considered getting rid of the child but had heard such horror stories about backstreet abortionists that she had chickened out and told herself that at least she had her mother's wedding ring to wear, and lodgings in a house not far from the docks, and a job making armaments. She felt lonely, but then the baby quickened inside her and suddenly it was company for her. Somehow, she told herself, she would cope. Perhaps she would have, too, if the Luftwaffe hadn't started dropping bombs on Liverpool and she had not met Ben, who had been just a youth then.

She had wanted to die when he had told her about Mick being reported missing presumed dead. Being angry and let down by him was one thing; his being killed was a different one altogether. Too easily she could imagine a ship ablaze and men screaming; hear the sucking sound of the sea as the vessel plunged beneath the waves, taking him with it. She did not know how she could bear that knowledge alone. In fact she hadn't because a raid had started and Ben had insisted on her fleeing to the sanctuary of the Arcadia's cellar with him. It was there she had given birth to Katherine a short while later, but the strain of the months before and the week-long bombardment, as well as the birth, had taken their toll. How much so she did not realise until later.

The barrier lifted and Celia walked across the railway line and on up Lower Aughton Street. It was seven-thirty in the morning and she had to be at the Seaview Hotel by eight o'clock. Her mind, though, was still in the past. She had never told the Mcleods that Mick was the baby's father. She could not remember why now. Perhaps it was because it was all too upsetting to talk about, and perhaps because deep inside her she believed Mick's mother knew already.

It had been obvious to Celia from the moment Katherine was born that Kitty Mcleod had taken her to her heart. Celia had been glad about that because her own nerves were in no fit state to cope with a baby, nor did she want to stay at the Arcadia being constantly reminded of Mick. His mother had always wanted a daughter so Celia decided to leave Katherine with her until she could sort herself out.

She had left without saying goodbye in case they tried to stop her going. She had planned on joining the WRNS, not wanting to go back into armaments but to get completely away from Liverpool. She had intended writing to Mrs Mcleod when she was settled but instead had collapsed in the street and been taken to hospital. Nervous exhaustion, the doctor had said, and within a fortnight they had moved her out of the city to a nursing home in Southport where it had taken a while for her fully to recover. When at last she managed to return to the Arcadia it was deserted and its windows boarded up. A neighbour told her the Mcleods had gone to live in Scotland.

Celia had pulled herself together and returned to Southport where she had a friend whom she had met in the hospital. Rita had got herself a job working for the government, issuing ration books, and suggested Celia did the same. Gradually they had both grown stronger and after the war the pair of them sought employment in the hotel business. Rita had risen higher but Celia hadn't the confidence to be the one giving orders. She only wished she had because money was something she would have liked more of, dreaming of the day she might go in search of her daughter.

What did Katherine look like? Did she take after Mick or herself? What had his mother told her about Celia? These were questions she had asked herself over and over again, and each time she came up with the same answers and did not like any of them.

A breeze blew a strand of hair into her mouth as she passed the Ribble bus station and was removed with fingers which still shook nervously when life got too much for her. She had never been able to harden herself against setbacks, heartache and pain, and so had kept herself to herself. After one bad experience she never risked getting involved with a man again. She guessed Rita was a bit that way too, although she had never said it was a man who had caused her to remain in her spinster state. Celia and Rita were not as close as they had been once but remained friendly.

She turned into the road where the Seaview Hotel was situated and hurried up a path flanked with laurel and holly bushes to a large redbrick Victorian building with revolving doors and a recently built sun lounge. She found Rita, now assistant manageress, in Reception.

'Morning, Cessy,' she said with a smile. 'What have you done to the weather?'

'Same as usual,' said Celia. 'Forgot to pray about it. Do you think it's going to be one of those summers?'

'Who knows!' Rita handed her the pass keys to the bedrooms. 'I got soaked the other day in Liverpool. By the way, I've something to tell you when you've finished.'

'Something nice?'

'Interesting. But I'll tell you later. Old Henny's on the warpath this morning. Must have lost at bridge last night.' She turned as a woman came downstairs.

Celia hurried away to hang up her coat and found the other cleaner by the broom cupboard. They exchanged hellos but Celia did not waste time listening to her stories about her husband and children that morning but started work. Later in the day she would go to the cafe off Lord Street where she helped in the kitchen around lunchtime. Sometimes, if the Seaview got really busy, she returned later in the day and helped out, peeling vegetables and washing dishes. She even waited at table sometimes, anything to make a bit of extra money, because she had a secret vice.

Celia daydreamed as she made beds and dusted, imagining what she would do if she won the football pools. First she would tell Mrs Henshall what she could do with her job, and secondly she would go in search of Katherine and tell her she never meant to desert her. Her daughter would believe her and Mrs Mcleod would be pleased to see her. She would be welcomed into the bosom of the family and they would all live happily ever after. Then every Saturday she and Katherine would have a good old root around the clothes shops and deck themselves out in the best Paris fashions, and they would certainly go on a cruise – *if* she could win on the pools.

If Celia won lots and lots of money she would buy her own little bed and breakfast place. It was a dream she and Rita had shared in their early days in Southport. Maybe she might even meet a man and get married. Someone like Mr Pritchard who came to stay at the Seaview with his sister towards the end of summer when the Southport Show was in full swing. He was tall and well-built with a ramrod-straight back from having been a professional soldier. He had served in India in the days of Gandhi and loved to talk about it. She imagined taking tea with him in one of the posher hotels in Southport and dancing to the music of Victor Sylvester at the Floral Hall. Then he would see her home and kiss her. He had a moustache so it might tickle. Celia smiled to herself and hummed as she hoovered.

She finished her stint, returned dusters, polish, vacuum cleaner, dry mop and dustpan to their cupboard, and went in search of Rita. As she handed back the pass keys, she asked, 'Well, what is it you were going to tell me?'

Rita leant across the desk. 'What was the name of that hotel you used to work at in Liverpool before the war?'

The question startled Celia and for a moment her mind went blank. Then she pulled herself together. 'The Arcadia. Why?'

'I thought it was.' Rita smiled. 'I was there yesterday!
Remember me telling you I was going to visit Beattie who
was cook at that vicarage where I worked as a kid? Well,
I'd gone early into Liverpool because I had to be back here
pretty sharpish in the afternoon. We went shopping and had
a cuppa in Reece's, and I'd just said tarrah after we'd seen
the Queen Mum when this girl had a fit right there on the
pavement in front of me! The woman with her needed a
bit of help so I gave her a hand and it turned out she was
the owner of the Arcadia! Out of all the boarding houses
and hotels she could have belonged to, she belonged there!
What d'you think of that for a coincidence?'

'Interesting, like you said. What was she like?'

'Friendly – grateful. Asked me in for a cup of tea. She
had a husband . . . big fella . . . Scottish . . . sixtyish.'

Celia went very still. It couldn't be! 'What was their
name?' she stammered.

'Mcleod. Hers was Kitty . . . Kitty Mcleod.'

The lobby seemed to spin and Celia gripped the edge
of the desk.

'What's wrong?' Rita's voice was concerned. 'Did I
give you a shock, love?'

Celia took a deep breath. 'It's OK. It's just that I thought
they'd left Liverpool. A neighbour told me they'd left
Liverpool!' she wailed. 'I don't understand . . .'

'They must have come back. You told me it was hit
by a bomb. They must have just gone away until the
repairs were done. You know what it was like in the war.
Sometimes it could take months and months for rebuilding
to be done.'

'You're right,' said Celia, although Rita's words did not make her feel any better. Then she remembered Katherine. 'This girl, what was she like?'

'Had quite a nice face. Nothing spectacular. Mrs Mcleod mentioned something about her daughter. Do you remember her daughter?'

Her daughter? Kitty didn't have a daughter! Celia was stunned.

Rita said helpfully, 'She would only have been a tiddler when you left, wouldn't she? Although come to think of it –'

But Celia had stopped listening. She was thinking: *Her* daughter! Was that how Kitty Mcleod explained my baby away? A child of the Change perhaps? She felt raw inside, as if the older woman had taken away not only her child's identity but Celia's own as a mother. She trembled with unaccustomed fury.

'Are you sure you're OK?' said Rita, placing a hand on hers. 'You don't look a bit yourself.'

'I'm OK.' Celia straightened. Forcing a smile, she said, 'See you in the morning,' and left.

All day it was as if a storm was going on in her head. Most of her life she had felt a nobody but at least in giving birth to Katherine she'd felt she had achieved something. Every year on her daughter's birthday she had imagined Katherine at a different stage in her life. She had skipped with her to school, bought her clothes and taken her to Wales on the steamer. She had even dreamed up a boy for her first romance. That way Celia had convinced herself that in a vague kind of way she had remained part of

Katherine's life. Now she realised she never had been. Kitty Mcleod had taken her over, lock, stock and barrel.

Until that moment Celia had endured a certain amount of guilt for having left her daughter, even though she had been able to blame circumstances for her never having claimed her. She had hoped that Kitty would have explained away her having deserted Katherine as one of those things which happened in wartime. 'It was sad but your mother Celia went missing. She could have been killed by enemy action . . .' Hopefully she might have gone on to tell Katherine something nice about her. Now Celia realised it was more than likely that her name had never been mentioned. All these years Mick's mother had been living a lie!

Anger and resentment burned inside her. She felt sick at the thought that she had deceived herself all these years, and became so worked up about the whole thing that she suffered blinding headaches. She was good for nothing and had to drag herself out of bed each morning and somehow struggle through her work. The pain was so bad sometimes she thought she was going mad. She blamed Kitty for everything. Even for not having left a message saying she was not staying in Scotland for good but would be back. Celia convinced herself that Kitty was responsible for Katherine's being an epileptic. Kitty Mcleod deserved to be punished, she told herself. But how? She wanted her to suffer the mental torture she herself had been through.

Celia thought and thought and as she lay on her bed one evening, her insides heaving, scared to move her

head in case the terrible pain returned, her eyes fell on
an Agatha Christie book by her bedside. Suddenly she
had an idea and slowly rose from the bed. Holding her
head steady, she went in search of a pair of scissors.
When she found them she took a newspaper from the
small pile she kept to make up the coal fire and stared
at the banner headlines. Then she began to snip out single
letters, knowing exactly what she was going to say.

Chapter Four

Kitty closed the bedroom door behind her and took an envelope from the pocket of her apron. She withdrew the single sheet of paper with fingers that trembled slightly and read YOU STOLE MY BABY! NOW I'M COMING BACK FOR HER, SO BE WARNED.

How dare Celia? How dare she after all this time? There was a definite threat in that 'BE WARNED' which really got under Kitty's skin despite her anxiety. When she considered how hard she had worked bringing up Katie she could have wiped the floor with Celia, or Miss Turner as she called herself. But of course the woman had been too cowardly to say any of this to her face and instead had waited until she got home.

Kitty read the words for the fourth time, hardly able to believe that the Celia she had known, employed and cared for, could have written them. Not that it was signed. She turned the page over to make sure but the reverse was blank. When she thought how she had lived with all kinds of fear throughout Katie's young life she could have screamed. There had been fear of disease, of accidents, even of gypsies stealing her beloved girl away, but never had she expected to receive a letter like this! She felt annoyed with herself for being so afraid, but telling the truth was one of her house rules. She had always been strict with Katie about the need for honesty, in families and in business, and it was the thought of that which worried her the most now. She herself had lied! She had lied!

Kitty gazed down at the newsprint letters again and it struck her that it was just like one of those anonymous notes one might read about in an Agatha Christie novel. Except it was *not* anonymous so why go to all the bother of cutting letters out of a newspaper and not signing it? What had got into Celia? Had she gone off her head? Yet the Miss Turner she had seen only a few days ago had appeared sane. Were the two women one and the same or not? Surely it couldn't be mere coincidence, the letter arriving so soon after she had been here?

There was a knock and Ben popped his head round the door. 'One of the guests wants to see you, Ma.'

'I'll be down in a minute,' she murmured, not looking up.

He came further into the room. 'Are you OK? You sound a bit funny.'

Kitty looked over her spectacles and realised with a sense of relief that she was not alone in this. There was John and Ben to share it with. 'I've had an anonymous letter. Having said that, I know who it's from.'

'Talk sense, Ma.'

'Have a look.' She handed the letter to him.

Ben sat beside her on the bed and after a few seconds lifted his head. 'She must be sick. But at least it proves Celia and Miss Turner are one and the same.'

'That's what I've been thinking. Although Miss Turner appeared quite sane.'

'I think this letter's working up to blackmail,' he said. 'The next one could be "GIVE ME SOME MONEY OR I'LL TELL HER YOU'RE NOT HER MOTHER!"'

Kitty stared at him and ice seemed to slither down her spine. 'I can't believe it . . . Celia wouldn't! Real people don't do that kind of thing.'

'Of course they do. Where do you think writers get their ideas from?'

'It doesn't happen to people like us.'

'You said that years ago, but you know from personal experience it's not just in films and books that people are evil.'

'But we're talking about Celia . . .'

'She's sick in the head, Ma. She must be, taking on two personalities.' He put an arm round her shoulders and hugged her. 'Now you're not to worry. I'll find that hotel in Southport and sort her out and this'll pass over.'

'As long as Katie doesn't get to know. I want her staying here under my roof where she belongs. She could never be happy with *this* Celia,' said Kitty, screwing up the letter and pocketing it.

Nor could Mick, thought Ben, feeling low. He had tried to speak to Sarah but she had cocked her nose in the air and said they had nothing further to say to one another. Mick was still going out with her and Ben was scared stiff where it might end. At the moment, though, his main concern should be his mother and Katie. Abruptly he said, 'Ma, you could stop all this by telling Katie the truth, you know.'

'No! And don't you dare! I want her enjoying her life, not worrying about who she is because I didn't give birth to her. You find Celia and warn her off. Tell her I'll have the police on her if she carries on like this.'

And without another word Kitty walked out to deal with the guest awaiting her attention.

If Katie had known what was going on she would not have been enjoying herself at all. Being the daughter of the owner of the Arcadia and heiress apparent was a role she loved to play. That afternoon she was entertaining Eileen, for whom she felt deeply sorry now she knew about the fits, and also a young male guest. They were in a coffee bar and she found it all very exciting, as her parents considered there was something alarming about teenagers meeting together to listen to rowdy music and drink foreign coffee.

Katie gazed about her at walls lined with tightly fitted lengths of lacquered bamboo and a poster of a frighteningly large black bull and a slender matador, just above the counter where an espresso machine hissed and gurgled. She gave a deep sigh of pleasure. From a juke box came the sound of the Crickets singing 'Maybe Baby' and a group of girls swayed to the music, a couple of them lah-lahing. Every table was crammed with young people and she felt really with it, sipping frothy Italian-style coffee.

'You look like the cat who's got the cream,' said the youth, who was from the Midlands and only staying a few days before emigrating to Canada with his parents and young sister. 'You've a cream moustache. Would you like me to lick it off?'

Was he teasing? Katie did not know but with slow deliberation leaned forward, aware of Eileen's eyes on her, and closed her eyes. His tongue flicked over her upper lip which tingled while a delicious shiver raced through her. It was the closest she had ever got to a kiss from a boy.

The record on the juke box changed and Pat Boone began to croon about April love being for the very young. They gazed deep into each other's eyes and it was so romantic.

'Like another coffee?' asked Eileen loudly.

'Yes, please,' said Katie and the boy in vague voices as Pat Boone's voice soared.

Eileen scowled. She was used to taking a back seat. It was where her parents had always kept her because they were embarrassed by her fits. Sometimes they forgot she was there altogether and that way she heard all kinds of things she shouldn't. She knew all about Katie but didn't consider this the best time to let the cat out of the bag. Katie was being kind to her in her way and so was Aunty Kitty. If things should change then she might have to rethink. It sure would be a lovely thing to take over the Arcadia if anything should happen to Katie and Aunt Kitty . . . After all, having epilepsy had never stopped Julius Caesar from conquering a large chunk of the ancient world!

'Where are you three off to?' asked Ben, his expression disapproving as he took in Katie's hand nestling in the crook of a different young man's arm. This one she had met in the market on a meat stall and apparently he shared her interest in music. She was looking lovely in a primrose sailcloth shirtwaister bought with Ben's birthday money and her hair was tied up in a ponytail. There was a flush of excitement in her cheeks and she looked so young and carefree that his heart ached for her. Sooner or later life would wipe that smile off her face, he realised gloomily, thinking of Celia and Sarah and Mick.

'We're going jiving at the Rialto,' said Katie, gazing up at the youth who was tall, fair and unusually dressed in cowboy clothes which his sailor brother had brought him from America, and which he wore when playing Country and Western.

Ben raised his eyebrows. 'That's what you think! They wouldn't allow him in there in that get-up. It's proper suits and strictly tempo. Why don't you try the YMCA?'

A tinkle of laughter escaped Katie. 'You're joking! I want to go further than across the road.' She did not feel at all pleased with Ben for making her feel an ignoramus about not knowing the Rialto was strictly ballroom.

'Try the Grafton or Locarno then. They're less classy. Should be just up your street if it's bopping you want.'

'They must be squares at that Rialto,' said the youth, tipping back his stetson and staring at Ben. 'They'll be closing down if they don't get with it.'

'There's still plenty of us squares around, mate, who like to do things in style,' snapped Ben. 'You just make sure you bring our Katie home at a respectable hour or there'll be trouble. She's only seventeen, you know.'

'I'm all of seventeen which isn't young,' said Katie sweetly, because she thought she knew why Ben was like a bear with a sore head. Sarah and Mick . . . She'd like to knock their heads together. 'Next birthday I'll be eighteen and I'll tell Ma I'm old enough to take over this place. 'Bye, Ben! Come on Eileen, Dougie.' And she swept out.

In no time at all they were entering the portals of the Grafton which was situated next to the Locarno ballroom. Eileen asked why two dance halls should be so close together. Katie thought, and remembered Kitty telling her that one had started life as the Olympia cinema, and said so. This was the first time she had been in a dance hall and she could not wait to get on the floor.

Overhead a shimmering ball twirled, reflecting shards of glittering light. The band was playing a waltz to which a few couples danced sedately. It was hard to believe the dance had once been banned in England. Clusters of girls sat on one side of the room, and on the other lads talked amongst themselves whilst eyeing up the girls.

'You grab chairs and I'll get us drinks,' said Dougie.

'Orange juice, please,' said Katie, handing him some money. He protested but she insisted. So he walked off in search of the bar.

The girls gazed about them, sitting on the edge of their seats, both longing to dance. Eileen had a net skirt on under her frock and Katie felt sorry for her because they weren't as fashionable any more.

Dougie hadn't been gone long when the waltz came to an end and a quickstep took its place. Immediately some couples began to jive and the girls watched as a youth skirted the floor and came towards them. He had dark hair perfectly styled in a fashionable Tony Curtis quiff and there were black velvet lapels to his jacket.

Eileen edged forward on her seat but it was Katie he addressed. 'Are you dancing?' His green eyes fixed on her face as his jaw moved rhythmically, almost in tune to the music.

Kitty did not allow Katie to chew gum and she was fascinated by that mobile mouth. 'I'm with a fella.'

He glanced around. 'The invisible man?'

Her lips twitched. 'Very funny.'

He grinned. 'Glad you appreciate the joke. How's about it then? It's not as if I want to take a lease out on you or anything. Just one dance.'

'No, thanks. He'll be back in minute.'

'A minute'll do me.' He wriggled his shoulders and did a soft-shoe shuffle. 'Just a quick bop, love.'

Katie did her best to hide a smile, and if she had not come to the dance with someone else, would have gone with him then. There was something very attractive about that smile and those eyes.

'I knew you could crack your face if you tried,' he said, holding one hand out towards her, but before she could do or say anything Dougie appeared on the scene.

'You're bothering my girl,' he said pugnaciously. 'Scram!'

Green-eyes looked him over. 'I preferred you invisible.'

'Is that meant to be a joke?' said Dougie, and poked Green-eyes in the chest.

The youth fell back a pace. 'I wouldn't do that again if I were you,' he murmured, combing back his quiff with his fingers.

Katie glanced around and saw that people were watching. 'Stop it!' she hissed. 'The pair of you could get us thrown out! Now will you go away?' she said to Green-eyes. 'I'm sorry, but I did tell you I was with someone.'

'If that's the way you want it.' He shrugged and walked away.

Eileen got up and followed him. Katie stared after her and watched, surprised at how badly she didn't want Eileen to dance with the green-eyed youth. When she saw them go on to the floor she picked up the smaller of the drinks and drained the glass.

'You shouldn't have drunk that so quickly!' exclaimed Dougie, looking alarmed.

'Why? I was thirsty.'

'It wasn't pure orange juice. I had them put gin in it.'

Katie stared at the glass as if it had been poisoned and almost choked. 'I'm not supposed to drink! Ma would have a fit.'

Dougie sat down heavily and sighed. 'This evening isn't going the least bit the way I wanted it. I thought the place would be jumping and we'd have a real cool time.'

Katie was starting to feel bored with him but they were here now and she supposed she had to make the best of it. She smiled and said, 'Why don't you take off your hat and we can dance?'

'I like my hat,' he said defensively.

Katie gave up on him and sat with her hands between her knees, waiting for Eileen to return. It was not long before she did. Katie wanted to ask her about the green-eyed youth but there was a tight expression on the Irish girl's face which somehow put her off.

As the evening wore on, the room became hot and crowded. The main band had a break and a younger group came on stage and eventually she got to dance because a bouncer ordered Dougie to take off his hat. As they jived Katie was aware of the green-eyed youth who had now taken to the floor with a girl whose hairstyle was startlingly like his. She wore a get-up much like the one waiting to see the light of day in Katie's wardrobe and, oh, how she envied that girl as the green-eyed youth jived with her as if to the manner born! She found herself blushing as his gaze suddenly caught hers, and looked away.

It was a relief when the last waltz was called and Katie glanced at her watch, wanting to dump Dougie as fast as she could. 'It's time we were going, I didn't realise it was so late. I'm going to cop it!' she said.

'Don't be a wet,' said Dougie, suddenly coming alive again and pulling her into his arms. 'We might as well stay to the end and have a smooch.'

'But people are starting to leave.'

'Let them.' He was suddenly very forceful.

'I'll dance with you,' said Eileen, flashing him a smile.

He looked at her disparagingly and without a word dragged Katie on to the dance floor. 'You could have danced with Eileen,' she muttered. 'That was unkind.'

'She's a gooseberry. Why did she have to come with

us?' he muttered, and pressing Katie against him, slobbered all over her neck.

After that she couldn't get out and home quick enough but to her dismay the queue at the bus stop was enormous. 'I'm walking,' she said. 'You coming, Eileen?'

'I'm coming too,' said Dougie, draping an arm round Katie's neck so she felt weighed down, much to her annoyance.

They headed past the registrar's office and the Hippodrome cinema towards Low Hill, accompanied by a stony-faced Eileen.

They were not the only ones walking. Katie could hear snatches of conversation and songs from the hit parade.

'Lollipop' mingled with Perry Como's 'Magic Moments', as well as a duet rendition of 'Hopalong Cassidy'. She guessed someone was taking the mickey out of Dougie and hoped he would ignore it, but some hope! Although it took a 'Where did you get that hat?' to make him turn and tell them to shurrup.

'The cowboy's getting tough,' said a girl's amused voice.

'He's not a cowboy,' added a male one. 'He's just pretending.'

'You!' said Dougie, clenching his fists. 'I might have known it would be.'

'Psychic, are you?' said Green-eyes.

'Perhaps he's an alien if he's not a cowboy?' said the girl, whom Katie now recognised as the one wearing the satin blouse and tight skirt, the one Green-eyes had danced with. 'You'd better watch it, Patrick. He might zap you.'

'Emperor Ming, you think?' Patrick smiled at Katie before his eyes came to rest on the youth at her side.

'Oh, you're so funny!' said Dougie, taking a step forward. Katie moved in front of him, not wanting them to fight. He tried to dodge round her but she shifted with him. 'Get out the way, Katie,' he yelled. 'I'm gonna punch him on the nose.'

The other girl's eyes widened. 'Touchy, isn't he? Will he remove his hat first?'

'Shut up, Bernie! Can't you see he's got no sense of humour?' said Patrick, eyes gleaming in the lamplight. He doubled his fists. 'Katie, let me at him.'

'No! You mustn't fight,' she said in a persuasive voice.

'No?' He dropped his arms and then unexpectedly caught her by the waist and swung her out of the way. 'But he wants to fight me,' he said. 'And I'm not chickening out.'

'But I'll be in deep trouble if I don't get home soon,' she said, struggling to free herself, but he was strong and that gave her a thrill.

'Where's home?' he said, breath fragrant with chewing gum.

'That's none of your business!' yelled Dougie in a fury as he attempted to drag her out of Patrick's grasp. The next moment Katie was on the ground and the two youths were trading punches.

Katie got to her feet, rubbing her hip and glancing round. She noticed that Eileen had vanished and wondered what to do next, then decided there was nothing she *could* do. So she watched the fight, eyes sparkling. She really didn't want the two of them to hurt each other, but what girl wouldn't find a certain amount of pleasure in the sight of two fellas grappling over her? Because she felt sure *she* was what this was all about.

Then a voice spoke and spoilt all her pleasure. 'Katie, you're not going to be allowed out for a week after this! Ma'll have your life!'

'Oh, hell!' she muttered, facing Ben and catching sight of Eileen at his side.

'He's the one causing all the trouble,' said the Irish girl, pointing at Patrick. 'Be careful, Ben, he might have a bicycle chain under his collar.'

'Don't be daft!' cried Katie, gazing at her in astonishment. 'He's not that kind of bloke. It's an act.'

But Ben had made his move and, seizing the pugilists by the back of their collars, forced them apart. For a moment their arms still flailed as their feet sought a securer hold on the pavement. 'You bloody onions!' shouted Ben. 'Think you're tough, do you? I'll show you what tough is! Turning the other cheek and walking away. Now shake hands and act like gentlemen.'

'You're jokin'!' said Dougie, managing to tug himself free. 'He was trying to pinch my girl.'

'One date does not make me your girl! So *you* can go home,' said Katie, incensed. She turned on Ben. 'Did you come looking for me?'

'What do you think?' he said.

'Oh!' she groaned. 'Why can't you accept I'm grown up?'

'Because you're not,' said Ben, throwing his arms up in the air. 'Doesn't what's just happened prove it?'

Patrick combed back his hair and stepped forward. 'It wasn't her fault.'

'I can believe that,' said Ben, shaking his head as he looked down at him. Dougie had made his exit. 'But the last thing she needs is someone like you around. Now, hop it.'

'Ben!' cried Katie, seizing his arm. 'He didn't do anything. It was –'

'Go on, blame Dougie,' said Eileen promptly. 'You know you were flirting with this other fella.'

Katie was flabbergasted. What had got into her? She stared helplessly at Patrick, who gave her a twisted smile. 'I wish it was true and you *had* been flirting with me.'

'Leave it, Patrick,' called Bernie, who was standing a few yards away, huddled into her coat, 'We'd best be going. You're going to get in trouble as it is with the state your jacket's in.'

He nodded but faced Katie once more with his hands firmly wedged in his pockets. 'Sorry, love. I didn't mean for it to get out of hand.'

She smiled. 'I know. Perhaps some other time . . . I live at the Arcadia Hotel.'

'See you around then.' He returned her smile and walked away.

Katie sighed.

Eileen said, 'Thank God for that. *He's* trouble.'

Katie turned on her and hissed, 'And what do you know about anything, coming from the backwoods of Ireland?

I'm really disappointed in you, I thought we were friends.'
She tucked her arm into Ben's and said in forlorn tones,
'Let's go home. And if Patrick does come round, you
won't frighten him away, will you?'

'I'll think about it. But really, you're too young, Katie,
to be having boyfriends. Think of the Arcadia. You've got
enough on your plate there.'

She nodded. But still hoped Patrick would call.

Chapter Five

There had been no more anonymous letters and Kitty was hopeful Celia had had second thoughts about what she had written. Even so during the first wet weeks of June she was all for Ben's searching her out, which he was doing with the help of the Southport Guide. She needed to know what Celia was up to because not knowing was causing her continuous sleepless nights.

Ben had sacrificed several of his Sundays so far but without any success. Near the beginning of the Guide it stated that Southport came into existence in 1792 when a small hotel called The Duke's Folly opened. For his purposes it would have been better if the town had not grown so much since then. He ran a finger down a page, considering where to go next. He had never believed it would be easy tracing the hotel but neither had he thought it would be so difficult. From page thirty-seven to eighty-eight were listed hotel after hotel, and following on from those were the names of boarding houses.

He had already tried several of the grander places such as The Clarendon in Hesketh Park – terms: seven and a half guineas weekly, sea and golf course at rear. *Comfort our keynote, service our pride*! His mother would have been interested in seeing what they had on offer. He had also visited The Prince of Wales which was situated on Lord Street and had four stars, was AA recommended and fully licensed. He had tried numerous smaller ones, walking the length of Lord Street which owed much of its charm to its Victorian architecture and leafy appearance, and tramping in the rain along Argyll Street and the Promenade.

It was sunny for once as he walked up the drive of a hotel called the Seaview in one of the lesser roads. He went through its revolving doors and entered a quiet reception area carpeted in pine green with a gold leaf motif. Its walls were painted in eau-de-nil and white. Soothing and tastefully decorated, he thought.

Behind a pale oak reception desk sat a middle-aged woman with her head bent so close to an open book that her narrow nose almost touched its pages. She did not look up as he walked towards her so that for a moment he wondered if she had dozed off, but as he reached the desk she said, 'Look at that figure! Would you say it's a five or a three?'

Ben's eyes followed her pointing finger. 'Five,' he said.

Her brow knitted. 'I thought it was three.' She slammed the book shut and blinked at him and he noticed she had a faint moustache. 'What can I do for you?'

'I'm looking for a Rita Turner. Does . . .?'

'Is she a friend of yours?'

Ben was so surprised at getting a positive response it took him several seconds to answer. 'So she does work here?'

'A Miss Rita Turner works here.' She looked disapprovingly down her nose. 'It's her day off, though, and I don't encourage followers.'

'I'm not a follower.' Ben's smile had a singular charm. 'Miss Turner knew my brother. He went missing during the war, was believed dead, and they lost touch. It's a sad story, Mrs . . .?' He paused.

'Henshall. Mrs Jemima Henshall.' She thawed slightly. 'I'm a widow and life can be so difficult for us widows. I've often wondered if Miss Turner lost someone. I've tried to encourage her to talk but –'

'She clams up?'

'A crude way of putting it, but yes. In fact, one could say she's downright secretive about her past.'

Ben felt a stir of excitement. Miss Turner and Celia had to be one and the same. He *had* to have her address but would Mrs Henshall hand it over? Perhaps if he laid it on with a trowel . . .

'My brother Mick was badly wounded and his mind affected after being afloat in a boat on the North Atlantic for weeks. He gets really down and I feel sure some of it's due to losing touch with Ce—' He caught himself up quickly. 'Er, Rita. Could you give me her address?'

Mrs Henshaw fixed him with an eagle-like stare. 'I'm sorry, Mr . . .?'

'Ryan. Ben Ryan.'

'Mr Ryan, it is not my policy to give out the addresses of my staff, but I tell you what I shall do – I'll inform Miss Turner that you called and then she can get in touch with you.'

'I'd much rather you gave me her address,' he said in what he hoped was a winning tone, but she was adamant.

'I have to protect my staff. It is possible she no longer feels anything for your brother and your visit could be an embarrassment. Now, if you don't mind, Mr Ryan, I have work to do. Good day.'

Ben accepted his dismissal with a show of good grace and thanked her. If nothing else, when the woman told Celia about his visit it would probably put the wind up her. He just hoped she wouldn't do a bunk.

As he walked out by the revolving door Celia came out of the lounge with a duster in her hand. 'Who was that?' she asked. 'There was something familiar about him.'

'He's no one you know, Celia,' said Mrs Henshall dismissively, adding sharply, 'Just because I'm giving you extra hours, it doesn't mean you have to know everything.'

'Yes, Mrs Henshall. I'm going off now. I need to darn some stockings.'

'Yes, yes! You go. You're looking pale. Go along to the pier and get some fresh air. But I want you back this evening. Oh, I do so hate it when Rita has a whole day off! It constricts me and I don't like being constricted. If you see her on your travels, tell her a man's been here asking for her.'

A man? Celia wondered who it could be as she fetched her outdoor clothes. She tied a chiffon scarf over her hair and thought about what Mrs Henshall had said about being constricted because Rita wasn't there, and imagined a boa constrictor choking the life out of the woman. She had seen one at the zoo once and had never forgotten being told they could eat animals whole. It had fascinated even as it sickened her because she could not get out of her mind a picture of the animal dying all of a piece in the snake's stomach, unable to get out.

She walked towards the front and found Rita playing cricket with her landlady's two children.

'Throw it! Throw it!' shouted the boy, Sammy, jiggling about on the sand as if he had ants in his pants.

Rita sent the rubber ball sailing through the air in the direction of the wicket and he caught it and sent the bails flying. He crowed with delight and Celia clapped her hands. 'Howzat!' she cried. Rita glanced in her direction and waved.

'It's not fair!' cried the boy's sister, Marie, dropping the bat and plonking herself on the sand. 'I'm not playing any more.'

'That's a relief!' said Rita, collapsing on to a towel. Celia sat next to her and gazed at the children, thinking of Katherine. She had lost her nerve after sending that one note to Kitty Mcleod but now could not stop thinking about her daughter.

'I hope you're not here because you've a message from ol' Hennie?' asked Rita, pulling a cardigan about her shoulders.

'She said a man's been in asking for you.'

'A man?' The smile faded from Rita's eyes. 'You must have made a mistake. I don't know any men who know where I work.'

'Can I have a swim?' said Marie, tugging at her frock. 'I'm hot an' sticky an' I need a swim.'

'You can't swim here,' said her brother scornfully. 'The sea's that far out, it's disappeared!'

'It's too cold even if the tide wasn't out,' said Rita.

Celia looked towards where the sea should have been and thought that was what made a mockery of the hotel's name. More often than not there was no sign of the sea and that was something she missed. Just as she had missed her daughter growing up. Her gaze fixed on the little girl as she threw a handful of sand up in the air and dodged back. She said to Rita, 'Wouldn't you like children of your own before it's too late?'

She shrugged. 'Maybe. If I could have them without a man.'

'The things you do say,' said Celia dispassionately. 'How would you manage to keep them without a man's wage packet coming in?'

'Widows manage.' Rita hunched her knees and wrapped her arms round them. 'But I'm not going to waste my energies worrying about not having children. I have these two to play with and I enjoy my work, despite ol' Hennie expecting far too much for the money she pays me.'

'At least you don't have to do two jobs. Don't I wish I could win the pools!'

Rita looked at her with interest. 'I never knew you did the pools?'

'I do a couple of lines, and I back the odd horse.' Celia got to her feet. 'My gran was a great gambler but so far her luck hasn't rubbed off on me.'

Rita smiled. 'You'll just have to keep on trying. See you tomorrow. Come on, kids,' she called. 'Time to get going. Your mum gave me the money for just one go on the fair.'

'Hurray!' shouted Marie, and Sammy did a somersault on the sand.

Celia watched them a few moments longer and then hurried home to her lodgings to darn the hole in her lisle stockings and make herself some cheese on toast.

She was back in the Seaview the next morning when Mrs Henshall almost leapt on Rita as soon as she entered the hotel. 'There's been a man here asking after you. Says his name's Ryan and you know his brother.'

'He's having you on,' said Rita, toying with a button on her green duster coat. 'I don't know any Ryans. What did he look like?'

'He seemed very positive he knows you,' said Mrs Henshall, glancing at Celia who had removed the bowl of flowers from the oval oak table she was polishing and was holding it in mid-air. 'Don't drop that!' she said sharply. 'Or it'll come out of your wages.' Then lowered her voice. 'His name was Ben and he said he had a brother who was in the navy and you thought he was dead but he wasn't.'

Celia gave up all pretence at polishing and stared at Rita who was shaking her head. 'Doesn't ring a bell.'

Mrs Henshall looked put out. 'Well, if you're going to be secretive, I might as well be off! I'm meeting my sister and we're playing bridge this afternoon. Telephone me if there's anything urgent.'

Celia said breathlessly, 'Did Mr Ryan say what his brother's name was?'

Mrs Henshall paused in the act of pulling on a pair of long white gloves. 'I don't think that's any of your business, Celia,' she said haughtily.

Rita said firmly, 'I'd like to know. His first name might jog my memory.'

Her employer stared at her hard. 'I think it was Mick – Mick Ryan. Very Irish,' she declared and swept out of the lobby.

Celia sank on to a chair with her cheeks paper white.

'What was all that about?' said Rita softly. 'Do *you* know these brothers?'

Celia nodded. 'I can't understand why they should ask for you, unless it has something to do with your going to the Arcadia that time?'

'Do you want to talk about it?'

'I couldn't! I'd have to –' She pressed her lips tightly together. Although they had become friends in the nursing home, she had never told Rita she had had a baby but let her presume she had lost someone in the blitz, just as Rita herself had.

'Have to what?' asked her friend gently.

'Nothing. Give me the pass keys, I've finished here.'

Rita handed them over without a word and as one of the guests came out of the dining room and approached the desk, no more was said between them.

Celia went upstairs and as she worked, the words 'Mick's alive!' kept repeating themselves in her head. She had forgiven him when she had believed him dead but now she was angry with him all over again. Why hadn't he come looking for her? Her life could have been so different if he had. She could have been married and had a little house and Katherine with her and maybe more children. She would never have had to work so hard in this place. The letter . . . That must be the reason why Ben had come looking for her. Her heart quailed inside her and her hands shook. But why Ben? Was there something wrong with Mick as well as Katherine? What should she do?

Celia asked herself that question over and over during the next few days, half expecting Ben to return to the Seaview, but as the days passed the waiting became unbearable and in the end she decided to take her courage in her hands and visit Liverpool. She felt thoroughly ashamed of herself now for sending that letter and wanted nothing more than to explain it away.

On her next afternoon off Celia put on her best frock, checked her seams were straight and brushed her hair neatly. As a booster she dabbed on some face powder and applied lipstick, a rare thing for her, and with her raincoat over her arm, set off to catch the train to Liverpool.

It was raining as she made her way across the city centre and now she was having second thoughts. Part of her hoped she might get away without being recognised but she knew she could not bank on that because surely once she started asking questions about Mick and Katherine, they would want to know why she was interested.

She came to the Arcadia and her stomach churned as she

gazed up at the building. It looked different from when she had last seen it; then tarpaulin had covered the hole in the roof and the shattered windows had been boarded up. Now it was all cream and primrose-painted, and the brass doorknob and name plate gleamed beneath a splattering of raindrops. She peered down the area steps wondering which way to go in, then decided if the whole family were down there she did not want to face them en masse. It was Mick and Katherine she wanted to talk to, and them alone.

Moistening her lips Celia mounted the steps to the front entrance and went inside. It was a relief to be out of the rain and she dragged her wet scarf from her head and stuffed it in her raincoat pocket. A girl who looked to be about eighteen stared at her from behind the reception desk and for a moment Celia's heart seemed to stop beating inside her breast. Was this Katherine?

'Can I help you?' said the girl.

Surely she wouldn't have an Irish accent? thought Celia. She cleared her throat. 'I'm looking for Mick Ryan.'

'I'm sorry, he's out.'

That was a blow and Celia could not hide her disappointment.

'I could fetch his mother,' said the girl. 'I'm sure she won't mind being disturbed. It's quiet here today. Otherwise she wouldn't be letting me do Reception. She's just having a rest.'

'No, no. It – it's OK. Is – Mick well?'

'He's fine. Haven't you seen him for a while?'

'Not – not for a long time. Do you think he'll be gone long?'

'Hours. He's got a day off and has gone to Rhyl with a friend.'

'A friend? Wh-what kind of friend? Man or woman?' Celia's fingers gripped the reception desk.

'Are you an old girlfriend of his?' The girl's eyes were bright with curiosity.

'You – you could say that,' said Celia, her hands trembling. 'I used to work here.'

'What's your name?'

'I – I don't know if that's any of your business!' Celia's nerves got the better of her. 'Who are you anyway?'

'I'm family. I'm Eileen, Annie's daughter. If you worked here, you'll remember my mam.' She leaned forward across the desk. 'If you tell me who you are, I'll tell you who he's gone out with. You just might know her because her family's been friends with the Mcleods for years.'

Annie's daughter? Celia remembered Annie all right! They had worked together for a while. She made a decision. 'I'm Celia Mcdonald. Is your mam living here again?'

Eileen stared at her and then her eyes gleamed with satisfaction. 'You're Celia? Fancy that now! You're going to come as a surprise for some. See, my brain can work fine. I've heard of you.'

Celia's smile almost dazzled her. 'I'm glad I haven't been completely forgotten.'

'Not forgotten, but I haven't heard you mentioned either. Where've you been hiding yourself?'

Celia brushed the question aside. 'Who's this woman Mick's out with?'

'They all call her Sarah O'Neill still but she's a widow woman. Do you remember her?'

Remember her? Of course she did! Celia could hardly believe Mick was walking out with that spoilt little madam who'd had so much when she'd had so little. Fury surged through her like a foaming tide. Life was so unfair! The only person who had ever spoilt Celia was her gran, and she'd been dead for years. She felt like smashing something and her hands curled into fists. She jumped when the door to the basement steps opened.

A girl came through and smiled sympathetically when she saw her. 'Still chucking it down? Poor you! You're soaked. Here, let me take your coat.'

'Katie, she's not a guest,' said Eileen. 'This is Celia. She wants to see your Mick. She knows him from years ago.'

Katie stared at the pale, raincoat-clad figure and recalled hearing the name before. Hadn't Ben mentioned a Celia in his quarrel with Sarah? Not a bit like she had imagined. 'Mick's out,' she said slowly. 'I'm sorry. Listen, why don't you go into the Smoking Room and warm yourself by the fire? You look like you need a cup of tea. I'll bring you one in and then I'll get Ma.'

'Ma?' asked Celia.

'My mother, Kitty Mcleod.'

Celia did not move but gazed and gazed at her with hungry eyes.

'It's on the house,' Katie reassured her. 'Perhaps you'd like me to show you where the Smoking Room is?'

Celia cleared her throat. 'I know where it is. I knew the place well in the old days.'

'Great! You just go in then. I know you were close to Mick so I'm sure he'll be glad to see you,' she called over her shoulder as she headed for the kitchen.

'Very close,' whispered Celia. The kitchen door closed and she thought, So that is my daughter. That glowing girl! And Kitty Mcleod and Mick have had years of her company while I've had nothing! Something snapped inside her. 'Very, very, very close!' She slammed her handbag on the reception desk. 'I thought he was dead but now I find he's alive and going out with bloody Sarah O'Neill! I could tear them apart!'

'Hell!' exclaimed Eileen, staring at her in amazement and sudden fear. She scurried from behind Reception and ran to the door leading to the basement.

Katie popped her head out of the kitchen. 'What was that you were saying?' Her friendly gaze rested on Celia's face.

Instantly she was ashamed and the anger drained from her, leaving her weak. 'I thought he was dead,' she whispered. 'I really thought he was dead. And you? Why do they call you Katie?'

Katie stared at her intently. 'My real name's Katherine.'

'Oh! So she did that at least.' Celia felt dazed and confused. 'I'm glad about that.'

Katie was starting to feel a bit strange herself and decided they could both do with that cup of tea. She went over to Celia and put an arm round her. 'You look all in. Come into the Smoking Room.'

Meekly, Celia went with her. Fortunately the room was empty and so Katie sat her down in front of the fire. 'I don't want Mick marrying Sarah,' she said in a conspiratorial whisper. 'I don't really want her marrying Ben, but he's potty about her and really hurt about the whole thing. Ma says it'll all work itself out but I don't see how, unless somebody does something. Now you're here, maybe *you* can do something? You do still care about Mick, don't you?'

Did she? thought Celia, feeling even more confused. Surely she must if she felt so jealous of Sarah? And it was true she had never forgotten him. She stared at her daughter and thought, You're so kind, so confident, so different from me.

'Well!' said Katie, smiling encouragingly. 'Tell me all about it.'

Celia did not know where to start but before she could say a word Kitty walked into the room. She was flushed and took up position immediately in front of Celia. 'Eileen told me you were here. What have you been saying to Katie?' Her voice was calm but there was nothing calm about her eyes. They were as cold as the North Pole.

'I haven't said anything,' stammered Celia, completely intimidated.

Katie glanced at Kitty and said, 'She told me she thought Mick was dead. That's why she hasn't been round for years. You should make her welcome, Ma. I'm sure Mick'll be glad to see her.'

'No, he won't,' said Kitty. 'The past is the past and it's best forgotten. Isn't that right, Celia? You burnt your boats when you left and there's nothing here for you any more.'

'Ma!' protested Katie. 'That's not very welcoming.'

Kitty did not look at her but said harshly, 'Go and make some tea.'

Katie hesitated. 'Now!' ordered Kitty. 'Or you can forget following in my footsteps!'

The girl frowned but left the room, leaving the door ajar.

Kitty went and closed it and placed her back against it. 'You don't want to ruin her life, do you?' she said fiercely. 'You can see how well she's turned out.'

'You never told her about me, did you?' said Celia in a dull voice.

'No. And you should be glad to hear I don't want her ever knowing! She's happy. She's got a good life here. You left her and she doesn't need you. I'd prefer it if she never saw you again.'

'Mick . . . did you deliberately lie to me about him being dead?' asked Celia, trembling.

'Of course not! I suffered along with you. But now I want you to leave. I don't want you here when Katie comes back. Follow me.' She led the way outside and Celia rose and followed, feeling utterly wretched.

Kitty paused by Reception and unlocked a drawer in the desk. She took out a tin box before moving in the direction of the vestibule. 'Come in here,' she said, opening the door and standing in the space between it and the front door. Celia did as she was told. She could not have spoken to save her life. 'Don't look like that!' said Kitty angrily. 'You never wanted her. Give me your handbag.'

Celia handed it over and she stuffed a handful of bank-notes inside it. 'There! Isn't that what you came for? Get yourself a taxi home. Buy yourself some new shoes, a new hat. Anything you want! Don't come back, though, expecting more, because I'll have the police on you if you do.' She clicked the handbag shut and closed Celia's fingers around the handle, then opened the door and waved her out.

Celia went, barely able to take in what had just happened. She felt sick, miserable and bereft as she walked through the rain in a dream.

It was not until she was sitting on the Southport train and had begun to thaw out that her mind started functioning again. The carriage was empty (who wanted to go to Southport on such a wet day?) so she opened her handbag and took out the money Kitty had placed in it and began to count it. There was over fifty pounds! She replaced the money and hugged her handbag to her. She had never been able to save and now here she was with a whole fifty pounds. What should she do with it? A hot meal, she thought. Steak and kidney pie with lashings of gravy, new potatoes and carrots and turnip. Her mouth watered. Clothes . . . She could buy herself a new frock and a pair of sheer nylons.

Blood money. The words seemed to come from deep within her.

'No,' she murmured. 'That's a payoff when somebody's involved in a killing. I've seen that in films.'

What is it then? said the voice. Blackmail money?

'No! I didn't blackmail her! I wouldn't! She couldn't

think that of me?' But of course Kitty Mcleod *had* thought that. Hadn't she said as much when she'd stuffed the money into her bag? But why? Because of that damn note, of course! Celia groaned. Why had she been so stupid as to send it? And why had she been so stupid as to let Kitty Mcleod walk all over her and send her packing? She did not want her blood money! Although, of course, it was nice having some money for once. But she had not enjoyed being treated like dirt. Katherine had not treated her like that. She felt warm just thinking of her daughter. It had made her proud to think she had given birth to such a pleasantly spoken and attractive girl. With a daughter like that at her side, she felt sure her life would improve drastically. She had made a big mistake in letting Kitty Mcleod force her out. What was money compared to a daughter? It was an insult. As if money could make up for what she had lost!

'Don't come back,' she had been told. Well, she had no intention of going back – but as for keeping out of Katherine's life, that was something different altogether. It was time her daughter knew the truth about her birth. It was wrong to tell people lies. Celia's gran had taught her that and she had been one of the best. A bit of a gambler, but where was the harm in a flutter now and again?

Celia opened her handbag. Fingering the banknotes, she considered what she should do next.

Chapter Six

Kitty closed the vestibule door and realised she was shaking all over. It had not come easy to her, behaving so harshly. Celia's face! But what else could she have done? She leant against the door and, closing her eyes, breathed deeply.

'Where is she?'

Kitty's eyelids fluttered open and she saw Katie standing near the open door of the Smoking Room with a tray in her hands. 'She had to catch the next train to Southport.'

There was a short silence then the girl said accusingly, 'You got rid of her! You sent her out in the rain all wet. It would have done her good to see Mick. She thought he was dead!'

'You don't know what you're talking about. That's all over and done with and best forgotten.' Kitty took off her spectacles and rubbed her eyes.

'Why did you do it?' demanded Katie. 'Because of Sarah? Why should you want her for Mick after the way she's treated Ben?'

'That has nothing to do with Celia. Now pour me a cup of tea and be quick about it!' said Kitty wearily.

Katie put the tray down on the desk. 'I felt sorry for her. She looked like she needed feeding up.'

'She's a grown woman, nearly forty! Will you *please* stop going on about her!'

There was a silence which was interrupted by Ben. 'What's all the shouting about? You'll be frightening the guests away.' He was standing in the doorway leading to the basement. 'Who's a grown woman and nearly forty?'

Katie turned to him in relief. 'Celia! She was here but Ma chased her away.'

'That's enough! I don't want to hear any more about it.' Kitty's voice shook as she brushed past Ben and went down the steps into the basement.

'What's Celia ever done to her?' said Katie.

He did not answer but said, 'How long since she left?'

'Five minutes at the most.'

'Thanks.' He ran upstairs and appeared a few minutes later, wearing a raincoat and a tweed cap and heading for the front door.

'You won't catch her,' called Katie.

He gave no sign of having heard. Katie wanted to know what he was going to do if he did catch up with her so hurried with the tray to the kitchen and dumped it on the table then ran upstairs, dragging off her apron. She glanced down into the road as she pulled on her duffel coat but couldn't see Ben. At least she knew where Celia was going! She took her umbrella from the wardrobe and tore downstairs and out of the hotel.

She ran most of the way to Exchange Station and was just in time to see a train leaving the platform. She was about to turn away when she spotted Ben on the platform. Could he have heard Kitty saying Celia had gone for the Southport train? It was the only thing she could think of to explain his being here. She wondered whether to join him but decided he might tell her to go home, so she bought a ticket for Southport and kept out of sight until he boarded the train. Then she jumped into the last carriage.

It was still raining when Katie arrived outside the Seaview after following Ben all the way from the station. He was already inside the hotel and she was unsure what to do. A vicious gust of wind tugged at her umbrella and that decided her. Without further thought she hurried into the hotel.

Ben was in Reception talking to an auburn-haired woman who stood behind the desk. Katie placed her dripping umbrella in a stand and tiptoed towards them. He did not turn so she sat on a straightbacked chair and took out the *Valentine* magazine she had bought at the station and pretended to read.

'There's three of us Ryans actually, Rita,' Ben was saying, 'but Teddy lives down South.'

'But it's your brother Mick Celia went out with, and it was him who was left in the Atlantic in an open boat?'

'We-ell,' said Ben, 'I can't tell you much about that. He doesn't like to talk about it.'

'What about you? Where was your war?'

There was silence and Katie lowered her magazine.

Ben cleared his throat. 'I did my bit during the blitz

in Liverpool and then – then I joined the Air Force in the last year, only to be shot down by enemy aircraft.'

'What happened then?'

Katie gave up all pretence at reading and waited for Ben's reply. 'I managed to get my parachute open but it was dark and I had no idea where I was,' he said in a dreamy voice. 'I should have stayed put until daylight but instead I began walking and ended up behind enemy lines. Stupid of me!'

'I think it was quite brave,' said Rita. 'It must have been tough.'

'It was!' He sighed. 'I was put in a prisoner-of-war camp. The food was terrible – what there was of it. Not a bit like home cooking.'

'You men!' said Rita in a teasing voice. 'You love your stomachs.'

'The way to a man's heart,' he said, and grinned.

Rita stared fixedly at him a moment then said, 'Changing the subject . . . fancy you thinking I was Celia!'

Katie's ears pricked up.

'It was Ma, as I said. Do you know where Celia is?'

Rita frowned. 'She should have been here by now. She's supposed to be doing extra hours and it's not like her to be late.'

'Maybe she got soaked and had to go home and change?' suggested Ben. 'If you gave me her address . . .?'

'We're not allowed to do that. I'd like to help, really,' said Rita, sounding like she meant it. 'Celia could do with someone to look after her. Her nerves aren't strong.'

There was a brief silence before Ben said, 'She never

told you anything about us and what happened in the blitz?'

'She told me she'd lost someone but didn't go into details. I understand that because – well, because I lost my mam and gran in the blitz and a brother at sea. That's why what you had to say about Mick interested me.'

'I'm sorry,' said Ben. 'Have you no other family?'

Rita hesitated. 'None that counts. Listen, if you want you could wait in the lounge until Celia comes in. Second door on the right. There's a good fire in there with its being such a miserable afternoon.'

Ben thanked her, and as he moved away from the desk Katie rose and walked towards him. She knew she had given him a shock because he blinked. 'How long have you been there?' he demanded.

She smiled and linked her arm through his, squeezing it. 'Long enough to hear you've led a more exciting life than I thought.'

'You shouldn't have followed me,' he hissed, dragging her in the direction of a door which had 'Lounge' written on it in gold lettering.

'You should be writing for the *Hotspur* or the *Wizard*.'

He grinned self-consciously. 'I got carried away. But you must have heard the tales our Mick and Teddy spin about their war experiences – do you believe them all? The one I spouted is based on something a mate of our Teddy's told me. The only difference is that this Jerry woman in the camp tore his wedding ring from his finger.'

'It was good as it was but I don't know why you had

to lie. You lived through the May blitz and I've heard people say that wasn't much fun.'

'It was definitely no picnic,' he said quietly. 'I'll never forget me and Celia running for home with bombs falling all around us and the docks ablaze.'

'There you are!' Katie smiled and said gently, 'Was that when she worked at the Arcadia?'

He hesitated. 'Naw! She was working in a factory as a welder making guns. She was bombed out, that's why she came to us.'

'So she was actually living at the Arcadia during the blitz?'

'She came and stayed for a short while. Then she left,' he said tersely. 'You'll have to ask her for the rest of the story. I've said far more than I should.' He opened the door of the lounge and ushered Katie inside.

She wondered what he meant by that but realised she was going to have to be patient for a little while longer if she wanted to learn more about Celia.

She looked about her with all the interest of one who worked in the business. The lounge at the Arcadia, which had housed the bar since the early-fifties, was long and narrow. She found herself envying the shape of this room which was a perfect square. Three easy chairs were occupied and pulled up so close to the fireplace she could not even see the fire, never mind feel its warmth.

'It's central heated but I'm sure it's not on,' murmured Ben, pulling up a chair near a window and waving her to it. He removed his coat and placed it on a nearby stool before seating himself so he could see the door and the rain-drenched garden. 'Ma should be thinking of having central heating put in before winter.'

'She said it'll create upheaval and cost a bomb.'

'It'll have to be done sooner or later. Unless she sells up.'

'Sells up?' Katie stared at him. 'You're talking about my future! Has she been saying something to you that I don't know about? She threatened me earlier that I wouldn't follow in her footsteps because I thought she was being horrible to Celia.'

'Did she hell!' exclaimed Ben, looking dumbfounded.

'I'm not surprised you're surprised,' said Katie, shaking her head. 'It really shook me.'

He hesitated. 'She didn't mean it, kid. She's getting on and can't take upset the way she used to. And maybe you showing an interest in boys lately has made her think that perhaps you might change your mind about wanting to take over?'

'How could she think that?' said Katie in astonishment. She was silent a moment. Lowering her head to stare down at her damp shoes, she said casually, 'If I was to meet someone, I'm sure they'd be glad not to have to go to all the trouble of looking for somewhere to live and have a readymade home.'

'Hotel life isn't everybody's cup of tea. Just think of our Mick!'

Katie glanced up and caught his expression. She reached out one hand and said gently, 'I don't understand why he's doing what he's doing. I can't believe he loves her.'

'Love's a damn nuisance,' muttered Ben, taking out his cigarettes. 'Take it from me, love, you're best without it.'

'Maybe you'll meet someone else?' said Katie.

'And the Liver birds might fly!' he said, lighting up.

Katie opened her magazine. 'You never know,' she murmured.

'Yeah! You could be right. Who'd have thought Celia would have turned up the way she did?'

'You think that's strange?'

'A bit.'

She raised her eyes and stared at him. 'How did you know you'd find her here?'

'How did you know how to find me?' he parried.

'Ah, but – what's up?' she asked as he got to his feet. She turned her head and saw Rita approaching.

'You're out of luck, I'm afraid,' she said. 'Celia's just phoned. She's not feeling well and won't be in.'

'Did she say what was wrong?' asked Ben.

'Feels she's got a cold coming on. Not surprising, considering the weather.'

'Could you give us her address then?' he said, stubbing out his cigarette. 'She might be glad to see a visitor.'

'Visitors,' murmured Katie, smiling at Rita.

'I mentioned you were here and –' She stopped.

'And what?' said Ben.

'She put the phone down. Unless she phones back, I think you'd better forget about seeing her today.'

There was silence and Katie was bitterly disappointed.

Ben grimaced. 'Thanks for trying anyway. Maybe

I'll come back another day.' He picked up his coat and walked out.

'I've upset him,' said Rita, staring at Katie. 'Are you related to him?'

'I'm his half-sister, Katherine Mcleod.' She held out a hand. 'What next, d'you think? It would be nice if Celia and Mick could get together.'

'There's nothing more I can do right now, love.' Rita smiled. 'I'm sure your brothers will be able to work something out.'

Katie nodded and hurried after Ben. 'What are you going to do?' she asked, putting up her umbrella and slipping her hand through his arm.

'Mind my own business and accept I'm going to be a bachelor for the rest of my life,' he said bitterly. 'I thought Celia would want to see us.'

'Ma was pretty unwelcoming, but I think that receptionist likes you. Why didn't you ask *her* for a date?'

Ben made a noise in his throat. 'It wouldn't be fair. I'm a one gal guy. Let's go home. And don't mention Celia to Ma. It won't do any good.'

Mick and Sarah were in the lounge when they arrived home. 'Where've you two been?' hissed Mick from behind the till. 'Ma and Pops have gone out and Eileen told us that Celia's been here, kicking up a fuss. I thought she was dead!'

'Why should you think she was dead?' asked Ben, going behind the bar and pulling himself a pint. He threw some money into the open drawer of the till.

Mick shrugged and waited until the guest he was serving had moved away. 'Just the fact that I've never heard anything from her and her name's hardly ever mentioned here. I thought maybe she'd been killed in the blitz. I mean, who was there to notify? The poor kid had nobody but us. I can't understand what she'd be kicking up a fuss about, though?'

'She didn't kick up a fuss,' said Katie hotly. 'She just wanted to see you, so far as I know. She was here during the blitz, wasn't she, Ben? So everybody here would know she hadn't been killed.'

'Yeah! She shared the cellar with us.' He glanced at Sarah. 'Funny, but Celia apparently believed Mick was dead all these years, too. Wouldn't it be romantic if they met up again and fell in love?' he added sardonically.

Mick frowned. 'We'll both have changed and probably have nothing in common. I wonder –'

'I'm going upstairs,' interrupted Ben. 'I'm whacked.'

'Do you want some supper?' asked Katie.

He ruffled her hair. 'If you'll bring it up, I wouldn't mind.'

'No trouble.'

As he went upstairs carrying his pint she was stopped in the lobby by Sarah's voice. 'Where've the two of you been?'

She gave Sarah a look. 'Southport. There's a woman there our Ben went to see.'

'A woman?'

'You heard,' said Katie with a smile, and went into the kitchen where she found Eileen.

'You had a visitor while you were out,' said the girl with a smirk, folding her arms across her chest. 'But Aunt Kitty chased him, too.'

It couldn't be? thought Katie. 'You don't mean . . .?'

'The ted? Sure it was him, and the way he looked didn't go down well here so I can't see him coming back.'

Katie felt like wiping the smile off her face but instead said, 'You told them about the fight, didn't you? Why? Even Ben didn't mention it. What is it you've got against me?'

Eileen shrugged her shoulders, the smile still playing round her lips. 'Nothing, to be sure. It's just that I don't want you going the way of your mother.'

Katie stared at her. 'What the hell d'you mean by that? Ma's –'

'Katie girl, if you're making something for our Ben, make us a meat sarnie,' said Mick, popping his head round the door. 'And, Eileen, the guest in number five wants a fresh towel. She's dropped the last one in the bath. Hurry up and get one to her, there's a good girl.'

She hesitated and he said, 'Well, get a move on!'

Eileen left the kitchen and Katie got on with what she was doing, wishing she had not gone after Ben because then she would have been able to talk to Patrick herself.

When Katie came out of Ben's bedroom she found Sarah sitting on the top stair. She sighed, feeling she'd had enough of her own sex for the moment.

'How is Ben?' asked Sarah.

'Why should you care?' said Katie, nostrils flaring with

annoyance. 'You've got our Mick on a string. Isn't he enough?'

'Hardly! Mick's no woman's puppet.'

Her words surprised Katie and she thought before she said, 'No, I suppose he isn't. But neither is Ben and I think you've treated him rotten, writing to our Mick on the sly while going out with him.'

Sarah's dark eyes flashed. 'How do you know that, you loathsome brat, and how dare you speak to me like that?'

'I don't want to speak to you at all,' said Katie, and instead of trying to get past her, went into her own bedroom.

To her annoyance Sarah followed and sat on the bed. The muted sound of distant traffic could be heard as well as a couple talking down in the street. Sarah glanced out of the window and stiffened. 'So this is where you do your spying! You were listening to me and Ben when we had that argument weeks ago, weren't you?'

'You didn't bother to lower your voices. Anybody could have heard you,' said Katie, opening her magazine. 'You were shrieking like an alley cat.'

'You cheeky madam!' Sarah crossed one Bear Brand sheerest nylon-clad leg over the other and glared at her. 'You could have let us know you were there.'

'You mean, shout down while you were arguing? Wouldn't that have woken the guests and the neighbours?'

Sarah's look was venomous. 'If you were my sister, I'd put you in a barrel and float you on the Mersey.'

Katie's voice was honeyed. 'But you're not my sister and I hope you never will be. Mick might make it up with

Celia and Ben has found someone else. So you can stop making sheep's eyes at my brothers!'

'I do not make sheep's eyes,' said Sarah indignantly. 'I have lovely eyes. I've been told they're my best feature.'

'By who?'

'Whom, you mean. Well, it wouldn't be your Ben, would it? He wouldn't say anything so poetic.'

'Which shows how little you know him. He reads the *Psalms* and *Song of Solomon* and they're real poetry and can be lovey-dovey. You don't know him at all and I think he's well rid of you.'

'You *would* think that! You don't want someone else getting the attention,' said Sarah in a silky voice. 'Well, I do know Ben. I've known him a lot longer than you have, and if I'm treating him in a certain way it's because I have my reasons. Ben and I go way back.'

'Yeah! You *are* a bit ancient.'

Sarah stood up with a wrathful expression on her face but before she could speak the door opened and Ben stood there.

'Why don't you try disturbing every guest in the hotel?' he said sarcastically. 'Now go downstairs, the pair of you!'

'You can't speak to me like that!' said Sarah. 'I'm not a kid like her.'

'Well, stop behaving like one. I want to get changed in peace before I go out.'

'But you've just got in! Where are you going?' demanded Sarah.

'None of your business,' he said, and closed the door.

'Swine!' Sarah ground her teeth. 'I could kill him!'

She flounced out of the room and Katie followed her at a more leisurely pace, pleased with the last ten minutes' work.

As Ben strolled down the Mount he felt a bit ridiculous, all dressed up with nowhere to go, but at least he had showed Sarah that he was not wilting away for love of her. Good ol' Katie for sticking up for him. She was as good as any real sister, but what had Sarah been doing upstairs? It was unlikely Katie had asked her up.

A sports car came to a screeching halt much too close to the kerb alongside him. 'I saw you leave. Can I give you a lift?' gasped Sarah.

Ben was flabbergasted but he hardened his heart and won his inner struggle. 'No, thanks.'

'Why not?' she demanded crossly. 'You never used to refuse a lift.'

'Things have changed. You're no longer my girl, and you're on the wrong side of the road.'

Her eyes darted from his face to the other side of the road and back again. 'Is that woman Katie mentioned the reason you won't accept a lift from me?'

Ben's expression froze and he thought frantically. 'Who else?' he said at last. 'Now will you go away before you get arrested for kerb crawling and dangerous driving?'

Sarah bit her lip, glanced behind her and shot across the road, narrowly avoiding a motor cyclist. Ben's heart leapt into his throat. 'You bloody idiot!' he shouted.

'Can't we talk, Ben?' she called, continuing at a snail's

pace on the other side of the road. 'I don't really want to be out of friends with you.'

'You have a funny way of showing it then, going out with my brother and insulting my sister. 'Bye, Sarah.' He lengthened his stride and did not look back even when she roared past him, leaving damp scraps of paper swirling in her wake.

He did not feel satisfied for long, though. It started to pour with rain and he got soaked as he walked back home, wondering what would be the outcome of Celia's visit and whether there was any way he could use it to win Sarah back for good.

Chapter Seven

Katie picked up the post and glanced at the envelopes. There was one addressed to her, a plain white one with a Lancashire postmark. She stuffed it into her apron pocket to read later, thinking it was from a guest she had made a friend of, and placed the others on the occasional table in the lobby except the one for Ma and Pops which was in Jack's handwriting. Katie had sent him a birthday card but he had not reciprocated. As usual Ma had included his name on theirs.

Katie went into the kitchen and removed toast from the toaster, placing more bread in it.

'Nothing for me?' said Eileen, sliding bacon on to a plate.

'There's one from your mother. I left it in the lobby. Perhaps she's writing to say it's time you upped sticks?'

'You think I'll be going home before I'm good and ready?' Eileen gave her a scornful look. 'I happen to like it here so you might as well get used to the idea. I could be here to stay.'

'Not when I'm running the place,' said Katie firmly. 'I don't get you. Don't you want to take over your parents' hotel in Ireland?'

'No, there's more life here. So I'm staying, whether you like it or not,' Eileen said confidently, and waltzed out, carrying a tray, as Kitty entered.

'Something's burning.'

Katie moved swiftly. 'This toaster's on its last legs,' she said.

'It'll last a bit longer. All you've got to do is remember to keep your eye on it,' said Kitty. 'What's that you've got in your hand?'

'It's for you from Jack. Probably wants to know when you're going up there for a holiday.'

Kitty smiled. 'Probably. His heart's definitely in the Highlands, just like Pops, because he doesn't come home often.'

'Oh, Ma! You say that every year at this time. But Pops is half-English. It's only because he's got the house up there that he keeps returning.'

'That's all you know about it,' said Kitty. 'He was brought up there from when he was seven and lived there until he joined the Medical Corps and went to war. He loves walking the hills, just like Jack.'

'OK, OK! I'm not looking to hear all about the old days.'

Katie picked up a toast rack and carried it into the dining room. She exchanged a few words about the weather with a singer who was appearing at the Empire but did not linger long because there was other work to do, and besides she wanted to see what Joan had to say.

Katie slit the envelope and saw two pages of beautifully written copperplate handwriting. She looked at the signature and read 'Celia Mcdonald'. Surprised, she turned to the first page and began to read. By the time she reached the end of the letter she had gone from hot to cold to hot again, and had to grip the table to steady herself. There must be some mistake. The woman was demented. It couldn't possibly be true. She was trying to get back at them because Kitty had chased her the other day – which wasn't surprising if this letter was the kind of rubbish the woman usually spouted. She ripped the letter up and placed the scraps in her pocket, returning to the kitchen to get on with her work.

But the contents of Celia's letter were not so easy to dismiss and as Katie was about to empty the torn scraps of paper into the wastepaper bin, the words *'Kitty Mcleod snatched you away from me. I'd no sooner given birth than she wanted you. I was weak and let her take you'* burnt into her brain. Katie shivered, feeling cold and drained of all energy. It couldn't be true! Ma would never steal or lie to her. The woman was just trying to poison her mind to get revenge on Ma for making her leave the hotel. She repeated that to herself and felt a little better.

Next Katie had the job of seeing to the post and got on with answering requests for accommodation, but even as she hammered out words on the old Underwood typewriter more of the letter forced itself into her consciousness. *'You're my baby. You're beautiful and I'm so sorry I didn't stand up to her but she was so strong and I'd had TB and my nerves were weak.'* Katie remembered Rita saying to Ben that Celia's nerves were weak. It made her feel a little better. There was definitely something wrong with the woman.

She finished her typing and then went out to post the letters. More words hit her as she was coming up the Mount and this time she felt so angry she ran the rest of the way to the Arcadia. *It's impossible! That sad, drab woman couldn't possibly be my mother. I don't look the least bit like her!* She entered the hotel in a rush and collided with Kitty.

'Careful,' she said, steadying her with a smile. 'What's the rush?'

For a breathcatching moment Katie was on the verge of telling her about Celia's letter. Ma would reassure her and they would laugh about it. No, not laugh because it wasn't the least bit funny. But just at that moment one of the guests came out of the Smoking Room and said something to Kitty about the summer sales and the two women began to talk bargains. Katie went into the kitchen and found Eileen making soda bread.

The girl glanced up and said, 'You're all rosy. Did something exciting come in the post for you?'

The flush died on Katie's cheeks, leaving her deathly pale. 'Have you been looking in the wastepaper bin?'

Eileen's eyebrows drew together. 'Is that where you'd put a letter from that Patrick? Sensible girl! You do surprise me.'

'P-Patrick!' she stammered. Her fear ebbed and she laughed. 'No, I haven't had a letter from him. More's the pity. But if he calls again, I'll make sure I get to speak to him and I'll tell Ma he's no ted. Now, have you started the soup?'

'No,' said Eileen, looking grumpy. 'I was waiting for

you to come in with fresh carrots and leeks, but you've a head like a sieve because where are they?'

'Like you said, I've a head like a sieve,' she said, trying to sound cheerful, and went straight out again.

For the rest of the day Katie was good for nothing. As much as she tried to forget Celia's letter, words kept popping into her head along with snippets of things people had said, such as her having been born in the autumn of her parents' lives and Celia's having been at the Arcadia during the May blitz. Could Ben know something about this? He had clammed up the other day and said she'd have to find things out from Celia. She felt cold all over again but convinced herself that he would never have kept such a secret from her. Even so she often found herself stopping and staring into space as she went about her work.

'What's got into you today?' said Kitty more than once.

'She imagines herself in love on one sighting,' said Eileen, rolling her eyes.

Katie forced a smile and did not deny Eileen's words but instead looked at Kitty and thought, You are old enough to be my grandmother. Her blood ran cold again. She did not want to think like that but could not help it. She hated the thought that Kitty wasn't her mother and Pops her father, that her brothers weren't even her half-brothers. Celia meant nothing to her and this family meant so much.

Katie could not sleep that night but lay on her back, staring up at the ceiling. I know hardly anything about the woman so how can she be my mother? *I would like to meet you again but away from the hotel,* Celia had written. Strange how she could remember so much of that letter. *'In Liverpool, if you like? Cooper's Cafe in Church Street next Tuesday at twelve. Please come.'* The last two words repeated themselves. *'Please come – please come – please come!'* She turned on to her stomach and pulled the pillow over her head, pressing her cheek against the cool white sheet. *Sad, drab – mad perhaps?* She needed to know if Celia was the latter of those three things and could only do that by keeping that appointment. Having made that decision, Katie determined to pull herself together and try to act normally until then.

On Monday, in order to avoid questions, Katie told Kitty she had an appointment with the dentist on the Tuesday. 'Do you want me to come with you, love?' said Kitty. 'I know how horrible it is going there.'

'No!' Katie could not conceal her alarm. 'I'm a big girl now, Ma.' She marvelled not for the first time at her own acting ability. She was as miserable as sin but felt sure no one could guess just how low she felt.

At a quarter to twelve on the appointed day, Katie left the Arcadia carrying her umbrella and wishing God could at least have made the sun shine. The rain seemed an omen and her mind was full of speculation on how her life might change if Celia proved to be telling the truth. As she passed Woolworth's and C & A Modes, with its display of summer fashions in floral cotton satin and rayon duster coats, her heart was thumping. Already she could smell the ground coffee for which Cooper's was famous and see a woman waiting in front of the store in a bright red mackintosh. Not so drab after all.

'You came!' Celia's voice was breathless and she clasped her hands to her chest and stared at Katie. 'I've been having palpitations thinking you weren't going to come. I thought maybe *she'd* keep you away.'

'If you mean Ma by "she",' said Katie in unfriendly tones, 'I didn't tell her I was meeting you. In fact, I haven't even told her about your letter.'

Celia's face fell. 'Why? Don't you believe me?'

Katie hesitated. 'I don't know what to believe. Shall we go in? I'm hungry.' She was not but felt a need to appear in control. Besides, her umbrella was dripping rain down her neck, compounding the misery and anger she felt as she gazed into the pale middle-aged face with its smattering of freckles.

'That's fine by me,' said Celia, hurriedly opening the door for Katie as the girl folded her umbrella. 'I don't know if I'll be able to eat a thing. You can't imagine what it took for me to pluck up courage to write to you! Seventeen years keeping a secret is a long time.'

'Why keep it then? If I had a daughter, I'd want to know her,' said Katie in a hard voice as she headed for the stairs which led to the first floor.

'That's easy for you to say,' said Celia, scurrying to keep up with her. 'There was a war on and I wasn't married and I'd been ill.'

Katie's heart sank. Of course she wasn't married! Stupid of me not to think of that. If Celia is my mother that makes me il–illegit – Oh, God! I don't even want to think the word! 'Don't say any more,' she said roughly. 'Let's get sitting down first.'

'That's fine by me.' Celia smiled. 'You really have got a nice face. You're much prettier than me, more like your –' She paused. 'At least you've got my eyes.'

Katie stopped and stared at her, and yes, Celia's eyes were a clear beautiful grey with her own hint of mauve and dark circle around them. She forced out the words: 'Lots of people have grey eyes.'

'None of the Ryans or Mcleods do, brown or blue only. I worked at the Arcadia long enough to know the colour of all their eyes. And did you know John is my godfather? He and my dad were in the Great War together. He's a good man and I can only think *she*'s got him really under her thumb to be able to chase me out. When I think of the kind of life I've had, and all because *she* wanted a girl. Anybody's girl! But you were somebody's. You were mine!'

'Shhh!' Katie scowled at her and ran up the stairs but Celia kept up, clipping Katie's heel at one point so that her shoe came off. It was only a petty little thing but it incensed her. She didn't want this woman for a mother! She had a mother and one was enough.

Katie found them a table and waved Celia to a seat opposite her. Obediently she sat down with a hesitant smile on her face. She gazed round her at the damask cotton-covered tables with their occupants and the uniformed waitresses. 'I always wanted to come here but I was too shy to come on my own. Besides, I couldn't afford to eat out then.' She fixed her eyes on Katie's face. 'What shall we have?' she said eagerly. 'You pick.'

Katie reached for the menu and used it to hide her

expression whilst trying to gather her racing thoughts. She chose the day's special for both of them and gave the order to the waitress who suddenly appeared at her side. Then she leant back and unbuttoned her coat. 'Where was I born?' she rattled off.

'In the basement, during the May blitz. It was the last night of the raids. Night after night of noise and destruction.' Celia's fingers trembled as she pleated the tablecloth. 'You were premature, and no wonder! My nerves were shot to pieces with the year I'd had before.'

'Who delivered me?'

'Annie's mam. Mrs Mcleod was there as well – and Hannah and Ben.'

'Ben!' She was stunned.

'He was only a kid and kept in the background but I remember him asking his mam did she want him to boil some water like they did in the films when a baby was coming.' Celia paused and held Katie's stare. 'Why did he come looking for me?'

'He's in love with Sarah. I told you, didn't I?' Katie covered her face with her hands. 'He was hoping you and Mick –' She stopped, hardly able to believe that the thought hadn't struck her before. 'Who's my father?' she asked, unable to keep the hope out of her voice.

'Nobody you know,' said Celia, who had anticipated the question. 'There was a war on. I had more than one fella fancying me. When young men go off to fight, you want to make them happy for a short while so you give them all you've got. I loved him, if that's what you're worried about.'

'Yes, that's what I was worried about,' said Katie in a subdued voice. 'Although – you did love Mick at one time?'

'Yes, I loved Mick.' Her voice had hardened. 'But we were both very young and people's feelings change.'

That was what he had said and Katie's hope of bringing them together died.

Their soup had arrived and Celia picked up her spoon and ate with relish. Katie was still not feeling hungry but she ate hers and when their plates were removed, said, 'What is it you want from me?'

'I'm lonely.' Celia smoothed the napkin on her knee. 'I don't suppose you know what that feels like, having lived in the Arcadia all your life, being spoilt, always having someone looking out for you?' She paused but Katie could not have answered to save her life because for the second time in the last few days she was trying to imagine living a different kind of life altogether. 'Nobody cares if I live or die,' said Celia.

Katie struggled to find her voice. 'Rita seemed to care about you.'

'Rita? Yes, I've got a lot to thank Rita for.' Celia smiled. 'If she hadn't helped Annie's daughter when she had a fit, I'd never have known the Mcleods were still at the Arcadia. I thought at first Eileen was you but Rita put me straight when I asked the name of the girl she helped.' Celia picked up her spoon. 'I went back to the Arcadia during the war, wanting to see you, but it was all boarded up and I was told the family had gone to live in Scotland.'

'So you did care that much?' said Katie.

'Of course I cared! Even though I never had the advantages Kitty Mcleod had, I think I could still have been a good mother to you if – if your father hadn't died. It's too late now to know how you'd have turned out,' said Celia. '*She's* left her mark on you. But that doesn't mean to say we couldn't give living together a chance.'

'You really want me to live with you?' Katie put down her spoon. She couldn't eat. 'You're asking a lot. I don't know you.'

'And whose fault's that?' Celia's voice was barely audible. 'I don't want to throw stones, Katherine, I know I failed you, but that woman's been living a lie all these years. *She* isn't your mother – *I* am. And I haven't been feeling very well lately . . . You're so young and strong. I'm sure with you looking after me, I'd soon perk up.' She spooned custard and jam sponge into her mouth.

Katherine! She called me Katherine, thought Katie. It made her sound like a completely different person. More grown up. And wasn't being considered grown up what she wanted? But still she protested: 'My life's at the Arcadia. Ma brought me up to take over when she retires.'

'I'm sure – she can give you – much more than I can,' gasped Celia.

'Are you OK?' Suddenly she felt exactly like a Katherine and pushed back her chair, thinking Celia was having a heart attack.

Celia made a choking noise and it was Katherine who forced her head down and whacked her between the shoulder blades. Jam sponge shot on to the tablecloth and

Celia dabbed at her mouth with her napkin. 'You saved my life,' she said hoarsely. 'See how useful it would be to me to have you around?'

Katherine stared at her and then she began to laugh helplessly. There was something about Celia that was beginning to make it impossible for her to walk away, and it wasn't just because she was starting to believe that this was in fact her real mother. Then the laughter died on her lips and tears filled her eyes. Dear God, what am I going to do? she asked.

'How was the dentist's?' called Kitty from behind Reception as Katherine entered the lobby.

She did not answer immediately but closed the vestibule door carefully after her. Raw misery and anger were tearing at her insides and she did not know who to blame the most for the way she was feeling. She placed her umbrella in the hallstand and wondered how and where to start, eventually realising there was no easy way. 'I haven't been to the dentist,' she said, striding towards the desk. She stopped close to it and said in a low voice, 'I lied to you about that, just like you've lied to me all these years about me being your daughter.'

The blood drained out of Kitty's face and she felt so weak she had to sit down but even so she did her best to make her voice sound normal. 'Who told you that?'

'Celia! Who else? She sent me a letter saying you wanted a daughter so badly you stole me from her.'

'And you believed her?'

'Why should she lie?'

'People do. I've never stolen a thing in my life!'

'You wanted a daughter, though?'

'I'd lost one. Of course I did. You were very welcome.' Kitty forced a smile.

Katherine fought against being charmed by that smile and her fingers gripped the edge of the desk. 'I didn't want to believe her, but why should she lie? She's nothing to gain.'

Kitty stared at her and felt suddenly furiously angry. 'You haven't known the woman five minutes and you're taking her word above mine? Have I ever let you down? Haven't I fed and clothed and cared for you? You're *my* daughter and Celia has no right to tell you any different. Now go and get out of those wet shoes and be down here in ten minutes. There's jobs you should be doing.'

Katherine did not move. 'I wish I could believe you.' Her voice cracked. 'I know you've done all the things you say and I'm grateful, but that doesn't prove you're my real mother.'

Kitty stared at her a moment. Getting up, she took her arm and ushered her into the tiny office, closing the door behind them so they were completely private. 'My name's on your birth certificate,' she said in a low voice. 'What proof has Celia got?'

'She told me Ben was there at the birth, that Annie's mother delivered me – that the maid Hannah went for her despite there being a raid on. That I was premature and born in the basement because of a raid. She seemed to know everything! About the bomb – how I was put in a drawer and wrapped up in cotton wool. She even told me she was moved up into the dining room and a bed brought down from upstairs.'

'I suppose she said I wasn't even there?' There was an angry flush on Kitty's face.

Katherine shook her head. 'She said you kept her spirits up when she was terrified that she was going to die.'

'Clever of her,' said Kitty grimly. 'I should have given her more credit. Still, all you've got to do is ask Ben if she's telling the truth. Would you take his word for it that you're my daughter?'

Katherine hesitated and Kitty's expression tightened. 'I don't believe this! Are you saying you don't even trust Ben? Hasn't he been the best brother a girl could have?'

'Yes, damn you!' Katherine's voice broke and her eyes filled with tears as she leant against the table holding the typewriter. 'But that doesn't prove a thing! He's kind and generous and I love him to bits, just like I love Pops, but he'd say what you wanted him to say. You're his mother and he loves you very much.'

'Pops?' Kitty was visibly trembling now. 'Would you believe him?'

'He'd say anything to please you too!' The tears were rolling down Katherine's cheeks and she had to swallow before she could continue, 'He wants you to retire so he can go to Scotland and walk the hills. You said so the other day. He'll be able to be near Jack then. So it's in his interest to keep me here.'

'And what's wrong with that? Don't you want to stay here?' Kitty held out her arms to her. 'You have a future here! From the moment I held you in my arms, I planned for you to take over the Arcadia. What girl could ask for more?'

'I know. You've given me a lot.' Katherine sniffed back her tears. 'But you vet all my friends and you chased Patrick away.'

'He wasn't right for you! He wouldn't fit in here. Besides, you hardly know him. I was looking out for you. Isn't that a natural feeling for a mother?'

'Yes, but – I don't believe you're my *natural* mother. I remember girls at school saying you were old enough to be my grandmother.'

'So you think I'm your grandmother now?' Kitty stared at her and there was hope in her eyes. 'Perhaps you think Mick . . .?'

'I did.' Katherine wiped her hand across her wet face. 'But I asked Celia and she told me I wasn't his child.'

For a moment Kitty was completely stunned. Deep down she had always believed Katie *was* Mick's child. 'She's lying,' she gasped. 'She's bloody lying! She left you here because she knew –' Her voice faltered and she felt terribly sick.

There was silence.

'So you admit it?' said Katherine at last in a faint voice.

Kitty nodded. 'I admit it. Even so, this was where you belonged. Celia didn't bother with you until a few days ago. We've loved you for years.'

'She tried to see me,' Katherine found herself defending Celia. 'She came back here but it was boarded up and we were in Scotland. She wouldn't have known that if she hadn't been here.'

That knowledge was a body blow to Kitty. 'I never knew,' she whispered, feeling as if the room had tilted.

'She's had such an unhappy life,' said Katherine, voice trembling. 'She lost both her parents early, had no money and nearly died from TB herself. Couldn't you have welcomed her? Why did you have to push her out in the rain? Why did you lie to me? Why couldn't you have trusted me with the truth when she was here? You were cruel. I hardly recognised you. I feel as if I don't know who you are any more. I feel as if I don't know who *I* am any more – Katie or Katherine or even "Katie girl" as Mick calls me. I need to be with her. I need to get to know her.'

'No, you don't,' said Kitty desperately. 'She can't improve on the girl you are. You're Katherine Mcleod. You were never Katherine Mcdonald.'

'I never had the chance to be! I could have been if I'd known the truth. I could have grown up knowing I was Katherine Mcdonald. She calls me Katherine. I could have got used to it.'

'You'd have grown up a bastard in that case,' said Kitty with brutal candour.

Katherine flinched and her throat moved but she could not get any words out.

'I'm sorry! I'm sorry! I shouldn't have said that.' Kitty moved towards her with hands outstretched imploringly but Katherine backed away.

'It's you that couldn't cope with that,' she gasped. 'It would have brought shame on you, and you've always worried about your reputation.'

'No!' Kitty's arms dropped to her sides. 'It was *you* I didn't want to feel shame.'

'I don't believe you.'

'Why don't you?'

'I've told you why. But if you want more – you've always worried about how things look. You dressed me like a little pink lady from when I was born. Well, I'm not yours, and I'm certainly no lady!'

Kitty felt wounded and utterly exhausted. 'What are you going to do?'

'Live with her.' With a weary gesture Katherine pushed back her hair. 'She almost had a nervous breakdown, you know. You brought me up to care about people and she needs someone to look after her.'

'You can't mean it! Let's talk about this, Katie.'

'I'm not Katie any more,' she said fiercely, hugging herself. 'I'm not a little girl with a stupid childish name.'

'Katherine then. There must be another way. Perhaps she'd like to come and live here? She could have her old job back!'

'As an all-purpose maid?' Katherine laughed. 'And what would be my job now I'm no longer one of the family – kitchen maid?'

'Don't be silly! We all muck in here. You change beds and wash dishes now. It's part of the job if we're short of money or short-handed. I do it, and I own the place.'

Katherine looked discomfited for a moment then jutted her chin and folded her arms. 'Celia wouldn't come and it wouldn't work.'

'Why wouldn't it?'

Katherine thought about it a moment. 'She'd resent you and you'd resent her. I'd be piggy in the middle. You'd both want a piece of me, in different ways.'

'What *do* you mean?'

She thought again. 'You'd want to carry on telling me what to do, and she – she'd want me to tell her what to do. And she'd have you telling her what to do as well!'

'What's wrong with that?'

'It's not right!' she said emphatically. 'She's my mother, and it's not what I want for her or me.'

'What *do* you want?'

Katherine hesitated because she didn't know what she wanted really. Part of her wanted to carry on living her old life and be Katie, despite what she'd said. Another part wanted to help Celia to have more *go* in her, and another part still wanted to run away from the whole thing and be somebody completely different. A Katie girl perhaps? She took a deep breath and stared at Kitty's familiar features. 'I want to do what I said and live with Celia for a while.'

Kitty's weary blue eyes gazed into hers. 'Where will you live?'

'She has somewhere.'

'What'll you live on?'

'I'll get another job. You've trained me well.'

'You're only young.'

Annoyance flashed in Katherine's eyes. 'I'm seventeen!'

Kitty was silent but felt a tug of anguish that this child she had raised was about to go out into the world, believing what she had taught her so far was enough. Well, she would learn. 'When are you going?'

Talking had calmed Katherine but suddenly she felt weepy again. Still, she kept a strong rein on her emotions and managed to say, 'In about an hour and –'

'An hour!'

'Yes!' Katherine pressed her lips together. Then she said, 'I don't want anyone knowing I'm going. I'll keep in touch. I'll write.'

'You will?'

'Of course I will.' There was a quiver in her voice when she added, 'I owe you a lot. This isn't goodbye, you know.'

'No.' Kitty blinked back the tears and took a firm grip on herself. What had John said years ago when her own boys had wanted to go their way? 'Let them.'

'Well, you go upstairs then and take what you need. You can always come back for anything you forget.'

Katherine nodded because she couldn't trust her voice and went out, hoping Ma wouldn't follow her upstairs or even wave her off at the door.

Kitty did neither because she could not bear to. Instead she did what she had always done at painful times. She got on with her work.

Chapter Eight

When Ben came in and was on his way upstairs it was Eileen who told him Katie had gone.

'What do you mean, *gone*?' he demanded, letting his rucksack slide from his shoulders and on to the landing.

'You ask your ma. It's not for me to tell tales,' she said virtuously, glad she hadn't let the cat out of the bag about Katie because Aunt Kitty was real upset. 'But it's to do with that woman who came here the other day – that Celia Mcdonald.'

Ben's heart sank. 'Where's Ma?'

'Where d'you think she is?' said Eileen in her lilting Irish brogue. 'Doing her duty. This place isn't going to fall down just because that miss who isn't related to any one of us has gone.'

'Who told you she wasn't related to us?' he said irascibly.

Eileen flushed. 'I've got ears, haven't I? I'm not saying any more. People are waiting for their pudding and I should be in the kitchen. So could you be getting out of my way, please?'

Ben moved aside and climbed the rest of the stairs

without any sign of haste. He would get washed and changed and then he and Ma were going to have a talk.

When he came downstairs he found only Eileen and one of the maids in the kitchen. So he went into the basement where he found Kitty with a cup of tea set in front of her on an occasional table and one hand clasped in John's large fist. Mick, still in his customs officer uniform, stood by the fireplace, an elbow on the mantelshelf, staring at them both. Ben thought his mother had aged ten years since they had both left for work that morning. He went over and rested a hand on her shoulder. 'What happened?'

'That's what I've asked,' said Mick irritably. 'I've only just come in and all I know is Katie's gone.'

Ben ignored him and addressed his mother. 'She knows?'

Kitty nodded. 'Celia wrote and told her . . . worked on her sympathy. It's my fault. I shouldn't have sent Celia out in the rain.'

'No, it's mine,' said Ben. 'I should never have gone looking for her.'

Kitty covered his hand with her free one. 'You did it from the best intentions. It was my stupid fault, thinking that Rita Turner could be Celia.'

'They work at the same hotel. I would have told you sooner about that if you hadn't been so worked up about Celia's having been here. Rita told me she'd told Celia about you inviting her in for a cuppa. It wasn't until they were talking the next day that she remembered Celia mentioning having worked here. Until then Celia thought we'd left and gone to live in Scotland.'

'We know that now, laddie. It's just a damn pity we didn't know it years ago for I never liked your mother not telling the girl the truth.' John's words seemed to resonate from deep inside his chest.

Mick slammed a fist down on the mantelshelf. 'I wish someone would tell me what the bloody hell is going on! I know I've been away at sea for years but I am part of this family. What is this about Celia and Katie? For God's sake, someone tell me!'

John's hand tightened on his wife's and Ben stared at them. 'You haven't told him?' He glanced at his brother in dismay.

'Well?' Mick demanded, feeling as if they were all ranged against him.

A pulse beat visibly in Kitty's neck and the words were just a thread of sound when she spoke. 'Katie – Katherine, I should say – is Celia's daughter and she's just found out.'

Mick could not believe it. 'Say that again?'

Ben repeated Kitty's words.

'*You* knew?' With a growing sense of outrage, Mick assimilated that information. 'How could you keep this from me all these years?' His voice shook and he had to pause to get a grip on himself. His mind was in turmoil as the memory of that day in the field with Celia came to him as clear as a picture. 'Why didn't you tell me? I don't get you all! Katie *has* to be mine! You must have known that!'

'We thought so,' said John heavily, 'but we didn't know for sure and now Celia says not.'

'She just went off and left the baby!' cried Kitty. 'We all thought you were dead at the time. Celia was in a state about you being missing, no doubt about it, and it hurt her to mention your name.'

Mick sank on to a chair and put his head in his hands. 'Katie has to be mine,' he repeated in muffled tones.

'You're admitting it's a possibility?' said Ben.

Mick lifted his head and there was a desolate expression on his face. 'What the hell does it sound like to you?'

'OK, keep yer hair on! How were we to know for sure? You never mentioned her name for years.'

'That's because I thought she was dead or didn't want to have anything to do with me. I wrote to her after . . . it happened but she never answered my letter.'

Kitty moved aside her cup and saucer and leant across the table towards him. 'Was it that time you were home on leave and your ship had been damaged and was in dock?'

'Yes, August 1940. We were nearly blown up by the Luftwaffe and were out of our heads with relief.' He stared at his mother and there was a tinge of red in his cheeks. 'I'd swear there was nobody else before me.'

'She told me you'd visited her.' There was a tremor in Kitty's voice. 'Katie was premature. The dates would be about right. She has to be yours. Celia even named her after me! Doesn't that prove something?'

'Then why say now that Katie's not mine?' he demanded.

'She's sick in the head, that's why,' said Ben glumly.

'She sent Ma an anonymous letter saying she'd stolen Katie and was coming for her.'

'What?' Mick gave a sharp laugh. 'Celia did that? I can't believe it! She was –'

'She almost had a nervous breakdown,' said Kitty, pleating the embroidered tablecloth with an unsteady hand.

'Rita said her nerves were bad,' confirmed Ben.

Mick stared at him. 'Who the hell is this Rita you keep mentioning?'

Kitty told him, with Ben throwing in extra information. 'Katie was right when she said Celia's had a hard life,' she finished.

'Whose side are you on?' said Ben, sitting down and gripping his hands together until his knuckles gleamed white. 'She's taken her away from us.'

'I know. But I can feel sorry for her now I know she's probably lied about Mick not being the father.' Kitty gazed at her eldest son. 'Katie's all confused. She thought it possible you were her father because she knew you'd been sweethearts, but after Celia's saying you weren't, she doesn't know who she is and has to find out.'

'Well, who did Celia say *was* her father?' said Mick, filled with sudden doubt.

'She didn't!' Kitty groaned, and put her cheek against John's hand. 'I should have told her the truth like Pops said.'

'That must be the understatement of the century!' said Mick with a touch of bitterness. 'And now we don't even know where Katie is! Only that she's with Celia whom you say is crazy.'

'I didn't say she was crazy,' protested Kitty. 'Anyway, Katie's a big strong girl.'

'We can get her back,' said Ben, lighting a cigarette. 'Rita knows where Celia lives.'

'Let's go then.' Mick got to his feet.

Ben flashed him a startled glance. 'Give us a chance! I haven't even had me tea.'

'What's more important?' said Mick, eyes glinting. 'Katie or your bloody stomach?'

'He needs something to eat after working hard all day,' said Kitty, whisking herself out of the room into the back basement where she kept an extra fridge and some treats for the family. 'I'll make you a butty, son, and you can take it with you.'

Ben thanked her and five minutes later the brothers were on their way to Southport.

'I could knock your block off for not telling me about Katie,' said Mick, frowning at Ben across the railway carriage. They had found one to themselves.

'It was Ma's decision.' Ben bit into a ham sandwich while at the same time attempting to rub a clear patch in the condensation on the window. 'It's supposed to be summer. Some joke.'

'As bad a joke as you lot keeping secrets from me! When I think of the times I put myself out for you when we were kids!' said Mick forcefully.

'You don't understand what it was like. You and Teddy were in the forces and Jack had been evacuated to Ireland. It was just Ma, Pops and me left at home to keep things going. I was only fifteen when Celia had Katie. There were bombs dropping overhead – I can tell you *that* was no joke! Ma, Pops and me became a team, and if Ma wanted things a certain way, we did it her way because she knew better than us how to keep a hotel going. It was only being hit by that bomb that stopped things for a while and you know about that.' He took another bite of his sandwich and chewed thoughtfully, reliving the excitement and terror of the blitz.

Mick stared at him, trying to imagine what it must have been like. 'Sorry. But I still think . . .'

'Jack doesn't know,' interrupted Ben. 'I don't think Ma intended it that way but the longer it was left, the easier it was to say nothing. And let's be honest, Mick, what could you have done for Katie that we haven't? You were at sea.'

'I could have signed on for a shorter term.'

'And what?'

'Done what you did, I suppose, and helped with money.'

'I've only been like a big brother to her. It's Ma who's done the looking after.'

'But I still should have been told!'

'I agree. But I've explained! So how about accepting that things haven't been easy for any of us? Anyway, if anyone should be feeling hard done by, it's me! You haven't exactly acted like you care tuppence for me being your brother over Sarah. Since you've got back you've –'

'OK!' Mick leant towards him. 'Let's get this straight, brother. Sarah made a play for me. She'd been writing to me and came on strong. I knew you two had fallen out because Katie told me so. Sarah might be an insecure demanding little bitch but she still has a way with her that makes a man sit up and take notice. The trouble is, she needs a strong hand and you're too soft with her. You shouldn't let her walk all over you. Try playing the kind of games she plays sometimes and keep her guessing. I tell you, if I was thinking of marrying her, I wouldn't let her rule me the way she has you.'

Bread and ham separated as they slipped from Ben's fingers. 'You bloody swine! You make me sound a right idiot. I suppose you think it's funny to play games with my girl?'

'Not half as funny as discovering my sister's my daughter, and hearing my favourite brother knew all about it!'

'Favourite brother? That's a joke!' Ben's tone was wrathful as he squashed ham and bread together again. 'I could kill you for the way you put on the charm when Sarah's around.'

'Save your strength. I think she's still in two minds about which one of us she prefers. She believes you don't love her enough in that romantic way women believe in. Now me, I might behave romantically but she's still unsure whether I can be trusted and that's got her in a dither. She might just decide to marry you yet, but I wouldn't be ready to fall into her arms if she starts making a play for you again. Do as I say and act hard to get.'

'I don't get you!' said Ben, shaking his head so a flaxen curl fell on to his forehead. 'I love her, for God's sake! But you –'

'Shut up, Ben! I've had enough. This thing with Katie and Celia has thrown me and I don't know whether I'm coming or going at the moment. Right now I'm trying to get into Celia's head. What kind of mother is it who leaves her baby when she could have stayed with her?'

'She had been through a lot and believed you were dead,' said Ben savagely.

'That's no excuse. I'm going to have it out with her when I see her.'

'What about Katie's feelings? Celia could carry on saying you aren't the father and she might believe her.'

Mick said grimly, 'Whether Katie believes me or not, I'm taking her home. It's where she belongs.'

'I hope it'll be as easy as you think. By the sound of it, she went with Celia of her own free will. You heard Ma. Celia played on her sympathy. I remember feeling sorry for her myself. There's something about her. An air of – vulnerability.'

Mick knew it. It was that which had drawn him to Celia in the first place. She'd had a lousy mother but had done her duty by her. Celia had always been a carer and that was why he found it difficult to take in all that had been said about her leaving Katie. He remembered the times when she had stood up for what she believed was right. She had made him feel uncomfortable at times. Perhaps she still could, he'd have to see. 'What's this hotel like where she works?'

Ben stopped staring out of the window and thinking of Sarah. 'For a posher clientele than ours, I'd have thought.'

'What's this Rita like?'

'Not bad-looking – in her thirties, good figure. Carries herself well. Seems confident and loyal to her friends, if her not telling me where Celia lives is anything to go by. Maybe she'll tell you if you use that fatal charm of yours.'

'I've heard people say *you've* got charm. Not that I've noticed it myself,' said Mick, with his tongue in his cheek.

'Oh, shut up!' Ben closed his eyes to shut out his brother and finished eating his sandwich.

Rita looked up as the two men entered the lobby and finished her conversation with one of the guests. 'Celia's not here,' she called to Ben. 'But I'm off duty soon. If you want to wait, I can show you where she lives.'

'Thanks! What's made you change your mind?' he said, resting an arm on the counter and smiling at her.

Rita's brows knit. 'I don't know if it's anything to do with you but she asked for her cards on Monday. Mrs Henshall nearly blew a gasket. Celia actually answered her back and called her a blood-sucking vampire!'

'You think she's got a job somewhere else?' interrupted Mick, looking her over and thinking Ben's description was fairly accurate.

Rita glanced at him. 'Who are you?'

He held out a hand. 'I'm Mick Ryan and I appreciate your help in finding Celia.'

Rita looked at Ben. '*This* is your brother? The one who . . .?'

'He's much better,' said Ben. 'It's amazing what doctors can do these days.'

Her lips twitched. 'He doesn't look a bit like I imagined.'

Mick fixed his brother with a hard stare. 'What have you been telling her?'

Ben's eyes gleamed wickedly and he said to Rita, 'He's a lot better since he had the brain transplant.'

'Oh, aye! Perhaps it's him who's responsible for Celia going off. He looks normal but –'

'Who said I'm not normal?' said Mick, giving his brother a suspicious look. 'What's this about my brain? I'm not Frankenstein's monster. What's he been saying about me?'

Rita shook her head in smiling reproof. 'In that case, I'll meet you both in a quarter of an hour. The bar's open if you want a drink?'

'Point us in the right direction,' said Ben, 'and we'll see you in a quarter of an hour.'

It was a silent trio that stood waiting at the level crossing in Aughton Road. Rita was wondering if she was doing the right thing taking them to see Celia, but her friend had been acting so strangely since Rita had mentioned visiting the Arcadia that she wanted to get at the truth. The train went by and a few moments later the barrier lifted and they crossed the railway track.

'Is it much further?' asked Mick.

'No. A couple of minutes' walk, that's all.' She averted her gaze. There was something about his looks that disturbed her and she did not want to dwell on why that should be. She took the two men past a line of shops and on beyond the Up Steps pub until she came to the house where Celia lodged. It had a small front garden bordered by a privet hedge which a woman was clipping.

'Is Celia in, Mrs Moore?' asked Rita.

The woman snipped off a particularly rampant length of privet. 'She's gone,' she said, mouth tightening. 'And not a word to me. I went upstairs and found the key in her door. Opened it and the room was empty of all her things. Not that she had much.' She eyed the brothers. 'You debt collectors? Is that why she's done a flit?'

'Do us a favour!' said Rita, laughing. 'Would I have brought them here if they were debt collectors? These men knew Celia when she lived in Liverpool.'

'Besides, we're not wearing bowler hats,' said Mick woodenly. 'I take it she didn't leave a forwarding address?'

Mrs Moore shook her head and pursed her lips. 'She's gone, that's all I can say. Now if you don't mind, I've this hedge to finish.'

They walked away and Ben said, 'Hell! That's put the kibosh on things!'

'You can say that again!' Mick's dark eyebrows almost met in a scowling line as he kicked a can in the gutter and sent it flying. 'How the hell are we going to find her and Katie now?'

'Katie?' asked Rita.

'Celia's daughter and mine,' he said.

Rita's jaw dropped but she recovered quickly. 'So that's what this is all about! She's a runaway wife with a child, and never mentioned a word to me because it was too terrible to talk about. Battered her, did you?' Her eyes glinted coldly. 'Well, the worm's turned. I'm glad she's got away!'

'Hang on,' protested Mick, scowling at her and digging his hands into his pockets. 'You've too much imagination.'

'I'm not the only one,' she said, glaring at Ben. 'I'm disappointed in you. I thought you were nice and caring.'

'I am!' he said. 'You've got it all wrong . . .'

'Too right she has,' said Mick. 'I'm not even married to Celia.'

Rita gasped. 'Have you no shame? You're worse than I thought!'

'I know I've got my faults, but why don't you shut up a minute and listen?' said Mick. 'There was a war on. I didn't know about the baby being mine and Celia left her with my mother who brought her up as her own. I haven't seen Celia since the day we –' He stopped.

A wave of colour flooded Rita's cheeks. 'Damn!' she said. 'Me and my big mouth!'

'That's women for you. You shouldn't jump to conclusions without having all the facts,' said Mick, smiling. 'But I'll forgive you.'

'I don't need your forgiveness,' she muttered. 'But perhaps your brother should have told me the truth instead of working on my sympathies, telling me you'd lost your wits when your ship blew up. He's made me feel a proper fool.'

'I said nothing about his ship blowing up,' said Ben, struggling not to laugh. 'Perhaps I should have! And maybe had him floating with only a lifejacket in the sea!'

Rita gasped again. 'You've no shame, either of you!

Anyway, I've said enough. I'm going home.' She turned away.

'Hang on!' said Mick, seizing her arm. 'We still need your help. You're Celia's friend and she might get in touch with you.'

Rita frowned at him. 'Why should she? She didn't trust me with the truth.'

'Aren't there things in your life you've never told anybody? Anyway, she probably knows you know now. She's bound to realise we'll come looking for her.'

'In that case,' interpolated Ben, glancing at his watch, 'it's unlikely she *will* get in touch. She might think Rita will tell us where she is.'

'And she mightn't!' said Mick emphatically. 'It depends how much she needs a friend.'

Rita felt a moment's bewilderment. 'I can't understand why she's gone off like this. I mean, if it's like you say, why run?'

'You're talking about someone who's got a sick mind,' Ben reminded her. 'Celia sent Ma a letter saying she'd stolen her baby and that she was coming to get it back.'

'She did that?' Rita could scarcely believe it. 'I know it upset her when I told her I'd seen your mother, but . . .'

There was silence for a moment and Ben glanced at the darkening sky and then at his watch again. 'It's not your fault. Anyway, we'd better be getting back to break the bad news to Ma. Thanks for trying to help us, Rita.'

'But I haven't really,' she said, suddenly aware that Mick was still holding her arm. 'What are you going to do?'

'No idea at the moment,' he said, grimacing. 'She *might* just get back to you.'

'We'll keep in touch,' said Ben.

Rita nodded. 'At least you know where to find me.'

'It would probably help if we gave you our phone number,' said Mick, freeing her arm and unclipping a fountain pen from his breast pocket. He wrote on a page of a small notebook and gave it to her. 'Thanks. You're a real mate.'

'Glad to help. 'Bye.' She pocketed the paper and walked away, thinking that was probably the last she would see of him.

When the two brothers arrived back at the Arcadia they found Kitty sitting in front of the fire in the basement. She gripped the arms of the rocking chair and her face registered disappointment. 'You didn't find her?'

'Sorry, Ma. Celia'd upped and left,' said Mick. 'She must have realised we wouldn't let Katie go that easy.' He sank down into a chair and rubbed his face with his hands. 'I feel whacked.'

'It's the shock. Sarah's upstairs, by the way.'

'I noticed her car but I'm in no mood to speak to her at the moment.'

'I think you should. Eileen's told her about Celia and Katie. She's in the bar with Pops.'

'Bloody hell!' he groaned. 'The whole road'll know soon. Even so, there's nothing I want to say to Sarah at the moment.' He glanced at his brother. 'You go up and see her. Here's your chance to make up to her.'

Ben did not move and Mick said irritably, 'Well, what is it? Changed your mind about wanting Sarah and fancy Rita now instead?'

'I'm not going just because you've told me to,' growled Ben, toying with his cigarette lighter.

'What is this?' said Kitty, getting to her feet in one weary movement. 'Hasn't there been enough upset today without you two arguing? It isn't the last we've seen of Katie. She did say she'd get in touch.'

'You didn't say that to us before,' chorused her sons, and resting their heads on the back of their chairs, stretched their feet towards the fire and closed their eyes.

Kitty poked them both with her foot. 'Wake up! That's because I'd rather you'd found her and persuaded her to come home now. I'd still rather. Otherwise she might think we don't want her.'

'She can't believe that,' said Ben, opening one eye.

'We don't know what's going on in her head. She believes she isn't one of us any more.'

'Poor kid,' said Mick, not moving an eyelid. 'But there's nothing we can do right now, Ma.'

'No, but what about Sarah? One of you should speak to her.'

'OK!' said Ben, accepting that his brother had had a worse shock than he had.

He got up and left the basement, thinking he was really in no mood to talk sensibly to Sarah. But then, having a sensible conversation with her wasn't the norm lately. He might as well get what he had to say over with.

Yet as soon as he entered the bar lounge and saw her

leaning against the bar talking to John, the breath caught in his throat. She was looking as vibrant as ever in a pillar-box red skirt and a white blouse patterned with huge poppies.

She noticed him straightaway. 'So the wanderers have returned,' she said, fingers wrapped round a glass. 'Did you find them?'

'If I had, Pops would be the first to know.' He rested an elbow on the counter and said to John, 'Celia's scarpered.'

'Your mother?' he asked anxiously.

'Seems to be bearing up. Mick's with her.'

His stepfather looked relieved but even so said, 'Perhaps you can take over here and I'll go and talk to her? We have to decide what to tell Jack.'

'Give us five minutes. I want a word with Sarah first.'

'Don't mind me,' she said with an artificially bright smile. 'I'll just go home. It's obvious you all want to have a family powwow.'

'Fine!' said Ben, not daring to meet her eyes in case his resolve weakened. 'You're showing real consideration. I'll see you to your car. Are you ready?'

'Let me finish my drink! And why don't you have one yourself? A pint – or maybe an Irish whiskey would be better? It'd do you a world of good.'

'I've had a pint,' he said, jingling the change in his pocket. 'Hurry up, Sarah. I haven't got all night and I've been working all day.'

'OK! Keep your hair on!' She drained the glass, and lifting her jacket from the back of a chair, click-clacked out of the room ahead of him.

'So Katie's gone?' she declared when they stood outside on the pavement.

'Why say it when you know it?' he said, glancing away from her and across the road.

'I was just – I wanted – I know you're fond of her,' said Sarah lamely. 'But I find the whole thing about her being Celia's daughter incredible. I think Aunt Kitty's a hero bringing up someone else's child.'

'Ma loves Katie! Loved her from the moment she was born. It's corny but true that she brought sunshine into our lives, and me and our Mick are both determined to get her back.'

'I think that's really noble of you both,' said Sarah, toying with her car keys.

'Noble?'

'I mean, you could both so easily not want her around – all the fuss Aunt Kitty made of her, and with her planning on handing the Arcadia over to her. After all, she's not really one of you, is she?'

Ben felt real disappointment in Sarah but her words had made him realise something. 'Of course she's one of us! Ma brought her up. She belongs here. Anyway, haven't you even thought how she landed up living with us? Haven't you thought about Mick and Celia being sweethearts? They saw each other during the war. They made love. Use your brains. Why d'you think Celia left her with us?'

Sarah stared at him and he had a mental image of the cogs slowly turning in her brain. Her eyes widened. 'She's Mick's daughter?'

'Got it in one! Fancy her as a stepdaughter, do you? You hate each other, I believe.' He turned and took the front steps in a stride.

'Ben!' Sarah hurried after him. 'You can't just leave it like that! What's going to happen? What's Mick going to do?'

'He's going to try and find them, of course.'

'And *then* what's he going to do?' She stared up at him. They were standing very close on the top step.

'Hadn't you better ask him? You've spent enough time in his company lately.' He fixed his eyes on a spot two inches above her head and tried not to breathe in the familiar fragrance of her favourite perfume, Coty's L'Aimant. 'I've other things on my mind.'

'Such as?' she demanded.

He said the first thing that came into his head. 'There's Rita.' His gaze dropped and their eyes met as he forced himself to continue: 'She's the receptionist at the hotel in Southport where Celia was working. She likes me just the way I am, which is good for both of us because I've no intention of changing – for her, for you, for anybody!' He turned and went inside.

'Ben, wait!' She sounded so stricken that he weakened and faced her.

Sarah pressed herself against him and looped her arms about his neck. 'Ben, Ben, I've made a terrible mistake.' Her dark eyes were drowning in tears. 'I'm truly sorry for the things I said to you. I know I've behaved badly. I did fancy your Mick a little bit – but it's you I love, really. Honest, I do!'

He stared down at her and his brother's voice suddenly echoed in his head and he thought: If I capitulate now, how will I know if she really means what she says and it isn't just because she thinks she might have lost our Mick to Celia? Ben thought he loved her enough to cope with her insecurities and moods for life, but needed to know for sure that she loved him. He loosened her hands from about his neck and brought them down to hold between his. 'I'll think about what you've said. But at the moment I'm too upset about Katie leaving to make any big decisions.'

'Katie! It's always her,' said Sarah in a petulant voice. 'She's no longer your responsibility but Mick's and Celia's! It's me that needs you, Ben.'

'Ma needs me. And if you had any heart, Sarah, you'd be thinking about her. All her dreams were wrapped up in our Katie. How do you think she's feeling now?'

'You know I've always been fond of your mother. She's always accepted me as I am.' Tears rolled down Sarah's cheeks and Ben was almost unmanned. He wanted to lick them away and kiss her better and have her arms go round him and for her to hold him in the way he desperately needed. Instead he dropped her hands and went inside and this time closed the door very firmly behind him.

Chapter Nine

Katherine pressed her forehead against the window as hailstones rattled on the glass like bullets from a machine-gun and wished herself out there where she could feel their icy sting upon her face. It would have been exhilarating to walk along the pier battling with the elements; much more fun than staying here in the boarding house where they had been for the last two weeks. The week before, they had gone to Rhyl and that had not been too bad because the weather had been better, but now it had changed again. Even so, the room was far too warm for her liking. But that was how Celia liked it, and who was she to complain? Celia had told her that when she was her age there had often been no coal to burn and no pennies for the gas meter so that now she was older she really appreciated the warmth of a good electric fire, even if she had to put shillings in the meter.

'Come away from the window, Katherine. You'll catch your death standing there,' she said, putting down her book and reaching for the box on the floor. 'What a summer! Have a chocolate, luv?' She gazed anxiously at her daughter. 'You can afford to put on a bit of weight. I bought these as a special treat.'

'No, thanks. I'm not hungry.' She had not felt really hungry since she had left the Arcadia. The first few days her throat had ached constantly as she fought against tears every time she thought of the family and not belonging to them any more. She had had to keep telling herself that they had deceived her and she was where she rightfully belonged now.

She moved away from the window and sat on one of the beds, thinking that Celia had bought so many special treat chocolates since last week that they were no longer special. 'When are you going back to work?'

'Soon,' she said, avoiding her daughter's eyes. 'You do like this room, don't you?' Again there was that anxious note in her voice. 'I thought it would be nice for us to have a little holiday.'

'It's a nice room,' she replied, and it was, but it was not the Arcadia. She swallowed a sigh. The boarding house was situated in a row of terraces and their room overlooked a street with trees. 'It's just that I'm thinking about money and wondering if I could get a job in the Seaview alongside you? I don't want you keeping me and using up all your savings.'

'What savings? I've never had any money to save.' Celia chuckled. 'Came into a little windfall, I did. I'm like me gran, I enjoy a little flutter.'

'You mean, you won some money?'

She winked. 'Somebody has to win. Why not me?'

'Did you win much?' Katherine caught herself up quickly. 'Sorry, I shouldn't have asked.' She was thinking of her own dwindling savings and having not written to the family yet because she did not know what to say.

'It doesn't matter, luv. But I'm still not going to tell you. I don't like talking about money. Too many people boast of what they've got and what others haven't.'

That was true, thought Katherine, but it was not an answer to her problem. 'It's just that I'm not used to sitting around doing nothing,' she murmured. 'Why don't we go to the Seaview and see if they'll give me a job?'

'No!' Celia pressed her lips tightly together.

'Why not? It makes sense,' she said in coaxing tones. 'With two wages coming in, we might be able to afford a decent flat.'

'We can't go back to the Seaview,' muttered Celia. 'Don't you see, *she* can trace us there! It'll be the first place they'll look and I don't want them finding out where we are. They might persuade you to go back to them.'

Katherine's heart leapt at the thought of the family looking for her, then plummeted again. She had to stick this out. Her eyes focused on her mother's face. 'Have you given up your job there, then?'

Celia nodded. 'I'll find us jobs, don't you worry.'

'Can't we go looking now?'

She sighed. 'Give it a rest, luv. I've worked all my life and I'm not young any more. D'you know, I've never had a holiday before so what's wrong with me taking a few weeks off now? I know of a few boarding houses who are always short of staff and they'll be glad to take us on later. Despite the weather, you can guarantee some people'll still be taking their holidays here. And there's the Southport Show at the end of this month and folk'll flock in to attend that.'

Katherine felt like saying, 'But if we haven't a proper home and need to earn the money for rent and board, it's the wrong time for us to take a holiday!' Besides, she didn't trust the kind of places Celia mentioned. If an employer treated their staff well, they stayed. She had not said so but when she had gone out for some fresh air on her own yesterday she had had an unsuccessful go at finding a job for herself, thinking perhaps it might be better if she and Celia were not in each other's company all the time. Mostly, though, it was because she felt a need to be doing something. 'I think I'll go for a walk,' she said now.

'In this weather?' Celia glanced in the direction of the window and shivered.

'Yes,' said Katherine firmly. 'I've got to have some exercise or I'll go mad.'

'You've got young legs, that's what it is,' said Celia, smiling. 'I remember when I was your age, I could walk for hours and not get tired.'

'Who did you walk with?' Katherine took a comb from her handbag and, gazing into the mirror on the chest of drawers, managed to twist her long hair up into a knot. She applied a dusting of face powder and lipstick and then went over to the window and rubbed a clear patch in the condensation. 'The sun's coming out. There's a rainbow over towards the sea.'

'That's a good sign,' said her mother, yawning. 'I learnt that in Sunday School. God places them there to remind Him never to destroy mankind again. That's why there's still some bad 'uns about, so you watch out for them!

You've been protected living at the Arcadia. Now you're out in the big bad world and, I can tell you, there's plenty of people around ready to knock a person down.'

Katherine thought, I wasn't that protected that I don't know there's evil in the world. Even so she said, 'I'll be careful.' She checked the seams of her stockings were straight before taking a yellow raincoat from the hook on the back of the door. 'See you later.'

Once outside she experienced an enormous sense of release and almost skipped down the road, breathing deeply of the cool damp air which tasted different from the Liverpool variety; despite all the talk in the *Echo* about cleaning it up, it still had a gritty texture to it sometimes. Tears pricked her eyes again as she thought of the family but she told herself not to be such a wet. It was not as if she was never going to see them again. She could go back anytime she liked – but she knew she wouldn't. Not just yet anyway. She needed to come to terms with who she was, now she was with her natural mother. Celia did need someone to take care of her much more than Ma did; she had three men to look after her. But Katherine *had* to find a job!

After a bit of a walk she came to Hesketh Park and the Clarence Hotel. With the sea, a golf course and park nearby, it was in a good position. She remembered seeing the hotel advertised in the Southport Guide left lying around in Ben's bedroom. '*Unanimous verdict – best value obtainable*' it had had blazoned at the bottom of the page. She had wondered who it was who had worded that banner recommendation, and drawing on the confidence of one brought up in the business, ran up the steps, only slowing down when she saw the woman arranging flowers in the lobby.

'May I speak to Mrs Ashton, please?' asked Katherine.

'You have a reservation?'

'No.' She smiled and said with an air of confidentiality, 'I've come to offer my services.'

The woman drew back slightly. 'I beg your pardon?'

'I'm very experienced. I grew up in the business and can do a bit of everything. Wait at table – clean – handle Reception – balance the books – cook.'

'You've come to the wrong place,' said the woman in a voice so frigid that Katherine almost winced. 'Cuisine is our speciality heah! We are not looking for a Jill-of-all-trades, so if you could take yourself orf?'

She almost did but a man came through a doorway at that moment and smiled at her. 'Who's this?' he asked.

'No one for you to concern yourself with, Albert,' said the woman with a twitch of her majestic bosom. 'If you could check today's newspapers are in a fit state in the lounge, I would appreciate it.'

The man, who was tall and gawky with a moustache and receding hair, continued to smile at Katherine. 'Have I seen you before?'

'Only if you've ever stayed at the Arcadia Hotel in Liverpool,' she said promptly, returning his smile.

'I'd guessed the Liverpool,' said the woman, tut-tutting. 'Southport is a very different kettle of fish, my girl. Now if you'd like to leave . . .'

'I'm going,' said Katherine with a wry smile. 'I can tell when I'm not wanted.'

'Hang on there,' said Albert, resting an elbow on the desk and cocking one mobile eyebrow at the woman. 'Maggie, old girl, haven't we anything?'

'No, we have not,' she said crossly. 'And for years I've been telling you that I hate being called Maggie!'

He turned to Katherine and said in a low voice, 'Sorry, my dear. Do come and see us some other time. Staff are inclined to come and go pretty smartly here.'

She thanked him and thought if she'd only had him to contend with she would definitely come back, but the dragon in Reception had rather put her *orf*.

She tried several more places but it was definitely a no go area at the Mayfair, where dogs were welcome at three shilling and sixpence a day but not Liverpudlians who were seventeen with no references and only a boarding house for an address. She tried several more places and some told her to apply in writing as they might need extra staff later in the season and others met her request with a straight refusal.

Her feet began to ache in her high-heeled shoes so that she was almost hobbling when she headed once more in the direction of the Promenade where she remembered seeing a medium-sized hotel called the Lancaster which had looked a decent enough place.

The sea breeze blew moisture from the striped awning overhead and splattered her raincoat as she took the two steps leading to the hotel's entrance. She turned the brass knob on the front door and went inside.

The entrance hall was much of a muchness with the

Arcadia and without hesitation she approached the man wearing a pinstripe suit sitting behind the reception desk. He had smoothed-back shiny brown hair and she guessed he was around the same age as Mick. He flashed her a smile. 'Can I help you, miss?'

She did not hesitate. 'Miss Katherine Mcdonald. Are you the proprietor?'

'That's right. I'm Mr Walsh.' He flicked open the leatherbound book on the desk in front of him and lifted his eyes, which on close inspection were lugubrious and had bags under them as if he hadn't slept much lately. 'Do you require a room, Miss Mcdonald?'

'I'm sure your rooms are very nice,' she said with a candid smile, 'but no. I'm seeking employment and wondered if you had any vacancies? I do have experience in the hotel trade and am prepared to do anything because due to family reasons I've had to leave my last job and –'

He interrupted her. 'You *are* Liverpudlian?'

She said frankly, 'Would you hold it against me if I said yes?'

He smiled. 'My wife's a Liverpudlian. I'm sorry, but we've just taken on extra staff.'

Katherine's spirits sank and she was about to turn away when he stopped her. 'You say you're prepared to do anything? Do you mean that?'

'Yes,' she said swiftly, knees unexpectedly weak with relief.

'And are you prepared to work in Liverpool?'

She could not believe it. 'What is this? You're offering me a job in a hotel in Liverpool?'

He opened a flap in the desk. 'Come with me. If you're not fussy, my wife may have something for you.'

Before Katherine could even think of asking him what he meant by 'not fussy' he vanished through a door to the right of the desk. She followed him into a small sitting room where a woman lay stretched out on a sofa with a plaid rug thrown over her legs. There was a Moses basket on two chairs beside her and from it came the mewling of a very young baby.

'Hettie, this is Miss Katherine Mcdonald and she's looking for a job. She says she'll do anything and I've told her you might have a job for her in Liverpool. I'll leave you two alone.' He smiled encouragingly at them before closing the door behind him.

'Well! The nerve of the man!' exclaimed Mrs Walsh as soon as he had gone. She looked to be at least ten years younger than her husband, with hair cropped close to her head and curled in an unruly fashion about her small face. She gave an impish smile. 'He didn't tell you what the job is, did he? You probably won't want it when I tell you.'

'I'll do it! Just tell me what it is,' said Katherine, almost jumping up and down with impatience.

Mrs Walsh shook her head. 'You won't want it. *I* don't want it! Even if I could do it, which I can't with the baby and this place to run. Besides, you're probably too young.' She looked doubtfully at her. 'Although young and strong is just what she needs . . .'

'Who?' cried Katherine, liking the look of the woman but wishing she would get to the point.

'My gran!' wailed Hettie Walsh, staring helplessly at

her. 'She's an awld bitch but she needs help . . . not that she'll admit it.'

'What kind of help?' asked Katherine cautiously.

'In her shop. She's almost crippled with rheumatism but refuses to give up the shop. It's been a way of life with her since before she was married. She's had more assistants than I've fingers since my mother died, but none of them'll put up with her because she's her own worst enemy. It's the pain that makes her like that, you understand. She hasn't always been that way. She won't come and live here – not that I believe that'd work – so the only thing I can think of is for me to pay for help so she can carry on as long as possible where she is.'

'But we've no place to live in Liverpool.'

'That's OK. If you're not fussy there's a couple of empty rooms above those which my gran uses over the shop. She could do with someone there round the clock. By the way, who's we?'

Katherine barely hesitated. 'My mother.' The job was not what she really wanted but it was better than nothing. Besides she was used to being nice to people, especially elderly ladies who came into town from the wilds of Lancashire or Wales to see a show or go shopping. Although sick, stubborn old ladies who wanted to carry on running a shop weren't her style – but maybe that was where her mother would prove useful.

Mrs Walsh sighed. 'You don't want the job? I knew it. It's a tough one, isn't it?'

'You've been very honest.'

'No sense in lying,' interrupted the older woman.

'You'd soon find out the truth. It would need a saint to take on the job.'

'It's not what I was looking for, but maybe I would be interested. What kind of shop is it?'

'A pet shop. That's another problem – not everybody can cope with animals.'

Katherine stared at her and vaguely remembered Celia mentioning something about her mother's having kept a pet shop. Perhaps this offer of a job could be the one to tempt her away from taking too long a holiday? 'My mother worked in a pet shop when she was a girl. If she can come too then maybe we'll consider it.' She felt certain that she herself would be able to find something else, if the job Mrs Walsh had described was not enough for two of them. After all, the country was supposed to be crying out for workers now the dark years of austerity were behind them.

A grin lit up Mrs Walsh's face. 'She sounds like the answer to my prayer, but perhaps the pair of you had better have a look at the place first and meet Gran?'

'No harm in having a decko,' said Katherine. 'Do you want to know something about us? I mean, you don't know us from Adam.'

'You look OK to me,' said Mrs Walsh cheerfully. 'Now let me give you Gran's address and you can get back to me as soon as possible.'

Celia was standing at the window looking out for her when Katherine arrived back at the boarding house. As soon as she entered the room, her mother pounced.

'Where've you been? I thought you must have gone back to *her*, the time you were!'

'I wouldn't go off without telling you,' said Katherine, as Celia helped her off with her raincoat and hung it on the back of a chair. She kicked off her shoes and wriggled her toes. 'How d'you feel about going back to Liverpool?'

Celia sat down heavily on a bed. 'Is that where you've been?'

'No! I've been looking for hotel work but with no luck. I've been offered something else instead.' She leaned forward. 'You did work in a pet shop when you were a girl, didn't you?'

Celia's grey eyes showed surprise. 'What's that got to do with anything?'

'This woman, Mrs Walsh, whose husband owns the Lancaster Hotel, has asked me if I would like the job of helping her elderly gran who has a shop in Liverpool?'

'I knew it! You're already fed up with me!' Celia's eyes filled with tears. 'Well, I suppose I shouldn't be surprised. I'm not much company and –'

'Shut up, Celia!' Katherine was tempted to give her a good shake.

'See! You can't even call me Mother!'

'No, I can't,' she said crossly. 'And I'm unhappy about that but it can't be helped. Maybe when we're more used to each other and I know you better I will. For now, listen while I tell you about this job. We can *both* go. There's rooms above the shop. They're empty but I'm sure we can buy some bits of furniture secondhand and do them up. The old woman's crippled with rheumatism, she needs someone to help her.'

There was a silence.

'Both of us! A pet shop, you say?' asked Celia cautiously.

'You've got it in one.'

Another silence.

'Where in Liverpool?'

Katherine glanced at the slip of paper Mrs Walsh had given her. 'Everton. Here, have a look. The old lady's a Mrs Evans. I know it'll be a big change from Southport but –'

'If it's Everton, it's far enough away from the Arcadia for me. Not that I know this part well and it's not too far from town, but still they won't know to come looking for us there.'

Katherine ignored all that. 'So you like the idea?'

'It depends on the old woman. But if you say we can both do it, I think it's worth a try.'

'Of course we can do it,' said Katherine positively. 'We'll have a decko in the morning and see how things go. Now isn't it time we were going down for dinner? I'm starving!'

Katherine only narrowly missed falling over a half-full sack of dog biscuits in the open doorway as she entered the shop. Celia was not so lucky but that was probably down to her stopping to admire a couple of silky-haired angora rabbits in the window and pausing to place a couple of pennies in the head of an artificial dog left outside for donations towards an animal charity. 'That needs moving,' she said, kicking the sack.

Katherine nodded absently and her nose twitched as different smells assailed her nostrils. A couple of flies buzzed as she glanced round the interior which was a mishmash of everything a pet might need. There were feeding bowls, rubber bones, thick studded leather collars and tiny ones with bells on. Dog leads hung from the ceiling as well as cages, millet sprays, and a fly paper with several flies stuck to it.

On shelves closer to hand there were more bells with tiny mirrors. There were chocolate drops, peanuts, sunflower seeds, rabbit food and sacks of straw bedding. Budgerigars twittered, several puppies yapped and a marmalade cat uncurled itself from a patch of sun on the counter where there was a marble slab, a pair of brass scales and various-sized weights, as well as a pile of newspapers.

The cat stretched and yawned before springing down from the counter and purring loudly as it stropped their legs.

'At least he's friendly,' said Katherine, bending to stroke the animal.

'Who's there?' There was the tap-tap of a stick and a curtain which hung beyond the rear end of the counter was pushed aside as the bent figure of an old woman appeared. She peered at them through thick-lensed spectacles as she rested a claw-like hand on the counter. A black shawl shrouded her shoulders and she wore a pine green frock buttoned up the front which almost reached her ankles. She wore slippers on her feet and her hair looked like it hadn't seen a brush in a month. 'Where's that lad?' she demanded.

'There was nobody here when we came in,' said Katherine.

The woman scowled. 'He's a blankety-blank nuisance! I'm not paying him to skive off as soon as me back's turned. You can't trust lads these days. What is it you want?'

'We've come to help you,' said Celia before Katherine had a chance to get another word in. She took off her coat and squeezed round the other end of the counter, her freckled face bright with excitement. 'I see you don't have mice?'

'Mice! Who sez I have mice? Why d'yer think I keep that no-good cat? Lazing about all day without a care in the world. What d'yer mean, you've come to help?'

'Your granddaughter –' began Katherine, only for Celia to get in first again.

'When I said mice, I meant white mice. We used to keep them years ago. Me mam had a pet shop Scottie Road way.'

'Did she now? And what the blankety-blank has that to do with me?' said Mrs Evans, attempting to straighten up but getting so far and no further. Her wrinkled face twisted with pain. 'One-two-three-four-five-once-I-caught-a-fish-alive,' she gasped.

'I know that one,' said Celia. 'Six-seven-eight-nine-ten – then I let it go again!' She smiled at the old woman and Katherine struggled not to laugh at the expression on Mrs

Evans's face. 'Your granddaughter sent us,' she managed
to say at last. 'She said you needed workers.'

'She had no right!' Mrs Evans glared back at them. 'If
I've told her once, I've told her a hundred times – I can
blankety-blank manage my own life!'

Katherine was about to say as tactfully as she could
that it didn't look like it to her, when a middle-aged man
stepped into the shop. 'Any dog meat, Mrs Evans?'

Katherine glanced at the shoulder-high shelves behind
the counter where there were tins of cat and dog food.

'I want none of them fancy tins,' sniffed the man. 'I
want fresh horse meat. And I need a pound of dog biscuits.'
He dipped a hand into the sack by the door and threw a
biscuit to the dog outside.

'Meat's in the fridge in the back, like it always is,'
said Mrs Evans. 'You can go get it yerself.' She nodded
in Celia's direction. 'You can weigh him the dog
biscuits.'

The man disappeared through the curtain and Celia
hurried towards the sack of biscuits. Katherine leant
against the counter. 'Do your customers always help themselves?'

'Not all. Some I wouldn't trust,' she grunted.

'None of them see to the animals, though, do they?'
asked Celia.

'The lad helps me there.'

Celia wrinkled her nose but made no comment.

'He comes cheap!' snapped Mrs Evans.

Celia reddened but carried on weighing the dog biscuits.

'Your granddaughter's willing to pay one of us, and

says if you're in agreement we could have the couple of rooms upstairs. She's worried about you,' said Katherine.

'Fine way she has of showing it, going all that way,' grumbled the old woman. 'How does she expect me to get there? It's not as if she has a car to come and fetch me in.'

'She visits you, though,' said Katherine.

'She doesn't have to bother. And I don't need a young flibbertigibbet like you telling me what's what.' She glared at Katherine from beneath bristling brows.

'I don't want to tell you what's what,' she said, smiling. 'I couldn't! I don't know what's what myself. We could work as a team, though.' It was how Kitty had always talked about running the Arcadia. Teamwork.

'Hmmmph!' Mrs Evans diverted her attention to Celia who had finished weighing the biscuits.

The man re-entered the shop carrying a handful of dark red meat and Celia removed the biscuits from the scales. The old woman peered through her spectacles at him as he threw the meat on the brass pan, brushing a fly away and fiddling with the weights. The scales went up and down on either side and Celia watched them carefully. 'Dead on a pound,' he said, and whipped the meat off quickly, wrapping it in a sheet of newspaper.

A frowning Celia handed him the biscuits but neither of them said anything as he slammed the money on the counter and hurried out. 'There was more than a pound of meat there,' she whispered to Katherine as soon as he was out of the shop.

'What was that, you – you, the older one?' snapped

Mrs Evans. 'Are you saying I don't know me own customers?'

'I wasn't saying anything of the sort,' said Celia, colour flooding her face as she folded her arms defensively across her chest. 'Perhaps there's something wrong with the scales and you both know about it?'

Katherine stared at her. 'You don't believe that?'

Celia hesitated then shook her head.

Mrs Evans made a noise in her throat and grunted, 'He's a good customer.'

'He's robbing you,' said Katherine. 'You'll soon lose your profits if they all do that.'

The old woman glared at her but made no comment as she walked slowly from behind the counter to the open doorway. Her mouth was set in a hard line and she leaned heavily on her stick. 'Where's that boy?' she muttered, gazing out across the road towards the post office and optician's.

'What do we do now?' whispered Celia.

'Wait,' said Katherine. 'What do you think of the place?'

'Plenty of work!' Celia went over to a cage of budgerigars and peered through the bars. 'Their water's clean and they've got food but there's feathers and seed husks and droppings all over the place. I don't know when their sheet of sandpaper was last changed. The lad's making sure they're fed and watered but that's about all.'

'It's too much for him,' said Mrs Evans without turning round.

'Golly! You've got sharp ears for your age,' said Celia, admiration in her voice.

The old woman snorted. 'If you're so worried about my animals, do something! Let's see what the pair of you are made of.'

Celia looked at Katherine for reassurance. 'Don't look at me,' she murmured. 'You're the one who knows about pet shops. What can I do to help?'

'Water and disinfectant is what we need first.'

'There's a sink in the back with buckets underneath,' said Mrs Evans, again without turning round.

'Hot and cold?' asked Celia.

'This isn't the blankety-blank Middle Ages! There's an electric kettle too. The girl can make me a cup of tea.'

Celia vanished through the curtain at the back of the shop but Katherine paused to ask. 'How many sugars?'

'Never heard of connie onnie, girl? I'll have three of them.'

'We used to make gorgeous coconut ice with connie onnie,' enthused Katherine. 'Ma made slabs of it in pink and white.' Tears caught at her throat unexpectedly.

'Toffee apples, that's what I remember,' grunted Mrs Evans, shifting round with obvious difficulty to face her. 'My brother worked at Tate's. He used to bring us molasses, thick and dark. It was good for us.'

Probably rotted your teeth, though, thought Katherine, as she went into the back where she found Celia standing in the middle of the room gazing about her with a tight expression on her face. Katherine let out a low whistle.

'Isn't it just!' her mother sniffed. 'There's a smell in here almost as bad as the shop.' She pounced on a saucer on the floor. 'Milk's gone sour.'

Katherine opened the fridge and recoiled before closing it swiftly. She picked up a blanket from an armchair in front of an unlit coal fire and didn't have to sniff it to smell it. 'I bet she's not even going to bed but sleeping in this chair.'

'Of course that's what she's doing! Your grandmother, my mother, did that when her chest was real bad. The old lady probably has difficulty getting up and downstairs on her own. When d'you think this place last saw a duster?'

'Or a hoover?'

'She probably hasn't got a hoover. It'd be too heavy for her to manage. A Ewebank, that's what she'll have.' Celia went over to the deep white sink and opened the cupboard underneath and took out a couple of buckets. Inside one of them was a floorcloth and a scrubbing brush. 'Doesn't anybody help her out at all?'

'She's probably too proud. Great-aunt Jane's like –' Katherine stopped, remembering she wasn't related to Eileen's grandmother any more and experiencing a sense of loss. 'I'll get cracking in here while you sort out the animals,' she said, flexing her fingers which itched to bring order out of chaos. 'And then we'll have a look upstairs.'

Celia murmured, 'You're supposed to be making her a cup of tea. And besides –'

Katherine looked at her. 'What is it?'

Celia finished lamely, 'I know it's not very Christian but what if we tidy this place up and I clean out the animals and she tells us to go? We'll have done a whole lot of work for nothing.'

'Mrs Walsh would probably pay us. Anyway, how

would your conscience feel if we just left it looking like a pigsty and those animals in their dirt?' Katherine picked up the kettle and went and filled it at the sink. She put it on the small table where it had been and switched it on.

'Watcha doin'?'

She jumped as a boy materialised on their side of the curtain and stood looking at them. He had an untidy crop of light brown hair and a lop-sided grin.

'Are you the lad?' asked Katherine dubiously.

'That's right.'

'You're only young,' said Celia, standing in the doorway of the scullery as she rolled up her sleeves.

'Don't go telling the whole world.' He dug his hands into his pockets. 'I want the money the ol' skinflint pays but I had to go and do a message for me granddad first, didn't I?' He jerked his head in the direction of the curtain. 'She sent me to see what yer were doin'.'

'Tell her Rome wasn't built in a day and she'll be having her cup of tea in a minute,' said Katherine cheerfully.

'And if she's thinking we might be thieves, tell her she hasn't anything I'd think worth stealing,' said Celia. 'After that, lad, you can come back here and help me.'

He disappeared through the curtain but was back again in a couple of minutes. 'She said there's some broken biscuits in a tin on the hearth and that yous can have a cup of tea as well.'

'Generous of her,' said Katherine. 'What's your name?'

'Donny Jones. I was named after me dad but he got deaded with me mam. They were in a charabang that crashed and it was a miracle I survived. I was only a little lad and asleep on the back seat. I live with me granddad now.'

'You can't half talk!' said Katherine.

'Talking's how I get noticed. If I said nuffink, people wouldn't know I was there. What d'you want me to do?' He addressed the question to Celia, gazing at her with a serious expression in his bright brown eyes.

She handed an empty bucket to him. 'You can put in all the water and food containers which can do with a wash. The sooner we get started, the sooner we'll finish and those poor animals and birds'll be clean and comfy.'

A couple of hours later Mrs Evans grudgingly admitted that their efforts had made a difference. The place reeked of Sanizal and down at the bottom of the back yard there were three sacks of smelly rubbish, around which blue bottles buzzed with a dizzy satisfaction.

'I suppose you can have a look upstairs,' she said, turning the shop sign to CLOSED. Donny had gone home for his tea and she was looking painfully exhausted. 'You can look at me flat and take a look at the rooms above. There's some old bits and pieces in there but you'd have to get yourselves a bed. There's no lavvy, that's in the yard. You'll have to excuse my place because I haven't been able to do much to it lately.'

Celia and Katherine looked askance at each other and Celia nodded. Katherine supposed there was no harm in looking but she was not too happy about there being no bathroom.

They helped Mrs Evans into her chair. 'There's two

lots of stairs,' she said, closing her eyes. 'You'll have noticed the ones at the front next to the shop entrance and the other –'

'We know,' said Katherine. 'It's outside in the yard.'

'The key's in the lock on the inside,' she yawned, and they left her.

They were both silent as they went up the staircase next to the shop entrance and were still quiet as they toured Mrs Evans's sitting room and bedroom. The living room was overcrowded with knick-knacks and large heavy old-fashioned furniture. Dust harbourers, Ma would have called them, thought Katherine.

There was plenty of that around and the windows hadn't seen a chammy and water for weeks, she reckoned. The fireplaces were a mixture of blackened cast iron and Victorian flowered tiles. On the landing there was a sink with cupboards underneath and a cooker. At the end of the landing towards the rear was the door which led to the outside wooden stairway down to the yard.

Katherine ran up the next flight of stairs which led to the attics and the two rooms which, if they decided to stay, would be theirs. Celia followed more slowly. The front room was larger than the back which had been used to deposit junk in. Faded floral wallpaper patterned the walls and the brown and green linoleum was worn in places. Light bulbs were naked in their sockets and no curtains draped the windows.

Celia dragged a dining chair from beneath a dirty green and gold damask curtain and sat down. 'What do you think?' she said, eyes darting about in her small, tense face.

'It's awful! I doubt if Mrs Walsh's been up here in years.'

'I know it's not what you're used to . . .'

'I wouldn't have thought it was what *you* were used to either,' said Katherine, resting her hip against the window ledge and flicking back her reddish-brown hair.

'I only had one room, and had to do everything in that! These rooms are bigger and we could have one each. We'll be cooking and washing on the landing. I don't mind doing that for the old lady if she'll let us have these rooms rent free for waiting on her and doing her washing and the like.'

Katherine admired her determination. 'You mean, you're really thinking of staying? We'd have to spend money and there's only that toilet down the yard. I bet it's filthy!'

'I told you, I've got money,' said Celia, mouth setting stubbornly as she folded her arms across her chest. 'If you don't want to stay, go! I didn't think you'd last the course.'

'And what course would that be?' said Katherine, annoyed by the slur on her character. She marched over to the window and looked out over the road to the post office and Walsby's the optician's on the other side. There was a Walsby's and post office on the Mount. Instantly that longing to return to all that was familiar overwhelmed her and she wanted nothing more than to run out of the building and catch a bus to Mount Pleasant, which she still secretly thought of as home.

'You know exactly what I'm talking about. Living in my world, not *hers*!' cried Celia.

Katherine spun round. 'Why do you call Ma *she* and *her*, and say *hers* in that nasty way? She helped you when you needed it.'

'Go on, defend her!' Celia's expression was unfriendly but Katherine could see she was trembling.

'Don't get upset. I'm not about to run out on you.' Katherine went over and put a hand on her shoulder.

'I know it's not Buckingham Palace,' said Celia.

Katherine snorted. 'More like the Queen's pigsty!'

'But I'm sure,' continued Celia, tilting her chin, 'that with a bucket of hot water and a whole lot of elbow grease and disinfectant, some nice curtains and covers and a few sticks of secondhand furniture, like you said, we can make the place better than it is.'

'Well, that's easy to believe,' said Katherine with a grin. 'It's just a pity we haven't got a wishing wand.'

Celia smiled. 'You like your joke, don't you?'

'If you can't have a laugh now and then, life's not much fun, is it?' she said, going towards the stairs.

'So who's going to say what to the old lady?'

'You!' said Katherine, glancing over her shoulder. 'I'm only the girl to her. I'll deal with Mrs Walsh. Who knows? She just might have something in her attic we may find useful.'

The trouble was, if Mrs Walsh did, how would they get it to Liverpool? How were they to carry any furniture they might get upstairs? Katherine had never had to handle anything like this before and for the hundredth time since she had left the Arcadia found herself missing the menfolk. She wondered what they thought about her leaving. At least she had probably made three people cheer. Which was a pity! Because the last thing Katie had intended was to make Jack, Eileen and Sarah happy.

Chapter Ten

Sarah was far from happy. Everything in her life seemed to be going wrong. Not only had she lost the attention and love of two men she really cared about but now her brother had informed her he was moving his shipping business to Southampton. Unless she went with him she was going to be out of a job and a home. Her emotions were in turmoil so she did what she normally did when in a state of indecision: she caught the Irish ferry and headed for the sanctuary of her parents' farm in the Wicklow hills.

She did not blame Davy for wanting to go South. Strikes at the Liverpool docks had not helped his business. Old markets were shrinking and there was growing competition from Europe and the Far East since the end of the war. Even the government was using Southampton more and more. The *Devonshire*, which had brought troops home to Liverpool a few months ago, would be the last ship to do so. In future trooping would be done elsewhere, so sadly another nail had been knocked into Liverpool's coffin and its future as a premier port was deeper in question.

But if Sarah went South, there was no guarantee Ben

would chase after her. Men had their pride, even normally easy-going blokes like him. It had been a real shock when he had failed to succumb to her tears and had left her standing on the steps, bereft and unable to think straight for quite some time. Since then she had spent many a sleepless night, wondering how to get him back. She had just never imagined Ben in the arms of another woman and blamed Katherine for encouraging him. For the first time since she and Ben had renewed their old friendship, she had an idea of how he must have felt about Max.

She sighed. Her marriage had been a mistake but it would never have happened if Davy had not walked in on them the evening she'd lost her virginity. Max had been from the Blue Grass country of Kentucky, mad on racehorses and quite charming. It was just after the war and she was nineteen. Even now she would squirm with the shame which had caused her to blurt out that they were going to be married. Max had behaved like a gentleman and gone along with what she'd said. If he had not, she felt certain Davy would have got rough.

As it turned out, Sarah had been pregnant on her wedding day but had lost the baby. Thinking about it now, she realised she was no better than Celia. They had both jumped the gun but Mick had not been around to marry Celia. How would she herself have felt if she had been pregnant with no man on the scene to give her a wedding ring, and no parents to turn to? It didn't bear thinking about. Even so, she could still wish Celia had taken her daughter with her when she was born instead of leaving her in Kitty's care. Sarah felt certain Ben wouldn't have

behaved the way he had, and she wouldn't be on her way
to Ireland right now, if Katie had not been around. But if
she was honest with herself, she could not blame everything on Ben and Katie. There was her own relationship
with Mick to be taken into consideration.

Sarah sighed. It was during a low period in her life that
the first postcard from him had arrived and she had been
thrilled, but the real Mick was different from her dream,
although he had still held an attraction for her. He was not
compliant like Ben and would walk away if she got into one
of her moods. That had brought her up short because she so
wanted his approval. She had eaten humble pie and it had
seemed to be worth it; he could be so charming and complimentary. Now she had gone completely off him because not
once had he hinted at what had gone on between him and
Celia, whilst she herself had told him all about Max.

She shifted uneasily and thought of Ben again. How
serious was he about this woman Rita? Could Sarah win
him back? Her confidence had received a severe blow and
she felt the need to talk to someone who knew Ben well.
As soon as she got off the ship at North Wall in Dublin
she would telephone her mother who had always had
a soft spot for him. At great expense her father had had a
line put into the farm, and it was at times like this she
was really glad of that because it was a long walk there
from the nearest village and she needed someone to pick
her up at the bus stop.

A truck drew up alongside Sarah where she stood waiting
not far from the church. The passenger door was pushed

open and she stared in astonishment at the tall lanky figure, dressed in khaki corduroys and a plaid shirt, sitting in the driving seat.

'Jack!' she exclaimed.

'Aye! It's me.' There was a tension about his mouth that reminded her of Ben when last she had seen him.

'Wha-what are you doing here?' She stumbled over the words because in all her musing she had not given him a thought.

'I could ask you the same?' He flung the words at her.

'I – I've things to discuss with Mammy and Daddy. Davy's leaving Liverpool.' She added in a rush, 'Has Aunt Kitty been in touch?' Sarah had no idea what had gone on at the Arcadia since Ben had left her standing on the doorstep.

'Nope! But Pops came up to see me.' He did not look at her as he stowed her suitcase behind the seat. 'I take it *you* know about Katie?'

'Yes.' She bit her lip, unsure what to add.

'Nice surprise, wasn't it?' he said sardonically.

'It was a shock. But why are you here? I thought you'd have gone home? Mick and Ben have been looking for her.'

'Don't I know it!' said Jack, getting behind the wheel and grinding the gears. 'Pops and I had a helluva row about it all. It made me see red, them keeping it a secret from me.' The truck roared up the hill out of the village. 'You know how much Ma's given to Katie and her plans for the Arcadia?'

Sarah nodded. 'She's been spoilt.'

'Aye! It just made me mad, knowing that all the time Ma knew she wasn't hers, and there was me coming home from Ireland and feeling an unwanted stranger. But then, I wasn't wanted in the first place!'

Sarah experienced a rush of sympathy. 'Who said you weren't wanted? That's an awful thing to say!'

'Eileen. When I went to Kinsale a couple of years ago to see Annie, whom I was always fond of. I don't think Eileen meant any harm but she'd heard Annie talking about when I was born and how Ma wanted a girl. Would you believe she dressed me in pink and put a bonnet on me?' He almost choked on the words.

'Poor Jack,' said Sarah softly. 'But they do care about you, you know.'

'Pops only cares about me being the doctor he always wanted to be. That's why I said what I did.' He paused and she could see the strain in his face.

'Oh, lor'!' she said, slumping down in her seat. 'What have you said?'

'I told him I'd fluffed my exams and wasn't going to be a doctor. That I wanted to be a farmer or a musician.'

Sarah gripped the edge of her seat as the truck took a corner too fast. 'You're mad! After all the money he's spent on you!'

A muscle moved in Jack's neck but he said nothing.

'Did you fluff them deliberately?'

A wry smile twisted his face. 'I didn't fluff them at all. I did very well, actually.'

'Then why are you here and not doing your final hospital year?' she demanded. 'You're an idjit!'

'I needed to get away from it all so I asked for some time off. I told them my sister was missing and I was needed at home.'

'But she's *not* your sister!'

'I know that!' he said with a scowl. 'But you tell that to my brain. Besides, I couldn't tell them the truth.'

There was silence then she murmured, 'Do your ma and Pops know you're here?'

Jack's dark brows drew together. 'No. But I'm thinking of getting in touch with them soon. I'd like to know why Katie's gone off with Celia when she had so much going for her at home.'

'You should ask Ben. He's closer to Katie than anyone,' she said gloomily.

'And you've never liked that, have you?' said Jack, carefully not looking at her. 'How's he taking it?'

'Hard! Not that I've seen him much recently. He's seeing someone else.' Her voice was bright. 'He blew up just because I said I wouldn't marry him and went out with your Mick a few times.'

Jack glanced at her. 'You're joking! Unless – did you go out with Mick to get our Ben going? I bet you did! But what a thing to do.'

Her eyes hardened. 'Shut up, Jack! I'm upset enough.'

'Our Ben and Mick?' he mused. 'I see why you've come home.'

'Shut up! You've no cause to think I've behaved any worse than you have – lying and upsetting your ma and Pops. Now I'm tired, I want a bit of peace.'

She closed her eyes and both were silent even when

the truck drew up in front of a whitewashed farmhouse with rambling roses round its front door. The perfect refuge for anyone wishing to escape reality, thought Jack, though no one could escape for ever.

Sarah's parents had heard the truck and were waiting for them. She flew towards them and flung herself into her father's arms to receive a bear hug. 'It's good to have you home,' he said.

'It's nice to be home.' She turned to her mother, who gave her a brief hug. 'You must be tired out with all that travelling,' said Becky O'Neill. 'As soon as you've had something to eat, you can have a bath and rest on your bed.'

Sarah felt herself starting to relax already. 'I can take the travelling. It's not knowing where I'm going in life that's driving me mad,' she said ruefully.

'You'll feel better after a cup of tea.' Becky's voice was soothing. She led the way into the large farm kitchen.

'Can I have whiskey in it like you used to give me when I had toothache as a child?' said Sarah, her expression warm as she seated herself on a large squashy sofa.

'Things that bad?' said her father, removing a copy of the *Irish Press* from the sofa and seating himself beside her. He took her hand and patted it.

'My heart's broken! Twice! I'm never going to get married again, the way things are going. Ben's carrying on with another woman and Mick'll probably marry Celia!'

'Poor you,' said her mother without emotion. 'But how's Kitty coping without Katie? She'll be short-handed.'

Sarah glanced at Jack who was sliding her suitcase beneath the open stairway. 'You didn't have to tell us. Jack did,' said Becky, putting an arm round him as he straightened. 'We're like a second family to him, aren't we, lovey?'

Sarah felt a momentary jealousy and thought: he fits in here better than I do. She remembered how miserable he had been when he had first arrived as a little boy, and how by the time he had to return to Liverpool he had been her father's shadow, following him everywhere on the farm.

'You haven't answered my question,' said Becky, going over to the huge fireplace where a cooking pot hung from a hook over the peat fire.

'She's coping as far as I know,' said Sarah, who had not given any thought to just how Kitty was managing without Katie's help.

'You hadn't thought of giving her a hand yourself now that Davy's going South?' said Becky with gentle irony.

'Me! She wouldn't want me! Besides, I came home for some breathing space.' She glanced at Jack. 'Isn't that true for both of us?'

'It was,' he said, hazel eyes pensive. 'But I've breathed, and now that I've seen you I've made up my mind that I need to see my parents.'

'You feel ready?' said Becky, looking concerned. 'You don't want to be upsetting Kitty by quarrelling over what she did for Katie. Your mother was only doing her best by the girl.'

'It's Ma I'm thinking of . . . because of what you said

about her coping. Anyway, I'm going. I have to face up to things sooner or later.'

Sarah stared and immediately said impulsively, 'If you're going, maybe I'll go back with you. Offer my help to Aunt Kitty as Mammy suggested.'

Her father groaned. 'I thought I was going to get to see something of you?'

'Another time, Daddy. Aunt Kitty's need is greater.'

Her parents exchanged glances but neither said a word about Sarah's lifelong habit of avoiding anything that in the least resembled housework. Perhaps Kitty would be glad of her help if she was *desperately* short-handed.

Eileen shrieked and her hands clutched at a tablecloth, dragging it several inches before she collapsed on to the floor. Everything on it would have gone with her if the man sitting at the table had not rammed his hands down hard. As it was, his dinner ended up in his lap and his wife's wine glass went over, turning a patch of tablecloth purplish-red. 'Someone, help!' he yelled, as Eileen went rigid.

John was there in seconds and bent over her.

'Not her!' snarled the man. 'My legs are bloody burning. This plate and these potatoes are damn hot!'

'Here!' Ben appeared at his side with a large cotton napkin and scooped the food up. 'We'll pay to have your trousers cleaned, of course.'

'I should damn well think so! And something off the bill as well.' He snatched his own napkin off the floor, dabbing at his trousers as he stalked out.

'The girl! How's the girl?' asked his wife, eyes darting from her departing husband to the figure on the floor. 'She looks like she's having some kind of fit.'

Eileen had begun to thrash about. 'She certainly does,' said John, who did not need to pretend to be surprised at the sight. It was only the fourth time it had happened but this was the worst. Suddenly the girl went limp and he scooped her up in his arms and carried her swiftly out of the dining room, followed by a buzz of excited chatter.

Ben reappeared and set about bringing order out of chaos. It was years since he had waited at table, but as adolescents all the Ryan boys had been expected to help where needed. Earlier in the day one of the part-timers had phoned in saying her daughter was sick so she wouldn't be able to put in extra hours today, and tired as he was Ben had volunteered to help out. He apologised to the woman, flirting with her a little, fetched a fresh wineglass and filled it, leaving the bottle with the compliments of the house. The woman responded with thanks and a smile but he guessed they would probably still have trouble with her husband. Ben intended leaving him to Kitty, who had just entered the dining room in a hurry.

'Eileen's not going to be able to wait on any more, Ma,' he murmured as he passed her. 'You can't chance this happening again.'

'I'll think about it in the morning,' she said, weary eyes darting round the room. 'Let's get this evening over with. If it's not one thing, it's another. Now where's that man Pops mentioned?' Ben told her he had gone up to his room and left her to it. He headed for the kitchen where he found Mick, still in uniform, making coffee.

'You've been roped in, too, I see?'

'Looks like it. Exciting life we lead,' drawled Mick. 'As soon as I can, I'm getting out. This isn't how I envisaged my evenings when I left the navy.'

'Come home, Katie, all is forgiven,' said Ben sotto voce.

Mick nodded. 'Maybe I'll go out looking for her at the weekend. Right now, it's supper and bed for me. I've got to be up extra early in the morning.'

Only John was up when Mick let himself out to catch a bus in Ranelagh Street for the Pierhead the next day. The sky was pale grey and it was raining. Passengers were spilling off the Irish boat as he made his way to the Customs shed with a message for one of the other officers. He had just dealt with the matter when he was brought up short by the sight of Jack and Sarah, looking dishevelled and droopy-eyed.

'What the hell are you doing here?' he said to his brother, ignoring Sarah.

Jack said pugnaciously, 'I've come home. What does it look like?'

'Off the Irish boat! Shouldn't you have come here first?' said Mick, his expression hardening. 'I don't know what you're playing at but you've really upset Pops after all he's done for you.'

'Done for *me*!' exclaimed Jack wrathfully. 'Me being a doctor was what *he* wanted. I never had the freedom of choice you Ryans had.'

'You've had more money spent on you.'

'That's not my fault!'

'I suppose not. But it's not Katie's fault she was born a girl and you hated her for that.'

Jack reddened. 'I don't hate her! Besides, what's that got to do with what we're talking about?'

'Plenty, I'd say! So get off and see Ma and Pops and say you're sorry, then go back to Scotland and work to pass those exams.' Without even a glance at Sarah, Mick strode off and did not look back.

'I know where I stand with him all right,' she said in a tight voice as she watched his tall upright figure go through a doorway.

'Ducks and drakes,' said Jack grimly, picking up their suitcases. 'You'll definitely have to make up to our Ben now if you want to marry into the family. Let's get a taxi and you can drop me at the Arcadia.'

'OK. Tell Aunt Kitty I'll call round later. I'm going to ask her for a job.'

Jack raised his eyebrows but made no comment as he headed for the floating roadway which had been built in 1874 to accommodate heavy horse and cart traffic. He was feeling angry after what Mick had said and did not need a crystal ball to guess what his father would have to say, but as it happened it was Kitty he had to speak to first.

'Where've you been?' Kitty frowned at her youngest son. 'You didn't answer my letter. I've been worried, and you've really upset your father failing your exams – as if we didn't have enough worry!'

'I never received your letter,' said Jack, experiencing a familiar hurt that she had not bothered even to make the effort to hug him. 'I've been in Ireland with the O'Neills.' His tone was sullen.

'What! You went there instead of coming here? That's hurtful, Jack,' she said, voice quivering.

He looked away. 'They make me welcome and I needed space to think, which I wouldn't have got here,' he muttered.

'Well, I hope it's done you some good! Your father wants you to resit your exams. It's nonsense your saying you want to be a farmer. What do you know about farming? It's because you failed, that's what it is. But doctoring's in your blood, son.'

'So is music,' he said, changing his mind about telling her the truth. 'Pops made sure I learnt to play the piano and the violin and I've been teaching myself the guitar.'

'Say no more!' She held up a hand as if to ward him off. 'You're not thinking you're going to become a pop star? That would be stupid.'

He shrugged. 'Someone has to do it. Look at Cliff Richard and Tommy Steele! I bet they're rich. Anyway, I haven't made up my mind. I might farm. The O'Neills would have me working on their place like a shot.'

The blood seemed to rush to Kitty's head. Her hand shot out and she grabbed his arm and pushed him into a chair, sitting down close beside him. 'This is all about Katie, isn't it, Jack? But it's not me you're hurting by what you're saying, it's your father. I don't care what you do –'

'That doesn't surprise me,' he said, trying to control his voice. 'You never *have* cared.'

'Shut up! That's a lie.'

'Like the one you've lived all these years, pretending Katie was the girl I wasn't!'

'You don't know what you're talking about! So I wanted a daughter and I pretended? I did it mainly for Katie – I didn't want her to feel unwanted or ashamed because she was illegitimate. We didn't know if she was Mick's child then. We still don't know for sure.'

'You didn't want *me*! You dressed me in a bonnet and made me wear pink!'

'I was ill. I got to love you eventually.'

'You didn't want another boy,' he droned, as if his mind was stuck in a rut. 'You didn't want *me*!'

'You're not listening!' She shook him. 'Becky O'Neill desperately wanted Siobhan to be a boy, but would you say she's unloved?'

Jack stared at his mother and shook his head. 'But she wasn't sent away from home at five years old, and she didn't come back and find someone else had taken her place in the family and was getting all the attention.'

'There was going to be a war!' Kitty's blue eyes pleaded desperately for his understanding. 'It broke our hearts sending you away but we wanted you to be safe. Everything we've ever done for you has been because we wanted what's best for you.'

'Sending me to Edinburgh wasn't best for me.'

'I didn't want you to go! But you loved Scotland and seemed to want to get away!'

'Because of Katie, that's why, and to please Pops. It was where he'd gone for his training.'

'I wish I'd known, but you never said anything or showed in any way that you didn't want to go.'

'No,' he said in a low voice. 'That's because I wanted your approval, but in the end it made no difference. You were still wrapped up in Katie because you wanted her, not just because she was a girl but for the Arcadia. That's the reason you've been living a lie all these years. You and Pops with your oh-so-strong principles! You lied to Mick. You lied to me. You lied to Katie. I almost feel sorry for her. Well, you're reaping what you've sown, Ma, and I hope you're satisfied!'

'Don't talk to your mother like that!'

Jack's head turned and he saw his father standing in the doorway with such a stony expression on his face that Jack got to his feet, fists clenching. 'It's true,' he said. 'I was never wanted here. I don't know why I came. Anyway I'm going back to the O'Neills.'

'So that's where you've been? But you're *not* going back there. You'll go back to Scotland to resit your exams, laddie.'

'See?' yelled Jack, exasperated. 'That's all that matters to you! You and Ma are both trying to fulfil your own dreams through me and Katie. You brainwashed her into accepting it was her duty to take over the Arcadia. Duty! I bet she's had as little fun as I have, really.'

John growled, 'Keep your voice down. I know it's come as a shock to you about Katie but you never liked her anyway, did you laddie? You'll no doubt be glad she's gone.'

Jack stared at him and hesitated before saying, 'I'm not answering that. I'm leaving. I'll be a farmer, I –'

He got no further. John brought a large hand across his son's face. The slap resounded round the kitchen. 'Then get out, you ungrateful wee sod!' he shouted. 'But you won't be able to go running to the O'Neills. After what I've got to say to them, they won't allow you near the farm.'

Jack could scarcely believe what had just happened. His father's handprint was a burning painful red on his cheek. 'You wouldn't!'

'Try me,' said John, eyes glinting. 'He owes me his life. Do you think he's going to go against me? Without money, a farm labourer is all you'll end up as. So think, laddie, what's it going to be?'

'Perhaps I'll be happy as a farm labourer,' said Jack in a hard voice, and stormed out.

Kitty stared at her husband and said in a trembling voice, 'You shouldn't have done that!' Then she hurried after her son but Jack was too quick for her. He had already left the building and was running down the Mount. She tried to catch up with him but suddenly collapsed in a heap outside the post office.

Sarah turned up at the Arcadia later that day expecting to find Kitty in the kitchen. Instead she found John peeling potatoes. 'Hi!' she said tentatively. 'Is Aunt Kitty around?'

'She's lying down. What is it you want, Sarah? If it's Ben or Mick, neither of them is home yet.'

'No, I didn't want either of them. I-I –' She toyed with

the handle of a saucepan. 'I've just come to offer my help.'

'You've what?' He stared at her, his surprise obvious.

She flushed. 'I mean it.'

John made an effort and smiled. 'How are you at making something simple?'

'Like what?' she said cautiously. 'I'm not much of a cook. I was thinking more like being in Reception and welcoming people.'

'Reception can look after itself. People can press the bell if they want us. I was thinking of you making a big rice pudding. I can tell you what to do. Eileen's gone to her grandmother's and we're short-handed.'

Rice pudding didn't sound too bad. 'OK,' Sarah said, taking off her swagger coat and hanging it on the back of a chair. John handed her an apron and began to tell her exactly what to do.

She was washing dishes when Ben entered the kitchen later that day. He thought he was hallucinating because he had pictured this kind of scene so often in his dreams: Sarah, domesticated and living in their own little house, cooking his tea and carrying his baby. Was it really her? He put his arms round her and cupped her breasts with his hands and nuzzled her neck, giving it little bites.

She yelped. 'What did you do that for?'

'You're real!' he said.

'Of course I'm real, stupid!' She gazed up at him from her great dark eyes. 'Are you nuts?' Her hair was untidy and wisps of it hung about her flushed face. He thought she looked lovelier than he had ever seen her before.

'What are you doing here?' he said as casually as he could.

She smiled. 'What does it look like I'm doing? I'm working. I thought your mum needed a bit of help so I volunteered.'

He could hardly believe it. 'There has to be a catch,' he murmured. 'You haven't given up on our Mick and this is your way of getting round him to forget Celia and his Katie girl?'

Sarah stuck her nose in the air. 'You're so suspicious, Ben. But I'm only doing what you said and thinking about your mother. I'm here because I genuinely care about Aunt Kitty.'

'So you say,' he said dryly, having come down to earth with a bump. Taking his dinner out of the oven, he added, 'Where've you been for the last few weeks? Ma could have done with you before now. Eileen had a fit right in the dining room last night and so Ma had to stop her waiting on. Eileen burst into tears and left. It's been pretty dire here.'

'Jack's gone too.'

'Jack! I didn't know he was home.'

She rested her back against the sink and told him what she knew before adding, 'Me and your Pops have been rushed off our feet. Aunt Kitty's in bed. She had a funny turn apparently.'

Ben stilled and his face wore the expression of an animal sensing danger. 'Ma never takes to her bed,' he rasped.

'Well, she's in bed now. You know, Ben,' she said

without pausing, 'you really hurt me last time we met.
But I realise now you've probably made Rita up to make
me feel jealous.'

'You ask our Mick about Rita. I think he found her
quite attractive.'

'*He* did, not you?' Sarah dried her hands and went over
to him and put her arms round his neck. 'I'm not going to
get angry with you. Now tell me what Rita's like?'

Ben hesitated, wanting to kiss her so badly, to run his
hands all over her body, to love her, to take her – but he
remembered what Mick had said about playing hard to
get. Almost as if he had conjured his brother up the door
opened and Mick entered. Immediately Ben and Sarah
stepped away from each other.

But he did not appear to have noticed anything. 'Hello,
Sarah. What are you doing here?' he said, taking off his
cap and putting it down on a chair.

She sighed and said, 'You tell him, Ben.' And reaching
for her handbag, she took out a tin of Nivea and began
to cream her hands which were not their usual smooth
selves.

Mick looked at his brother. 'Well?'

'Sarah's practising discretion but apparently Jack's
been here and gone, Eileen's at her gran's and Ma's in
bed. It'll be us doing the guests' supper drinks tonight,
mate.'

'Ma never takes to her bed,' said Mick, frowning. 'I'm
going up to see her.'

'I was just thinking of it,' said Ben, and moved towards
the door.

Sarah placed the lid on the Nivea and hurried after them. They met John on the stairs, looking grim again. 'Have you told them?' he said. Sarah nodded. 'I'm going to telephone your parents and have a word with them about Jack,' he said.

'Right!' the three of them replied and carried on upstairs.

Kitty was sitting in bed propped up against a couple of pillows. The light was on but she was not reading or sewing but just gazing into space.

'You all right, Ma?' said Mick, sitting on the side of the bed and covering one of her hands with his.

She focused on his face but did not smile. 'Jack said I was reaping what I sowed in Katie leaving – and now he's gone too,' she murmured. 'Where did I go wrong, Mick? I just did what I thought was right. I gave out love and worked my fingers to the bone, doing my best to make your lives happy.' She sounded bewildered. 'Perhaps Katie'll never return? I feel like chucking my hand in right now.'

'You're tired, Ma. You've had a bad few weeks. Things'll look better in the morning.'

'That was what I used to think but I don't know any more.' She moved her head restlessly on the pillow.

Ben said, 'Remember our Teddy going missing and turning up just like a bad penny? Our Mick did the same, except he came back from the dead! You've just got to keep your chin up, Ma.'

'I'll try,' she sighed. 'But it isn't easy at my age.'

Sarah looked shocked. 'Never confess to being old!

That's what Mammy says. I'll bring you up a hot drink and you just think happy thoughts. I remember you saying that to me once when I stayed here.'

'All right, love,' said Kitty in a docile voice, and closed her eyes.

'Hell!' said Mick, as they went downstairs. 'She's not a bit herself.'

'We've got to find Katie,' said Ben. 'It's no good us sitting around waiting for her to get in touch. We don't know what she's up to or what she's thinking. She might believe she's not wanted here any more.'

'So where do we start?' said Sarah.

Ben looked at her and could not forget the things she had said about Katie. 'I couldn't trust you,' he said abruptly.

'Thanks very much!' She sounded hurt. 'What do you think I'm going to do to her?'

'You just mightn't crack on if you find her.'

'Shut up, you two,' hissed Mick, smiling as he made way for one of the guests to pass and saying, 'Good evening.'

None of them spoke about Katherine again until they were in the kitchen and the men were eating their dinner. Ben took from a drawer the well-thumbed Southport Guide. 'Right, Mick! How are we going to do this? Do we let Sarah help us?'

'If she wants to and has the time, working here. We'll get there quicker if the three of us share the task. Pass me the Guide.'

Ben did so and Mick opened the book and ripped pages out.

'What the hell are you doing?' said Ben, frowning as his brother passed him several sheets. 'This isn't the best way. We'll be coming back on ourselves. It would be easier to take a street or an area each.'

'That'd mean more time sorting it out. Have you seen how many hotels and boarding houses there are?'

'Of course I have.'

'There you are then,' said Mick. 'Just take what you've got and do what you can with it. And while we're all walking round, who knows? We just might spot Katie and then we'll take it from there.'

Chapter Eleven

'Have yer gorrany puppies?'

'No. You'd see them if we had any,' said Katherine, resting her elbows on the counter and wondering when Celia would return with Mrs Evans from town. She had promised to be back well before Katherine went to work that evening at one of the pubs down the road. By slapping on make-up and putting up her hair, wearing her tight black skirt, white satin blouse and best high heels, she had persuaded the owner that she was older than she was and he had taken her on to help out in the bar. Celia did not approve but Mrs Evans had surprised them both by chuckling when Katherine had paraded in front of them, saying she was as good as the films and that it wouldn't do Celia any harm to do something with herself.

'Will yer be gerrin' any in?' said the youth.

'There's none down in the book.'

'When d'yer think yer'll be gerrin' any in?'

'I don't know.'

'Well, when yer do gerrany in, d'yer know if they're gonna be girls or fellas?'

Katherine could not believe it. 'I'll be able to tell you when we get any in,' she said slowly.

He beamed. 'Right yerrah, lah. I'll see yer on Saturday.' He left the shop.

Katherine groaned and dropped her head on her arms. She and Celia had been here two months now and this was only her fifth stint working in the shop but that did not mean she had been sitting twiddling her thumbs for the rest of the time. Decorating and sorting out upstairs had taken some doing and she had marvelled how in this day and age, when high-rise flats were going up all over the place and people were buying televisions and washing machines, they should be living in conditions that were more thirties than fifties.

'Can I have some cuttlefish, ducks?'

'We've got no fish,' she said, without lifting her head. 'I don't know when we'll be getting any in or what kind they'll be if we do.'

'Are you feeling all right? You've got some on that shelf just behind you.'

Katherine lifted her head and the old lady in the black straw hat with artificial magnolias on its brim smiled at her. 'You're new, aren't you? I want it for Bluey, me budgie. He sharpens his beak on it. It's that white bony-looking stuff. He can talk, you know.'

'What does he say?' Katherine's eyes scanned the shelf behind her and after a 'To your right a bit', from the old lady, she found the cuttlefish.

'And some millet. He says "Pieces of eight".'

'Isn't that what parrots say?' said Katherine, finding the millet.

'Two sprays,' said the old lady, and smiled roguishly.

'He's a bit of a wild one and I didn't want him saying "Who's a pretty boy then?" He's a very good-looking budgie, but pretty . . .?' She wrinkled her nose.

Katherine smiled as she wrapped the woman's purchases in newspaper. 'He doesn't sit on your shoulder, does he?'

'Yes! And he nibbles me ear.' She placed some money on the counter and waved as she went out.

Katherine fluttered her fingers, trying to imagine a wild ear-nibbling budgie and wondering what Ben and Kitty would have made of her customers so far. A lump came into her throat. She kept meaning to telephone but something held her back. What would she say to them? What questions would they ask? She had thought of writing but whenever she took out a writing pad Celia seemed to be there, hovering at her shoulder, asking who she was writing to. When she told her there would be a look on her face which upset Katherine and completely put her off what she was doing.

She knew it was emotional blackmail but away would go the writing pad while she promised herself she would get it out again when her mother was not around. The trouble was that when Celia wasn't there, then Katherine was either at the pub, doing housework or in the shop. Sometimes she would settle, only for Mrs Evans to ask her to do something for her. The old lady was much happier these days and took an interest in all they did. She was still grumpy at times because the pain didn't go away but at least her granddaughter had said that their being there had made her life that little bit easier.

Katherine went over to the window and looked out.

The angora rabbits had been sold and so had some hamsters and puppies. Now they had kittens, three black and white and one completely black but for a white patch on its tiny nose. She picked him up, cuddling him against her neck as she gazed out of the window.

A dark-haired youth dressed in a black leather jacket came out of the post office opposite and walked past the optician's. There was something familiar about him and as he disappeared from her sight Katherine went and stood on the step for a better look. He was passing the china store now and had a canvas bag with pockets on it slung over his shoulder. Her eyes narrowed and suddenly she was thinking of that dance at the Grafton. He stood looking in the window of the photographer's shop for a moment before going inside.

Katherine waited for him to reappear but he still had not when another customer arrived and she had to deal with him. He wanted corn for his pigeons and could have won prizes for the length of time he talked non-stop about his birds, ships, and life in general. At last she got rid of him and followed him outside. She could see no sign of the youth in the black leather jacket and presumed she had missed him. 'Damn!' she muttered, thinking it might have been fun meeting him again if he was who she thought he was.

'Watcha doin'?' said Donny, making a sudden appearance.

She glanced down at his thin face and, smiling, said, 'Don't be nosy.'

He looked affronted. 'I won't learn nuthin' if I'm not

nosy. Me granddad says there's millions of questions he doesn't know the answers to, and he knows all sorts of things! He remembers there being wounded soldiers from the first war in his ol' school when he was my age.'

'How old is your granddad?'

'Old. He's got wrinkles round his eyes and his hair's all white. Although he sez it's been like that since he was in his twenties. He can still kick a ball. He works at Bibby's down by the docks but he's off at the moment because a machine chopped the top off two of his fingers.'

Katherine winced. 'Your poor granddad.'

'He's OK. He'll probably get some money for it and then he says we can have a little holiday.'

'Lucky you!' She thought how she had spent all her savings, except for seven and sixpence, on a new bed and bedding, a chest of drawers and a beautiful china po with roses round it for emergencies. There was no way she would use the enamel bucket Celia said they could make do with indoors at night. Even using the po made her feel like she had come down in the world, but using a bucket or descending the outside steps into the dark yard was something she would not countenance.

'Is there anything yer want me to do?' Donny looked anxiously up at her. 'I wanna earn some spends.'

Katherine's expression softened. Their arrival had made him redundant. 'You're good at doing messages, aren't you?'

'Yer want me to go somewhere?'

'The photographer's. I want you to go inside and see

if there's a fella in there wearing a black leather jacket and carrying a bag over his shoulder.'

His eyes brightened. 'Is he a Russian spy? D'yer want me to follow him?'

'Don't get carried away,' she said, a quiver in her voice. 'Just do as I tell you. Although you could ask the owner if he knows if the fella's name is Patrick?'

'Yer knows him?' He sounded disappointed.

'I might. When you come back I'll give you a penny, a biscuit and a drink of pop.'

His thin chest swelled and he made to dart across the road but she pulled him back by his Fair Isle pullover. 'Don't you ever look both ways?'

A cyclist went past. 'I knew he was there,' snorted Donny. 'I saw him out of the corner of me eye.'

'Maybe. But just slow down. It's not a matter of life and death.'

He pulled a face and was off. She watched him a moment and then another customer appeared wanting rabbit food.

Donny returned ten minutes later and in that time Katherine wondered if she had run quite mad in sending him in the first place. Did she yearn for the past that much, that even the sight of a vaguely familiar face from happier times caused her to behave in such a way?

'He's gone! I told the man you was a girlfriend,' panted Donny when he returned. 'He helps the man take photos of weddings and babies and develops the pictures himself. He'll be back later.'

'You didn't tell him where you'd come from?'

'Not me. I told him yous was from the pet shop. Where's me pop?'

She took him inside feeling somehow more cheerful and he chattered to her and told her all about his granddad's accident.

Celia and Mrs Evans rolled home in a taxi with several bags and parcels. Katherine had made a steak and kidney pie but they said they weren't ready for it yet. 'Did you have a good time?' she asked.

'I'm knackered,' said the old woman, shifting in her chair as if every bone in her body ached. 'It was worth it, though. I got some good warm fleecy knickers from TJ's.'

'Cool,' said Katherine, taking a lipstick and compact from her handbag. She glanced at Celia. 'What about you? You're looking a bit like you've lost a shilling and found tuppence. You didn't see anything that took your fancy?'

'I'm tired,' she said crossly. 'Everything been OK here?'

'Some bloke thinks I can foretell whether a puppy is a dog or a bitch before it's born.'

Mrs Evans's face broke into a smile. 'You do get them. Now hadn't you better be off, girl? You're going to be late for work.'

'I'm going!' She kissed their cheeks and left and was just wondering whether Celia had lost money on the gee-gees as she walked along the pavement when her arm was seized and she was spun round to face the young man in the black leather jacket.

'So you're my mystery girlfriend,' he said, a smile

lurking in the green eyes which gazed straight into hers. 'You look different.'

She blushed. 'The girlfriend was Donny's idea. I just sent him to find out if it was you. I could scarcely believe it was possible, seeing you again just out of the blue like that!'

'Why not?' His smile deepened. 'God works in mysterious ways. Where are you going? Back to the hotel where the fire-breathing dragon lives who doesn't approve of me?'

'No.' Katherine glanced into a shop window so he could not see her expression and said brightly, 'I've left there. Things changed. I'm going to work now just up the road.'

He looked puzzled. 'But I thought you worked in the pet shop?'

'I do some of the time but I have another job. How about you? Are you really a photographer?' She noticed the hand on her arm was stained with what looked like ink or dye.

'Part of the time. I use Mr Angler's dark room. I'm a trainee photographer looking for that picture that'll get me into the big time.'

'There's money in it then? I always thought taking pictures was more of a hobby than a job.'

'Unfortunately that's how lots of people look at it, including my mam and dad. They run a chip shop and I help out there. Where is it you work when not at the pet shop?'

'In a pub.'

His expression changed. 'Is that why you're all made up? You'll ruin your skin.'

It was what Celia said and it annoyed her. 'So what?' she said chirpily. 'It's my skin and really none of your business.'

'Sorry!' His eyes twinkled down into hers. 'It's just that it'd be a pity to ruin such beautiful skin.'

'Flatterer.' She blushed again.

'It's true,' he protested. 'And you've got lovely hair but having it up like that makes you look older.'

'That's the general idea!' She tilted her chin.

He looked mournfully at her. 'Don't get on your high horse. I've never forgotten you, you know. Your smile, your eyes . . .' He looked her up and down. 'Your legs. A pub's not a nice place for a young girl like you.'

She drew herself up to her full height which was above average. 'You don't know how old I am. I could be older than you.'

'I'm eighteen going on nineteen.'

'Then you should be in the Army or the Air Force or even the Navy, doing your National Service!'

'I had polio as a child and it's left me with a weakness in the muscle of one leg.'

'Oh, I'm sorry! But I'd never have known it from the way you danced that time.'

'That's the way I want it but I often pay for it afterwards, and I couldn't march or stand for hours on end in the forces. How d'you feel about going dancing?'

'With you?'

He glanced around. 'There's no one else here doing the asking, luv?'

She smiled. 'OK, Smarty Pants, that was a daft question. I'd love to go dancing. The only trouble is getting a night off. I work evenings.'

'Lie to them,' he said. 'Say your granny's ill in hospital and you have to go and see her.'

They had reached Sturla's departmental store and she paused to look in the shop window, avoiding his eyes. 'I don't lie,' she said gruffly. 'Truth's important to me.'

'My mistake!' He pulled a face and gazed at her thoughtfully. 'Don't you even tell little white ones? I don't believe in telling whoppers, but the odd little one not to hurt people's feelings?'

Katherine hesitated. 'I might have in the past but I try not to now.' She walked on.

'Right! We'll always be honest with each other,' he said seriously.

'You're a fast worker, aren't you?' She tried to hide a smile.

Two tiny dimples appeared at the corners of his mouth. 'It was you that made the first move, Chicken Licken. Think about when we can go out. I'll be seeing you.' He raised a hand and left her at a trot to catch the bus that had drawn up on the other side of the road.

Chicken Licken! The cheek of him calling her that but she supposed he hadn't meant any harm by it. There was a grin on her face as she pushed open the door of the saloon bar and went inside.

Four hours later Katherine clattered wearily up the stairs to the flat and let herself in. Celia was sitting near the window sewing. 'You smell of beer and smoke,' she said, lifting her head and staring as if accusing her of some great sin.

'Mrs Evans in bed?' said Katherine, ignoring the criticism as she went and put the kettle on.

'Well, I haven't murdered her yet,' said Celia, putting down her sewing and gazing at her daughter as she sat in the other comfy chair and eased off her shoes to rub her aching arches. 'I don't like you having that job,' she said. 'Perhaps you should work more in the shop and I'll look for another job? You get on with the old lady better than I do and I really hate you smelling of pubs. I don't mean to be rude, luv, but you're young and pretty and that smell isn't the best of perfumes.'

Katherine shrugged. What she smelt of was the least of her worries. She'd had her bottom pinched and a lewd suggestion made to her tonight and had not handled it very well. The head barmaid had come to her rescue but had told her she had to develop a far tougher skin and learn to laugh such things off. Katherine had felt far from laughing and had longed for Ben and Ma to be there to take her side. As it was she had forced a smile and said she'd do her best. She really missed Ben and their little chats.

She glanced at Celia surreptitiously, thinking they seldom joked or discussed the big questions in life. Neither was her mother forthcoming with information about the man who had been Katherine's father. She kept herself pretty much to herself, seemingly content for them to live together but for their lives to run along parallel lines. It was not the way Katherine had imagined things when she had left the Arcadia.

For a moment she wondered what kind of reception she would receive if she went back to the family right now. She allowed herself a luxurious moment imagining them welcoming her with open arms but it did not last. Why should they want her back? She wasn't one of them. Besides, she had thrown all they had done for her in their faces by leaving. She felt desolate for a moment and glanced at her mother, wondering if she would end up like her, prepared to settle for anything and scared of life?

Celia caught that glance and smiled unexpectedly. 'Do you think you could give my hair one of those colour rinses?'

'What?' She was really startled. 'You mean, you want a rinse?'

Her mother's cheeks pinkened. 'I never realised my hair looked so drab until I saw it alongside yours. Rich . . . that's what your colour is. Rich. And I'd like mine like that!'

Katherine's mood changed and she laughed. 'You know what'll happen if you do have a rinse? You'll want a whole new look and then you'll be rushing off to the shops to buy some glamorous clothes instead of sensible ones.'

'You think that'd be wrong? That I'd be like mutton dressed as lamb?' said Celia, looking dismayed.

'No! I think it's great, you wanting to change your appearance.'

'So you'll do it?'

'I'll do my best. You go to the chemist and pick your colour.'

Celia smiled. 'Thanks. Maybe you can even do a home perm for me?'

Katherine was not so sure about that. 'Why don't you go to the hairdresser's? There's a couple up the road. I mean, I could make a mess of the colour – turn your hair green and fuzzy. Unless you don't have enough money?'

'Oh, I'm OK for money.' Celia shook out the folds of the dress she had been hemming and held it against her. 'What do you think of the length?'

'About right, I'd say.'

'Rita gave it to me. Did you meet her? She buys several new outfits a year because she says a girl has to look smart, being an assistant manageress. Not that she's rich but I do see what she means.'

'Ma always said a woman had to look smart in business.'

Celia pursed her lips and said in a tight voice, 'You still can't get out of the habit, can you?'

'It just slips out,' said Katherine, immediately on the defensive. 'I don't do it on purpose.'

'No, I don't suppose you do,' murmured Celia. 'Sorry. I'm going to bed. It's been a long day.'

A very long day with so many different things in it, thought Katherine, remembering Patrick and what her mother had said about giving up the pub job and working longer hours in the shop. She would prefer that but until Celia found another job, things would have to stay as they were.

'Can I have a kitten?'

Katherine looked up from reading *Reveille* and met Patrick's smiling eyes. Her mother was having her hair done and Mrs Evans was sitting on a chair in a patch of mid-September sunlight near the shop entrance. 'Why do you want a kitten?'

'Why shouldn't I want a kitten?' He propped his arms on the counter so they rested against hers. 'It'll have a good home.'

'Did I say it wouldn't?'

'No, but you looked like a surprised pussycat yourself, as if you couldn't believe that was my real reason for coming in here.'

'Is it?' she chuckled. 'Children and unmarried ladies are kitten people. They think they're so cute and sweet.'

He looked injured. 'Are you saying I don't think they're cute and sweet – that I can't be moved by that pleading look in those kittens' eyes, which says: "*Buy me and you'll never regret it. I'll be faithful for life!*"'

She smiled. 'Which one do you want?'

'The all black with the white nose. He looks a man's kitten. I'm thinking of putting him in a Father Christmas hat with some tinsel and taking his photo. Real chocolate box, don't you think?'

'You mean it?' she said with a quiver in her voice as she went over to the window. 'He's my favourite, you know. I don't really want to part with him.'

'You could always come and visit. Make sure I'm not beating him up or feeding him to the dog.'

She picked up the kitten and stroked its head. 'He's not much more than a baby.'

'Don't be turning soft on me,' he groaned, leaning against the counter. 'How old was he when he left his mother?'

'Six weeks.'

'Hand him over! It's time he went on his travels like Dick Whittington's cat.' She passed him the struggling kitten and his fingers brushed hers. His skin was cool and slightly rough and she noticed the staining on his fingers was still there.

'It's developing fluid,' he said apologetically. 'It sometimes ruins my shoes as well but it's part of the job. I have a mate who's a printer. He can never get the ink off his fingers altogether. It's not so bad with me.'

'Celia says I smell of beer and cigarette smoke when I come in. You'd best have a box.'

'Thanks. You want to smell my family! It's a meal in itself. D'you live over the shop?'

'That's right.' She hoped he wasn't going to start asking questions. 'D'you want a tin of cat food? Would you like a basket for him?' She was aware that Mrs Evans was probably listening and wanted to appear efficient.

'The box'll do. And I'll take one tin. I'm not made of money so this kitten'll have to work for his living.'

'What are you going to call him?'

'Rover.'

She bit back a laugh. 'It sounds a suitable name for a Dick Whittington cat,' she said gravely.

'That's what I thought.' Patrick dug in a pocket and brought out a handful of change. 'I want to know if you suit your name. Which is it? Katherine or Katie? My sister read all the *Katy* books but she never would tell me *What Katy Did*! Have you thought any more about going dancing, or maybe we could do something during the day?

You could be my assistant and carry my bag. I don't just take pictures of happy couples, squawking babies and sweet kittens. Have camera, will travel! You never know when a calamity might happen. Fire! Flood! Gas explosion! Housing getting pulled down . . .'

'Maybe.' She was interested. 'Tell me more.'

'A picture has to say a thousand words! It doesn't always have to be dramatic. It could be the first colours of autumn in Sefton Park or mist across the Mersey on a November morning with a ship looming through the fog.'

'You sound like a poet. Let me know when you're going. And look after that kitten.' She smiled at him and patted the box. Scrabbling noises and a smell came from inside.

He screwed up his nose. 'Perhaps –'

Aware of Mrs Evans again, she said politely, 'Sorry, sir, no refunds.'

He blew her a kiss and walked out.

Katherine's smile lingered until the would-be purchaser of a puppy entered the shop and she had to draw on all her reserves of patience to explain why she didn't know yet whether the puppies they had heard were due were dogs or bitches. She reassured him, though, that she would let him know as soon as possible.

Celia moved her head tentatively as she stepped outside the hair-dresser's. Her scalp was still warm and a little sore but she told herself that was the price a woman had to pay if she wanted to make an impression at her age. She had scarcely been able to believe it was *her*, Celia

Mcdonald, looking out from the mirror in the hairdressing salon. Not only was her hair beautifully set but she was blonde as well.

To go blonde had been a last-minute decision while gazing at photographs of perfectly coiffured heads on the walls of the salon. Gentlemen prefer blondes! she had thought, with a particular man in mind. She was thinking of taking dancing lessons, having seen classes advertised in the *Echo*. She tightened the belt of her red raincoat and walked swiftly along the road.

She came to the pet shop and automatically her hand went to her hair before she took a deep breath and stepped inside. Katherine had her back to her and appeared to be doing something with the cage where there was a new lot of hamsters. She was with Donny and his granddad. 'They're from Abyssinia, that's what Mrs Evans told me,' the lad was saying.

'I think she means the breed originally came from there,' said Katherine. 'These ones have just come in. They were born over here so I don't know if that makes them British or Abyssinian. What do you think, Mr Jones?'

'It's a tricky one,' said the man in a rumbling voice. 'Like, I have a West Indian bloke living next door to me and his wife's a nurse, a nice woman. They were born in Jamaica, like, but their kids were born here. Does that make the kids Jamaican or Liverpudlian?'

'I don't care about them,' said Donny disparagingly. 'I wanna know about the hamsters, Granddad. Can I have one?'

'You just wait, lad. Like, don't be interrupting yer

elders. I'll think on it, and in the meantime we'd best get doing the messages.' Mr Jones turned, saw Celia and his mouth dropped open.

'Mr Jones,' she said, with a little nod of her head.

Katherine's eyes widened. 'What have you done to yourself? I thought you were going auburn?'

'You don't like it?' Her mother's voice trembled.

Katherine hesitated and Celia said, 'I look tarty, don't I? Is that what you're thinking?'

'No!' she said swiftly. 'You just look –'

'Different,' piped up Donny. 'Yer hair's like a film star's, all white and shiny.' He approached her slowly and peered at her. 'How did yer get it like that? Can I touch it?'

'It's a bleach. Peroxide,' said his granddad, smiling at Celia. 'Yer look a fair treat, girl. Although yer could do with a bit of make-up on, like. Yer face looks kinda bare with yer hair like that. Me dead wife used to swear by a bit of rouge and lippy for finishing herself off.'

Celia smiled. 'I just wanted a change.'

'You've got that all right,' said Katherine, still staring at her. 'Red's your colour now, being blonde. You look completely different. Do you feel different?'

A film star! thought Celia, and nodded. 'I feel like I shouldn't be here but going somewhere.' There was a dazed look in her eyes. 'I'm all dolled up with nowhere to go.'

'You'll have to go somewhere then,' said Donny seriously. 'Come to the pictures with us? We're going to the first house of the Gaumont later, aren't we, Granddad?'

'That's right. But I should think Mrs Mcdonald's probably too posh for the Gaumont, lad.'

'Posh! Me?' Celia laughed and went on laughing. It just seemed so incredible that a change of colour and hairstyle could make such a difference, but would she have the courage to go and take those dancing lessons on her own? Mick had been a lovely dancer and she had sometimes wished she could match up to him. She squared her shoulders and told herself she did not know why she had to think of him right now. There were plenty of other fish to fry for a woman who had the looks of a film star. She would take those lessons but would keep it a secret. In case Katherine or Mrs Evans laughed at her.

If only she had known it, Katherine would have been delighted because she had other fish to fry herself that she did not want her mother knowing about.

'It's Lord Nelson's two hundredth birthday on the 27th,' said Patrick, as Katherine pulled the door shut behind her.

'Are you going to send him a birthday card?' she said with an innocent look.

'It mightn't get there.' He looked thoughtful as he fell into step beside her, on her way to work.

'So why mention it?'

'Newspapers and mags love anniversaries. There's going to be celebrations on the *Victory* on the day, but that's down South. I was wondering what I could do to link him up with Liverpool's great seafaring tradition.'

Katherine's eyes gleamed. 'What about pictures of streets named after a couple of admirals, and their photos, and an article? You've Rodney Street for a start – he was a naval hero who fought the French and kept Jamaica for the British – and then there's Gambier Terrace. Admiral Gambier was another who fought in the Napoleonic wars. You could go further. You could start a series on ordinary street names if they didn't want your idea for Nelson's anniversary.'

Patrick stepped back and stared at her. 'You amaze me. A girl who knows something about naval history and has an eye for what might catch the public interest!'

She giggled. 'I don't! not much, anyway. Mick was in the Royal Navy and he'd tell me the odd thing, but it's the guests who started me off.'

'What guests?'

She hesitated and then said with a shrug, 'At the hotel in town where I used to live. There was the odd guest, as I said, who wanted to see places of historical interest so I started finding out things. The Yanks are real keen. Did you know the American wild-life artist John James Audubon came to Liverpool and held an exhibition at the Royal Institution in Colquitt Street? Liverpool still has some of his pictures.'

'Well, blow me over with a feather! I never knew that, and if I didn't then there's probably loads of people who don't know either. I could become famous for this! It'll have to be a series of pictures for the *Daily Post*. But will you come with me?' said Patrick, eyes ardent as they rested on her face.

'Where to?'

'Rodney Street, of course! It's always good for a picture

with all those Georgian houses, and Gambier Terrace is right close by. It could look marvellous if I can get the right angle just before sunset.'

She hesitated. 'I don't know . . .'

'Why not?' Some of the light died from his face. 'I'm not going to ravish you in broad daylight.'

'As if I was scared of that!' She rolled her eyes.

He sighed. 'You're not taking me seriously. What is it then? Why don't you want to come?'

She knew she could not explain. Not yet. How did you tell a bloke you weren't ready to bump into the family you'd been brought up with but no longer belonged to because you were illegitimate! Better to go with him and chance it. 'It's OK, I'll come,' she said, smiling. 'But it'll have to be late afternoon.'

His face brightened again. 'That suits me. I'll meet you outside Lewis's at half-three. See you tomorrow then. I'm frying tonight!' He blew her a kiss and ran for the bus that had just drawn up at the bus stop on the other side of the road. Something he always seemed to be doing these days, she thought, already looking forward to seeing him tomorrow.

Chapter Twelve

Sarah was feeling the strain of being nice to people when she would much rather tell them exactly what she thought of their complaints. For one, she didn't have two pairs of hands that she could be in Reception, dish out food, fetch and carry and still be running up and downstairs checking things with Kitty, who spent more time in bed than getting on with the job of running the hotel.

Once the doctor had reassured John that all his wife needed was to rest and stop worrying, he had gone up to Scotland in search of Jack, having discovered that he was not at the O'Neills' farm. This left Sarah with more responsibility than she cared for, and if it had not been for the part-timers and one of Kitty's cousins turning up part of the day, and Mick and Ben helping in the evening, she would have found it impossible to cope. Eileen was still at her grandmother's, refusing to go home to Ireland, making the old lady's state of health her excuse.

Katherine's bedroom had been put at Sarah's disposal so she could sleep in if she wanted, which suited her fine, and at least her mornings and evenings were lightened by the occasional intimate encounter with a half-naked

Ben or Mick coming out of bedroom or bathroom. Mick exchanged pleasantries but it seemed to her that his mind was elsewhere most of the time. As for Ben, there was nothing lover-like in his attitude; rather it seemed he could not get away from her quick enough, although he did say he appreciated her stepping into the breach and helping his mother. Sarah had had to be content with that but was starting to believe she was going to have to do something to get things moving again between them.

Sometimes she worried what would happen to her new position if they found Katherine, but so far there had been no news of her. Sarah harboured suspicions that Ben might be seeing the mysterious Rita whilst in Southport, and that did not make her feel good about herself. So to buck herself up she decided to go shopping and treat herself to a new frock.

Lewis's had been advertising the latest fashions and so whilst Kitty's cousin held the fort, Sarah went mooching round the women's department. She bought a new uplift bra and two dresses which were fitted snugly to the new high waist-line just beneath the bust (she had slimmed down with all the running around). Wide-skirted and with a multi-coloured screen border, they were made of brightly coloured needlecord cotton. She had noticed there was an Over Thirties Night advertised for next Wednesday at Wavertree Town Hall where the dancing would be strictly tempo and she hoped to persuade Ben to take her.

It was as she was coming through the first set of double doors on the corner of Lewis's facing Renshaw Street that she saw Katherine standing outside. For a moment Sarah froze. Since being at the Arcadia she had come to realise just how hard Katherine must have worked. Her returning now could really lighten Sarah's load yet still she stood there unmoving, thinking of Ben and how she and Katherine had wrangled over him. If the girl returned, would that result in more arguments and she herself needing to leave before she could sort things out between them?

Even as Sarah hesitated a young man in a leather jacket stopped in front of Katherine and spoke to her. Her face lit up and Sarah felt a softening of her heart as she watched the pair cross the road together. She had been young herself once. She came to a decision and hurried after them as best she could in high heels and with her parcels bumping against her legs. She thought perhaps they intended to go up Mount Pleasant to the Arcadia but instead they went along Renshaw Street past Pollard's, the babycare shop. A second time Sarah hesitated then followed them.

It was when she was toiling up the hill where the Anglican cathedral stood on St James's Mount that she began to ask herself why on earth she was bothering tailing them. If Katherine intended visiting the Arcadia whilst in the area, it would be much more sensible if she herself was there behind Reception, very much in control, when the girl arrived.

Ben had arrived home early that day and was whistling as he clattered down the area steps into the basement.

'What are you doing home at this time?' said Kitty, as she swirled a lace-trimmed linen tablecloth over the gate-legged table which her mother had brought from the house where Kitty had been born in Crown Street.

'You're up? Great, Ma!' He picked her up and swung her round.

'Put me down, you daft lummock! This won't get the work done.' She cuffed him lightly across the head and he lowered her to the floor.

'You feel like work? Good!'

'No! But I've decided I've had enough lying in bed and eating off a tray. And besides, I might have to go out later.'

'What's up?' His blue eyes were suddenly intent. 'Is there news of Jack?'

'No. Pops hasn't seen him. He hasn't been to his flat, the hospital or the house.' Kitty placed fine bone china cups and saucers on the table. 'It's Eileen. She's had another fit and one of my cousins came round here demanding I do something.'

'It's not your problem, Ma! She's *their* niece.'

'That doesn't mean a thing to them. Annie put her in my care and they have their own families to see to. They're worried it'll all be too much for Aunt Jane and will see her off.'

'So what are you going to do?'

'I'm wondering if you would take Eileen to Ireland? I mean, you could call in on the O'Neills at the same time. Go for the weekend . . .'

'Ma, Eileen lives the other side of Ireland from the O'Neills,' he said patiently.

'I know. I was wondering if Jack could have gone there after John phoned.'

He put his arm round her. 'You're still not thinking straight, are you, Ma? Why should he go there? It'd cost him and he has no money of his own.'

Kitty twiddled abstractedly with a knife. 'Someone might have lent him the money. He might have written to Annie who always had a soft spot for him.'

'He's not going to remember that! Besides, if Jack was desperate to return to Ireland, he only had to wait and ask me for the money.'

'You'd have lent him it?'

'He's my brother,' said Ben shortly. 'And he's studied bloody hard for the last few years and I've seen little of him. It's no wonder he sees Uncle Daniel's farm as Paradise. Sarah told me they love the bones of him there.'

'I'm sure they do. We were very grateful to Daniel and Becky for having him.'

'Sure. But what happens when he comes back here? No spoiling for him then because there was Katie and the pair of you doting on her. No wonder he resented her. I feel sorry for the kid!'

'Have you finished?' Kitty's face had a pinched look to it. 'He is *not* a kid! He's twenty-four, and at his age I'd been working for years!'

'So had I! But it was Pops who wanted him to be a doctor, just like *you* wanted Katie to take over here.'

'That's what he said. But what's wrong with that? You thought it was a good idea . . . you all did.' Her voice was trembling and she sat down abruptly.

Immediately he was ashamed of himself for upsetting her. 'Sorry, Ma. I'd better get cleaned up and changed if I'm going to wait on.' He brushed her brow with his lips and hurried out.

Kitty sighed and dropped her head into her hands, wishing she could run away. Tears trickled between her fingers. She had always loved the hotel business but since Katherine had gone, she had lost heart. Why couldn't the girl have written, just a few lines to say she was OK? Surely Kitty was entitled to that? But young people these days had different ideas on how they should behave towards their elders. She thought with an unexpected fierce anger: She owes me something! She mightn't be Mick's daughter but I still gave her so much. Oh, Katie girl, where are you? Just as suddenly her rage ebbed, leaving her exhausted.

She lifted her eyes and gazed about the basement, feeling a loathing for it, wondering how she could have been so content living here for over thirty years. There were so few of this world's goods in it because so much of their money had gone into improving and making the hotel a success. Suddenly she decided she would get shut of the place. What had she been thinking of, wanting the same kind of life for her girl? Work, work, work! That was what *her* life had been! She had to get away! Perhaps she would go to Ireland. The O'Neills might have lied about Jack being there if they were as fond of him as Ben said. But now there was a meal to prepare so she had better get up to the kitchen.

*

Sarah arrived back at the Arcadia in a breathless state and found Ben in Reception. 'Why are you home so early?' she demanded, her cheeks glowing with exertion.

'That's a nice welcome!' His blue eyes flicked over her face. 'Aren't you in need of help tonight? I thought you'd be glad to see me.'

'Of course I'm glad to see you,' she stammered. 'It's just that you took me by surprise.'

'Obviously.' He moved from behind Reception and began to help her off with her coat. 'You look flustered,' he murmured against her ear. 'You've got to remember, Sal, you're not getting any younger and shouldn't be dashing round the shops when you've work to do here.'

'I'm younger than you,' she retorted.

'Don't remind me! Remember when we were seven and you were mad at me because I was a few months older?'

She glanced up at him. 'They were happy days.'

A smile tugged at his mouth. 'Yeah, they sure were.'

'Remember us pretending to be detectives when we were eleven and how you borrowed Mick's mack and trilby? I used to love it when we dressed up. Remember us playing doctor and nurses with that stick of limp celery?'

'That was your idea for a stethoscope, but then you made that joke and were in stitches.' He sighed. 'The trouble is, we're not kids any more and life's got too serious, what with Katie,' he groaned, 'and Jack's still missing and Ma's upset. I feel I have to do something to find them before I can think of myself.'

'I saw Katie!' she burst out.

'You what!' He gripped both her arms and his eyes blazed. 'Where?'

'That's why I'm all flustered. I spotted her outside Lewis's but before I could speak to her this fella came up and she went off with him.'

'Where did they go?'

'I thought she might have been coming here but they went up by the cathedral. They might still be there.'

'Bloody hell, Sal! Why didn't you tell me straight away?'

'You didn't give me a chance! What are you going to do? She might still come here.'

He hesitated on his way to the front door. 'Wouldn't she have come here first if she was going to do that?'

'I don't know. Anyway there'll be someone here if she does come while we go and look for her,' said Sarah.

Their eyes met and his face softened. 'If you're coming with me, you can get those high heels off or you'll be holding me back.'

'Give me five seconds!'

She hurried behind Reception where she kept a pair of flatties. He was already outside by the time she'd put them on and grabbed her coat. He seized her hand and they ran. It was exhilarating and she felt like a child again. 'Remember Green-teethed Ginny?' she panted as they jogged in the direction of Rodney Street. 'How she was supposed to haunt the cemetery?'

'I remember you calling me a coward because I didn't want to go down there.'

'You did, though. My hero!' She planted a kiss on his

chin and his hand tightened on hers and suddenly they were oblivious to everyone else as they slowed to a walk.

'I love you, Sal,' he said unsteadily.

'I love you too,' she whispered, tears welling up in her eyes.

He kissed her mouth gently and murmured, 'We'll just find Katie and then you and me are gonna make some plans.'

She nodded, knowing this was no time to feel jealous over his still wanting to find the girl, but she held his hand firmly, unable to bear to let him go.

They circumnavigated the cathedral and its graveyard without seeing any sign of Katherine. Sarah knew he was disappointed so kept quiet as they returned to the Arcadia, hoping for all the family's sake that Katherine would be there.

She was not and Ben did not have the heart to mention her to his mother. Sarah squeezed his hand and said, 'It was worth a try. Maybe she came so far and then felt she couldn't come in – was unsure of her welcome?'

'Maybe,' he said.

'I'm sorry, Ben,' she said ruefully. 'I should have spoken to her, but with her being with someone I wasn't sure what to do.'

'What was the fella like?' he asked.

She described Patrick as best she could but it didn't get them far. 'At least it looks like she's getting on with her life,' he said with a twist to his mouth. 'Let's forget her for now. Shall I carry your parcels upstairs.'

'Thanks!' Sarah's heart was suddenly light.

She went with him, hoping that before they made for the kitchen they could talk about themselves for a few moments. She needed to know for sure he had really meant it when he'd said he loved her. Ben dumped her parcels on the bedroom floor and sniffed. 'You've made it your own. I've always liked that perfume.'

'I didn't mean to take Katie's bedroom over.' She hesitated. 'It's only since I've worked here that I've realised just how much she did.'

'I'm glad to hear you say that, but you've done your fair whack since you've been here. I'm proud of you, Sal.' His eyes were full of warmth as they rested on her face.

Tears shimmered in hers. 'Oh Ben, why did we ever fall out? It was all my fault! I wanted to change you and that was stupid. You're kind and generous and easy-going – and perfect. I never loved your Mick.'

'And I've never even been out with Rita.' One giant stride brought him close to her and his arms went round her. 'Marry me, Sal?'

'Yes, please. I want to be with you for ever.'

They kissed passionately and went on kissing, just could not get enough of each other. Everything else was forgotten. He lifted her up and carried her over to the bed. He sat astride her with his knees pressing against her thighs and they gazed deeply into each other's eyes.

'You said we'd never even made love properly. Well, I'm going to do it now, Sal, because I want you really to belong to me. If that's all right with you?'

'Oh, Ben!' she whispered, and brought his head down to hers. She wondered if this was the first time for him. They were both trembling and she guessed that once they went all the way he would never leave her. With him the commitment would be for life. She unfastened his shirt and trousers and soon they were both naked. He was not completely gentle with her as she had expected, but passionate when it came to taking her. It felt so right and the sex was so delicious that she marvelled at her own stupidity for putting this moment off for so long.

It was not until Sarah was in the bathroom afterwards, staring into her luminous eyes and noting the softness of her mouth, that she thought about it happening on Katherine's bed. It seemed fitting somehow. She owed the girl for this moment and knew she would never feel the same antagonism towards her again if she came home.

Katherine had no intention of returning to the Arcadia. She was enraged. Her heart had leapt into her throat when she caught sight of Sarah and Ben but it had come as a shock that neither of them had noticed her. They had had eyes only for each other and had even kissed in the street! She felt choked, thinking about it days later. She had prayed for Ben to see her but nothing had happened so she had given up on God as well.

She stepped into the new skirt she had bought that day and pulled it with some difficulty over her hips, easing inside the waist band a black cotton sweater. She clipped on a waspie belt before gazing at her reflection in the full-length mirror. Her eyes wore a wounded expression and she realised she must have looked like that when it happened because Patrick had asked her what was wrong. Perceptive of him, she thought. A deep sigh escaped her and despite wearing a roll-on she sucked in her stomach because she had bought the skirt a size too small so it would fit really snugly. Too snugly.

She hobbled over to the secondhand chest of drawers painted flame orange and picked up a comb. She swept her hair up into a ponytail then fastened on a pair of round black plastic earrings before applying mascara and orange lipstick. She shuffled backwards and picked up a chiffon scarf, which almost but not quite matched the lipstick, and fastened it about her neck so the knot was at the side. Then she slipped her feet into a new pair of red high heels and looked at her reflection again. That was better, she thought. Bright and cheerful is the name of the game!

'You're not going out like that, are you?' said Celia.

Katherine jumped and turned round from the waist only. 'I wish you wouldn't creep up on me like that,' she said crossly, taking tiny steps over to the bedside chair and picking up her jacket.

'You're never going to get down the stairs.'

'Little ray of sunshine, aren't you?' she said sarcastically.

'You are in a mood! I can't do with moods. But you'll see . . .'

Katherine went along the landing until she reached the stairs and knew then that Celia was right. She was watching, which infuriated Katherine even more. She was getting as bad as Ma, the way she fussed, she thought, and felt weepy all over again. They didn't want her, that was for sure. Otherwise Ben wouldn't have looked so happy. But she was not going to think about him and Sarah.

She tilted her chin, determined to prove Celia and the invisible Ma wrong by going out dressed as she was. She put a hand on the banister rail and jumped with both feet together. By taking tiny jumps in such a manner she managed to reach the living room, slightly breathless but triumphant. 'See!' she said to Celia, then her legs gave way and she sank on to the floor.

'You're a right mad alec,' said Mrs Evans, chuckling.

Celia shook her head. 'I'm not owning up that she's mine.'

Katherine stuck her tongue out at her and somehow managed to get up. She glanced at the clock and saw it was time she was on her way. She checked there was money in her handbag and swayed out of the room. Celia, who was going dancing with a woman she had met at her dancing class, followed, hoping nothing would come of Katherine's wearing a skirt which she considered completely outrageous.

Katherine was determined she was going to have a helluva good time this evening. She would flirt and have drinks when customers offered. She was not going to give a damn what people thought of her.

By ten o'clock the pub was crowded and Katherine had downed four Babychams and a couple of Cherry Bs and was getting more and more melancholy, thinking how different things would have been if Mick had been her father and he and Celia had married. She felt annoyed

that he wasn't and her mood changed until she felt quite
pugnacious. It was Saturday and there had been a win for
first-division Everton. Their fans were happy but some
Liverpool supporters were not and were getting rowdier
and ruder the more pints they downed.

'Keep it down, gentlemen,' said the landlord in a weary
voice. 'There's ladies present.'

'Show me one,' said a young Liverpudlian with a
cheeky grin.

'Thus no ladies 'ere, whack!' muttered another
morosely, jutting out his thick lips. 'Only ol' frilly knickers
here,' he said, indicating the chief barmaid. 'And the other
one thinks she's queen o' the midden,' he added, twisting
on his stool and staring at Katherine, who was collecting
empties. 'Give us another pint of mother's milk and make
sure yer fill it to the top this time, girl.'

'Listen, slobbergob, I always do,' she said belligerently,
remembering this supporter from another Saturday when
the roars from Anfield had been heard in the shop. 'Your
trouble is, you think you're God's gift to women.'

'Yer saying I'm not?'

'Who'd have you?'

'Plenty.' He leered in her face. 'I could do yer with
one hand tied behind me back.'

'You've got as much chance of that as winning the
Pools,' she retorted, and made to move away.

He placed his hand on her bottom and immediately
she swayed round. Banging the glasses down on the
table, she hissed, 'Keep your filthy hands off me, you
swine!'

'I'm a bloody customer!' he yelled, stumbling to his feet. 'Hey, landlord, yer wanna drown this one in a keg!'

'What's going on?' said the landlord, bustling over. 'I've told you, gentlemen, to keep it down.'

'She insulted me!'

'He touched me!' said Katherine wrathfully. 'He's got no right to touch me.'

'He probably meant no harm. It could have even been an accident,' said the landlord, looking harassed.

'She wus asking furrit,' said the man. 'Dressed like a bleeding tart!'

'That's it!' said Katherine in a fury, and picking up a glass, flung the dregs in his face. 'I quit! I'll be back for what I'm owed in the morning!'

She stormed out in as dignified a manner as possible, notwithstanding how tipsy she was and how hard it was to keep her balance wearing her new high heels. She was thinking if her mother dared say 'I told you so' she would slay her. But the evening was not over yet.

Celia had enjoyed herself. She had been asked to dance several times and one of her partners had said she was a natural dancer, but when he then asked to see her home she had refused. Even so she was in a happy mood as she hurried along the road. The pubs had begun to let out and men lingered on pavements. A figure emerged from the doorway of the photographer's ahead and crossed the road. Her eyes followed him and suddenly she noticed Katherine by his side, hips swaying seductively in that too-tight skirt. Celia felt anger, annoyance and anxiety as another man detached himself from a group outside the pub and made a grab for her daughter. Katherine managed to avoid him. He went after her again and this time seized hold of her.

Celia flew across the road. The stupid girl, flaunting herself in such a way! There were now two men tussling, with her daughter in their midst. Celia reached the pavement and, lashing out with her handbag and umbrella, managed to floor one of them while the other she punched in the back.

'Hell!' he said, clinging on to Katherine.

'What did you do that for?' she said, putting her arm round the youth and blinking at her mother. 'This is Patrick! He came to my rescue. He's the baddie on the ground.'

Celia said in a vexed voice, 'How was I to know that? Anyway, let's get away from here.' She seized Katherine's left arm and hustled her towards the pet shop with Patrick holding on to the girl the other side. 'You've never mentioned a Patrick to me,' muttered Celia.

Katherine blinked down at her. 'Why should I? D'you tell me everybody you meet?'

'I'm your mother! I don't have to. And if you'd taken that skirt off, things would have been different!'

'I've been saying that to her,' said a limping Patrick.

Katherine giggled. 'You know how that sounds?'

'Yep.' He smiled, winced and touched his lip. 'I'm bleeding.'

'I'll kiss it better!' She swayed in his direction but missed his mouth by a foot and almost fell over.

'Will you behave yourself?' hissed Celia. 'You're

making a show of us and I want the people round here to respect me.'

Katherine attempted to pull herself together. 'You're getting to sound more like Ma ev-verry-day!'

'Don't mention her here,' snapped Celia, opening the door. 'Will you get inside!' She tried to force her in but Katherine clung to Patrick.

'Hang on! What about him?'

'He's got a home to go to, hasn't he?' said Celia, feeling harassed.

'Yes – but he's bleeding.' Katherine looked soulfully at Patrick. 'He-he at least de-deserves a cup of cocoa.'

'You're drunk!' said Celia, turning on her. 'I knew no good would come of you working in that pub! I don't know what Mrs Evans will say . . .'

'She won't say anything. She-she likes me!' said Katherine, dragging on Patrick's arm. 'Come in, come in!'

Celia ground her teeth. 'Oh, I wash my hands of you! I'm going to put the kettle on.' She hurried upstairs.

Patrick frowned after her. 'Who's Ma if *she's* your mother?'

'Oh, never mind that now,' said Katherine, clutching at him. 'Carry me upstairs. I'll fall down if I try to walk up.' She attempted to control a yawn but could not.

'Who do you think I am – Superman?' said Patrick, giving her a stern look. 'She's right. You're going to have to give up that pub, Katherine.'

'Oh, shut up!' she said, jiggling about. 'And lift me up.'

Somehow he managed to sweep her up in his arms. 'If we both fall down, it's your fault,' he warned.

'You won't drop me, my nice strong Patrick,' she murmured, head lolling against his shoulder. 'But you mustn't go picking fights with people any more. You'll get hurt.'

'I never pick fights!' he exclaimed. 'It's only when you're around I get into trouble.'

'Be honest. You picked that fight with Dougie!'

'Shhh!' said Celia, as they reached the landing. 'Who are you talking about now?'

'Nobody important,' sighed Katherine as Patrick carried her into the living room and put her down on the sofa.

She gazed up at him and tutted. 'You're bleeding.' She dragged herself up and swayed across the room to where she knew there was a biscuit tin with first-aid things inside. With her eyes shut and her head resting against the wall above the sink, she dampened a ball of cotton wool and click-clacked back into the room. 'My brave hero,' she said, jerkily dabbing the cut on his face.

'A lot of good it did me being a hero,' he said glumly.

'Shush! You've made your lip bleed again.' She drew away from him a little. 'You look a bit better now. How's the cocoa coming on, Ma?' she added, without looking up.

'Don't call me Ma,' said Celia.

Katherine sighed. 'I can't win. Nobody loves me.'

Celia said impatiently, 'Of course people love you! But not when you get drunk and act daft.'

'I want someone who'll love me all the time.' She sighed and smiled at Patrick. 'You poor boy. I suppose you deserve a kiss.' She leant towards him and their mouths brushed, leaving her lips tingling as if touched by thistledown. 'Nice,' she said.

He shook his head at her but there was a slight smile on his face. 'I think I'd best get home. I'll see myself out.'

'Goodnight, sweet prince!' She wiggled her fingers and closed her eyes.

There was silence as his footsteps receded.

'You're naughty,' said Celia. 'Flirting with that young man.'

'I like having a fella around.'

'It shows! But you shouldn't encourage him. And what happened to you to get in this state? I never thought you'd be so much trouble,' she said severely.

'I threw beer over a customer for pinching me bum.' Katherine yawned. 'And I quit me job.'

'Well, that's one good thing. You can carry on here and I'll start looking for other work,' said Celia, pouring boiling water on the cocoa. 'It shouldn't be difficult. As for you liking the opposite sex around – I've lived without them for years.'

'Perhaps that's why you're the way you are?' murmured Katherine.

'What d'you mean by that?' said her mother indignantly.

'Now me, I wish – I wish –' Katherine's eyes closed again.

'What do you wish?' asked Celia agitatedly.

'Mick –'

'What about him?'

But Katherine did not answer. She had fallen asleep.

Chapter Thirteen

Mick strolled up the drive to where the lights of the Seaview shone through the fog like beacons in the darkness and was about to push his way through the revolving doors when Rita came out.

'Just the woman I'm looking for,' he said with a smile. She was wearing one of the new Empire-line winter coats in royal blue bouclé wool and he thought the style suited her. There was colour in her cheeks and her hair was loose about her shoulders, which he liked. 'Have you finished for the day?'

'Can I help you, Mr Ryan?' She pulled on a green glove, smoothing the fingers one by one with careful deliberation.

'You remember me?'

'Of course.' She flashed him a brief smile. 'It might be months ago but I'm not senile yet.'

'Had a bad day?' he said sympathetically, falling into step beside her as she walked down the drive. 'I don't know how you put up with the job. Although, not owning the place, you can get away from it instead of having to live with it twenty-four hours a day.'

She glanced at him. 'I like the work. You haven't been making enquiries about me today, have you?'

'No. Why?'

She frowned. 'Someone's been ringing up asking questions about me.'

'You've no idea who?'

'I wouldn't have asked you if I did,' she said dryly. 'Anyway, I'm sure you're not here to talk about me. Is it Celia? Have you had any luck?'

'Not a sausage!' he said soberly. 'But Katie's been seen in Liverpool with a young bloke so we did wonder whether she and Celia have separated. I take it from what you've just said you haven't seen her?'

'Obviously not or I would have been in touch.'

'It's not that obvious,' he murmured. 'You could be lying because you don't quite trust me.'

She stopped and stared at him. 'What do you mean by that?'

'I was under the impression you thought me the kind of man who treated women rotten?'

'I'm sure I said I was sorry about that.' She was glad it was dark so he could not see her face which felt hot with embarrassment. 'Actually I'd forgotten about that until you reminded me,' she lied. There was no way she had forgotten him which annoyed her because of course he belonged to Celia. 'I have got a life of my own to live, you know, without thinking about you all the time. I like the theatre and dancing . . . I do all kinds of things.'

'I'm glad you lead such an exciting life,' he drawled, digging his hands deep into the pockets of his overcoat. 'Which way are you going? Perhaps I can walk you home? It isn't a nice night for a woman to be out on her own.'

'I'm quite used to looking after myself, Mr Ryan,' she said contrarily, having thought earlier it was not going to be pleasant going home past Hesketh Park. The fog made even the most familiar landmarks look strange and spooky.

'OK, if that's how you want it, I'll leave you to it. Bye.'

He stayed where he was and for a moment she was at a loss. 'Well, aren't you going?' she said after a minute or so, knowing that if he was catching a train to Liverpool they would be walking in the same direction.

'I thought I might go inside and have a drink. You do serve non-residents?'

'I'm sure they'll serve you, Mr Ryan. Goodbye.' She watched him walk back up the drive before turning away.

Her heels made a ringing noise on the pavement that echoed in the silence. The distant sound of a dog barking enhanced the atmosphere which was starting to take on the mood of a Hammer horror film. After several minutes she began to think she could hear footsteps behind her but convinced herself it was all in her imagination.

Think of something else, she told herself, but feet were still on her mind and suddenly she was remembering her father repairing her shoes on the cobbler's last which had been his father's before him. She had never known her grandfather but had heard a lot about him from her own father, who had been a man for telling tales. She had adored him but when she was nine years old he had left and never returned. He had been a good-looking, gentle man, different from any of her playmates' fathers in that he made her dresses and liked to cook; much to her mother's disapproval, who put his behaviour down to his having to fend for himself when he was in the army during the Great War. Rita had never been able to accept that because his ex-army chum, Uncle Bert, who had a bad chest and lived with them, had not been a bit that way. He had disappeared the same time as her father.

She remembered her mother, red-eyed with weeping, telling her that her father was catching a ship that would take him to Australia where he hoped to make his fortune. Rita had wanted to go with him so she ran all the way down to the docks but she had not been able to find him. For months she had expected a letter but it had never come.

'How do you manage to walk so fast in those high heels?'

She nearly jumped out of her skin and whirled round. 'You swine!' she gasped. 'How dare you frighten me like that?'

Mick quirked an eyebrow, something he had practised and practised when he was younger because he had once seen a cowboy do it in a film. 'Who said I was following you? I happen to be going this way and now I've caught up with you, if you don't want my company I'll just go on ahead.'

'You do that,' she said crossly. 'I'd rather have you where I can see you.'

'Really?' He smiled and walked past her.

She could have kicked herself for having responded in such a way but trust a man to pick it up and turn it to his own advantage!

'Why aren't you married?' Mick's voice floated back to her through the fog.

'None of your business!'

'You're not bad-looking.'

'Am I supposed to say thanks for the compliment?'

'Not necessarily. I suppose you have been asked?'

The cheek of the man! 'I don't want to get married! I'm happy with my life the way it is,' she said loudly.

'They all say that, the ones who haven't been asked.'

She was indignant. 'I'll have you know I've had two proposals! One from a guest and one from a policeman during the war. He – he'd helped dig out my mother's and gran's bodies when our house received a direct hit.'

'Sorry.' He turned and looked at her. 'How about having dinner with me?'

'No, thanks. I've eaten. Now, if you would please go away, I've nothing else I want to say to you.'

He sighed. 'OK, if that's the way you want it. But if Celia gets in touch, will you give us a ring? She could send you a card at Christmas and Katie just might still be with her. Ma's talking of putting the Arcadia up for sale – which, little as I like the place, is a sign that she's giving up hope of Katie returning and I don't like that. I'm moving out myself. Buying a house in Waterloo near the front. See you sometime.' He walked away.

Rita stared after him. There was a hollow feeling inside her. She decided if he was buying a house it was probably for him to live in with Celia and Katie one day. She was right keeping him at a distance, but was he right in thinking Celia would get in touch at Christmas? And if she did, what was Rita to do about it when she was inexplicably attracted to Mick? At the moment she had no answer.

Katherine closed a cage door and walked over to the tinsel-decorated window as she heard a taxi draw up outside. It was Celia bringing Mrs Evans back from Southport after spending a couple of days over Christmas with her granddaughter. Her mother had found herself an early-morning cleaning job which left her free for such excursions, despite Katherine's protesting at her taking on such a strenuous job at her age. Celia had become quite uppity at that and said she wasn't in her dotage and better she did it than Katherine. She wanted her daughter further up in the world than working in a pub or cleaning.

Katherine had responded, 'You call working in a pet shop up in the world?'

'Yes!' Celia had said firmly. 'You think, girl. At least Mrs Evans gives you a certain amount of leeway here to do things your way and you're getting to know how to run a business.'

Katherine had accepted there was some truth in that but it had only served to remind her what she had given up in leaving the Arcadia. She often thought of the family and had sent them a Christmas card, saying she hoped to visit them on New Year's Day. She had finally come to terms with Sarah and Ben's being back together. After all, she told herself, she could not expect him to worry about her feelings when she had not considered his and left without even thanking him for all he had done in accepting her as part of the family. Now he had his life to live and she had hers, and there were certain compensations in that. She was free to come and go as she pleased and already shouldering responsibility in a way that she might not have if she had stayed at the Arcadia. There was also Patrick to think about but she did not intend thinking too much about him. That only led to worry about Ma's disapproving of him and what that might mean if she returned to the Arcadia . . .

She went outside to welcome them. 'Had a good time?'

'Lovely!' said Mrs Evans, accepting her assistance getting out of the taxi. 'I'm whacked but it was worth it. I'm going back there for the New Year. That great-grandson of mine is a real cheeky monkey!'

'Great!' said Katherine, glancing at Celia. 'Did you enjoy your day out?'

'It was very nice,' she said, taking the old woman's other arm. 'I really enjoyed looking at the shops along Lord Street. Mrs Walsh came with us and we went in Matti and Tissot's. I'd always wanted to go in there but I didn't like to on my own. We had coffee and these gorgeous Charlottes Russes.'

'There were chocolates made on the premises, too,' said Mrs Evans, smacking her lips. 'Expensive! But Celia treated us both to a quarter after she met a man she knew there.'

'I didn't know him the way you make it sound,' she said, going red. 'He was just someone who used to stay at the Seaview, and who's staying there now because he missed out on his week in the summer when his sister was ill. He couldn't even remember my name!'

Mrs Evans snorted as Katherine helped her into her chair. 'He kept you talking long enough!'

Celia went even rosier. 'He's a very talkative man and we have a common interest.'

'So are you seeing him again?' said Katherine, intrigued.

'Of course not! He's a different class from me. He was a sergeant-major in India.'

Katherine winked at Mrs Evans. 'One of the big guns, hey? Kept the Empire going till it started to collapse.'

'That's not funny,' said Celia, colour still high. 'He's not a bit snobby.'

'What's he got to be snobby about?' said Katherine, raising her eyebrows. 'Just because he's staying at the Seaview and was a sergeant-major doesn't make him any better than you. What does he do now? I bet he has to work for a living?'

'I didn't ask him,' said Celia, and smiled unexpectedly. 'But you're right. I mean, it says in the papers that the class barriers have come down since the war.'

'Hmmmph!' said Mrs Evans. 'You tell that to some of the nobs. They still think they're running this country! Money talks.'

'You think so? I thought they were all poorer because of taxes?' said Katherine.

'There's them that blankety-blank are and them that aren't,' grunted Mrs Evans. 'Mind you, there's also the nouveau riche who don't have breeding, as they call it, but have made their own money, and lots of it!'

'It would be nice being rich,' mused Katherine.

'Aye,' said Mrs Evans. 'But it doesn't buy you good health. Now how about a cup of tea, girl?'

'Okeydokey,' said Katherine and went to put the kettle on. When she returned she said, 'So when will you be going to your granddaughter's again?'

'New Year's Eve. Your mother'll take me there so don't think you're having the morning off. She's going to some dance or other in Southport. Who's playing, Celia?'

'Tommy Speakman and his orchestra,' she said. 'It's at the Floral Hall!' She tried not to sound excited but the sergeant-major had said he would be there and would look out for her.

'Are you going with your friend from dancing class?' said Katherine curiously, sensing her mother was keeping something back. 'And will you be coming home?' They had discovered about the dancing classes the other week.

'Of course!' she snorted. 'You don't think I'd be leaving you here on your own!'

'I won't be lonely,' said Katherine with a twinkle. 'I'm getting to like my own company. And besides, Patrick said he'll come round about ten and we'll go out. He's nice and dark and knows what to bring to first foot properly.'

Celia shot her a look. 'You'll keep him in his place, make sure he doesn't misbehave?'

Katherine's eyes opened wide. 'Whatever do you mean, Mama! I know he doesn't look it, but Patrick's the perfect gentleman.'

'Maybe,' said Celia dryly. 'But it's New Year's Eve

we're talking about, and if he gets a few drinks down him he mightn't stay such a gentleman.'

'I'll keep him in his place, don't you worry. So you just go out and enjoy yourself and forget about me.'

Celia had every intention of doing that but did not say so. Instead she thought of the dress she had bought and how, hopefully, it would make the sergeant-major's eyes pop out!

The wind whipped a long strand of hair across Katherine's face as she stood outside the shop. It was Wednesday and New Year's Eve and there had been few customers, probably because the weather was threatening to get worse. She just hoped the rain would hold off. December had been a terrible month with planes grounded at Speke airport and a tanker stuck in mud at Bromborough dock. She hoped the weather would not spoil Celia's evening because she had taken to Southport with her a lovely dress, all sequins and shiny satin. She said she had bought it secondhand but it had looked pretty new to Katherine. Still, it was none of her business what her mother did with her money, as long as she continued to pay her way. A gust of wind caught the door and hastily Katherine seized it before it could slam.

The wireless was belting out Connie Francis singing 'Stupid Cupid!' when Katherine opened the door to Patrick. 'So you made it then?'

He felt his own arms and chest. 'Yes! It's me. I'm here!'

She chuckled, and seizing an arm, pulled him inside.

'You don't have to act dafter than you are. D'you want a cup of tea before we go for that walk?'

'Is that all that's on offer?' His arm slid round her waist and he whirled her round the small space at the bottom of the stairs and with his mouth against her ear, crooned along with Connie Francis about being in love.

'Shhh! Don't be silly. You've been drinking.'

'It's New Year's Eve! What do you expect? But I swear I've only had twenty pints.' He kissed her enthusiastically until she scarcely had any breath. He had never kissed her in such a way before and she wished he wouldn't now because it made her feel even more muddled up about returning to the Arcadia.

'Twenty pints!' she gasped. 'Who are you kidding?'

'Twenty-two then. Or perhaps it was the three helpings of Desperate Dan's cow pie that made me feel great!' He began to croon about how easy it was to fall in love as the Crickets took over from Connie Francis. He held Katherine tightly and kissed her ear, her cheek, her chin.

'Patrick! Behave yourself,' she said, managing to get her hands against his chest.

'Why? Don't you like it? All you've got to do is let yourself go!'

She pushed him away. 'I can't,' she said. 'Not until I know where I am with Ma!'

'Ma?' He looked at her in surprise. 'You mean Celia? What's she been saying about me?' He took Katherine's hands and placed them round his waist, holding them there with his own and swaying from side to side, singing, '"Tea for two, cha, cha, cha!"'

She danced with him cheek to cheek, ignoring that remark but wondering where tonight was going to end. 'How much have you really had to drink?' she murmured.

'None of your business if you don't want to love me.'

She thought of Ma and of the Arcadia and of the future there for which she still longed. 'What are you doing talking about love?' she managed to say in a light voice. 'We hardly know each other. And besides, we're too young to get serious.'

He released her abruptly so that she fell on to the stairs and his expression was suddenly sombre. 'I'll wait down here while you get your coat. Don't be all night.'

'What did you do that for? It hurt!'

'Sorry! But I'm not a saint, kid. Go and get your coat if we're going out.'

She went, feeling awful for rejecting him when all the time she needed him and didn't want to lose his friendship. Her fingers shook as she applied fresh lipstick.

'Hurry up!' he yelled.

'Coming!' She felt relieved he had not left while she was upstairs. She glanced at herself in the mirror one last time, thinking she looked pretty good, then dashed downstairs.

Patrick already had the door open. 'Got your key?'

She nodded and fell into step beside him. She would have liked to have slipped her hand into the crook of his arm but thought he might misconstrue her action. He looked distant and she waited for him to crack a joke or speak but he did not and the longer the silence lasted, the more difficult it became for her to say anything. This is stupid! she thought but still they walked on in a silence that was starting to feel as heavy and thick as fog.

Eventually, after she felt they had walked a couple of miles and the pubs had let out, she managed to say, 'We thought this was going to be fun. You've brought your camera because you said you hoped we'd see something worth taking that you could sell to the newspapers. But it's not fun when we're not speaking to each other *and* you haven't even taken one shot.'

'It's not fun because we're at that point where I can't pretend this is a passing romance,' said Patrick in a tight voice. 'Walking in the wind and the rain's fun for lovers! But we're not lovers, are we, Katie? So rain's just rain and we get miserably wet.'

'I'm not miserable,' she said with a sinking heart. 'And besides, it's not raining.'

'It feels like it's raining to me,' he murmured. 'And *I* am miserable. Bloody, bloody miserable!'

'Oh, Patrick! Don't swear and sound like that!' He was wringing her heart and she wanted to hug and comfort him, but she didn't because she knew there would be no going back then, and besides she didn't know if it was real love she felt for him. 'I'm very fond of you.' He made no answer, only stared at her. She felt her cheeks burning and her heart began to thud.

'So you've said,' he murmured. 'I think I'll go home.'

'Home!' She couldn't believe it. 'Home!' she repeated, losing her temper. 'You *can't* go home! You were first footing for us! You've got the coal, salt, everything! And you're a man and I'm a woman and it has to be a man if we're to have a healthy, happy New Year! So don't be blinking selfish!'

'OK, OK! Keep your hair on!' He glanced at his watch. 'If we go past Barker's and along Belmont Road we should time it just right to arrive at the pet shop for midnight. I'll let the New Year in and then I'll go home.'

'Fine!' she said brightly. 'We'll do just that.' They walked on, not speaking.

There were people milling around at the junction between Oakfield Road and Belmont Road. The two of them attempted to skirt round the crowd but instead became caught up in it. Someone came between them and linked arms and others joined the chain. People began to sing and dance the 'Hokey Cokey' and 'Knees Up, Mother Brown'. Bells rang and ships' horns began to blow. A roar went up and people cheered and began to sing 'Auld Lang Syne'. Then on every side people were kissing complete strangers and wishing them a Happy New Year. A dark man with a moustache kissed Katherine and so did a woman and then someone else. She wiped away their kisses and looked for Patrick but there was no sign of him and suddenly she felt bereft. Then another person was shaking hands and greeting her. It seemed to go on forever as she forced her way through the crowd, trying to find Patrick. Several men made a grab for her, seizing her by her coat or a sleeve. Somehow she managed to tug herself free and find her way on to the pavement.

She stood outside Reuben Berg's china shop, looking back at the crowd, and noticed a fight had broken out. She was reluctant to leave, wondering where Patrick was.

Could he have gone home as he had said? Where was he? she wondered fretfully. She wanted him to first foot. If he didn't they wouldn't have a happy, healthy and prosperous New Year. A man came up to her and suddenly she recognised him as the one from the pub whom she had thrown beer over.

'Look who we have here,' he sneered, touching her hair and breathing alcoholic fumes over her face.

'Go away,' she said, avoiding looking directly at him and staring over his shoulder in an attempt to spot Patrick.

'Nah! You owe me! How's about a nice sloppy kiss?'

'No, thanks.' She moved aside but he grabbed hold of her and forced her against him. She struggled but he was too strong for her and the next moment his mouth was all wet and slack over hers. Wrenching her face away, she let out a scream but the noise was such that nobody took any notice. Then he was feeling her over in a way that hurt and angered her, sucking her neck as if he was a vampire. She tried to break free, managed to yell, 'Patrick, Patrick, help!'

And the next moment, miraculously, he was there, dragging the man off her. She leant back against the shop window, her breath coming fast, watching them grapple with each other. Then there was the flash of steel. She gasped and moved forward but before she reached them the man was lurching away and Patrick was on the ground, clutching his arm.

Katherine went down on her knees and stared in horror at the blood welling up between his fingers. 'I – I'll dial 999,' she babbled.

'Not on your nelly!' he panted. 'You'll give me mam a heart attack if the police go knocking on her front door. Help me up.'

'You should see a doctor!' She was near to tears but managed to get her shoulder beneath him and hoist him to his feet.

'Get me to the shop. We'll talk about it there,' he gasped.

'I don't know,' she gulped. 'The things you'll do to get me alone upstairs.'

'Very funny!' He leant on her heavily.

Her arm went round him and slowly they drew away from the crowd which was beginning to disperse.

The coal fire still glowed in the living room because Katherine had banked it up with slack before Patrick had arrived earlier that evening. She was glad of that as she led him to the sofa in front of it. They were both shivering and she stuck a poker into the slumbering fire and moved it around until the coal burst into flames.

She glanced down at Patrick and saw that his eyes were shut and his face white but it seemed to her the blood was not flowing so quickly now. She took off her coat and covered him with it and went and put the kettle on before taking a bottle of Christmas sherry out of the sideboard cupboard. She filled two glasses and drained one before kneeling in front of him and placing a cold hand against his cheek.

His eyelashes fluttered open and he stared at her. 'Drink this,' she ordered. 'Then we're going to have to get your jacket off.'

He drained the glass and forced himself upright. With difficulty they removed not only his jacket but sweater and shirt as well; his shirt sleeve had stuck a little and he gritted his teeth as she eased it off. Then he flopped back on the sofa and closed his eyes again.

Katherine felt full of pity for him and a little scared but she had noticed the wound was only bleeding sluggishly now, although it looked ugly. 'It's only a flesh wound.' Relief caused her voice to crack.

'It hurts like hell!'

'I'm going to have to clean it.' She bit her lip. 'I think we'd both better have another sherry.'

They had emptied the bottle by the time she had mopped the wound clean and painted it with iodine and bandaged it up. She was feeling woozy by then so sank down beside him. She had covered him with a blanket because he was still minus his shirt and sweater. His eyes did not open but his head lifted and shifted on to her shoulder. She took hold of his hand beneath the blanket and squeezed it before closing her eyes. What a start to the New Year, she thought, and the next moment was asleep.

It was Celia who woke her, looming over her in her sparkly frock. 'What's going on here?'

Katherine yawned but did not move. Patrick was still flat out but the blanket had slipped, revealing one bare shoulder. 'What time is it?' she asked.

Celia glanced at the clock. 'Gone two. He should have left by now. I hope you two haven't been up to anything?'

'Chance would be a fine thing.' Katherine yawned again and blinked. 'Anyway, what time is this for you to be coming in?'

'I ask the questions,' said Celia, looking worried as she picked up the empty sherry bottle. 'I hope he didn't get you drunk and . . .'

'Have his wicked way?' Katherine laughed shortly. 'No chance, Mama! He came to my rescue when I was attacked, and got stabbed for his pains.'

'Stabbed!' Celia looked shocked. 'Why isn't he in hospital?'

'He didn't want it. Anyway, I've bound up his wounds and he's exhausted. Now you're not going to send him out into the cold, are you?' She cocked her head to one side. 'I mean, he's not doing any harm sleeping on the sofa.'

'Me heart's not that hard! But you can get to bed and leave him here.'

'I'll disturb him if I move,' she murmured, watching Celia from beneath drooping eyelids. 'Did you have a good time?'

'Lovely!' Her face lit up. 'I really enjoyed it. But you're still leaving him here and going to bed. I'll fetch another blanket for him and maybe he should see a doctor in the morning.'

Katherine agreed to that and slowly got up so as not to disturb Patrick. She gazed down at him and her heart melted. Any visit to the Arcadia was definitely out of the question now.

Chapter Fourteen

The wind had whistled all night and was still howling as Rita came downstairs. She saw her landlady bend to pick up the mail from the coconut mat and flick through the letters. 'Any for me?' she called, hoping there might be a late Christmas card from Celia.

'As it happens, yes!' said the other woman. 'It's got an Australian stamp on. Who do you know in Australia?'

'Nobody!' Rita stretched out a hand to take the letter and suddenly remembered there was somebody. But surely . . . Her thoughts went no further. She tore the envelope open and took out an extremely official-looking letter. She read it swiftly and then more slowly.

'What is it? Who's it from?' said her landlady.

Rita lifted her head and there was a dazed expression in her grey eyes. 'My father's dead!'

'I thought he was long gone?'

'No.' Rita moistened her lips. 'It – it's just that I haven't seen him since I was a child. He went to Australia and we never heard any more. I presumed –'

'Well, I am sorry, love.'

'Thanks,' she murmured, placing the letter in her handbag before leaving the house. It was New Year's Day and despite the weather she was thinking that maybe it might be going to be a good year after all. The letter was from her father's Australian solicitor and the fact that he had hired one to see to his affairs seemed incredible to Rita. He'd had nothing when he left Liverpool! The letter requested that she contact the Liverpool firm of Mason, Carshaw and Mason in Castle Street. There must be money involved! As soon as she arrived at work she would telephone and make an appointment.

Rita hummed the lyrics of 'A Certain Smile' as she totted up figures.

'Someone sounds happy,' said Andy Pritchard as he stopped in front of the reception desk. He was a tall man with a soldierly bearing, a reddish face and gingery moustache. His pale blue eyes were slightly protuberant but he wore his fifty years well.

'It's Johnny Mathis. Did you enjoy yourself last night?'

'Wonderful!' He clapped his large hands together and flashed a toothy smile. 'Met a lady who used to stay here. Name of Mcdonald. Perhaps you remember her? Blonde and small and with private means.'

'Can't say I do,' said Rita. 'Does she have a first name?'

'Celia.' The name rolled off his tongue. 'Rather a nice name, don't you think? Makes me think of nymphs and things.'

Rita stiffened. 'Celia Mcdonald!'

'That's right. You remember her?'

Rita hesitated. 'I'm not sure I do. We have so many people staying throughout the year and not all are regulars like yourself.'

'Or so hard to forget,' he said roguishly, patting her hand. 'I'm off! There's a matinée dance with Rex Hilton and his band this afternoon at the Floral Hall where I'm meeting Miss Mcdonald. Then my sister wants me to take her to the pantomime this evening. Don't know what she sees in them but I suppose she's never quite grown up. We'll be leaving in the morning so if you could have the bill ready?'

'Certainly, sir.' She watched him ascend the stairs, a frown furrowing her brow. It was her day for surprises, it seemed. Could the Celia Mcdonald he had met be *their* Celia? She felt certain if another woman of that name had stayed at the Seaview she would have remembered it. But Celia a blonde and with private means . . . That was incredible!

She nibbled on a fingernail. Was this the breakthrough Mick Ryan had hoped for? What should she do? Let him know about it or ignore it? She'd had difficulty getting him out of her mind since November and realised how much she wanted to know how he was getting on. There and then she decided she would visit the Arcadia whilst keeping that appointment with the solicitor.

The next day the wind was still howling but Rita dressed in her Sunday best, putting on a coat in russet brown and fastening a gold-coloured scarf about her neck with a marcasite brooch in the shape of a leaf. Then she donned a neat little mustard-coloured hat with a feather in it, pinning the hat on firmly with a couple of hat pins. She glanced in the mirror, was pleased with what she saw then made her way downstairs.

*

Rita had to hang on to her hat as she toiled up Mount Pleasant. There were several smashed slates on the pavement and she kept glancing up at buildings, thinking it would be awful if now she had come into money, she was knocked stone dead by a falling chimney pot or slate. She felt as if she was living in a dream. It seemed her father and Uncle Bert (they had gone off together) had bought some land dirt cheap to grow market garden produce. Then Uncle Bert had died and the Australian Post Office Company had wanted to buy the land. So her father had sold it and put the proceeds of the sale into the bank and lived frugally for the rest of his life. He had actually left the money to her mother and his two children but as Rita was his only living relative she came in for the lot. She felt now she could go some way to forgiving her father because he had not completely forgotten her.

Rita stopped in front of the Arcadia and stared up at it. For a moment she hesitated, thinking of Mick, and then of his mother and him saying she was thinking of selling up. She remembered how Kitty had spoken so fondly of the girl she had called her daughter and felt sorry for her. She climbed the steps and tried the door. It was locked so she rang the bell.

Kitty had stayed in the whole of New Year's Day, expecting Katherine to come. She had read and re-read the words on her Christmas card and planned exactly what they would have for dinner but Katherine had not come and Kitty's imagination had run riot, picturing her run over by a bus or killed by a falling tree on her way. Commonsense told her it was more likely that Celia had somehow prevented her from coming but that made her just as unhappy. Mick and John had ordered her to stop fretting, suggesting Katherine might turn up another day. So Kitty was clinging to that hope as she got on with preparing for the next influx of guests, due to arrive on Saturday.

It had been a quiet Christmas. Sarah and Ben had gone to Ireland to talk over the final arrangements for their wedding which was to take place in Ireland on St Valentine's Day. There had been no word from Jack so the hotel had felt very empty with only Mick and themselves and the puppy they had bought him for Christmas. At least Nelson had provided them with some entertainment but soon he and his master would leave to go and live in Waterloo.

When the doorbell rang Kitty thought it was Sarah and Ben back home despite there having been gale warnings for shipping in the Irish Sea, so it came as something of a surprise when she saw a lone woman standing on the doorstep hanging on to her hat.

'I don't know if you remember me,' gasped Rita, 'but I helped you that time when your cousin's girl was having a fit?'

Kitty's face broke into a smile. 'You're Miss Turner. How nice to see you. Come in. What a terrible day!'

'Yes. I always feel sorry for sailors in this weather.'

'It said on the radio there's been earthquakes in the Channel Isles,' said Kitty, shaking her head in bewilderment. 'Here, let me take your coat and hat. You'll have a cup of tea?'

'Love one,' said Rita, peeling off her coat and handing it to her. 'How are you, Mrs Mcleod?' She was thinking that Kitty looked older than she remembered. 'How's Eileen?'

Kitty led the way into the kitchen. 'She had to go. Her mother came for her just before Christmas but she refused to go home and has found work in another hotel.' She smiled at Rita. 'I must thank you for doing your best to help the boys find Celia and Katie.'

'They're the reason I'm here.'

'You've heard something?' Kitty sat down abruptly and there was a hopeful expression on her face. 'You know where they are?'

'Not exactly. It's only a small lead I've got, I'm afraid.'

Kitty tried to hide her disappointment. 'Tell me it all the same.'

Rita told her and Kitty's brows puckered as she listened. 'I know it's not much,' said Rita.

'Oh, but it is! It's something and that's better than nothing. Katie sent me a Christmas card but there was no address on it, which means in my book that she doesn't want us visiting her. She could be having it real tough. She said she would come on New Year's Day but never arrived. I'm worried, of course.'

'Of course. But how disappointing for you – and Mr Ryan.'

'Mick was annoyed. For my sake more than his own. I brought her up, you see.'

The doorbell rang and Kitty said, 'That could be Mick now. With the way the weather is, there won't be many ships docking. You know he's with the Customs? Or maybe it's John and he's forgotten his key.' She hurried out, leaving Rita feeling slightly in a twitter at the thought of seeing Mick.

Kitty hurried to open the door, thinking it wasn't a day to keep anyone waiting, and this time received a real shock. On the step stood a tall, dark, rain-drenched, bearded figure.

'Hello, Ma! Happy Hogmanay!' it said.

'Jack!' she gasped.

'Sorry I didn't make it for the day but better late than never, hey, Ma?' He flashed her a rather tight smile.

She pulled him inside. 'You're all wet! You'll catch your death out there!'

'It is a bit chilly.' He rubbed his hands together and gazed about him as if in a daze. 'Nothing's changed but it looks strange somehow.'

'You haven't seen it for a while, that's why. Where the hell have you been? We've been worried sick!'

'You shouldn't have worried.'

'Why not?' she snapped. 'You are our son, whatever you think, and that matters to us. We – we love you.'

He raised his eyebrows but said nothing. For a brief moment their eyes met and she motioned with her head in the direction of the kitchen.

He followed her in but paused when he saw Rita. 'This is Miss Turner, Jack. My son, Miss Turner,' said Kitty. 'He's . . . been away.'

'Listen, if you want me to go, I can. I've done what I came here for,' said Rita.

'No!' said Kitty, glancing at her son as he went over to the fireplace. 'You're not going out in that weather without something hot inside you after coming all this way. Please, sit down.'

Rita sat, wondering what was wrong between this rough-looking young man and his mother. She could not remember Ben or Mick mentioning a Jack at all.

'You'll be hungry?' said Kitty, looking in his direction.

'I didn't come for food,' he muttered, pulling off sodden woollen gloves.

'You'll have some soup, though?' She switched on the gas beneath a large pan before going to the refrigerator.

Rita was starting to feel slightly uncomfortable but was sure if she made a move towards the door Mrs Mcleod would be there before her, insisting she stay.

'Where's my father?' said Jack abruptly.

'He's taken Mick's puppy for a walk. Should be back soon,' said Kitty.

'You've allowed our Mick to have a dog? You never allowed me one!' There was a tremor in his voice.

'He's taking it with him. He's bought a house and'll be moving out soon.'

'Katie turned up then?'

'No. But she sent us a Christmas card, which is more than we got from you.'

'But I'm here and she isn't!' He shot the words back at her.

There was silence. The pan began to steam and Kitty poured soup into three bowls and called her son over to the table. She placed one of the bowls in front of Rita, who did not like to refuse. She picked up a spoon and dipped it into the soup and it was then that they heard voices in the lobby. She half rose but Kitty waved her down. 'It's only Mick and John. Eat your soup.'

'But surely you'll want to be on your own?' said Rita.

'Later. Mick'll want to talk to you.'

Of course, thought Rita. Finding Celia and his daughter is the most important thing to all of them here.

The two men entered with Mick carrying a King Charles spaniel which was licking his face. Both stopped abruptly. Mick's eyes went to Rita whilst John stared at his son who had got to his feet.

'Miss Turner's brought us some news,' said Kitty hastily, gazing at her husband as if to say: 'Don't lose your rag!'

'Celia's got in touch?' said Mick, going over to Rita.

John had not moved, neither had Jack, and there was a strained atmosphere in the room.

'Let's go into the lounge,' murmured Mick, taking Rita's arm.

Without a word she rose and followed him out.

'Want a drink?' he said, placing the puppy on the floor and going behind the bar.

'You don't have to,' she said, as the dog sniffed her shoes. She bent and stroked him.

'Don't have to what? I'm afraid it's a bit cold in here. I should have taken you downstairs where there's a fire.'

'It doesn't matter. I can't stay long. I told Mrs Henshall I'd be in later this afternoon.'

'So what's the news?' he said, eyes on her face as he poured sherry into a glass and handed it to her.

'Thanks. It isn't much.' She told him what she knew as he poured himself a double whisky.

'You'll have this man's address?' said Mick.

'I brought it with me.' She opened her handbag and took out a slip of paper and handed it to him.

'Thanks.' He placed it in his pocket before sitting back on the dark green leatherette couch which stretched along one wall. 'And how are you? Still walking down dark lonely roads on your own?'

'Not for much longer,' she murmured, lowering her gaze and wishing he would look anywhere other than directly at her.

'I'm glad to hear it.'

She drained her glass and stood up. 'I have to go.'

'Can't you stay longer? Let's talk and get to know each other better.'

Rita said quietly, 'What would be the point? There's Celia.'

'So?'

'So!' She was flabbergasted. 'If you can't see it makes a difference, then you're stupid.'

'I'm not married to Celia!'

'Not yet, but you might –' She walked over to the door.

He rose and followed her. 'You're jumping the gun. Celia mightn't want to marry me. If she did, she wouldn't have gone missing.' He paused but Rita was silent. 'Anyway, why won't you be walking down dark lonely roads on your own? Have you met someone? Are you getting married?'

Rita smiled unexpectedly. 'No. But I've come into

money. So I'm packing the job in and going on a cruise.'

Mick's face lit up. 'Congratulations! It's nice to hear of someone having some luck.'

'Thanks.'

They both looked at each other and he said softly, 'You must keep in touch. You'll want to know if I find Celia, surely?'

She hesitated before nodding. 'Yes, I think I'd like to know.'

'Don't leave it too long. In fact . . .' Mick unclipped a fountain pen from his breast pocket and, picking up a beer mat, scribbled on it before handing it to her. 'That's my new address. Come and see the view over the river from the house sometime.'

'I might just do that,' she murmured.

He followed her out, helping her on with her coat.

The last she saw he was standing at the bottom of the steps, nursing the puppy. He raised a hand and impulsively she blew him a kiss before hurrying on down the Mount.

Slowly Mick went back indoors and found the others still in the kitchen. They were all drinking soup. 'So what have you been doing with yourself?' he asked Jack as he took down a tin of dog food from a shelf.

'Wandering around. Working,' said his brother, shooting him an uncertain glance.

'Doing what?'

'This and that.'

'Digging potatoes,' rumbled John.

'You did it yourself once,' said Jack defensively, staring

at his father. 'At least I earned an honest crust and that's what matters . . . and I told you, it wasn't the only thing I did!'

'OK! Calm down, both of you,' said Kitty, getting up and ladling out soup to put in front of Mick.

'So why did you come home?' he said, picking up a spoon and sitting down.

Jack gave a hollow laugh. 'It ain't no fun living the wandering life in this weather. I came home because I couldn't stay away any longer.'

'How did you get about?'

'Walked, hitched, caught the odd bus when I was in funds.'

'Did it teach you to appreciate your home and parents?' drawled Mick.

'Sure. But it also showed me I didn't like being out in all weathers so I'm not going to be a farmer.'

'Then you're going back to finish your training?'

'No, but –' Jack put his tongue in his cheek. 'I might be a musician.'

'Yer what, laddie?' said John, half rising from his chair. 'You didn't say that before.'

Kitty placed a hand on his shoulder and pressed him down. 'He's joking.'

'Am I?' challenged Jack, hazel eyes glinting. 'I'm still thinking about medicine but I need more time. I want to stay at home for a while. I don't expect you to keep me so I'll find some way of earning money. A bloke I met when I was playing piano in a pub told me the music scene is going somewhere in Liverpool.'

'Jazz. Rock'n'roll,' groaned John.

'You don't have to do that,' said Kitty hastily. 'You could work here.'

'You can do a job for me right now,' said Mick, taking a slip of paper from his pocket. 'This is the address of a man Rita thinks Celia's been seeing. You can go and keep a watch on his place and him. You're looking to his meeting a forty-year-old blonde, I'll pay you.'

Jack hesitated.

'Don't want to take my money?' said Mick impatiently. 'Don't be so darned proud!' He took his brother's hand and slapped the paper into it. 'You'll be doing me a favour if you find her. I've got to sort this whole Celia and Katie thing out before I get too old.'

Jack flushed a dull red. 'OK, I'll do it! But you don't expect me to be there every hour of the day, do you?'

'No. I should think weekends and evenings would be OK.'

Jack glanced at his mother. 'I could do a few hours here, work for my keep?'

'Fine,' she said, eyes softening as they rested on him. 'It'll be nice having you home for a change.'

So it was settled.

Jack decided to start his detective work the next afternoon, reckoning it was worth having a look at the place in daylight. He had shaved off his beard, considering it best if he was going to be hanging around, and now cleanshaven and wearing one of Ben's caps, stood across the road from Pritchard's Toy Emporium in Old Swan.

The shop was on a corner and took up twice the space of the sweet shop next door which had *Dolly's Sweet Mixtures* painted in large letters above. Suddenly he realised he would not recognise Mr Pritchard unless he went inside the shop or peered through the window because customers would be coming and going and some of them were bound to be men.

He crossed the road and gazed in at the window. Instantly his interest was kindled as he realised this was not your ordinary kind of toy shop but was filled with a mixture of old and new. The large dappled rocking horse which had pride of place must have come from the nursery of a large house, he decided, and was surely only there for show. No family in the streets round about was likely to be able to afford the space or the money to house such a beauty. He spotted a kaleidoscope which had been one of his favourite toys and had always fascinated Katherine. Despite the ravages Christmas must have made on the stock there were dolls with rosebud mouths and eyes that opened and closed. He remembered pulling the limbs off one of Katherine's dolls and suddenly felt uncomfortable. His gaze shifted to teddy bears and Bendy toys, wooden jigsaws and a host of other playthings.

He tried the door but it did not open. Then he noticed a small card with 'Be Back Soon' printed on it in coloured pencil. He walked slowly past the window display until he came to the sweet shop and stopped. This shop window was worth looking at, too. There were small round jars and tall ones with glass stoppers, filled with sweets in more colours than the rainbow; cherry lips and pontefract cakes, jelly beans and chocolate drops, sherbet lemons and banana-flavoured toffees, bonbons and dolly mixtures. There were open boxes displaying artificial chocolates and paper doily-covered glass cake stands on which stood pyramids of cubed Turkish Delight and rounded heaps of sugared almonds and chocolate dragees.

Just as he was beginning to think of giving in to temptation, the door opened and out came a tall middle-aged man with a moustache, followed by a young woman. They hurried past him and went into the toy shop next door. He waited a few moments before sauntering back along the front of the emporium and looking in through the open doorway. The man was using a telephone on the wall behind the counter, speaking rapidly into the mouthpiece in agitated tones. There was no sign of the young woman. Jack went back outside and along to the sweet shop and waited.

Ten minutes later came the noise of an ambulance bell and within seconds the vehicle had drawn up outside the toy shop. Several passers-by paused to watch and the man whom Jack took to be Mr Pritchard came outside and spoke to the ambulance men before leading them indoors.

There was a buzz of conversation and a crowd quickly gathered. The ambulance men reappeared carrying a stretcher with a blanket-covered figure on it. Mr Pritchard locked the shop door and after exchanging a few words with the young woman from the sweet shop, climbed into the ambulance. It drove off and she came towards Jack. Their eyes met only briefly but it was as if he had received an electric shock. He waited until she had vanished inside the sweet shop before opening the door.

A bell tinkled as he entered the small interior, its dimness relieved only by a shaft of sunlight coming through a fanlight above the door. There was no one there but a voice called, 'Won't be a minute!'

Jack waited, tapping his fingers on the counter as he breathed in the sweet smell of so many different flavours and was transported back ten years to an outing by char-abanc to Blackpool, which had been arranged by his Great-aunt Jane and her neighbours. He and Katherine had been invited. Sweets had been on ration but there was still Blackpool rock and candyfloss to be had. They had been irresistible and he remembered Katherine's hand being all sticky when she had slipped it into his as a group of them went on the ghost train. Not that he had let it stay there!

A beaded curtain parted and a little woman appeared. She had iron grey hair cut as short as a man's and a small pointed face. She smiled at him with eyes as shinily brown as Uncle Joe's mint balls. 'Sorry to keep you waiting, young man. What can I do for you?'

'A quarter of pontefract cakes, please.'

He watched her weigh the sweets in a brass pan and wondered where the girl had gone. She must be related to Dolly surely? He waited, eyes on the measuring needle as it reached the right weight. She dropped on an extra pontefract cake and he liked her for that.

'Anything else? Some chocolates for your girl or mother, perhaps?'

Jack did not hesitate, despite his pockets being some-what for let. 'My ma. A quarter of dragees, please.' He bit into a pontefract cake as he waited and looked around. 'Nice little shop you have here.'

'It's been in my family for years. I was born upstairs in the days when we used to make our own sweets.' She gave him a bright-eyed look.

'What about next door? I noticed an ambulance outside.'

'Ethel Pritchard! Now she was here before I was born and has been getting frailer and frailer by the minute. Had a break in Southport but it doesn't appear to have done her any good. Heart, my daughter reckons, but she's got a strong will. Still, none of us can live forever.'

'Your daughter was the girl who went next door?'

'That's right. My Vicky!' Her face shone. 'She's a good girl, passed all her exams and works at the Royal. She's on nights so she's gone back to bed for a bit more shut-eye. It was she who told Andy to dial 999.'

So she was a nurse! Jack rested his arms on the counter. 'Is he Ethel's husband?'

'Goodness me, no! They're brother and sister. She's a good ten years older than him and I'd say has more business sense. He made a career of the army and when he came back wanted to take over the running of everything, but her mother had left the lease to Ethel with her being an old maid. She knew she'd need to provide for herself, having no man to do it.'

'What about him? Has he ever been married?'

Dolly pursed her lips. 'No. And I can't see it happening now. He's over fifty is Andy, and set in his ways. Although there are women who'd find his kind of looks attractive, I suppose.'

'What about means? Has he any that would be attractive to a nice little widow, perhaps?'

Dolly gave him a severe look and placed the paper bag of dragees on the counter. 'You're asking a lot of questions, young man?'

'I'm just interested in people, that's all, Dolly.' He pocketed the dragees and paid for them.

'And what do you do?'

He hesitated before saying, 'I'm a medical student.'

She looked at him approvingly. 'Now there's a coincidence. Are you doing your training at the Royal?'

'No. Edinburgh. My father's half-Scots.'

'You should have done your learning here,' she said, leaning towards him across the counter. 'They've got a nice new building attached to the university, opened by the Queen Mum.'

'I've only got my year's hospital training left.'

'The Royal then! That's where you should go, young man.'

'Thanks for the advice!' He smiled and left, thinking he knew where he would find Mr Pritchard that evening, as well as Nurse Vicky, and it was almost on his own doorstep.

The Royal Infirmary, a Victorian redbrick building, stood in Pembroke Place and backed on to the university on Brownlow Hill. Jack telephoned the hospital asking about visiting hours and that evening set out for Pembroke Place, carrying with him the Liverpool *Echo*.

He was there on the opposite side of the road, hiding

behind the newspaper, ten minutes before Andy Pritchard came marching along. Jack watched as he went inside the hospital and was halfway through perusing what was on at the cinema – *The Son of Robin Hood* and *The Sheriff of Fractured Jaw* with Jayne Mansfield – when the visitors came spilling out of the hospital again.

Jack folded his *Echo* and set off in pursuit of Mr Pritchard, thinking he might lead him to Celia, only to end up outside Pritchard's Emporium once more. He did not mind that at all because he had remembered Nurse Vicky was on nights. So he waited and it was not long before his patience was rewarded by the sight of her emerging from the sweet shop, now wearing black stockings and mackintosh and nurse's cap.

He followed her to the bus stop but was separated from her in the queue by several people. Still, he kept his eyes open and saw her go upstairs and again he followed, only to have his chance of starting up a conversation with her thwarted by an elderly woman sitting next to her. The two women began to talk as if they had known each other for years. He took a seat behind her and watched for glimpses of her profile. Her skin was what the poets might call peaches and cream and her voice was low-pitched. He could easily imagine Nurse Vicky calming the most troublesome patient or relation. He liked her flaxen hair, too, and by the time they had reached their destination knew exactly which way every curl lay beneath her cap.

He followed her off the bus, a plan already formulated in his mind, and when he caught up with her, said, 'Excuse

me, but I think you might have dropped this on the bus.'
He held out a silver cigarette case.

She gazed at him and their eyes met on a level. She
was tall for a woman and long-limbed with it, but with
what his mother might call a bit of meat on her. And there
was a twinkle in her blue eyes. 'No, I haven't dropped it.
But have we met before?'

He looked dubiously at the cigarette case. 'I was sitting
behind you on the bus and I could have sworn –'

'If you were sitting behind me, you'd know I didn't
smoke. Nice try, though. But what would you have done
if I'd laid claim to that cigarette case?'

'Handed it over.' He grinned. 'I've given them up.
Can't afford them, really. I keep thinking of pawning it
but my brother gave it to me for my twenty-first birthday.'

'Sensible man! Any doctor would tell you they're bad
for your chest.'

'I know,' he said ruefully, 'but good for the nerves.
I'm in the profession myself.'

She looked surprised. 'Not at the Royal?'

'No. I've done most of my training in Edinburgh.'

'Then you'll be doing an extra year. Isn't that the
Scottish way?'

'That's right.' They had come to the hospital entrance
and both stopped. Vicky folded her arms across her chest,
hugging herself. The wind had dropped in the last day or
so but it was still very cold. 'You're from Scotland then?'

'No, I was born in Liverpool. My family are still here.
I was thinking maybe of changing cities and perhaps doing
my last year at the Royal.'

She glanced at the red brick building behind her. 'Ever read *Her Benny*?'

He nodded. 'One of my mother's favourites and written by a Victorian clergyman. The Royal Infirmary gets a mention. Heartwrenching stuff.'

They stared at each other. 'You could do worse than work here,' she said softly.

He nodded. 'I think so too.'

There was silence. 'I'll have to go,' she said, holding out a hand, that twinkle still in her eyes. 'It was nice talking to you.'

'The name's Jack Mcleod.' He took her hand.

'Vicky Bartholomew.'

'Perhaps we can see each other again?'

'I'll be catching the same bus every evening at the same time this week.' She withdrew her hand and walked away.

The following evening Jack sat next to Vicky on the bus and she told him how her father had been knocked down by a car during the blackout and how her mother had been a nurse for a short time so it had seemed natural she should follow in her footsteps.

'What about *Dolly's Mixtures*? I would have thought she'd have wanted you to take it over.'

'No. She was pleased when I said I wanted to be a nurse. She thinks nursing is a gift. That you're born with it.' Vicky slanted him a sidelong glance. 'Do you think that's true? That something like nursing or being a doctor is in your blood?'

Jack would have agreed with anything she said because

he was already head over heels in love. On Saturday he planned on asking her for a proper date. But it was then that Andy Pritchard spoilt his plans somewhat by not taking the bus home after visiting his sister.

He was extremely late coming out of the hospital and when he did he was looking agitated. Jack was undecided what to do but when the man quickmarched down London Road in the direction of Lime Street, he followed. His destination turned out to be the Odeon cinema and Jack watched as he stood waiting several minutes before going inside the foyer but he was soon out again. He walked round the block and only then did he catch a bus heading for Old Swan.

Jack glanced swiftly at the clock that hung on the wall outside the jeweller's in London Road and raced to the hospital. His luck was in because Vicky was hovering on the pavement outside. 'Sorry!' he panted. 'But I couldn't help it. Something turned up.'

'It's OK, you're here, but I'm going to have to go in a minute,' she said, her voice tinged with regret.

He took her hand and held it tightly. 'Listen, are you off duty tomorrow afternoon? Will you go out with me?'

Her smile dazzled him. 'I thought you were never going to ask. Of course I'll go out with you. Where will we meet? And don't say here!'

'Lewis's corner!' He planted an exuberant kiss on her mouth and thought if he never had anything else to thank Katherine for all the rest of his life, he had something to thank her for now.

Chapter Fifteen

Andy Pritchard had not turned up and Celia could have wept as she caught the bus home. She had waited over an hour but in the end had to accept that he was not coming. Perhaps he had never meant to come? Perhaps there had been something in her behaviour that had made him suspect she was not all she claimed to be? Yet he had seemed so keen on New Year's Day and she was sure she had not put a foot wrong, even explaining why he could not call for her by inventing a domineering mother who hated men.

Mrs Evans . . . What was she going to say to her when she arrived home far earlier than expected? Knowing the old woman, Celia expected the third degree as soon as she got upstairs. Perhaps she should walk round for a bit? But then, she was not wearing the right kind of shoes. The pictures! She glanced at her watch and thought she might just catch the big film.

There was a crowd coming out of the Royal cinema and immediately she saw Donny and his grandfather. The boy's face lit up when he caught sight of her and without looking he ran across the road towards her. She let out a scream as a car came towards him but it swerved and missed him by inches. She caught hold of him as he reached her side of the road and shook him. 'That was silly, Donny! You could have been killed!'

'I wasn't, though.' He grinned up at her. 'Are yer going to the pictures all dollied up? Yer've missed the black and white film and it was a detective one and real good.'

'Never mind that,' she said severely. 'You must look both ways when crossing the road.'

'He can't be told,' said Mr Jones, reaching them. 'I've tried to drum it into him, like, but it goes in one ear and out the other.'

Celia looked at him and saw a man at least fifteen years her senior with a prominent nose and deep-set eyes hooded by thick eyebrows. He was only a couple of inches taller than herself but had a thick head of hair and was much more smartly dressed than when she had last seen him.

He smiled and said, 'You look really nice.'

Her cheeks flushed. 'I was meeting a friend in town but they didn't turn up and I thought it was too early to go home.'

'All dressed up and nowhere to go, like?'

She nodded and gave an involuntary sigh.

Donny tugged on his grandfather's hand. 'She could come and have supper with us, couldn't she, Granddad?'

'She could,' he said gravely. 'But she mightn't want to. Ours is a bachelor household and not what she's used to.'

'Ours is a place!' said Donny scornfully. 'Yer should have seen owd Mrs Evans's place before Mrs Mcdonald and Katherine got to work on it.' He slipped his free hand into Celia's. 'We've got chocolate biscuits. Yer'd like them.'

The feel of the boy's hand in hers made Celia's sore heart feel a little better. 'Me favourites,' she said.

'Let's go then!' He swung on her hand as he beamed up at her, so she went.

The Joneses lived in an area known as the Lake District. There was a Windermere, Rydal, Ullswater, Coniston and Grasmere Street, but a district less like that northern countryside could not be imagined despite most of the terraced houses being looked after with housewifely pride. Celia knew from having walked the streets during the day that most had their brassware gleaming, steps scrubbed and sandstoned, and upstairs and downstairs curtains matching beautifully.

She was ushered into the front parlour. Two glass-fronted bookcases filled the alcoves to either side of a tiled fireplace where a single-bar electric fire stood. There was a painting of a bluebell wood on the wall above. Flowers and ornaments were conspicuous by their absence. The floor was covered in green and brown linoleum and a multi-coloured rag rug lay between hearth and brown leatherette sofa.

'Me owd lady made the rug,' said Mr Jones, switching on the fire. 'She and the daughter. I sorta hang on to it even though the room would probably look better with a carpet square from Sidney's.'

'It looks nice,' said Celia reassuringly. 'I remember making one just like it. We couldn't afford oilcloth in the old days, never mind carpets!' It was a confession she

would never have made to Andy Pritchard. Her heart
seemed to skip a beat just thinking about him and then
plummeted again.

'The good owd, bad owd days, like,' he said, smiling
as he stood with his hand on the open door.

'More bad than good if I remember right,' she
murmured, sitting on the sofa and gazing at the picture
of the bluebell woods, feeling warm at the sudden memory
of an outing to Kirkby.

'Aye, well, I'll go and see how Donny's getting on
making the tea,' he murmured. 'He's keen, like, but he
tries to do everything in a hurry.' And Mr Jones closed
the door behind him.

Celia leaned back and shut her eyes, telling herself to
forget the 'owd days'. She concentrated on trying to visu-
alise Andy Pritchard's face. Why had he let her down just
when her confidence was building up? A heavy sigh
escaped her and, getting up, she went over to the bookcases
and peered inside. There was a whole row of Dickens,
some R.L. Stevenson and several large thin books.
Curiously she opened one of the glass doors and took one
out: *Bibby's Annual 1922*. There was a knight in armour
on the cover. He had his arm round a woman but he was
not looking at her but sternly at some distant enemy. Celia
thought, I want a man who enjoys looking at me!

Clothes were so important and she had spent some of
her Pools win in November (her private means) on a new
coat, two dresses, shoes and a decent pair of soft leather
gloves, as well as a Christmas present for Katherine. She
needed to recoup that money and there had been horse

racing over the sticks that day so she had bet ten pounds on a horse the bookie's runner had tipped to win. It had fallen at the first fence, though, so she had lost her money. Accidents could happen to anyone, she had told herself, but decided not to trust that runner again.

A thought suddenly struck her. Maybe Andy had had an accident? How could she find out? She did not know where he lived but someone as important as he would surely get a mention in the *Echo*. He could have been run over by a bus or fallen down a coal hole! There could have been a fire and he'd stopped to help rescue people! What if . . .?

The door opened and her host entered bearing a tray. Donny followed, carrying a plate of biscuits and a milk jug. He walked carefully with a solemn expression on his face and the tip of his tongue protruding. Celia's heart was touched. He was so young, so earnest! She moved away from the bookcase and sat down, still holding the book. Tea was poured and biscuits offered. She placed the book on the arm of the sofa and Mr Jones picked it up.

'I've worked for Bibby's since I was a lad. Me dad worked there and wasn't always sober, like. He fell in the East Waterloo dock one day and drowned.'

Celia made a sympathetic noise in her throat. 'You've had your fair share of upsets, Mr Jones.'

He smiled. 'That was a blessing, luv. He used to beat me mam and us lads something rotten. But after he kicked the bucket Bibby's were good to us. Gave me and another brother a job. And I'll be getting a nice little lump sum, like, for me accident. They're a good firm to work for. Have social clubs – not that I can get to them often with Donny to look after. But I'm chunnering on and I don't want to bore yer, like. Donny, pass Mrs Mcdonald another biscuit.'

Celia accepted another biscuit. She found the man's and boy's attention soothing, and besides, whilst Mr Jones talked she could let her mind drift to her next meeting with Andy Pritchard, hero! It was Donny who brought her back to where she was.

'Was Katherine's dad Scottish?' he asked. ''Cos yer name is, like Flora Mcdonald who helped Bonnie Prince Charlie escape. Me granddad's told me all about them.'

Celia felt the colour rush up under her skin and her knees were suddenly shaking. What would this good man think if he knew she'd never been married? That Katherine was illegitimate? She thought swiftly and with a bright smile said, 'That's right. He was a sailor and his ship went down in the North Atlantic. He was a very brave man.'

'A hero,' said Donny, resting his head against her arm. 'Yer must have been sad?'

'I was, but it's a long time ago now.' She realised then that the thought of Mick no longer had the power to hurt or anger her. When had she stopped feeling like that?

'It's ages and ages since Gran died, isn't it, Granddad?' said Donny. 'Yer wanna see her picture?' He scrambled off the sofa. 'Here she is wiv a veil over her head and a big bunch of flowers.'

Celia rose, expecting to see an ethereal figure, but Mrs Jones had been a big woman with a very determined expression.

She sought for something complimentary to say but could only wonder how the little man sitting in the armchair opposite had coped with her. Perhaps her death had been another blessing? She was shown a photograph of Donny's parents and he talked about them with affection and sadness in his voice. They chattered about this and that and Donny fell asleep against Celia's shoulder. By then they were Frank and Celia to each other and he offered to see her home.

'No! It's time Donny was in bed. It's been very nice but I'll manage on my own.'

Frank helped her on with her coat. 'Yer welcome to come again,' he said wistfully. 'We've both enjoyed yer visit.'

She smiled but made no promises, her mind still on scanning the pages of the *Echo* for mention of Andy's heroics.

There was nothing in that evening's newspaper and Celia was downcast all the next day but on Monday Mrs Evans, who always got to read the newspapers first and was a keen peruser of the Births, Marriages and Deaths, prodded a finger on the newspaper and said, 'Eight mentions for ol' Agnes Moore who I used to know at school. Got more money than sense some families – sisters, brothers, nieces. Look at them! They've all put something in.'

Celia looked, read, and read on. *Ethel Pritchard, dearly loved sister of Andrew, passed away peacefully on . . .*

Her spirits soared and she read no further. A death! She had never thought of a death. Of course he could not come to meet her when his sister had died! She glanced again at the newspaper to see when the funeral was to take place and where, and also more importantly the address where flowers could be sent. She was surprised but thought the word 'Emporium' did have an impressive ring to it. She would buy herself a little black suit and a hat with a discreet wisp of veiling and go and pay her respects. Katherine had asked her to look after the shop that afternoon but that was out of the question now.

But when Celia told her daughter she was going out that day, Katherine was vexed. 'You have to! You promised! I'm going out with Patrick. He's still getting over that wound, you know.'

Guilt caused Celia to go on the defensive. 'You'll have to tell him you can't go. I've a funeral to attend.'

'I can't do that! I don't know where he lives.'

'That's stupid! Fancy not knowing where yer fella lives,' said Celia irritably.

'I've never had to know where he lives!' Katherine scowled and paced the floor. 'Oh, why do you have to mess up my day!'

'It's not intentional,' said Celia sniffily. 'But I feel I have to go to this funeral of a dear old friend.'

Katherine looked at her suspiciously. 'You told me you had no friends but Rita?'

'Well, I had this one! It's just that I forgot about her for a moment.'

'She couldn't have been that dear, then.'

Celia put a hand to her chest and took a couple of deep breaths. 'You're giving me palpitations. It's important I go. A last farewell. You're too young to understand the need for that yet.'

'OK! But Patrick's going to be disappointed.'

'Well, I'm sorry about that, luv. But he'll understand if he's worth having.' Celia hurried out of the room before Katherine could say any more.

Thursday came. 'You'd think she was a widow at a husband's funeral feast,' said Mrs Evans, from her position near the Aladdin paraffin heater in the shop. 'All dressed up like a dog's dinner.'

'Black suits her now she's blonde, you have to admit that,' said Katherine reluctantly. She didn't know what had got into her mother lately. She was changing and Katherine sometimes didn't know where she was with her.

'She was all right when she was that reddish colour. She's gone flighty since she's become a blonde,' commented Mrs Evans.

Perhaps that was it? thought Katherine. Now she had a flighty mother instead of a nervous one!

Patrick breezed in but his smile quickly faded. 'You're not ready!'

'Celia's had to go to a funeral,' she said gloomily.

'Damn!' He rested both elbows on the counter and looked straight into her eyes and she felt a flutter in the region of her heart.

'Less of that language, young man,' said Mrs Evans from her chair.

'Sorry.' He straightened up before facing her and saying in wheedling tones, 'Couldn't you mind the shop?'

'No, I could not! That's what I pay Katherine for.'

'Couldn't I pay you then to play out so we can be alone?'

A quiver raced across Mrs Evans's face. 'That's impudence, young man! But if you could buy me a new pair of knees I'd take you up on the offer. I was young myself once.'

'My gran has bad knees,' he said conversationally. 'She reckons it was all the scrubbing she did years ago.' He turned back to Katherine. 'So when?' he said softly.

Before she could answer a man entered the shop and asked for rabbit food. Patrick moved away from the counter and went over to the cage where several budgies were making a fair old racket. When the man left, Patrick went back to Katie. 'Well?'

'Shop closes on Wednesday. We'll go out then.' She kissed a couple of fingers and pressed them against his mouth. He took hold of her hand and kissed its palm a dozen times. Katherine found that really sensual and romantic and looked at him with stars in her eyes. He seemed about to say something more when another customer entered. 'This is hopeless,' he whispered. 'Wednesday it is! See you then, love of my life.'

She stared after him, wanting to be with him, and was annoyed with Celia for having to choose today for supposedly going to a funeral. A man! she would bet. There was definitely a man on the scene somewhere.

Celia stood on the edge of the gathering which had just emerged from St Oswald's Church and shivered in the cold wind that blew across the gravestones. Her faith was a simple one taught her in elementary school and by her grandmother who had taken her along to church when the mood took her. The service had been a Requiem Mass and Celia had quite enjoyed the solemnity and ritual despite not understanding the Latin bits. She had sat at the back near the aisle, having decided that was the best place to be noticed, and sure enough Andy had seen her as he followed the coffin out of church. His astonished smile had been worth all the expense of her new clothes.

The mourners started to make their way to the church gateway and suddenly there was Andy in front of her, dressed in a black pin-stripe suit. 'Celia! I'm so pleased you've come.'

She beamed at him. 'I saw it in the *Echo*. I had to come and say I'm sorry about your sister.'

His smile was replaced by a more sombre expression. 'It was so sudden. You do understand that was why I wasn't at the meeting place? It happened that evening, would you believe! You will forgive me?' He had taken one of her black leather-gloved hands in his and was pressing it gently.

She was thrilled by his touch. 'Of course I will! I was just worried you might have had an accident.'

'It's nice to have you worrying about me. You'll come back and have a glass of sherry and a bite to eat?'

'If you want me to. Although I won't know anyone.' She gazed anxiously up into his ruddy face.

'You know me and that's the important thing. The rest don't matter. Unfortunately this graveyard's full so we have to go to the Yew Tree cemetery first. I'll see you into one of the cars.'

He did just that, squeezing her in with two middle-aged women and an elderly aunt who snuffled and blew her nose all the way to the cemetery and on the return journey to Prescot Road.

Celia had been astonished when she had read where Andy lived. She had not expected a man of his stature to live in a flat above a shop but that was forgotten when she set foot inside Pritchard's Toy Emporium. Even now a toy shop was a wonderland to her. The joy of playing with toys was something she had missed out on. Her mother had considered them a waste of money and her grandmother had always been instructed to buy her shoes or clothes instead. Now here was this magical place crammed with so many beautiful playthings.

She would have liked to linger but instead had to go upstairs which was very different altogether. It was as if time had passed it by. The windows were curtained in heavy green velvet and the net runners were lace-edged. The furniture was dark and heavy; Celia reckoned it was mostly good stuff but pre-Great War. The gloominess of the room was exaggerated by every mirror being draped in black crêpe.

Andy left her sitting in a chair while he went to get her a drink. She gazed into the fire, not wanting to catch anyone's eye in case they should come up and talk to her. For some reason she was nervous about explaining how she came to be there and who she was. But she was not to be left alone.

'Hello! I'm Dolly from next door. You look lonely sitting here all on your own,' piped up a voice at her shoulder.

'Oh, no! I'm fine,' stammered Celia, gazing at the bright-eyed, elderly woman hovering beside her chair. She rose to her feet. 'I was just having a warm because it was a bit cold in the graveyard. Please, have my seat.'

'That's kind of you.' Dolly sat in the chair and stretched her lisle-stockinged legs towards the fire. 'I think we're in for more bad weather.' She held her head to one side. 'Family, are you?'

'No, friend,' said Celia swiftly, and could have bitten off her tongue. She was at least twenty years too young to be one of Ethel's friends.

But the woman smiled. 'Used to come in the shop years ago as a nipper, I suppose? Left the area but still come here for your children's toys?'

Celia did not know how to answer that without having to think up another reason for her being there so just smiled as if in agreement.

'You've probably been in my shop,' said Dolly. 'All the kids came in my shop for a penny bag of mixtures before the war. My mam was in charge then.' She looked up at Celia. 'What were your favourites?'

'My f-favourites?' she stammered.

'Your favourite sweets?' Dolly's tone was encouraging.

Celia said the first thing that came into her head. 'Cherry lips! And those violet-flavoured ones that made your breath smell nice.'

'Nice to be kissed,' said Dolly, and winked.

Andy approached with two glasses in his hands. 'I see you're keeping Miss Mcdonald company, Dolly?'

'Miss?' Dolly chortled. 'And there was me giving her

a husband and a handful of kids. I thought she was one of those mothers that comes back.'

Celia smiled but let him carry on speaking. 'Ethel and I met Miss Mcdonald in Southport. She, like us, had been going there for years, staying at the same hotel,' he explained.

Dolly's bright eyes went from one to the other of them. 'How nice for you both,' she said, in a way that made Celia feel hot all of a sudden.

'Yes, isn't it?' said Andy, smiling. He touched Celia's hand. 'You'll have to excuse me a moment. There are people I have to speak to. I'll be back as soon as I can.'

'Perhaps I shouldn't have come? I don't want to be in the way,' she said hurriedly.

'Don't you dare disappear!' He looked alarmed. 'You stay right there and don't let Dolly play twenty questions with you.' He moved away.

Celia looked at Dolly apprehensively and took a large sip of sherry to brace herself.

'So will we be seeing more of you round here, Miss Mcdonald?' she asked.

'Maybe!' Celia's tone was bright and there was a flush on her cheeks as she took another sip of her sherry. 'Tell me, Dolly – I hope you don't mind me calling you Dolly? – is it any business of yours?'

Dolly's mouth closed like a clam and Celia drained the sherry glass and moved away, feeling slightly ashamed of herself for being so rude. She did not know quite what to do with herself and wandered over to the window where she tried to peep out but the nets deterred her from doing so. She was just starting to think about leaving when Andy came up to her.

'I'm sorry I haven't been able to spend more time with you but I'm sure you know how it is.' He took hold of both her hands and inclined his handsome head towards her. 'I'm going to be tied up for the next few days. Paperwork, you know, and getting rid of things. Ethel was a hoarder. I'm not looking forward to it at all.' He sighed as if he had the weight of the world on his shoulders.

'Perhaps I could help there?' she suggested eagerly.

His face brightened. 'You are an angel! Perhaps you could come on Wednesday afternoon? The shop'll be closed then.'

Celia hesitated because she had promised to take Mrs Evans to Southport that afternoon. Then she decided he needed her more, and after all she could always fall back on Katherine to look after the old woman.

'Me?' said Katherine the following Tuesday when they were feeding the pets and Celia mentioned the matter. 'I can't! I'm going out with Patrick. I let him down last week because you went to that funeral. I can't do it again.'

'But this is important,' said Celia crossly. 'It's not often I go out and I can only meet this – this other old friend I met at the funeral tomorrow afternoon because it's hi— her day off.'

'Well, you'll have to get in touch with them and cancel.' Katherine folded her arms, her expression decisive.

'I can't do that!' cried Celia.

'If you can't, then tell Mrs Evans you can't take her

to the pantomime in Southport. And by the way, Mr
Jones called and said if you wanted to quit your cleaning
job, he could put a word in for you at Bibby's. We had
a nice little chat.' Her eyes gleamed. 'You didn't tell me
you've been to his house? Donny was full of it! They
were both really interested when I told them we'd worked
in hotels.'

'You didn't tell him the truth about the family at the
Arcadia?' said Celia, alarmed.

'Why not?' said Katherine defiantly. 'He was very
sympathetic and understands why I can't produce a refer-
ence. People always think if you can't produce one it
could be because you're a thief. Well, I'm not dishonest
and I wanted him to know that. He's a nice man and I
trust him.'

Celia had paled, remembering what she had said to
them about her supposed husband's death. 'You really told
him everything? Good God! You'll be telling Mrs Evans
next and then we'll never hear the end of it. I feel so
ashamed. What must he think of me?'

Katherine shrugged. 'He said these things happen in
war and I bet Mrs Evans would say the same. She's not
all that strait-laced. She has a sense of humour and is
more tolerant than you think.'

Celia shook her head and gnawed on her lip, wiping
a rabbit's head absently with a cloth. 'It's easy for you to
say that but there's lots of people who would think I was
dirty and spoilt goods.' She began to tremble. 'You've no
idea how it felt when I first started showing and had to
try and disguise it.' Her hands shook.

Katherine took the cloth from her and put it on the counter. 'I understand,' she said quietly.

'I'd never done it before,' said Celia, flushing. 'We just got carried away. It's easier than you think, so you be careful with that Patrick. Have you told him?'

'Not yet. Although he knows I used to live at the Arcadia. But I will tell him.'

Celia closed her eyes tightly before opening them again and blinking. 'Do you have to be so honest with everyone?'

'I do with Patrick,' said Katherine firmly. 'But it's getting to be alone with him that's the problem.'

Celia sighed. 'You're too trusting. Just like me.'

Katherine said nothing. She could not see that she was like her mother in any shape or form. Perhaps Celia's trouble came from never having trusted the family at the Arcadia with the name of the real father. She knew they would still have helped her. It was in their nature to care for people. There was an ache inside her still when she thought of them. She wanted to see them again but in the meantime there was Celia's problem.

'What are you going to do about seeing your friend?'

Her mother's expression hardened. 'You don't have to worry about me! I'll sort it out. You just get on with your own life and leave me to get on with mine.'

'OK,' said Katherine, shrugging. 'If that's the way you want it.' She reached for some millet sprays and got on with tending the budgies.

Chapter Sixteen

'There's that woman!' hissed Dolly. 'That colour's not real.'

'What colour? What woman?' said Vicky, coaxing a curl into place so that it nestled against her cheek. She had finished the night shift and was meeting Jack in town. They were going for a drink at the Grapes and then on to the Cavern.

'That Miss Mcdonald! The one I told you about who came to the funeral.'

Vicky put down the comb and went over to the window.

'You won't see her now, he's let her in. Nice goings on, I must say!' Dolly wobbled her chin, wishing her bottom teeth would stay put. 'Who's to know what they'll get up to inside there?' she mumbled, and pressed her teeth back into place, allowing the net curtain to drop before sitting in her armchair and picking up her by now luke-warm cup of tea.

'You shouldn't be so nosy.'

'He said he met her in a hotel in Southport. I'd like to know what kind of hotel that was! You hear about these places,' said Dolly with relish.

'What places?' said Vicky, trying to keep her cool,

remembering how Jack had explained his reasons for being in this part of Liverpool. He had asked her to keep her eyes and ears open for just such a woman.

'Never you mind,' said Dolly, who strangely enough had always tried to keep her only daughter ignorant of certain ways of the world, despite knowing she was bound to learn a thing or two nursing. 'Where are you going, miss?'

'I told you.' Vicky glanced in her direction and smiled. 'And you're not to start asking questions as soon as I get home. I'll bring him in when I'm ready.'

'If I'd dared to speak to my mother like that, I'd have got the strap! You haven't even told me his name!' Dolly's tone was scandalised.

Vicky shrugged on a green coat with black piping round the collar and hem. 'It's a plain honest to goodness name: Jack. I like it.'

'Jack and the bean stalk and Jack and Jill went up the hill,' mumbled Dolly, peering out of the window again. 'It's a nursery rhyme name. She's still in there! Jack be nimble, Jack be quick, Jack jump over the candlestick!'

'Your memory, Mother. And give them a chance. She's only had time to take off her coat.' She picked up a black patent leather handbag and pulled on a pair of gloves. 'I'm going. I've got my key, don't wait up.'

'I won't,' said Dolly. But they both knew she would.

Celia gazed round the bedroom with its floral wallpaper and wished she had kept her coat on. It was cold in here, unlike the living room where Andy was doing some paperwork. It was her own fault for landing herself with the task in hand. First she had apologised about tomorrow and then she had volunteered to clear his sister's room for him this evening. He had instantly taken her up on her offer and she could see why. The place was a mess, as if someone had been searching for something. He had suggested that when they had both finished, they could go out for a drink.

She squared her shoulders and opened the wardrobe door and was immediately assailed by a strong smell of mothballs. She coughed as the smell caught her by the throat but set to work emptying everything out. As she did so she dreamt of the moment when Andy would ask her to be his wife. Then she would do over this flat, which was larger than the rooms over the pet shop and had an upstairs lavatory. They would run the toyshop together! She was already looking forward to meeting mums and children and being accepted as the owner's wife. The only trouble was Katherine. It was Celia's dream of being Andy's wife which had caused her to keep silent about her daughter. There could be no pretending to be a widow in this case because she was pretty certain that widows who remarried had to produce some sort of evidence to prove their previous husband dead. That was really thinking ahead, she thought proudly – but Kitty could have told her that even the best laid plans can go awry.

When Celia had boxed and bagged all Ethel's clothes, Andy took her to the Cygnet pub and soon they were settled in a corner of the lounge with drinks in front of them. 'I'm thinking of getting rid of the toys,' he said without preamble.

Celia stared at him in dismay. 'Why? It's a lovely shop! A real Aladdin's cave of wonderful things for children.'

'I don't like children. Never have.'

That was a disappointment. Celia would have liked one more go at having another child before it was too late. Still, a woman her age couldn't have everything.

He sipped his whisky. 'I'm going to turn it into a bicycle shop. That's more your man's kind of thing. There used to be a good one round here. The bloke had a penny farthing on display. I've never forgotten that.'

'But can you change what you're selling?' asked Celia, forcing a laugh.

'What?'

'Turn it into a different kind of shop. Isn't there something in the deeds that says you can only sell certain kinds of things?'

He stared at her blankly and for the first time she noticed how protuberant his eyes were. 'What do you know about deeds? Women shouldn't be filling their heads worrying about such things.'

She hesitated. 'I know the owner of a pet shop and she told me in her deeds it states it can't be turned into a fishmonger's nor can there be any tallow or glue making on the premises.'

He smirked. 'How many people would know such things? I reckon I can get away with it. What the eye doesn't see . . .'

'You should check,' said Celia quickly. 'There's bound

to be someone at the Town Hall or somewhere who knows. Haven't you ever seen the deeds?'

'I've looked for them,' he said in a disgruntled voice. 'Not a sign. You didn't find them when you were going through Ethel's stuff?'

'Surely she'd keep them in a safe place? Have you asked at her bank or does she have a strong box anywhere?'

'I can't think of everything! I am a man suffering a grievous loss.'

'Of course you are,' she said warmly, and touched his knee. He covered her hand with his and pressed it down on his thigh. She felt the colour rise to her cheeks and glanced round, hoping no one could see. She managed to tug her hand free and, not wanting him to think she was a prude, changed the subject swiftly, asking how it came about the shop had not been left to him.

'I was in India, up to my neck in mud and bullets. You've no idea how handy a Gurkha can be with a knife in a fight,' he said with relish. 'I've seen Everest, you know.'

'How exciting,' said Celia, who was really more interested in the shop. 'You must tell me all about it.'

His eyes shone. 'I'll get myself another whisky and then you can pin your ears back and hear just what kind of man you're sitting opposite.'

It was later than Celia intended when she let herself out of the shop after leaving Andy, having imbibed several more whiskies than he should have, snoozing in a chair. She had had to be firm with him when he made a rather coarse remark and attempted something she was definitely not ready for, but she had done it with a dignity befitting the kind of woman she was supposed to be. She hurried in the direction of Green Lane, having barely noticed the couple canoodling in the doorway of Dolly's shop, her mind definitely not on love but on finding those deeds when she returned later in the week.

'That must be her,' whispered Vicky, eyes following Celia's retreating figure.

Jack murmured, 'She fits the description. It has to be her. I'll have to go, love. See you tomorrow.'

He kissed her quickly, and with his hands in his pockets strode in Celia's wake, his breath a cloud of vapour in the cold night air. She caught a bus and so did he and when she got off there was a bit of a walk but he felt well rewarded when he saw her enter a pet shop just after midnight.

A light went on in an upstairs room and he saw her draw the curtains and was pleased with himself. He knew exactly where he was because he and Ben had often gone to Anfield football ground when he came home, but he was not about to tell anybody back at the Arcadia just yet. Tomorrow he would be back and hopefully see and talk to Katherine and then he could present her to them, much as a magician produces a rabbit out of a hat, and they'd all be pleased with him.

The next day it was raining and lunchtime by the time Jack found his way to the pet shop because Kitty had wanted him to help John move furniture. He was just in time to see the 'CLOSED' sign being turned on the door.

Damn! His plan had been to go inside as a customer and, presuming Katherine worked in the shop, to try and persuade her to come home. Now what? He decided to wait a while and see if she came out so stood outside the optician's facing the shop, watching.

After half an hour or so a taxi drew up, obliterating the doorway of the pet shop. Hurriedly Jack crossed the road and stopped outside the chemist's a couple of doors up. He pretended to be absorbed in a display of shampoos, hair dyes and perfumes but really it was three large bulbous bottles filled with some mysterious brightly coloured liquids that fascinated him.

The pet shop door opened and Celia emerged with an elderly woman, who was obviously having difficulty walking. Rheumatism, thought Jack with interest. What a pity they couldn't give people new knees or hips. A young couple followed and Jack recognised Katherine in a sunshine yellow raincoat and a headscarf. She looked slimmer and was wearing what Kitty used to call her mischievous look as she inclined her head towards the old woman as they helped her into the taxi. Jack heard the murmur of Katherine's voice and it seemed to be that of a stranger. Even so it had much the same effect on him as the sight of her. He felt guilt, as well as relief that she looked OK.

The taxi moved off, leaving her and the young man behind. He said something to her which made her smile. She linked her arm through his and they began to walk towards Jack. He was not ready for a confrontation and pulled the peak of Ben's cap further over his face, huddling closer to the shop window. They went past and Jack caught the name Patrick and a mention of Celia. The two carried on walking past the Baptist church and on round the corner.

He followed, thinking Katherine seemed to be having plenty to say to this Patrick as their heads were very close together. He thought about love making the world go round and of Vicky.

They came to the Gaumont cinema and went inside. Jack followed, glad to be out of the rain. He saw them go through into the stalls and bought a ticket and a bag of popcorn because he was starving. The lights had dimmed and the title *Me and the Colonel* was showing on the screen. An usherette appeared at his side and he realised he was going to have difficulty spotting Katherine and her companion in the dark. Deciding there was nothing for it but to take off his cap, open his popcorn and enjoy the film until the lights went up again, he relaxed.

The last few days had been busy and exciting for Jack. He had fallen in love and had had an interview at the Royal Infirmary about finishing his medical training there. Last night he had got to bed extremely late and this morning he had worked physically hard. He fell asleep and did not wake until someone shook his shoulder and asked could they get past.

Jack stumbled to his feet, pressing himself against the folding seat. The neon sign that flashed TOILETS was a few feet away and suddenly he saw coming out of the door Katherine!

She spotted him the same time he spotted her and he guessed from her expression she didn't believe her eyes.

In a flash he remembered how he had felt a few months ago when he'd needed time to think about his future and it occurred to him that the decision to return to the Arcadia should not be forced upon her.

Jack allowed his gaze to wander past her as if he did not know her and when next he glanced in that direction she was no longer there. He looked around and noticed the boyfriend coming up the aisle with ices and followed him with his eyes until he saw Katherine. The way they smiled at each other caused Jack to search for Ben's cap where it had fallen down the side of the seat and drag it over his rumpled hair. Another time, another place, he would talk to her, but now was the wrong time.

Katherine took the Orange Maid from Patrick and smiled at him as if in a dream. 'Do you think everyone has a double?' she mused.

'You mean, is there another you somewhere, or even another me? Real cool thought! Perhaps they'll get it together instead of us?' murmured Patrick.

'We will get it together,' said Katherine. 'Didn't you listen to a word I said on the way here? Didn't I explain it all perfectly?'

'If you say so.' He scooped out ice cream with a small wooden spoon. 'Who was the double you thought you saw?'

'It was my brother Jack!'

'I thought you said he was nothing to you now?'

She sighed. 'Not related but I still haven't got the hang of thinking of him like that.'

'So what are you going to do? I don't want you thinking of me like a brother,' said Patrick forcefully. 'I know you said that at one time you thought of me like that but I don't want that, Katherine, and you know it.'

'Of course I know it, but we can't get engaged until I sort things out.' She took a large bite of the Orange Maid and gasped as the chunk slithered down her throat. It was several seconds before she could speak and when she did it was still not the words he expected. 'I wonder if it could have been Jack and he just didn't want to know me?'

'I'm not surprised from what you told me,' said Patrick, exasperated that he could not pin her down to making a decision now. 'He must have felt you were a right cuckoo in the nest and that he'd been shoved out of it to make room for you!'

Katherine was silent and Patrick glanced at her and saw there were tears rolling down her cheeks. 'Sorry,' he whispered, shocked that his words could have such an effect. Putting an arm round her, he wiped away her tears with the side of his hand. 'I'll try and be patient.'

'But you're right,' she sniffed. 'It must have been like that for him. And you're right, I have to do something soon.' She rested her head on his shoulder and it felt so comfortable she wished she could keep it there for ever. 'It's just that I'm torn in two,' she whispered. 'I want to go back but I don't know what to expect, and part of me is worried that Ma'll be so anxious to prove that I still belong to the family that I might have trouble standing up for myself and just allow her to run my life for me again.'

'I'm sure you'll stand up for yourself after all you've been through,' he said in a low voice as the lights dimmed. 'You're a tough cookie.'

'That's only window dressing,' she said forlornly. 'There's also the thought that they mightn't want anything to do with me – and I need people to like me.'

'Shush!' said someone in front of them. 'You two don't half go on.'

'Shush yourself,' said Patrick belligerently.

'You looking for a fight, mate?' said the youth in front, standing up.

'No!' exclaimed Katie before Patrick could answer. She snuggled closer to him and thought, He needs me to keep him in order and what if Ma really shows her disapproval of him? Doesn't think he's good enough for me? She decided then that the folk at the Arcadia had to stay in her past.

February blew in and it was a picture in the *Echo* which caused Katherine to change her mind. She took the newspaper and waved it under Celia's nose. 'Have a look at this,' she said, incensed. 'It's Ben and Sarah. They've got married and I wasn't there to see it!'

Celia put down a mascara brush and picked up the newspaper. 'Nice frock,' she said with a sigh.

'Ivory figured satin,' said Katherine gloomily, stretching out on the bed and gazing up at the ceiling. 'The bridesmaids wore apricot and a single artificial flower in their hair. Mick was the best man. I wonder if they missed me?'

'I should think they did. Isn't it time you went back to them?'

Katherine lowered her gaze and looked at her mother in astonishment. 'What did you say?'

Celia hesitated and then went over to the bed and sat beside her. 'Perhaps this is the right time to tell you something . . .'

'Like what? You've had a win on the horses and that's why you're wearing another new frock?'

'No!'

'You've got a man?'

'Why should you think that?' Celia laughed lightly and Katherine raised her eyes to the ceiling in disbelief.

'What is it then?'

'I've told you a terrible fib – Mick Ryan *is* your father!'

Katherine thought, I'm tired, I've had a bit of a day with dropping that rabbit and it dying on me. My ears aren't working properly. It's a good job I'm lying down . . .

Celia cried, 'Haven't you anything to say? Aren't you going to shout at me?'

Katherine turned her head and realised Celia was trembling. She was serious! 'Could you repeat that, please?'

'Mick Ryan's your father.' Celia's voice shook. 'I'm sorry I didn't tell you the truth but I knew if I did you wouldn't have left them. You'd still have felt part of that family and I didn't want that. I wanted to hurt *her* and Mick.'

Katherine got up and went downstairs to the living room and put the kettle on. Celia followed. 'Don't you believe me?' she whispered, aware of Mrs Evans dozing in front of the fire.

'Does everybody tell lies?' Katherine said to the wall.

'I'm sorry. She thought she could buy my silence and I didn't like that.'

Katherine spun round. 'She offered you money?'

'She was frightened! Terrified of losing you! She loves you much more than I ever could. Even though I've grown very fond of you.'

'Fond of me?' repeated Katherine, thinking that her mother was right. It was love that made someone terrified of losing the object of that love.

'Don't look like that!' Her tone was fretful. 'Be honest, Katherine, isn't fondness all you feel for me? I left it too late for us to feel more. I didn't give you all you needed when you were growing up.'

Katherine did not answer. Her head was suddenly aching and she needed to think straight and the pain made it difficult.

'You do see you can go back to them now? Mick *is* your father! I'm telling the truth this time,' insisted her mother.

Still she did not answer.

'Why don't you say something? Don't you believe me?'

Mrs Evans started in her chair and blinked her eyes.

'I believe you,' said Katherine in a low voice. 'But will the family?'

'You'll go and see them then?' said Celia eagerly. 'Today would be a lovely day to go, the week after the wedding when Mrs Mcleod will be missing Ben.'

Katherine gnawed on her lip. 'I don't know, I have to think.'

'What is there to think about?' said Celia, that fretful note in her voice again. 'It's perfectly straightforward. You're one of them. You can go home.'

'It isn't that simple!' blazed Katherine, turning on her. 'Do you realise how you've made me hurt them?'

Celia flinched. 'You can put it right. They'll be pleased to see you.'

'How do you know? And why do you suddenly care? It's not like you to care about them,' she said scathingly.

A flush spread from Celia's face to her neck. 'Conscience! I do have one. The Mcleods were good to me years ago but I wouldn't let myself dwell on that after she gave me that money. I felt tainted, dirty! Getting to know you has changed me. I understand now why she did what she did. I do care for you, Katherine, I do. But we both have our different lives to live.' There were tears in her eyes.

'What's going on?' asked Mrs Evans querulously.

They ignored her, too intent on what was happening between them.

'I know we have but you're not telling me the whole truth,' pressed Katherine.

'What else d'you want to know?' Celia's colour deepened. 'How it actually happened?'

'No! It's just so sudden, you telling me about Mick and wanting me to go back to them.'

'I explained that. My conscience has been bothering me.'

'Aye, your conscience,' said Katherine dryly. 'I think there's more to this than your suddenly feeling guilty but I won't argue the point right now. I'm tired, I need to think.'

She walked out of the room. She wanted to be comforted but Patrick was working at the chippie this evening. Despite the early hour she filled a hot water bottle and went to bed, to think and remember the times Kitty had been there for her, and to long for the security of her previous life, before Celia had disrupted it. To have Ma chiding and comforting her, and Pops there, as strong as a rock if a little distant at times. They had always known who she was and still treated her as their own. Perhaps things could be just the same if she went back?

On that comforting thought she eventually fell asleep, only to dream that she was hunting for something but it kept eluding her and she was running and running until she came to the edge of a cliff with a sheer drop. She recognised it as a place up in Scotland where sea birds nested. She went over the top and was falling, falling. Then suddenly she was flying but she was still searching. When she woke, her mind was made up. She had to see the family and tell them what Celia had said. She would not know where she belonged until she did.

Katherine gazed through the swirling fog at the familiar frontage of the building she had called home for most of her life and thought: It looks different from how I remember it! Whether that was due to the weather she was unsure but she was in no mood to confront any guests. So after the barest of hesitations, she climbed down the area steps where she found a pint of milk and tried the door to the basement. It did not open so she peered in at the window but the room was empty and the fire unlit. The tension which had started to build up in her since yesterday evening increased. She so wanted to get those first moments of seeing Ma again over with!

She picked up the milk and retraced her steps and tried turning the hotel door knob but the door remained closed. She pressed the bell but no footsteps came in answer to her ring. Could they all have been gassed or have gone away for ever, forgetting to cancel the milk? The fear gave her a cold, sick feeling and her nerves felt ready to snap. She pressed the bell again, hearing it ringing and ringing inside. She did not want to believe no one was there. How could the place be empty? The Arcadia was a hotel, for goodness sake!

But eventually she had to accept the truth that there was no one there. She sank on to the doorstep and huddled against the door, reluctant to leave but shivering in the cold.

'Katie!'

It was so long since Katherine had been called that, that she did not respond immediately. It was not until it was repeated and the person came and stood in front of her that she glanced up.

'Eileen, so you're still here? Thank God!' she said, scrambling to her feet, forgetting how she had felt about the girl last time she had seen her. 'Hurry and open up and tell me where everyone is?'

'I can't,' said Eileen, dismay in her eyes. 'I haven't got a key.'

It was then Katherine noticed the other girl had a suitcase with her which she dumped on the step. 'You've been away?'

'Sure and you could say that,' said Eileen in her Irish brogue, flicking back her tangled hair. 'I haven't worked here for months but when I saw Ben and Sarah had got married, I thought maybe Aunt Kitty would take me back. I've been thrown out of the other place.'

'What other place? What's been happening here?' demanded Katherine. 'Where are they all?'

Eileen shrugged narrow shoulders clad in a thin woollen checked coat. 'Ask me another! You don't still have a key?'

'I've never had a key! Ma always said when I was twenty-one I'd get one, but not until then.'

'Hell!' Eileen sagged against the area railings. 'What am I going to do? I can't go back to Gran's! The aunts would get on to Mam and Dad and he'd come and drag me back home then.'

'Why don't you want to go home?'

'They treat me like a child because of me fits, and other people treat me like the village idjit! I'm no loss to them. I know it's horrible for them but it's no fun for me either,' she said gloomily. 'I've just lost me last job and now I don't know what to do.'

'I know the feeling,' said Katherine, leaning against the front door.

'You've got no job? Is that why you're here? What happened with your real mother?'

'No, I don't mean that! I'm still living with her and I've got a job. It's just that –' She paused and gazed at Eileen, who was shivering now in the thin coat. 'Perhaps you'd best come home with me? We'll both catch our deaths if we stay here.'

'Katie!'

Katherine turned and saw a dishevelled-looking Jack carrying a small suitcase. 'What are you doing here?' she gasped.

'I could ask you the same question but I'm just glad to see you.'

'Are you?' she said in surprise.

'You don't know how much,' he said in uneven tones.

'And me?' asked Eileen in a small voice.

He glanced at her and smiled. 'And you. Look, let's get inside. It's freezing out here and you'll both end up with pneumonia. I've got to go out again but I'll need to make the fires up first because the part-timers are coming in this afternoon. We can have a cuppa if nothing else. You've got the milk, good girl, Katie!' He put a key in the lock and opened the door.

'What *are* you doing here?' asked Katherine, following him in. 'The wedding was in Ireland, wasn't it?'

'I've been there. But I actually came home here when you went missing, had a row with Pops and went roaming. I came back New Year. I've got loads to tell you but first things first. Are you here to stay?'

'Maybe! If I'm wanted,' she said swiftly. Her eyes met his. 'Why? What's wrong? There *is* something wrong, isn't there?'

He nodded. 'Ma's had a heart attack!'

The blood seemed to drain out of her and she felt for the wall behind her.

Jack reached for her. 'I shouldn't have sprung it on you like that.'

'Is – is she . . .?'

'No! It happened in Ireland the day after the wedding and she's in hospital there.' His eyes fixed on Eileen. 'Annie's been worrying herself sick about you. It's time you went home but you can't go yet. I need your help. There's guests due and we're Ma and Sarah short.'

'She's – she's not going to die, is she? I'd like to see her,' said Katherine, her teeth chattering.

'You can't! She's got to be kept quiet. But we'll telephone and say you're back. That'll speed her recovery. So let's get to work.'

'You're working here? What about Edinburgh and medicine?' They went into the kitchen, followed by Eileen.

'I've applied to do my final year at the Royal Infirmary. I've met someone, a nurse, and we're going to get married. But . . .'

'You? Married!' She could scarcely believe it. 'She must be a very special person.'

'To put up with me, you mean?' he said with a twisted smile. 'I confess I've been pretty rotten to you in the past but –'

'I'll put the kettle on,' said Eileen.

They both ignored her.

'It can't have been easy for you,' said Katherine in

rapid tones. 'You were so young when you went to Ireland, and coming back to find me here can't have been fun.'

He studied her closely. 'You've been giving that some thought while you've been away?'

'I've thought about a lot of things.'

'Me too,' he said with a touch of awkwardness. 'The others aren't the only ones who've missed you.' He placed an arm about her and gave her a swift hug. For a moment she rested her cheek on his sleeve and then they drew apart, both feeling slightly embarrassed.

Some of the tension had eased out of Katherine but now it was back. Gazing about her, she saw things through a blur of tears and had to clear her throat before saying, 'When are the guests expected?'

'Tomorrow! We closed the place down because of the wedding and Ma –' He stopped abruptly. 'Is it the wedding that brought you home? Did you see the photo in the *Echo*?'

'Yes! And it upset me, I can tell you!'

'I saw it, too,' said Eileen. 'Sarah got him after all!'

'Yeah,' muttered Katherine, going over to the fridge and touching things as she passed.

'Sarah's been working here and sleeping in your room,' said Jack. 'There might still be a few of her things around. She didn't do the job as well as you, although Ma said she was doing her best.'

'I left Ma in the lurch, it was wrong of me.' Katherine turned and faced him. 'Do you know all about me not being your sister?'

He nodded slowly. 'It came as a shock and I'm still

not sure if I'll ever get used to thinking of you as my niece.'

'Pardon?' she said, startled. 'You said your niece? How do you know that?'

Jack raised his eyebrows. '*Aren't* you my niece?'

'Yes, but Celia only told *me* last night that Mick was my father.'

Jack grinned. 'He believed it from day one. They've been looking for you.'

'Where?'

'Southport. Tried all different hotels and then Rita came up with . . .'

'Rita?'

'She works at the hotel where Celia used to work.'

Katherine remembered her. 'So what did she come up with?'

'Let's take things in order,' he said, his brow creasing with concentration. 'Before she came up with a man's name whom Celia had been seeing, Sarah saw you.'

'Sarah did? But she kept quiet about it?'

'No! She followed you then went for Ben but the pair of them lost you.'

'I saw them but I didn't realise they were looking for me,' said Katherine in a low voice. 'They looked so happy with each other, I was angry – jealous. I didn't like seeing them together at all. It made me feel an outsider. Is that how you felt when you used to come home and find me ruling the roost?'

'Something like that, but it's behind me now. Jealousy's

a waste of energy. I should have said how I felt years ago but it wasn't easy.'

'Because I was always there. Have you talked with Ma and Pops about it?' He nodded.

'So my going away has done some good?'

'Loads, I'd say. Anyway, to get on with the story – and I'm not sure if you're going to like this bit –'

'Why?'

He accepted a cup of tea from Eileen. 'Wait till I tell you.' So he told her about Rita and how Mick had paid him to watch Andy Pritchard's place.

Katherine was flabbergasted. 'So it *was* you in the cinema! But why didn't you speak to me?'

'There's a right time for everything. I didn't feel that was it. I thought you'd come back when you were ready.'

'But what did you tell Mick?'

'I told him that the lead didn't go anywhere. Wrong of me in view of what happened to Ma, but I thought you and the bloke you were with looked pretty wrapped up in each other.'

Katherine blushed. 'We are but – Ma didn't approve of Patrick when she met him.'

'Patrick!' exclaimed Eileen. 'You've met up with him again?'

'Yep! Seems like fate,' said Katherine brightly. 'But I can't go mentioning him to Ma yet. Anyway, when will Mick be home?' she asked Jack.

'He won't be. He's left. Has a house in Waterloo near the beach and got himself a dog. He doesn't know about

Ma because he only stayed in Ireland for the wedding, but he calls here at least three times a week to see if there's any news of you and Celia.'

'He really wants to find us?'

'I think he's desperate to.'

Desperate! That surprised her. 'I'll have to go and see him.'

'You haven't time. He'll turn up here tomorrow, expecting Ma to be here.'

'I should never have left,' groaned Katherine, feeling guilt-ridden. 'It's my fault!'

'I felt it was mine but Pops has been telling her for years she should take it easy. Anyway, it's not going to get us anywhere, blaming ourselves. We've got to keep the Arcadia a going concern. So you'll stay?'

'Of course. Although I'll have to dash back to the pet shop and get some clothes and let Celia know what I'm doing. I don't want her worrying about me, although she's been very sneaky about this Andy Pritchard you've mentioned.'

'That's great!' Jack looked in the bread crock but it was empty. 'Right! Who's going shopping, you or me?'

'You get the fires lit, like you said,' said Katherine. 'Eileen and I'll do the shopping, then sort out bedrooms when the part-timers arrive.'

For several hours it was all go and it was not until early evening when the fog had cleared that she left the hotel.

The shop was closed by the time she got there but she found Celia upstairs on the landing cooking bacon and eggs in the cramped space. Katherine felt she had been away ages.

'Well! Did everything go off OK?' said Celia eagerly. 'They've accepted you?'

'Ma and Mick weren't there.'

Celia's face fell. 'What do you mean?'

'Ma's had a heart attack and is in a hospital in Ireland. Jack was there and we had a –'

'A heart attack! Oh, lor'!' cried Celia, dropping the fish slice and putting a hand to her mouth. 'What are you going to do? Did they blame me for it?'

'Of course not. Although only Jack was there. He seems to think she's going to be OK and he knows something about medicine.'

'I'll say a few prayers for her,' said Celia.

'You do that,' said Katherine dryly. 'But I'm needed at the Arcadia so I'll be going back there.'

'They do want you then?' Celia's tone was eager.

'Aye, they want me.'

Her mother beamed. 'I'm so glad. You'll want your things. I did right packing them for you, I thought it'd save time.'

Katie gave her a shrewd look. 'Anyone would think you were trying to get rid of me.'

Celia's smile vanished. 'Of course I'm not. I just want what's best for you.'

Humph! thought Katherine. Something is up with that man. I wonder what she's told him about me? 'Mick's been looking for us,' she said loudly. 'Jack says he's desperate to find us. Wouldn't it be romantic if you two got together again? He has a house in Waterloo. I bet he bought it with us in mind.'

Celia's colour came and went. 'I don't believe it!'

'Honest to God! Cross my heart and hope to die if I dare tell a lie! I'll be seeing him soon. Why don't you come along tomorrow, Ma, and we can give him a surprise?'

'Don't call me Ma!' There was a tremor in her voice.

Katherine sighed heavily. 'There was a time when you wanted me to call you that.'

'Never,' said Celia with surprising vehemence. 'Mum or Mam, yes, but never what you call Mrs Mcleod.'

'OK! If that's how you feel,' said Katherine, putting on a cheerful voice, 'I'll take me things. Has Patrick been in, by the way?'

'Yes. But I didn't tell him where you'd gone.'

'Why not? He knows the truth.'

Celia groaned. 'It's a wonder you haven't told the whole neighbourhood.'

'I didn't see the need,' said Katherine, a sparkle in her eyes as she gave her mother a hard look before going up to her bedroom.

She did not feel a bit sentimental about leaving that bedroom but felt weepy when she had a few words with Mrs Evans, promising she would see her again soon. After that it was just a matter of heaving the suitcase Celia had packed for her down the stairs. She left it at the bottom for a moment and ran over to the photographer's but Patrick was not there and was not expected until tomorrow. She left a message, fetched her suitcase and caught a bus into town.

It was strange going into her old bedroom but still like coming home. Katherine switched on the light and wrinkled her nose. If Jack had not told her, she would have known Sarah had been there. The place reeked of her perfume and as well as that she had left a pair of stockings hanging on a chair and a lipstick on the chest of drawers where there was a framed photograph of two children. They were unmistakably Sarah and Ben and she touched his face with a gentle finger and wondered when they would return from their honeymoon and where they had gone and whether they knew about Ma's heart attack.

Tears started in her eyes. Not wanting to think of Kitty in pain, she said a prayer. She took the top off the lipstick. It was that bright red Sarah favoured and almost used up. Katherine pocketed it, intending to put it in the bin. She opened the top drawer to find it empty. She opened all the drawers and only in the bottom one did she find some underwear of Sarah's, the unglamorous kind. She had probably bought new for her trousseau. Patrick was suddenly in Katherine's mind and a smile softened her mouth.

She went over to the wardrobe and discovered several skirts and blouses of her own. She took out a skirt and held it against her. She had lost weight and Ma wouldn't be pleased about that. Katherine gnawed on her bottom lip, thinking of Kitty. Jack had telephoned Ireland before going out to meet his girlfriend and had told her on her arrival that Ma was comfortable. She hoped he was telling her the truth. She began to unpack her suitcase, filling wardrobes and drawers. She checked there were clean sheets on the bed and was grateful to see there were. She felt certain she had Eileen to thank for that but there had been no sign of the girl when she had arrived back. Perhaps she had gone to see her gran after all.

Katherine was feeling more at home every minute. She ran water and poured in bubble bath before lowering herself into the hot steamy water. This was something she had missed while she had been away so she soaked luxuriously whilst reading a Georgette Heyer novel. Going to the local baths or having a wash down was no substitute for your own tub, she had long decided.

Afterwards, when she was pink and wrinkly, she went and filled two hot water bottles, made a cup of cocoa and took it upstairs with her. She could feel the space like a tangible thing around her. She felt King of the Castle – Queen of the May – in charge! This was her domain. She put a hottie in Jack's bed, glad, so glad, they were friends at last. When she went into her own bedroom she knelt on the bed looking out of the window at the YMCA building across the road and knew she had come home. Even so, she knew now things could never be the same again. There was Patrick. How would he fit in here? She needed to see him soon but first there was tomorrow to get through and that first meeting with Mick.

Chapter Seventeen

Katherine stood at the bottom of the steps, leaning against the area railings, having left Eileen in the kitchen with the part-timer and Jack in Reception. She would have to go in soon but as Jack had said this was the time of evening when Mick generally arrived she wanted to see him first on their own. She was muffled up against the cold in a green coat and the long scarf in drop stitch which Mrs Evans had knitted her for Christmas. She remembered that evening when she had sat on the step waiting for Mick to come home from sea for good. She had not been so nervous then as she was now.

Suddenly there were footsteps coming up the Mount and she lifted her head and saw him with a small dog trotting at his heels. Affection swelled inside her and she remembered Celia telling her about the dog she had given Mick when he was just fifteen and how the gift had changed things between them and they had become sweethearts. Katherine waited no longer but ran to meet him, only to stop a foot or so away as he looked at her as if seeing an apparition.

'It's me, Katherine,' she said, her smile uncertain. 'I've come back.'

He raised an eyebrow. 'I'm not blind! I know it's you. The last eight or nine months might have aged me but I haven't forgotten what you look like.'

Her spirits plunged. 'You're not pleased to see me?' The words were just a whisper.

His expression changed. 'Of course I am,' he said roughly. 'But I'm bloody angry with you as well!' His eyes glinted. 'What could Celia possibly mean to you compared to Ma? Going off without leaving an address where we could get in touch with you . . . What if something had happened to her?'

She felt as if he had slapped her in the face. 'I wasn't thinking straight! I'd had a shock. As it is –'

'Don't you think I don't know how you felt?' he interrupted. 'Suddenly my half-sister's my daughter! It wasn't funny! Especially with you missing and Ma looking like she might have a heart attack.'

'Don't say that!' she said in a choking voice. 'She *has* had a heart attack!'

'What!' His face whitened in the lamplight and he sprang forward. The dog yelped. 'My God! Where is she? Is that why you're here?' He groaned. 'But that's stupid! How would you have known?'

'Exactly! She's in a hospital in Ireland but she's getting better now but has to have rest and not get too excited,' babbled Katherine. 'I'm here because Celia told me two days ago she'd lied and I *am* your daughter after all, and Jack said he wanted me to stay and help at the Arcadia because there was no one else. So here I am and I thought you'd be pleased and –'

'OK, OK! Slow down.' His eyes were dark and unfathomable as he looked into her face. 'So you are my daughter?'

'Yes. I wouldn't blame you, though, if you didn't believe me.'

'Why did Celia lie?'

'To hurt Ma! To hurt you! I think she went a bit crazy when she discovered you weren't dead, but she's OK now. You two should meet, Mick. You really should.'

His expression was suddenly wary. 'She's not in the Arcadia now, is she?'

'No, she has a job . . .' Katherine clapped a hand to her cheek. 'Hell! She has double the work to do now I've come here . . . Damn!'

'What d'you mean?'

'We live over a pet shop. I've been working there. She'll have to do my job now as well as her own. Damn, damn!' she said through gritted teeth. 'I've made a mess of things again.'

'Stop crucifying yourself.' He seized her arm and hustled her towards the Arcadia. 'At least you haven't wasted any time coming here and it seems you came at the right time. Pity Celia didn't tell you sooner, though. Ma's putting the Arcadia up for sale.'

Katherine felt she had received another smack in the face and could only stare at him.

'Sorry to fling it at you like that.' He put his arm round her.

'It's OK.' Her voice quivered. 'Why should I expect her still to want me to have it? And yet –'

They stood at the bottom of the steps. 'She hasn't done anything final,' he said in a low voice. 'I think she's been hoping you'd come home. She said she didn't want you to turn up and find us all gone.' His hand tightened on her shoulder and he looked worried again. 'You are sure she's going to be all right?'

'Jack said so and he should know.' She blinked back tears. 'I really have failed Ma. Me taking over the Arcadia was her dream. It's what she trained me for.'

Mick sighed and said, 'I think she started to believe that her dream could be a nightmare for some. I don't know what you'd have to do to change her mind, kid, but maybe you should be thinking of doing something else with your life.'

'Don't you care at all about the Arcadia?' she said fiercely. 'After all, it was your home. Wouldn't you like it to stay in the family?'

'It doesn't bother me. I've seen Ma slog her guts out to keep this place going. Why should I want a life like that for you?'

'Things are different now,' she said, putting a hand on his chest and looking up into his face. 'There's hoovers and washing machines, fridges and central heating. This place is all I've ever wanted. It won't be as hard for me.'

'I thought you might come and live with me?' There was a mixture of exasperation and tenderness in his expression. 'But if Ma's going to have to rest, she'll want you to live with her and Pops. It's not going to be an easy situation for you to cope with when they come back.'

'I know.' She thought of Patrick and a tear trickled down her cheek. Life had become extremely complicated. She could not go upsetting Ma now by mentioning she wanted to get engaged to the young man Kitty had taken against.

Mick hugged her against him and they were silent a moment, each thinking their own thoughts. Then Katherine said abruptly, 'I've become quite fond of Celia. She's a funny mixture. She can stand up for herself but there's times when she's as daft as a brush.'

'But this isn't just a flying visit, is it?' he said against her hair. 'You aren't going back to live with her?'

'I'll want to keep in touch.'

'Despite what she did by leaving you when you were a baby?'

Katherine lifted her head and stared at him. 'She's still my mother. It wasn't easy for her.'

'I wouldn't argue with that, but still – to leave you?'

'We all make mistakes.'

He said wryly, 'There's more of Ma in you than I realised. That's what she would say. I'm glad I've given her a granddaughter.'

'You and Celia both,' she said firmly.

'OK! Keep your hair on. Me and her both. But I still think she's a lot to answer for, and when we meet I'll tell her so.'

'You do that if you must but now I'm going to have to do some work. You can talk to Jack. He'll tell you more about Ma than I can. His girlfriend's expected soon, by the way.'

'She's OK, is Vicky,' said Mick conversationally, and lifting Nelson up in his arms, followed her inside.

It was hours later, after he had spoken to his stepfather on the telephone, been reassured about his mother and departed for his own home, that Katherine had a chance to speak to Vicky about Celia. 'Jack tells me the man my mother's seeing has a shop next to your sweet shop?' she said, passing her a cup of cocoa.

'That's right! So if you want her off your hands, you could be in luck. She's there quite a lot.' Vicky smiled.

'It depends on what he's like,' said Katherine thoughtfully. 'I wouldn't like to come between them if he's a nice man, but the fact that she hasn't mentioned him makes me suspicious.'

'In that case – I think he's a big blow,' said Vicky bluntly. 'Mum says he's always had a high opinion of himself but now he's worse. He's going on about what a marvellous place the shop's going to be now he's in charge. I don't know where he's getting the money from but he's planning all kinds of changes and getting the flat done up. I wouldn't have thought old Ethel would have left that much. She was generous to a fault and often gave to good causes.' Her eyes twinkled suddenly. 'Listen, Katie, if you want to have a butcher's at him, come to tea with Jack on Sunday. My mum'll be pleased to meet you.'

'Thanks! I'd like that,' she said eagerly.

First she had to see Patrick. She only hoped that when he did come to call Eileen would not start any of her old tricks again because she had noticed the girl giving her strange looks a couple of times when she mentioned his name. But before Katie could call on Patrick or take a decko at Celia's fancy man, something happened to rid her of that worry.

Eileen's room was still in darkness when Katherine went to wake the girl the following morning but she could hear her thrashing about. Katherine's hand froze on the switch but when all went silent she pressed it down and light flooded the room to reveal Eileen lying on the floor.

Katherine hurried over and knelt beside her with a pounding heart. The Irish girl looked so still that she fumbled for her pulse. A sigh of relief escaped her but the next moment Eileen started to twitch and her eyes flew wide open and her limbs began to flail about again. Katherine fled the room and ran for Jack, who was keeping his eye on the porridge.

'Eileen!' she gasped, clutching his arm.

'She's had a fit?' he said, eyes brightening with a medical man's interest.

'More than one,' she whispered. 'Jack, you're going to have to go up to her! It really scared me. I thought she was dead for a moment but – but people really can't die of a fit, can they?'

'Of course they can. Here!' He flung a wooden spoon at her. 'I'd better go up.'

'The guests are stirring. Try not to alarm them.'

'I'm not daft,' he said, and hurried out.

Katherine got on with the breakfasts but her mind was elsewhere and she splashed her wrist with hot fat, which hurt like hell. She had no time to do anything about it and determined to ignore the pain. Rushed off her feet, due not only to Eileen's non-appearance but to Brenda the part-timer's late arrival, an hour passed and still Jack had not come down.

What was happening? wondered Katherine, fearing the worst. If Eileen was dead, what would she do?

She was starting to feel quite dreadful, picturing the scene as the girl was carried off. Running through her mind were memories of all the times she had not really got on with the girl or been sympathetic to her. She remembered Eileen saying she wouldn't be a loss to anyone. Poor, poor Eileen, she thought. So young, but perhaps it was a blessing . . . She had even got as far as mentally writing out a notice for a new kitchen-cum-chamber maid when Jack and Eileen entered the kitchen.

Katherine dropped a plate and stared at them.

'You look like you've seen a ghost,' said Eileen.

'You're OK?' she demanded.

'Still a bit wonky but Jack's made me feel a lot better.' Eileen smiled at him and hugged his arm. 'He says I'm very brave to cope with all I have to put up with.'

'You are!' agreed Katherine, going over to the girl and hugging her. 'I don't think I'd have your determination to carry on working here.'

'It's been hard,' sighed Eileen. 'And now he tells me Aunt Kitty might sell the place, I've made up my mind to go home.'

'To Ireland, you mean?'

She nodded. 'I'll book my ticket later today. Now what d'you want me to do?'

Katherine told her, feeling a rush of relief mingled with

a sudden new liking for the girl. As for Jack, he told her later he had decided to do research into epilepsy and brain disorders.

It was the following Monday before Katherine had a chance to visit the pet shop but she found only Mrs Evans and Donny there. 'What are you doing off school?' she asked, smiling down at him.

'Got a whitlow and can't write.' The boy held up a bandaged finger.

'Painful things them,' said Mrs Evans, casting an eye over Katherine. 'And when are you going to be back, miss? Or have you left us for good as Celia sez?'

'Has she told you everything then?'

'Aye.' Mrs Evans pressed her lips tightly together and made a noise in her throat. 'But I won't talk about it in front of the boy.'

Katherine nodded. 'Where is she?'

'I don't bloody know!' said Mrs Evans crossly. 'She's always coming and going at the moment.'

Donny and Katherine gasped. 'You never swear!' they chorused.

'I'm upset,' she muttered. 'Celia's supposed to be looking after Donny and the shop! She said she'd be back half an hour ago but she's still not here. Your mother's up to something but she's not saying what. You couldn't stay till she comes back, could you?'

Katherine glanced at her watch. 'I was hoping to go over and see if Patrick's at the photographers but I'll give you twenty minutes.'

'Better than nothing, I suppose, your ladyship,' grumbled

the old woman. 'Running a hotel, indeed! At your age! I've never heard the like.'

'I'm only filling in,' said Katherine, her voice severe. 'Ma – my grandmother's had a heart attack so she needs me there. Now would you like a cup of tea?'

'If you're making one, I won't say no.'

Katherine had no sooner put the kettle on than old Mrs Taylor came in carrying an empty cage and with tears running down her cheeks. 'He's gone,' she wailed. 'My beautiful boy's gone.'

'Shall we get a fishing net and go looking for him?' suggested Donny eagerly.

'No, you don't understand! He's dead!' She placed the cage on the counter and the magnolia in her black straw hat dropped as more tears flowed. 'I came downstairs and there he was with his little legs, all stiff, sticking up in the air!' She dabbed at her eyes.

'We'll get you another,' Katherine said, patting her hand.

'It won't be the same.'

'Of course it won't! Your beautiful boy was special because you made him like that. You could do the same to another.'

Mrs Taylor glanced at her from tear-drenched eyes. 'He must be a talker,' she said with a sniff.

'You'll teach him, just like you did your beautiful boy.'

'We've got some young ones coming in next week,' said Mrs Evans. 'You come in then and I'll see to you special.'

'OK!' The old woman gave a watery smile and, leaving the cage, she went out, dabbing her eyes.

'It's sad,' said Donny, nodding solemnly.

And Katherine had to agree. She felt almost as upset at leaving the pet shop now as when she had waved Eileen off at the Pierhead because most of the customers who had come into the shop she was friendly with. She knew she was going to miss them and the pets almost as much as she would miss seeing Donny, Mrs Evans and her mother every day but she could not see that there was any way she could combine her two lives. One had to go.

Celia had not returned by the time Katherine left the shop, promising she would see them soon. She was also out of luck when she arrived at the photographer's, hoping Patrick might be there. 'He hasn't been here for the last few days, luv,' said the assistant. 'But I'll tell him you called and want to see him.'

Katherine went back to the Arcadia feeling slightly down in the dumps to be greeted by the news that there had been a telephone call from Ben and Sarah. 'Where are they?' With so much happening she had not thought to ask where they had gone for their honeymoon or where they would be living when they returned to Liverpool.

'They went to Paris for a week and now they're at the house in Scotland, seeing what needs doing up there. They were pleased to hear you were back but shocked by the news about Ma. They're going over to Ireland to see her before coming home,' said Jack, glancing up from the table he was laying with cutlery. 'You do know, by the way, that Scotland's where Ma and Pops are planning on retiring to? Her plan was to do bed and breakfast during the season. Whether she'll do it now or not . . .' He shrugged.

Katherine wondered about that, too, as she made a couple of apple pies. What if Ma expected her to go up to Oban with them? She would be parted from Patrick! She gnawed on her lip. Here was something else she was going to have to face. Unless she could change Ma's mind about selling the Arcadia? But that was something that would have to wait. In the meantime Vicky had reissued her invitation to tea, and so on Sunday afternoon, after lunch was served and leaving a cold supper, which would be seen to by one of Kitty's cousins who had volunteered her help any time Katherine needed it, she caught the bus with Jack to Old Swan.

Dolly welcomed her with an air of excitement. 'I hope you don't mind, luv,' she said, her bright eyes sparkling, 'but our Vicky's told me all about your mam and I've been keeping my eyes and ears open because there's been talk that she's been seen coming out of the priest's house.'

'The priest?' Katherine's mind worked swiftly. 'And?' she demanded.

'I went to Mass this morning and there they were! And . . .' she paused, and her audience of three gazed at her expectantly '. . . the banns were read, and for the third time of asking, would you believe? And not a word to us about a wedding!' She shook her head. 'It must be going to be a real hole-in-the-corner affair, if you ask me!'

It would be, thought Katherine wrathfully. How dare Celia not tell her about it? What had she got to hide?

'Did you find out when it is to be?' she asked.

'Wednesday! Half-day closing. I wouldn't have thought Andy Pritchard would have had so much business sense, but there you are.' She gazed intently at Katherine. 'So what are you going to do, luv?'

She gnawed on her lip again. 'I'll have to think. It's no use me appealing to her to have second thoughts if she's gone this far.'

'Do you really care that much who she marries?' asked Jack.

Katherine almost opened her mouth but realised she could not say before an audience that she had had hopes of her father and mother marrying. So it was Vicky who answered for her. 'Of course she cares! Why else d'you think she's here? Anyway he drinks and I saw him giving her a shove the other day. Who knows what he might do to her in private?'

'She wouldn't be marrying him if he knocked her around,' said Jack. 'Anyway it's a bit late for Katie to do anything.' He turned to her. 'You're just going to have to accept it, kid.'

Like hell I will, she thought. Although she had not yet set eyes on Andy Pritchard, she decided her mother was probably besotted with the man. But what had Vicky said the other evening about him? *He was making plans and she wondered where the money was coming from* . . . Suddenly Katherine realised where it was coming from. Her gambler mother must have had another win on the Pools. A large one this time and he was marrying her for her money.

That put the kibosh on the wedding so far as she was concerned. She could not allow her mother to marry a loud-mouthed ex-soldier who drank and might knock her around. She had to think up a plan!

Katherine was pretty quiet for the next half hour or so but by the time she caught the bus home she had it all worked out. Her idea was pretty drastic and she had certain qualms about it but told herself faint heart never got a girl anywhere and she was doing it for her mother's good.

Chapter Eighteen

Katherine stood in the graveyard of St Oswald's Church, having concealed herself behind an ancient lichen-encrusted stone cross to watch Celia go inside. She looked rather nice in a peach suit and large-brimmed cream hat, thought Katherine, and gave her a few minutes before creeping in after her. There was only a small congregation up at the far end but even so when she saw them and the ornately robed priest she almost got cold feet. Then she reminded herself what was at stake and tiptoed down the central aisle, slipping into a pew halfway down.

Scarcely breathing, she listened carefully to the words, some of which were in Latin. She crossed her fingers and prayed that she would not miss them and almost jumped out of her skin when the priest began to intone, "'If anyone here knows any just cause or impediment why these persons here should not be joined in holy matrimony then ye are to declare it . . .'"

There was a deathly silence and it took Katherine all her courage to speak out. 'Me! I object!' Her voice came out as a squeak. Gaining courage, she waved a hand and said much louder, 'It was me! I object!'

There was a gasp and a ripple ran through the tiny

congregation. She saw bride and groom turn their heads, straining to see who had spoken. The priest held up his hand. The noise subsided. 'This is a serious matter, young lady. Come here. Why do you object?'

Katherine moved out into the aisle and said loudly, 'I don't want this man to marry my mother. My father's still alive!'

A noise like a swarm of angry bees buzzed through the congregation despite the priest's attempt to hush the people. Katherine could see Andy staring at her even as Celia threw down her bouquet and, taking to her heels, fled up a side aisle. Immediately Katherine turned and ran after her but Celia had a good start and was out of the churchyard and halfway across the road by the time Katherine reached the gate.

'Mother, wait!' she cried. But Celia ignored her and headed in the direction of Prescot Road.

Katherine raced after her but the breath was burning in her throat by the time she reached the toy shop, the door of which stood open. Celia must have already gone inside. There was no sign of her mother so she waited, having decided not to venture up the stairs she could see through the door at the other side of the shop. By the time she had her breath back, Celia was descending the stairs, carrying a suitcase. She was stony-faced and there were signs of tears on her cheeks where her mascara had run.

'I'm sorry, Mum, but I had to do it,' said Katherine after the barest of hesitations.

'Don't speak to me,' said Celia in an icy voice. 'You shamed me! How could you do that to me? Dear God,

I'll never be able to look those people in the face again – nor him. And I wanted this shop!'

'He's no good for you. I've heard he drinks. And I think he's after your money.'

'Do you think I don't know that?' cried Celia. 'I'm not bloody daft! I've fancied him for years though he turned out not to be quite what I thought. But still, I'd have got this shop if I'd married him!' She clenched her fist and hit the nearest wall. 'Ouch! Now see what you've made me do!' Her face screwed up with pain as she dropped the suitcase and nursed her hand.

'Sorry,' said Katherine meekly, struggling against giving way to hysterical laughter.

'Stop saying sorry!' yelled her mother. 'What good is that?' She sucked her knuckles, closed her eyes and opened them again. 'Well, I've been paid back good and proper. I sinned and this is what happens. I should have drowned myself in the Mersey when I found out about you and then I wouldn't have suffered the way I have.'

'Thanks very much! I'd have been dead too,' said Katherine indignantly.

'Exactly. You've been nothing but trouble! Better we'd both drowned.'

'I'll go then!'

'You do! I don't ever again want to see you!'

'That suits me,' said Katherine. 'I only did what I did to save you from yourself! And I thought you might have liked a share in the Arcadia!' She marched out of the shop, glanced up at Dolly's window and saw the net curtain move but did not delay in case Andy Pritchard turned up at any moment. She walked along Prescot Road until she reached the Cattle Market pub and was just wondering what the awful smell was when Celia caught up with her.

'What was that about the Arcadia?' she panted, struggling with her suitcase.

Katherine stopped and stared at her. 'I thought you never wanted to see me again?' she said in a hoity-toity voice.

'Oh, shut up! Tell me about the Arcadia.'

'I have it on good authority that my grandmother is putting it up for sale,' she said, very politely. 'I thought you might have liked to put some money into it?'

Celia stared at her and laughed. She plonked her suitcase down on the pub step and sat on it and laughed and laughed.

'What's so funny?' said Katherine, herself unable to resist a smile.

Celia did not answer but a man came out of the pub and told her to shift herself. She did not move, still laughing. So he grabbed hold of her by the back of her jacket and even as Katherine protested, pushed her mother in her direction. 'Gerra out of here. She'll be giving us a bad name.'

Katherine steadied Celia and, picking up her suitcase, pulled her away from the pub. Celia continued to laugh until Katherine thought she would choke. She shook her. 'Stop it!' she ordered. 'Stop it!'

'You want my money?' cried Celia. 'You'll be lucky! I only won a few hundred pounds, not the bloody seventy-five thousand jackpot! But he thought the same as you and I *let* him think it!'

'You're joking?'

'Sorry, luv.' Celia took a handkerchief from her pocket and wiped her eyes. 'What a lousy day this is turning out to be for both of us. Can't Mick give you the money?'

'I told you, he's bought a house.' She hesitated before saying persuasively, 'Why don't you come back with me to the Arcadia now? He might just drop in.'

'No, thanks! I still feel bloody cross with you. I left a note with Mrs Evans saying I was getting married and wouldn't be back. Hopefully she hasn't read it yet.'

Katherine shook her head. 'You are mean, Mum. You should have told her. The poor ol' thing . . .'

'I couldn't risk you finding out,' said Celia fiercely. 'How did you, by the way?'

'Jack's girlfriend lives next door to the toy shop. Her mother told me the banns had been read. I didn't even know you were a Catholic!'

'I'm not. I lied about that too. Said the church where I was baptised was bombed in the war.' She sighed. 'Trust Dolly to tell you. I was rude to her. It's true what they say: do a bad turn and you'll get it back.' Her brow creased. 'How did Jack meet her daughter?'

'Mick sent him to watch Mr Pritchard's place.'

Celia frowned. 'But how did he know to do that?'

'Rita! Mr Pritchard told her he'd met you at the dance in Southport.'

'You don't have to say any more.' Celia sighed again.

'Mick wanted us found,' explained Katherine. 'He wants to meet you. Why don't you come with me and do that now?'

'No, thanks,' she said again, stretching out a hand for her suitcase. 'I'm all wound up inside . . . and I'm hungry. I'd prepared a buffet in the flat. I should have taken something from it to eat. I was daft to leave all that food there.'

'You're not going back, are you?' said Katherine in alarm. 'I mean, you wouldn't do it because you still fancy him?'

Celia frowned. 'I do a bit. But you're right, he did drink and he got a bit rough at times and he'd have found out sooner or later I didn't have seventy-five thousand pounds. Anyway he's not going to want me now he knows you exist so I might as well go home. Bang goes me honeymoon in Blackpool.'

'Sorry, Mum.' There was a sympathetic expression on Katherine's face. She opened her handbag and took out a ten-shilling note. 'Buy yourself some fish and chips and a nice cake from Sayers. I'll see you soon.'

'It's the least you owe me,' said Celia, snatching the money from her hand. Without even a goodbye, she crossed the road and was soon out of sight.

Katherine turned away and hurried in the direction of Dolly's shop. It was half-day closing so she rang the bell and a few minutes later the door opened and Dolly stood in the doorway. 'What's going on?' she said, giving a little giggle. 'My, my, girl, you are a one! What have you done? I saw you and your mother, and you'd just left when *he* came in. He's in there now, rampaging around. Most likely he'll get drunk.'

'Most likely.' Katherine sighed. Now it was all over she was suffering from a sense of anticlimax.

'Like to come in and have a cup of tea and tell me all about it?'

'I would but I'd better not. I've a three-course meal to prepare.'

'Well, just step inside and tell me what happened then.'

Katherine decided she could spare a minute and soon had Dolly shaking her head and saying she marvelled at her courage and couldn't wait to tell Vicky all about it. Katherine guessed that it would soon be all over the neighbourhood.

With no sense of misgiving she stepped out on to the pavement, only to bump into the erstwhile bridegroom himself as he came out of his shop, still with a carnation in his buttonhole. Seeing him close up as he blocked her path, she wondered afresh what on earth her mother had seen in him. He glared at her from bloodshot eyes and although she was pretty certain he did not have the faintest idea who she was, she thought she had better vamoose. He did not look like he was going to move so she stepped round him and hurried towards the bus stop. She glanced back once and saw he was staring after her but did not let that bother her. Instead she began to devise a way of bringing her parents together.

Chapter Nineteen

'Who's been sleeping in my bed?'

'Mmmph?' Katherine came up from sleep that appeared to be fathoms deep and struggled to open her eyes, recognising the voice and experiencing a once familiar irritation. 'Oh, go away, Sarah! It's too early for a telling off!'

'You've got a cheek, coming back and taking over,' said Ben's wife.

'*I've* got a cheek!' croaked Katherine, managing to force her eyelids open. 'What about you, moving into my bedroom as soon as my back was turned? What time is it?' She yawned. 'Should I be up?'

'Yes! Ben's downstairs. He's talking to Jack but should be here any minute. Then you've got the job of explaining why you walked out without a word to him – and it had better be good!'

Katherine was about to say: 'It's none of your business!' but of course Sarah would think it *was* her business now she was Ben's wife. Besides, Katherine remembered they had come straight from seeing Kitty and would have news. She sat up. 'How's Ma?'

Sarah's face softened. 'Getting better, thank God, but she won't be home just yet.' She moved off the bed. 'I believe you've been short-handed here with Eileen going off home?'

'Yeah! It's been hard work,' said Katherine, sliding from beneath the covers and dragging on a dressing gown. She yawned.

'It was a good job Jack was here,' said Sarah.

'I couldn't have done without him.'

'So you two have made up your differences?'

Katherine nodded and was about to go to the bathroom when the door opened from the other side and Ben popped his head in. 'You decent?'

She flung her arms round him and hugged him tightly.

'It would have been little use if she wasn't,' said Sarah, with only the slightest edge to her voice. 'You're going to have to get into the habit of knocking, husband of mine.'

'Yes, luv,' said Ben, grinning happily at her over Katherine's shoulder. 'But I'm not going to be living here, am I? So isn't it time you two kissed and made up?'

Katherine pulled away from him. Looking at Sarah with a gleam in her eyes, she said, 'We could shake hands?' and suited the action to the words.

'Right!' said Sarah afterwards, rubbing her hands together. 'Now that's done, I'll leave you two to talk and go and help Jack start the breakfasts.'

'I'll be down in a minute,' said Katherine swiftly.

'Don't rush yourself. I can cook, you know!'

'Two eggs for me, luv,' said Ben.

Sarah blew him a kiss before closing the door.

'You've tamed her,' marvelled Katherine.

'Don't you believe it! If you knew how she beats me

when we're alone . . . She's a terrible woman. Now tell me, what's this I've been hearing from Jack about someone called Patrick?' he teased.

'He told you about Patrick!'

'Only because he thought I should pave the way for the two of you with Ma.'

'That's not going to be easy,' she said gloomily. 'He's been here and Ma didn't exactly approve of him – and you've met him as well.'

'Have I?' Ben looked surprised. 'Can't remember.'

Well, if he didn't remember she was not going to remind him of the circumstances.

'With a name like Patrick he must be a Catholic,' said Ben, 'and it's taken Ma and Pops all their energy to keep their mouths shut with Vicky being one as well. But Jack is over twenty-one so there's nothing they can do there.'

Katherine's brow furrowed. 'Patrick and I've never spoken about religion.'

'Perhaps you should. Pops is Presbyterian and Ma's always been C. of E. And you know what it's like in Liverpool on the Twelfth of July with the Orange and Green. His family might have strong feelings about you.' He put an arm round her and pulled her against him. 'Still, you're not eighteen yet. You're only young so I wouldn't worry too much and maybe keep quiet about Patrick for now. At least until Ma's feeling a lot better.'

'OK.'

'That's my girl! It's great to have you back. We'll have a proper gab later. Now I'd best get a call put through to our Teddy before he leaves for work and tell him the latest news on Ma.'

Katherine stared after Ben, glad that things did not appear to have changed much between them, but she had not liked the insinuation that she was still only a kid. In her eyes almost eighteen was grown up and she was not going to revert to being treated like a child. She had to see Patrick as soon as possible.

Katherine was to see him sooner than she'd planned because he called the next day. Unfortunately she was doing reception work and was up to her eyes dealing with an influx of guests and could only excuse herself for a moment. 'Hello, you,' she said softly, wishing Kitty was there to see him now. He was wearing a suit and looked quite different. Even his Tony Curtis quiff had been subdued with what smelt like Brylcreem. 'Where are you going, dressed up to the nines?'

'Look who's talking,' said Patrick laconically, resting his elbows on the reception desk. 'Off to visit the Queen, are yer?'

She was wearing a navy blue suit and her hair was twisted in a neat knot. 'It's window dressing. Goes with the job when I'm standing behind here. What can I do for you? Sorry, I can only spare a minute.'

'Nothing.' He straightened up. 'Just came to tell you the *Daily Post* have accepted our idea for a series of pictures and articles on street names. Remember the *Echo* turned my Nelson idea down?'

'Great!' Her face lit up. 'See! You'll be a success before you know it.'

'They're giving me the odd assignment too.'

'I'm real made up for you!'

'I'm off on one now. Some do or other at the Town Hall. It would have been great if you could have come with me.'

'I'm sorry,' she said regretfully. 'But there's no one to take over from me.'

'Pity!' He pulled a face. 'Anyway, how's your grandma? Mrs Evans told me about her heart attack.'

'She's coming on, but if she sells the Arcadia and goes to live in Scotland I might have to go with her.'

'What! *You* go and live in Scotland? That's a bit much to . . .'

'Excuse me, dear,' interrupted a woman's voice, 'but how long are we going to be kept waiting?'

Katherine rolled her eyes and said clearly, 'Sorry, madam. I'll be with you right away.' In a whisper she added to Patrick: 'Hang on, I'll be back in a minute.' But when she returned from seeing the guests to their rooms he had gone.

She expected to hear from him the next day and the next but a week went by and there was still no sign of him. She could not think what had happened to him and thought of nipping to the pet shop to see if he had called at the photographer's, but there was a telephone call from Ireland saying John and Kitty were coming home and she decided she really had to make sure everything was just right for them.

Katherine was shocked when first she set eyes on Kitty. She looked frail and as if she had shrunk somehow.

Katherine felt wracked with guilt. Was this all her fault? She did not know what to say to her and the words that did eventually come to mind seemed to stick in her throat.

'So you're back, and about time too!' said Kitty in brisker tones than they would have expected. 'There's no need to be looking like I'm going to bite your head off! I'm just glad I'm here to see you. Now, go and put the kettle on and let's forget you ever went.'

'Ri-right, Ma!' Katherine glanced at John for his reaction and saw he was smiling. She hurried out, considering herself fortunate. She passed Jack on the way and, glancing back, saw him hug his mother. At least everything was OK there, she thought, but was not sure how she would cope if Kitty started on about Celia because she did feel a certain loyalty towards her mother and did not want her to become a bone of contention between them.

She had already set a table in the basement with cakes and scones but first served some warming lentil soup with crusty bread. Conversation was on a mundane level until Jack began talking to his father about his plans to do medical research. It was then Kitty turned to Katherine and filled her with dread by asking, 'How's Celia?'

'Fine! We – we seemed to rub along OK.' She managed to get the words out with a bright smile.

Kitty returned the smile. 'Glad to hear it. She'll have to come to tea so we can have a chat. I owe her an apology.'

Katherine could not believe her ears but she took Kitty up on her words immediately. 'Next Sunday would be a nice day for her to come. It's Mothering Sunday and the pet shop'll be closed.' She was thinking Mick would be coming too so it would be a perfect opportunity for them to start getting to know each other again.

'Jack said something over the phone about a pet shop. Did you like it there?'

'Loved the shop.' Katherine's face broke into a smile. 'Some of the people were really funny.' She told Ma about Pretty Boy the budgie and his owner, and it was not until she came to the end of her tale that she became aware Pops and Jack were listening too.

'It sounds fun,' said John.

'It was but – it wasn't home.'

John and Kitty glanced at each other but said nothing and it was not until father and son left the room to check something in a medical book that Kitty murmured, 'Did the boys tell you I'm selling the Arcadia?'

Katherine felt as if everything had suddenly gone still and the muscles in her face had frozen. She could not have spoken to save her life.

'You see, love,' said Kitty earnestly, leaning towards her, 'I need the money. Ben wants to go into business and be his own boss, and now he and Sarah are married there could be babies and I'd like to help him. He's been a good son to me all these years and never asked anything for himself.' She paused but still Katherine did not speak and Kitty sighed. 'Then there's our old age, love. Pops and I need some money to fall back on if we get ill or the roof falls in on the house in Scotland. Try and understand how it is?'

Katherine took a firm grip on her bottom lip which was trembling due to her intense disappointment and said,

'Of course I understand. I think Ben deserves all the help he can get, and you've worked so hard all your life you need a rest. I felt terrible when I heard you'd had the heart attack.' She was visibly trembling now.

Kitty placed a work-worn hand over hers. 'It wasn't your fault. It was my own stupidity. I should have practised what I preached.'

'You did,' said Katherine in a low voice. 'You were loving and kind to me always.'

'Well, I did my best. And don't be thinking I'll leave you with nothing. You'll all get something, but you and the other grand-children won't benefit until you're all twenty-one.' She smiled. 'I don't know what your plans are, love, but I wouldn't have you homeless. If you don't want to live with Celia or Mick, who I believe has offered you a home, you could come and live with us up in Scotland? You'd come in real handy up there. Although I know it mightn't be much fun in the winter with just us two old fogeys.'

'You're not an old fogey,' she whispered, touched.

'Not yet, love, but it won't be long.' Kitty patted her grand-daughter's hand. 'I've said enough. You just let me know what your plans are when you've had a chance to think about what I've said, but we'd love you with us.'

Katherine nodded, thinking Ma had not even considered there might be someone else in her life other than the family or that she was old enough now to set up her own household! How was she going to break it to her that she was in love with Patrick? Then she remembered what Ben had said about not upsetting Ma and kept her mouth shut.

Instead she said, 'Did you mean it about Celia coming to tea?'

Kitty was gazing into the flames but turned her head as Katherine spoke. 'Yes, love, I did. Why?'

'Could she come on Mothering Sunday as suggested? You didn't answer. I'd like to be with both the women who've mothered me.'

Kitty was silent a moment. Then she squared her shoulders and said, 'Anything you like, love, so long as you don't expect me to get up and start cooking for her.'

Katherine felt a rush of affection and bent and kissed her cheek, thinking her generosity of spirit made some things just that bit harder. 'Thanks,' she whispered, and hurried out before her emotions got the better of her.

With Pops back and the new girl assisting, Katherine was able to get to the pet shop the next day. As she let herself in, she could hear the wireless and ran upstairs.

'So you're here again, are yer?' said Mrs Evans, smiling. 'Can't keep away from us, hey, girl?'

'You could say that. Seen anything of Patrick?'

'Not a sign of him,' said Celia, glancing up from the ironing board and giving her a sharp look. 'Have you?'

'Not for a week or so. How are you?'

'I'm surviving. You still welcome at the Arcadia?'

'Until it's sold,' she said moodily, sitting at the table and placing her chin in her hands. 'You're invited to tea on Sunday. Grandma says she owes you an apology. You will come, won't you? I want you there. It *is* Mothering Sunday.'

Celia said tartly, 'You don't have to look so glum about it. I'll come, and I won't let you down.'

Katherine was surprised she had agreed so easily. 'About four o'clock? Is that OK?'

'That's fine. I won't be late.'

Katherine took her word for it and after chattering to Mrs Evans for ten minutes or so, made her excuses and went over to the photographer's shop but although there was a light on upstairs and she knocked and knocked and rang the bell, no one came. She frowned, wishing she had thought to ask Patrick his address, despite her being a bit apprehensive of calling at his home because she was unsure what kind of reception she would get from his mother. But what was the point of thinking like that? She didn't know. She just had to hope he would get in touch soon and hope she had not put him off with her talk of going to Scotland to look after Ma.

Any apprehension Katherine might have felt about Celia's visit to the Arcadia vanished when she opened the front door and saw her mother dressed in a muted gold knitted jersey suit, with her hair newly set and her make-up carefully applied. She wore matching black gloves, handbag and patent leather high heels. In her ears were large black circular earrings shot through with gold and about her neck were beads of the same colour.

'You look great!' cried Katherine, clapping her hands and grinning. 'I'm proud of you.'

'I felt I had to make the effort,' said Celia, touching the back of her hair in a self-conscious gesture. 'This was all part of me trousseau.'

'You'll knock hi— them dead,' she said.

'That'll suit me,' said Celia, a slight quiver in her voice. 'I haven't forgotten how I felt last time.'

'You look like a star,' said Katherine.

'I remember Donny saying something like that when I first had me hair done. He touched it to see if it was real.'

'Come in. We're eating in the dining room.'

Celia stepped inside. 'The family always used to have their meals in the kitchen or the basement in my day.'

'They still do most of the time. But we're not that busy and there's quite a crowd of us because Teddy and his daughter Wendy turned up this morning.'

Celia looked alarmed. 'I hope there's not going to be a big fuss! I mean, I haven't always behaved the way I should.'

'You're here now so you'll just have to make the best of it. You look great, just remember that.'

Celia swallowed and squared her shoulders. 'You're right. Deep breaths.'

It seemed to Celia as Katherine flung open the door to the dining room that it was full of people. Then a silver-haired woman moved forward, holding onto the arm of a tall dark man in his late-thirties. Mick, thought Celia, and still as handsome as ever! But poor Kitty Mcleod, she thought with a sinking heart, wondering if it was her fault that her hair had turned white since last they met.

'Well! You *have* changed,' said Kitty, surprise evident in her eyes.

'Me daughter's influence,' said Celia, tilting her chin

and slipping a hand through Katherine's arm. 'You made a smashing job of bringing her up. She knows how to encourage a person.'

'Whereas I didn't give you much encouragement last time,' murmured Kitty.

'Best not to go into that now,' whispered Katherine.

'No,' said Mick, raising an eyebrow. 'We don't want an atmosphere at the table.'

'I haven't come for an argument but to make things up,' said Celia, gripping Katherine's arm the tighter. 'But I will just say I think she's grown up a lot in the time she's spent with me, so maybe it was a good thing I got in touch.'

'There were times when I could gladly have strangled the pair of you,' said Mick softly. 'But as you say, let's not argue. You're sitting between Katie and me. It's how she's arranged it.'

'She can be a bit bossy at times,' said Celia, still hanging on to Katherine's arm as she followed him and Kitty over to the laden table.

'You can say that again,' he murmured.

'D'you mind, both of you?' said Katherine, pleased they were behaving quite naturally.

Most of the people were known to Celia, even Jack's and Vicky's faces vaguely familiar. Only Wendy, Teddy's daughter, was a complete unknown.

'Pity Patrick's not here,' said Vicky in a low undertone across the table to Katherine as plates were passed round.

'Who's he?' asked Wendy, her brown eyes bright as she gazed at Katherine.

'Katie's boyfriend,' said Jack.

'Shush!' hissed Katherine. 'I'm keeping quiet about him.'

'What was that?' said Mick, taking some cold cooked meat from a plate.

Celia pursed her lips and said, 'They're talking about Patrick. A lad Katherine's been seeing. He takes photographs. I think it's a funny way to earn a living. Not a proper job at all.'

'It *is* a proper job,' stated Katherine. 'It'll just take time before he's famous enough to make a lot of money.'

'Are you and he serious?' asked Wendy.

Katherine darted a glance at Mick. 'I'd rather not talk about it.'

'Why?' persisted Wendy. 'Does he look like the creature from the Black Lagoon?'

'No! He's quite nice-looking actually.' She tried to frown the other girl down but like her father she was nothing if not persistent.

'Then why isn't he here?'

'Leave her alone, Wendy,' put in Ben. 'She has her reasons.'

'Tell us them then? I'm out of touch with what's going on up here.'

'What are you out of touch with?' asked Kitty, leaning across the table.

Katherine groaned as Wendy said, 'Katie's boyfriend.'

'She doesn't have a boyfriend,' said her grandmother in a severe voice. 'Now eat up that meat or you'll soon be slipping between the bars of a grid because there's nothing of you.' She turned to Sarah and began to talk to her about her mother.

Katherine heard Mick say to Celia, 'I did write, you know.'

'I wish I'd known. It would have made me feel a bit better about everything,' she said.

'In that case, perhaps we should discuss this whole thing on our own so we can both feel better? We could go for a walk later and get everything off our chests. What d'you say?'

'If you think we should, that's OK with me.'

Katherine could have cheered and wished she could go along with them but knew that could defeat the object.

The meal over, Celia was claimed by Kitty who asked if she would like a liqueur.

'I wouldn't mind an egg flip,' Celia said, not showing any apprehension at all at the thought of a tête-à-tête with the woman who at their last meeting had shown her the door. Once fortified by the drink she took a plain brown envelope from her handbag and placed it on the table between them. 'That's yours, with interest,' she said, a quiver in her voice.

Kitty did not touch it but said in embarrassed tones, 'I should never have insulted you by forcing money on you but after that letter you sent I feared the worst.'

'I must have been a raving loony! I could make excuses for meself but what's the point? Take the money. You did me a favour by forcing it on me. I bet on an outsider which pipped the favourite at the post and that was the start of a run of good luck for me. I've even won on the Pools twice.'

Kitty managed to smile. 'I'm glad. And I'm pleased you're looking heaps better than the last time I saw you. Katie thought you looked half starved.'

'I probably was. You can't gamble and eat three square meals a day. Katherine's made sure I get proper food since she's been with me. She's a carer, for all she drives me nuts at times.' She glanced around, noting the improvements since she had worked here before the war. 'It's a pity you're selling the old Arcadia. I reckon given a few years she could have made a real success of running this place.'

Kitty looked tired all of a sudden. 'It's too late! I've explained to her. I didn't think she'd go complaining to you.'

'She hasn't!' exclaimed Celia indignantly. 'She's very fond of you. I just wish I had the money to give her, but I haven't. What she needs is a rich husband to buy another hotel, not that Patrick who's after her.'

'Who is this Patrick?' Kitty's head drew closer to Celia's. 'He sounds Catholic. Not that I've got anything against them but she wasn't brought up that way. I hope she isn't serious about him?'

Celia was silent a moment then murmured, 'I think she'd soon forget him if she didn't see him for a bit. If you said you really needed her, I'm sure she'd go to Scotland with you. Not for good, mind, because I'd like to see her now and again, but a few months would get you on your feet, wouldn't it?'

Kitty took a sip of Drambuie. 'I don't want her unhappy, but she is only young . . .'

'Much too young to know her own mind. We're only thinking of what's best for our girl.'

Kitty nodded, understanding her perfectly.

Mick approached them. 'Have you two finished? Nelson's waiting for his walk.'

Immediately Celia drained her glass and stood up. She held out a hand to Kitty. 'I've enjoyed everything. Tarrah for now.'

They shook hands and Celia went out with Mick.

'We'll go this way,' he said, leading the way up the Mount.

She followed, a slight smile on her face as they crossed the road and walked along Rodney Street.

'Remember that Sunday after Dr Galloway was burgled and you came down the street with your hair flying behind you?' he said abruptly.

'Fancy you remembering my hair being like that,' she marvelled, feeling as if it was in another lifetime.

He grinned. 'I only remember because it was the day after we'd been to see *Dracula* with Bela Lugosi, and I'd been told off for being late.'

'I was fifteen,' murmured Celia. 'Far too young to be thinking of love.'

'I was mad about you but you weren't really that mad about me. You were always pushing me away.'

'I *was* in love with you,' she said indignantly. 'But a girl has to keep her head. Where would we have been if I'd have started a baby then?'

'I would have married you.'

She laughed in his face. 'D'you think they'd have let

us! I'd have been sent off to some home for unmarried mothers and they'd have taken the baby away. I'm glad I kept my head!'

'OK, OK! I would have married you later, though, when we both lost our heads! But you vanished.'

She stared at him. 'It was you that scarpered after it happened. Why didn't you ask me then instead of running away?'

Mick looked uncomfortable. 'I was all mixed up and I still feel bad about that. So how about it?'

Celia looked at him stupidly. 'Pardon?'

He said impatiently, 'How about it? Me and you getting married now – making Katie legal.'

'Are you serious?'

'Of course I'm bloody serious,' he said irascibly. 'I can offer you a house and I've a good job. Katie could live with us and we'd be a proper family. What d'you think?'

'I think you must be mad! You can't throw questions at a woman like that and expect an answer right away. I don't even know you any more.'

'I haven't changed that much.'

'That's what I'm thinking,' she muttered.

He smiled. 'I have changed in some ways, Cessy. I'm really not as selfish. I do care about Katie and want her to feel we both want her.' His smile held all its old charm and, oh, for a moment she really was tempted! What he was suggesting had been her dream all those years she had been on her own but . . .

'Well?' he said.

'I'll think about it.'

He stared at her, eyes narrowed, and there was a pause before he said, 'Right! Do you want to go back now then?'

'What about Nelson?' She looked down at the dog. 'The poor little lad has had hardly any exercise. You should at least take him round the block.'

'You're right!' And with that Mick walked away, leaving her standing outside the house where he had once kissed her so passionately on the front steps.

For a moment Celia was tempted to run after him and say she would marry him, just to see the dismay in his face, but he had done what she supposed he thought was the decent thing by asking her, even if she really did not want to accept.

She set off to walk to Lime Street and catch a bus but had only reached Lycée Street when a hand took her by the shoulder and forced her round. She stared up at Andy Pritchard and her knees went weak, while at the same time her heart did a somersault.

'Who was that bloke you were with?' he snarled. 'Yer bloody husband!'

She yelped as he squeezed her shoulder. 'I – I haven't got a husband.'

'Liar! What was all that in the church when we were supposed to get wed, then? Practising to go on the stage, were yer?' He thrust his ruddy face into hers.

She coughed. 'You're drunk! Let me go!'

'Like hell I will!' He shook her and she cried out.

A couple stopped and stared in their direction.

'Let me go, you brute!'

'Shut up!' yelled Andy, and slapped her across the face.

Celia saw red and hit out with her handbag.

'Hey!' shouted a man's voice. 'Leave that woman alone.'

'Yeah! You leave her alone, yer big bully!' said his companion.

Another couple and a man had stopped. Andy looked at them, and thrusting Celia against a shop window, hissed, 'You haven't heard the last of me.' Then he lumbered off in the direction of Renshaw Street.

'You all right, luv?' asked one of the women, peering into Celia's face.

'I'll live,' she said shakily, touching the cheekbone where the blow had landed.

'Far to go?'

'Everton. I'll be OK on the bus, thanks!'

'If you're sure?' said the woman, looking at her curiously.

She nodded, thanked her again and changed her mind about the bus she would normally take and went home by a different route.

Still shaken by the encounter, it was with dismay that she saw Andy standing outside the Windermere Hotel when she got off the bus. She stopped in her tracks and realised he must have drink on him because he was in a worse state than he had been earlier, swaying as he leant against the wall. She wondered how he had managed to trace her when she had given him a false address, but that was irrelevant at the moment.

She told herself she was stupid to be frightened in broad daylight. Someone would come along just as they had earlier. She just had to stand up to him and show him he couldn't frighten her. She eased back her shoulders, one of which was giving her pain where he had gripped it, and walked in the gutter towards the pet shop, keeping her distance from him.

He came across the pavement at a run and lunged at her. 'I've been waiting for you! You bloody humiliated me in that church!' he yelled, grabbing hold of her.

'You're hurting me, Andy,' she gasped. 'Let go of my arm or I'll call the police.'

'Don't care! You should be punished! You and that bitch of a daughter.' He swung her round by her arm and then released her. She went flying and would have landed on the road if someone had not caught her.

It was Frank Jones and she clung to his overcoat while her head swam.

'You all right, girl?' He steadied her with both hands.

She nodded mutely and he turned to Donny and said, 'You look after Mrs Mcdonald.'

'Right, Granddad!' Donny thrust his hand into Celia's and held it tightly as Frank faced Andy.

'I think, like, yer're bothering this lady,' he said. 'I don't want to cause a disturbance, like, but I think yer should gerrout of here.'

'Eff off!' snarled Andy, looking down at the little man and doubling his fists.

Frank shook his head. 'That's not nice language in front of a lady.' He half-turned and then he spun round fast and caught Andy with a beautiful left hook to the chin and then a right one on the side of his face. Then another on the chin. The ex-sergeant-major crumbled at the knees and slid slowly to the ground.

Frank turned to Celia who stared at him with admiration and surprise on her face. 'I was going to marry him,' she said in wonder.

'Oh, heck! I'm sorry, luv. I didn't –'

'No! I'd already changed my mind, that's why he got rough. I must have been desperate, that's all I can think.'

'You desperate! A luvly woman like you?' said Frank, his voice as gentle as a caress.

Celia saw the glow in his eyes and her heart lifted. 'You say the nicest things, Frank.'

'It's true,' he said simply. 'Now would yer like me to see yer home?'

'Yes, please.' She tucked her free hand under his arm and together she, Frank and Donny stepped over Andy and made for home.

Chapter Twenty

The FOR SALE sign had finally gone up outside the Arcadia and Katherine was feeling down in the dumps. Not only had she not heard from Patrick, she had had no word from Celia about how she had got on with Mick.

Ma had taken to using a walking stick and was constantly saying how she hoped Katherine would come up to Scotland with them; after all, she already had friends up there from holidaying at the house. She mentioned one particular boy called Alastair who was the local doctor's son. As if that was not enough to persuade Katherine up North, she added that Wendy was thinking of spending the holidays with her grandparents to help them out and would be good company. Katherine did not mind the girl but much preferred male company, namely Patrick's. Katherine decided she had to see him as well as Celia before Ma wore her down.

She went to the photographer's first, only to be told, 'You've missed him, dear. Although I haven't seen much of him lately. He was talking of finding a flat where he could have his own dark room. You had a lovers' tiff?'

'Of course not!' she said stiffly, and walked out feeling hurt that Patrick had not mentioned anything about a flat to her. She met with as little success at the pet shop in her search for her mother.

'She's gone to the pictures with Mr Jones and Donny,' said Mrs Evans. 'How are you, girl? You're not looking your normal cheerful self. Things not working out?'

'They're OK.' She forced a smile. 'It's just that I haven't seen much of Patrick. I've been told he's getting himself a flat but I've no idea where.'

Mrs Evans clucked her tongue against her teeth. 'You young people! Careless, that's what I call it. But cheer up! He did call here the other day and was talking to your mother. Perhaps she knows his address?'

Katherine's spirits lifted. 'I'll come tomorrow. No! Ask her to come and see me instead. Mick's coming too.'

But the next day Katherine returned from shopping to be told Celia had rung to say she could not make it that evening, but if Katherine would like to meet her outside Cooper's on Friday, she would treat her to lunch.

It was obvious as soon as she saw Celia that she was in a bit of a stew. Katherine seized her arm and whisked her inside the store. 'I'm being followed,' said her mother, linking arms with her and hurrying her upstairs.

'By who?'

'Andy Pritchard. He's proving a bit of a nuisance. He's out for revenge!'

'You're joking?' Katherine stopped in her tracks but Celia hurried her on.

'Believe me, this is no joke.'

They had reached the restaurant and managed to get a

table by a window. Celia's eyes searched the street below and, leaning across the table, she grabbed Katherine's arm and hissed, 'See down there? The man in the raincoat and trilby with the orange scarf? That's him! If it weren't for Frank, I'd be a nervous wreck by now.'

'Frank?'

Celia resumed her seat and flushed as she toyed with a fork on the table. 'Frank Jones – Donny's grandfather. He's been awful good to me.'

A pucker appeared between Katherine's eyebrows. 'What happened with you and Mick? I thought you were making friends?'

'We have! And he did suggest we get married, for your sake, but . . . it wouldn't work, luv,' she said earnestly. 'We're not what each other needs. He wants someone stronger than me to stand up to him otherwise he can get a bit above himself. I know he can be kind and a real charmer when he wants but he's not for me.'

Katherine swallowed her disappointment. 'Well, if you feel like that, there's nothing I can say.'

'No, there isn't, luv, because I'm going to marry Frank and we're going to tie the knot soon. He'll keep me safe from Andy.'

'But he's only little and he's *old*! Could he defend you?'

'He already has,' said Celia proudly. 'He used to be a flyweight boxing champion when he was young! I know he's a bit older than me but he loves me and he'll do anything for me. It sounds kind of sudden but he has shown an interest before and he's got a nice little house that'll suit me down to the ground – and it's handy for the pet shop. I don't know how Mrs Evans'll manage without us living there but I'll do me best to help her, and Frank says I don't have to give up me work altogether. He wants me just to cut me hours so I can be there for Donny and him when they come in.'

She looked so happy that Katherine could not help being happy for her. 'It sounds perfect,' she said sincerely.

'Doesn't it just?' Her mother's eyes shone.

A waitress came to the table. 'Are you ready to order, madam?'

'Give us a few minutes more, luv,' said Celia, waving her away.

Katherine stared at her, remembering the first time they had had lunch here, and thought how much her mother had changed. And that's down to me! she realised. In so many ways her leaving the Arcadia had been a good thing. She had matured as Celia had said on Mothering Sunday and whatever happened in the future with Patrick, she would be always glad she had done what she had and gone with her mother. So many people had come together because of it: Jack and Vicky, Ben and Sarah, Celia and Frank. Suddenly she realised that although strictly speaking she no longer had four brothers, she would be taking on board a stepbrother in young Donny and could not be happier about that because she was fond of the boy.

'When's the wedding to be?'

'Next month. We don't see any point in hanging around but it's going to be a proper wedding with banns read at St John's and invitations sent out. I haven't many friends but the ones I've got, I'd like to be there.' Celia's grey eyes were suddenly anxious. 'Do you think Pops would give me away? He is my godfather.'

'I'm sure he would.'

Celia smiled. 'And you'll be my bridesmaid?'

'Why not! Although – are you sure you wouldn't like Rita? If it hadn't been for her, you might have ended up with Mr Pritchard.'

'Don't!' Celia gave a tiny shiver and glanced towards the window. 'It's getting that I feel I'm being watched all the time.'

'OK. But what about Rita? She's more your age.'

Celia hesitated then shook her head. 'I'll send her an invite but I want you. If it wasn't for you, I'd never have met Frank. You'll have to come round the shops with me one Saturday and we can pick frocks.'

'OK, if that's what you want.'

'I'll go to the Arcadia with you after we've eaten, but will you tell Mick I've decided not to marry him? I know you might have liked the idea, luv, but I don't think he's going to be that disappointed.'

Katherine nodded, wishing she could find someone for him. At the moment it was looking like that old Spanish gypsy had got it all wrong.

It was when their soup was set in front of them that she asked Celia about Patrick and whether he had told her he had found himself a flat. Her mother gave her a wide-eyed look. 'Me, luv! Why on earth would he do that? Why do you ask? Hasn't he been in touch?'

'Not for over a week. I know that doesn't sound long

to you but it is to me!' She put down her soup spoon, her appetite having deserted her for the moment, and gnawed on a fingernail. 'Who knows when the Arcadia'll be sold and I'll be whipped off to Scotland? I might never see him again!'

Celia avoided her eyes, crumbling a piece of bread into her soup. 'If he's for you, he's for you, luv. Why don't you wait and see what happens? And in the meantime, let's decide what colour bridesmaid dress you want and think of a way of avoiding Andy outside. God only knows what's happening to the toy shop while he's drinking and following me. You know what he did . . .' She proceeded to tell Katherine about his attack on her.

Katherine was angry but also felt slightly guilty for bringing this upon her mother. 'Still,' she said reassuringly, 'he's not going to do anything now with all the crowds around. Let him follow us! If he comes near the Arcadia, Jack or Pops will soon see him off.'

Despite her words Katherine had to admit it felt a bit spooky, knowing someone was following you with ill-intent, and had to resist the temptation to keep looking over her shoulder. Still they arrived at the Arcadia without Andy's making a move to harass them. When they spoke to John about him he went outside but there was no sign of Celia's erstwhile bridegroom and they both hoped that was the last they would see of him.

Mick appeared unmoved by the news that Celia was marrying someone else when Katherine told him. 'I can see you're disappointed, kid,' he said. 'But she's showing sense. We got over each other years ago.'

'Then why did you ask her to marry you?' she demanded. 'Was it because you were thinking of me?'

He raised an eyebrow. 'Aye! But also to give her the chance to turn me down.'

She smiled and linked her arm through his. 'You are funny. Why should she want to do that?'

'It's women who are the funny creatures. Anyway the wedding's off and I'm still alone and so are you. Do you mean to go up to Scotland with Ma or will you live with Celia and her new husband when the Arcadia is sold?'

Katherine's smile faded. 'I'll probably go to Scotland. Ma looks like she's going to be in a wheelchair by the time she gets there, the way she's been limping.'

'I didn't think she was that bad.' His eyes were thoughtful as they rested on her face and he said gently, 'What would you really like to do? You could always come and stay with me for a while, you know.'

'Thanks, but . . .' She glanced around the basement living room, at the well-worn familiar furniture and the picture of her great-grandmother on the wall. 'I really would like to stay here and carry on what *she* started. I know it's impossible but . . .' She shrugged.

'What about this Patrick I've heard about?'

Katherine stared at him in surprise before averting her eyes and gazing into the fire. 'I haven't heard from him and he's probably Catholic and Ma's met him and doesn't approve!' Her voice sounded strained.

'I doubt she would approve of any boy you brought home so I wouldn't let that bother you.'

Katherine pulled a face. 'She's been going on about

this doctor's son up North. I think she wants someone rich and settled for me.'

'Understandable. But it's your life, Katie, and Ma has Pops.'

'But he's old!'

'He's only in his late-sixties and *his* grandfather lived to a ripe old age.'

'But Pops mightn't and then she'll be all alone!'

'I'd say face that when it comes. Anyway, I've come straight from work and poor ol' Nelson will be waiting for his dinner. I'll have to go.'

'I'll see you out.' She thought how strange it still felt, accepting he was her father and not an elder brother.

They stood at the top of the area steps and he said, 'Come and see the house soon. I think you'll like it. It's right by the river.'

She smiled. 'I'll come.'

'Good girl!' He touched her hair with a gentle hand and she watched him walk down the Mount before turning and going back inside with a heart that felt lighter because he had seemed to understand a little of how she felt.

When Mick left the Arcadia to catch the Southport train he did not get off at Waterloo but instead travelled to the end of the line, having made up his mind to find Rita if he could. He was to meet with disappointment because she was no longer working at the Seaview and when he visited the address the woman behind Reception gave him, he was told she had gone on a cruise and they were unsure when she would be back.

'Will you tell her Mick Ryan called?' he said.

'Mick Ryan,' repeated the woman, smiling. 'I'll tell her.'

Mick had to be content with that but was soon imagining Rita meeting a millionaire and coming home married. He felt gloomy at the thought and began to envisage a lonely future for himself. Like his daughter, he began to believe that Spanish fortune teller had got it all wrong.

Rita returned home a week later, sunburnt and refreshed. Although she had enjoyed the Mediterranean cruise there had been times when she had felt lonely despite having attracted the attention of several men. But they were either too old or too polished and none measured up to Mick Ryan. So it came as a welcome surprise when her landlady told her he had called, but once she started thinking about his visit, she found herself worrying. What if he had called to tell her he was going to marry Celia?

She was thinking about that as she opened her post and took a silver-edged card out of an envelope. For a moment she felt sick. Then she read the card and sank into a chair. Why Celia was marrying a Francis William Jones instead of Andrew Pritchard or Michael Ryan she did not know but she felt euphoric about it and immediately made up her mind to visit the address given on the card.

There were puppies in the pet shop window. Nice little dogs all curled up in a heap in a jumble of heads and tails and paws. They were slumbering, all but one who opened an eye and gazed at her for a brief sleepy moment. Rita thought: Celia seems to have gone from one kind of caring to another! She gazed a little longer at the puppies and then opened the door and went inside.

An old woman sat on a chair knitting while Celia leant on the counter reading from a pile of newspapers.

'I'd like a puppy, please,' said Rita in a lilting voice.

'Right.' Celia straightened and instantly her features registered astonishment. 'It's you, Rita. Blinking heck! I never expected to see you here so soon.'

'I got your invitation and felt I had to come. There were questions I wanted to ask you.'

'About the wedding, you mean? Come right in!' Her expression had changed to one of delight and she waved a hand in the direction of the old woman. 'This is Mrs Evans, by the way. She's my employer and friend. Mrs Evans, this is Rita who I used to work with. You'll have a cuppa, won't you, Rita?'

'When have I ever been known to say no to such an offer?' she said in a teasing voice.

'You just wait then,' said Celia, reaching for the coat that hung behind the curtain. 'I'll run up to Sayers for some cakes. We always have one at this time of day.'

'You don't have to bother running for me,' said Rita, glancing over her shoulder as she shook hands with Mrs Evans.

'It's no bother. Mrs Evans'll take care of you while I'm gone. Did you really mean that about a puppy?' Celia babbled. 'They're gorgeous, aren't they? But your landlady, won't she mind?'

'I'll explain about that. You go and get the cakes.'

'OK.' Celia laughed. 'I feel all excited, seeing you again. I've got such a lot to tell you . . .'

'Me too.' Rita gave her a friendly push in the direction of the door before turning towards Mrs Evans who was regarding her with interest.

'She's talked a lot about you,' said the older woman briskly. 'But business first! Which puppy do you want? We can't keep them for long or they cost us too much to feed so the sooner we're rid of them the better.'

'The dun-coloured one but I'll leave him here until I'm ready to go,' said Rita, and asked advice on what she would need and how to look after him.

When Celia returned the kettle was put on and then she found a chair for Rita.

'This is a nice shop,' she said. 'I take it you have a flat upstairs?'

'For now. But it isn't where I'm going to be living,' said Celia, as if to reassure her friend that she had not gone down in the world. 'My Frank's got a nice little house not far away. He's a widower.'

'How did you meet? You could have knocked me over with a feather when your invitation came.'

Celia told her, adding, 'He's had a sad life has Frank, but he doesn't harp on it like some.'

'So you're happy?' said Rita.

'Oh, yes! Now Andy Pritchard's stopped following me around,' said Celia, and told Rita all about that.

She expressed amazement but only said it was a good job her friend hadn't married him.

Celia agreed before making tea and seeing to Mrs Evans. Then she sat next to Rita and said, 'You're looking well. I take it you haven't strangled Hennie yet?'

'Felt like it but I don't think I ever will now.' Rita bit into a cream and jam cookie and said in a muffled voice, 'I didn't realise how hungry I was. It must be the excitement.'

'The excitement of us meeting up again?' laughed Celia.

Rita swallowed and took a sip of tea. 'Of course! Where's Katherine, by the way?'

Celia's face softened. 'She's back at the Arcadia. It was my idea. I told her the truth about Mick's being her father and she went.'

'And how did she take the truth?'

'She was made up, of course! She was one of that family again, wasn't she? Not that we didn't get on, and she still comes to see me. She's going to be my bridesmaid.'

Rita stared at her. 'I take it your husband-to-be doesn't know the truth?'

Celia's eyes widened. 'What d'you take me for? Of course he knows the truth! Frank's a very understanding man. It's a pity you couldn't find one like him.'

Rita made no answer. 'Is Mrs Mcleod still selling the Arcadia now Katherine's gone back there?'

'How did you know about that?'

Rita explained and so Celia told her about Mick asking her to marry him. 'He didn't really want to, though. I think he did it because he thought it was the right thing to do, but I knew by then we weren't right for each other despite us both wanting to do the best by Katherine. But she's not a little girl any longer and she'll be going to Scotland soon.' A sigh escaped her.

'Scotland? Why?'

'Because of Kitty Mcleod having had a heart attack. I'll miss Katherine, of course, but it's best for her. She's always been fond of them.'

Mrs Evans butted into the conversation. 'She loves Patrick.'

'Who's Patrick?' asked Rita.

Celia looked uncomfortable. 'He's just a lad Katherine knows. She'll get over him.'

Mrs Evans scowled at her. 'How do you know? Just because you got over her father doesn't mean she'll be the same. She doesn't want to go to Scotland and it's wrong to pressurise her into going. You're her mother, you should help her to get what she wants. Mrs Mcleod has a husband to look after her.'

Celia was silent.

'What does Mick say about it?' said Rita.

'I haven't the foggiest idea what he thinks!' said Celia irascibly. 'But I should think, like his mother, he'd want her to do better for herself than marry a photographer!'

'I'd have thought he'd want her happiness above anything else and I'd have believed the same of you until now,' said Rita.

'I *do* want her happy! And it's not that I've got anything against the lad but he does seem to be always getting himself into some scrap or other. Just – just look at this!' Celia got up and went over to the counter and took a newspaper off the pile. She handed it to her friend and put a finger on two photographs. 'That's him – and that!'

Rita stared at two faces and there was a funny feeling inside her.

'Let me see,' said Mrs Evans.

Rita read the words beneath the photographs before handing the newspaper to the old lady. After a couple of minutes she said, 'So that's why he's been missing? You have to show the girl this, Celia.'

'I'll give it to her, if you like,' said Rita, eyeing Celia as she took the newspaper. 'I'm going to the Arcadia. I have something to say to Mrs Mcleod.'

'Well, if she gets to see Patrick,' said Mrs Evans, 'tell her he can have the flat Celia's vacating if he wants it, and to come and see us soon!'

As Rita walked up Mount Pleasant, carrying the puppy and with the copy of the *Daily Post* tucked under her arm, she wondered if she had run mad. It would have been wiser to wait before buying a dog but she had acted on impulse and now was doing the same thing again. She pushed open the door to the hotel and went inside.

Katherine was behind Reception totting up some figures. How efficient she seemed, and how smartly dressed. The girl looked up and smiled and immediately it was like being hit between the eyes because the smile was pure Mick. 'Can I help you?' she said.

'You don't remember me, do you?'

Katherine stared at her and after a moment said slowly, 'The Seaview . . . You're Rita Turner!'

'That's right. I've just been to see your mother.'

'You got your invitation to the wedding?'

'Yes.' She placed the newspaper on the counter and the puppy on the floor. Immediately it wet the carpet. 'Damn!' said Rita ruefully. 'I am sorry.'

'I'll get a cloth. Did she play on your good nature to buy the puppy?'

'No.' Rita smiled. 'Sandy and I fell in love at first sight. I've come to see Mrs Mcleod. Is she in?'

'She's in the kitchen. I'll show you through.'

Rita held her back with one hand. 'There's no need. I know the way and I'll get the cloth and put Sandy in the yard. You read that newspaper on the counter. Celia gave it to me because she thought you might find one of the articles interesting.' She picked up Sandy and went into the kitchen where Kitty was making a pie with tinned golden plums, but she responded swiftly to Rita's request to put the puppy in the yard and asked the younger woman what she could do for her.

Rita was starting to enjoy the look on people's faces when she told them she had come into money and this time was no exception.

'How lovely!' said Kitty, delighted at her good fortune. 'So what are you going to do with it?'

'I'd like to buy the Arcadia.'

'You're joking!'

'Why d'you say that? Don't you think it's a good buy?'

'Of course it is but . . .' Kitty sat down heavily on a

chair. 'Yours is the first offer we've had. I was starting to think . . .'

'You wouldn't sell it? I hope I haven't given you too much of a shock.'

'You have a bit.' Kitty smiled unexpectedly. 'But if you want to buy, I'm selling. Would you like to see over the place now? It's probably the best time for you to come. In a few weeks it's the Grand National which is our busiest time. We generally throw a party for the guests on the day of the race.'

'Sounds fun,' said Rita lightly. 'I presume your staff'll stay? Katie seems very efficient.'

'She is but . . .' Kitty's expression changed. 'I don't think her staying would be a good idea. She expected to take over and I don't think she'd enjoy working under someone else. Besides, I'm going to do bed and breakfast and I need her in Scotland with me.'

'Why?' asked Rita bluntly. 'You managed without her when she wasn't here. Surely you can find a local girl who'll do just as well?'

Suddenly Kitty looked tired and Rita's conscience smote her. 'I'm sorry. I know it's nothing to do with me.'

'Of course it is,' said Kitty slowly. 'My girl knows the Arcadia and our regulars. But we've always worked well together and we don't need words half the time. She knows what I expect of her.'

'What *you* expect? What does she expect of you?'

Kitty looked at Rita. 'What are you trying to say?'

Rita shrugged. 'I'm not sure. I've been to see Celia

and she was telling me you both think Katie can do better for herself than a boy called Patrick.'

'You think I'm being cruel, trying to separate them? He's a teddy boy with one of those haircuts and a leather jacket! I only want what's best for her.'

'Who knows what's best for each of us?'

'I love the girl.' There were tears in Kitty's eyes.

'I'm sure you do. And I've no right to say this – but ask yourself is there a part of you that wants to hurt her even while you're trying to hang on to her? And all because she went with Celia and you fell ill and ended up having a heart attack?'

Kitty gripped her hands together tightly. 'I don't know how you can think that!'

Rita grimaced. 'I know! Terrible of me, isn't it? Perhaps I should come back another day and we can talk about the Arcadia?'

'Yes! I need time to think about whether I want to sell it to you.' She looked up at Rita with unfriendly eyes.

Rita nodded, thinking she had ruined her chances, and went and got Sandy. She left Kitty still sitting in the kitchen staring at the wall.

As soon as she stepped into the lobby Katherine pounced on her. There was a glow about her that had not been there before despite the anxiety in her eyes. 'Do you know what this is all about?' she demanded.

'A boy called Patrick.' Rita smiled. At least she had made someone happy.

'And Mam gave you this?'

'Yes! And the old woman in the shop told me to tell

you that if you get to see him, you're to tell him there's a flat for him over the shop if he wants it.'

'Cool!' She flung the newspaper up in the air.

'You know where to find him then?' said Rita.

'The hospital. Thanks!' She picked up the newspaper. 'Did you see Ma?'

Rita nodded. 'We've still got some unfinished business. But now I'm going to see Mick.'

'Mick?'

Suddenly Rita felt self-conscious and could feel the colour flooding her face. 'He came to see me and I was away.'

'You have his address?' asked Katherine with lively curiosity in her eyes.

'I have his address,' she murmured, and left.

Rita took the beer mat with Mick's address on it from her mock crocodile skin handbag as she came out of the railway station in South Road and walked towards the river. She received no answer when she rang the doorbell so put a note through the letter box and headed for the beach, thinking to return in half an hour and check if he was in before catching the train back to Southport.

The tide was out and the wind was chilly but immediately the puppy began sniffing and tugging on his lead. Rita did not let him run free but huddled into her coat and hung on to him, remembering that when she was young and had played here with her brother there had been patches of sand which had warranted a danger notice. She thought of Mick and Katie and the Arcadia and its mistress and hoped she had not made a complete hash of things. She wanted the hotel badly but perhaps Mick could help her there.

It was on her return journey that Sandy came nose to nose with Nelson. Rita gazed at Mick and felt a warmth inside her which flooded her whole being. 'Hello!'

He reached out his hand and took her free one and held it tightly. 'I'm glad to see you.'

'Likewise.'

'You're looking good. Enjoy the cruise?'

'I could have enjoyed it better. There's nowhere quite like home,' she murmured, shivering slightly in the stiff breeze from the Mersey.

'Doesn't that depend on where home is and who's waiting for you there?'

His dark eyes searched her face and she said unevenly, 'It's a long time since anyone was waiting for me. It can get lonely.'

'I know the feeling.' He cleared his throat. 'Perhaps we should do something about it?'

'If it had been this time a couple of weeks ago last year I could have asked you to marry me,' said Rita boldly.

'It was a leap year?' And he added huskily, 'Ask.'

'Marry me?'

'Yes.' He caught hold of her by the shoulders and pulled her against him and his mouth covered hers in a kiss that expressed his relief and just how much he wanted her.

It was later, when they were in his kitchen feeding the dogs, that she told him about wanting to buy the Arcadia.

'You what?' His face fell. 'Why d'you want to do that? You can't!'

Two spots of colour appeared high on Rita's cheeks. 'There's no need to raise your voice, Mick. I can do what I want with my own money. It would be a good investment and owning a hotel has always been my dream.'

'But – but what about me? I've got this house and I don't want to live at the Arcadia! You can't go buying it, darling!' He put his arms round her. 'I hated the life. We hardly ever had a moment to ourselves and I don't want that for us.'

'I haven't had a yes on it yet.' She rested her head against his shoulder. 'I want Katie and your mother doesn't want me to have her.'

'Scotland!' he groaned.

She looked up into his face. 'I have it from the old lady at the pet shop that Katie doesn't want to go.'

'She wants the Arcadia.'

'I don't blame her but she can't have it. She could have second best, though.' Her voice softened. 'I'd have her living in as deputy manageress. She's young but she knows the business and could be a great help to me.'

Mick was silent a moment. 'You've got it all worked out without a word to me, haven't you?'

'I'm having that word now. I'm nearly forty, Mick! I don't know if I could have children or even if you want them. But I do know I can't sit at home and just be a housewife after working all these years.' He did not speak and after a minute she added, 'I should have said all this before you said yes. I don't know what kind of wife you want?'

He released her reluctantly. 'I want you. I'm not that bothered about babies because I'm pretty sure I'll find them a nuisance. Being the eldest, I remember when . . .' He broke off before continuing, 'Anyway we've got Katie to think about and she's enough at the moment. You say Ma hasn't given you a yes on the Arcadia?'

Rita nodded and told him exactly what had transpired between them and about the newspaper article. He heard her out without interruption, although he shook his head several times. 'So what do you think we should do?' asked Rita, when she had finished.

He rubbed a hand across his eyes. 'Sort it out as soon as possible. Have to speak to Ma – and Katie – on neutral ground. Away from the Arcadia where there would be too many interruptions. I'll get them here tomorrow afternoon on some pretext or other.'

'Phone now then,' said Rita. 'The sooner it's sorted out the better.'

Mick got up and telephoned the Arcadia.

Chapter Twenty-One

Katherine felt she had to tell someone about the article in the newspaper so she could get away for an hour or so to the hospital but knew she could not approach Kitty. She went in search of Jack and found him in the basement making toast in front of the fire.

'Have you seen this?' she said, placing the newspaper on the rug in front of him and stabbing the words beneath Patrick's picture with a trembling finger.

'Seen what?' he murmured, screwing up his eyes as he tried to focus on the page.

'It's Patrick and he's been hurt and I must see him! He's in the Royal!'

Jack handed her the toasting fork and picked up the newspaper, glancing at the date before focusing on the photograph of Patrick's smiling face and the shot next to it showing a bruised and battered one with a black eye. He read swiftly how Patrick had been attending one of the Lord Mayor's social occasions for the *Daily Post* and was on his way home when he saw an old lady about to walk in front of a car. He had pulled her back and in the process been hit himself.

He put down the newspaper and stared at Katherine. 'A hero, hey?'

'Is that all you can say? He's hurt!'

'It says he has a slight concussion and that swelling and bruising will go down within the week. He'll be OK now.'

'How can you say that?' demanded Katherine, flinging the toast on a plate. 'You medical people make light of everything! He'll think I don't care if I don't go and see him. Will you take over Reception for me?'

'If you want, but I doubt he'll be in the Royal now.'

She frowned. 'What do you mean?'

Jack tapped the newspaper. 'This is last week's. He'll have been discharged.'

Katherine snatched up the newspaper and stared at the date and moaned, 'He *will* think I don't care!'

'There's nothing stopping you from seeing him now.'

She flopped down into a chair. 'I don't know where he lives.'

'What?' Jack picked up the butter knife.

'I just never got round to getting his address. He used to call at the pet shop and I'd cross over to the photographer's when I wanted him for something.'

'Well, of all the harebrained ways to carry on!' Jack's teeth crunched into toast. 'Vicky could get it for you.'

Katherine sat up straight and there was a hopeful gleam in her eyes. 'Of course! The hospital'll have records.'

'Of course they'll have records. I'll be seeing her tomorrow. She'll be able to get you the information on Monday.'

Katherine's body sagged and she moaned, 'I've got to wait until Monday?'

'Patience, my child.' He patted her head. 'We'll get him sorted out but it's you that'll have to sort Ma out if you decide not to go to Scotland because of him.'

All the effervescence went out of her and she stood up. 'I'll have to get back to work but don't you forget what you're doing for me!' She left the basement, intending to talk to Kitty, but there was no sign of her anywhere. When she asked John where she was, he said she had been feeling tired and had gone to bed.

It was much later after meals and bedtime drinks were over that Katherine went upstairs to see how Kitty was. Her hand was raised to knock on the door when she heard her voice saying, 'I can't leave her behind, John! I can't!'

Katherine's heart sank, thinking, She can only be talking about me and Scotland! Oh, hell! She stepped back and stumbled over a ridge in the carpet. The door opened and John stood there. 'How's Ma?' she said swiftly, thinking she was having as much trouble calling Kitty Grandma as she'd had with calling Celia Mum.

'Still resting,' he said, giving her a smile but looking tired himself. 'I've got a message for you, lassie. Mick phoned earlier. He wants you to go and see him tomorrow afternoon.'

'What for? It's Sunday! He generally comes here.'

'Says he wants to throw a party and wants yours and Ma's advice but I've decided she can't go. He said that's OK. You'll do.'

She was astonished but pleased. 'There's flattery for you! But what's he throwing a party for? Is it anything to do with that Rita Turner?'

John's expression changed and he frowned. 'He said a house-warming. Why should you think Miss Turner has anything to do with it?'

'She was going to see him. He'd been to see her, apparently.'

'I see,' said John with slow deliberation, and without another word closed the bedroom door.

Katherine turned and went into her own room, thinking of Mick and Rita and whether the party might be to announce their engagement. She had not forgotten the way Rita had blushed when she had mentioned Mick's name. She could not wait to find out.

Katherine had never thought she would be glad to get away from the Arcadia but she had not slept well, dreaming she was looking for something she could not find though she did not know what. As well as that there had been an atmosphere all morning and dinner had been a nightmare with Kitty grim-faced and untalkative, so that Katherine felt she could not approach her. In the end she had made a telephone call and vanished upstairs which meant Katherine had to cope with just the help of the two men so both she and Jack were late leaving the house.

She caught a bus to Skelhorne Street that took her to Waterloo. To her annoyance when she reached Mick's house there was no answer to her rat-a-tat on the door knocker but she could hear a dog barking. The back gate proved to be only on the latch so she went through into the small walled garden to be greeted by Nelson.

'Where's your master?' she demanded. The dog

answered her with a woof and capered round her before going over to the gate and barking. 'You want a run, do you?'

He woofed again, so after peering through the windows and trying the back door, Katherine reopened the gate and went out with him. When she reached the front of the house she took out a pencil and a used envelope and wrote on the back of it and posted it through the letter box. Then she headed for the beach.

Nelson was away with her in pursuit, the ends of her long scarf flying in the breeze. Her spirits lifted and she decided it was real cool Mick's house being so near the river. The sand stretched for what seemed miles. The tide was out and the sea and sky seemed to merge into one. She thought of Patrick and his poor bruised face, and of Ma looking like death, and wished there was an easy answer to her dilemma. What if Patrick no longer wanted her? That would be a miserable way out of her problem. But what if Ma died? That would be another. Katherine shivered at the thought. She did not want her to die.

She gazed across the sand to where the waves lapped the shore and saw a dredger and a liner making their way towards Liverpool. She watched them a moment and then began to look for pretty seashells but could only spot cockleshells with the odd razor amongst the broken glass and a few bits of washed up wood and scraps of seaweed at the tide line.

Nelson came flying up the beach with something in his mouth. He dropped it at her feet and she saw it was a blue rubber ball, one of those solid ones that can bounce really high on a pavement but not here on the beach. He was jumping up at her, letting out little yelps. She threw the ball and he went skittering after it.

'Enjoying yourself, are yer?'

Katherine jumped and whirled round and stared into the bloodshot eyes in the unshaven, ruddy face of Andy Pritchard. He wore a pith helmet and a sort of tunic with baggy leggings and well-worn cracked boots. Her heart bumped uncomfortably against her ribs because he looked so weird. She made no answer but instead ran after Nelson. What was Pritchard doing here? He must have followed her from Liverpool. She did not really believe he could do anything to her here in the open because there were a few other people around but decided to keep as much space between him and her as possible. She glanced over her shoulder and saw he was coming after her, not running but marching, left, right, left, right, as if he was still in the army.

She felt apprehensive because there was something disturbing about that figure and so she increased her speed, picking up the ball as Nelson brought it to her and throwing it on the run. Then two things happened at once. She heard her name being called and the ball disappeared into one of those patches of sand that Mick had once mentioned but which she'd forgotten about until now.

Katherine screamed at the dog even as he leapt after the ball but it was too late. He landed and immediately began to struggle and being only a little dog was sinking fast. She did the only thing she felt she could and went in after him.

She caught him up and held his trembling body against her chest. Realising she was up to the top of her thighs in the horrible soft, sticky mud and sand, she instantly froze. She had heard tales of sinking sands, seen films of swamps and read of quakemires in Devon where ponies and grown men disappeared in a swirl of bubbles never to be seen again, but she had never believed it could happen to her.

Andy Pritchard stamped to a halt on the edge of the patch of sand and his grin was wicked. 'So how're you going to get out of there, girl? Isn't funny, is it? Just like what you did to me wasn't funny. I wanted Celia, I did, but you had to go and spoil things. I hope you die!'

'You're sick,' she said in a trembling voice.

'I've no effing money and I'm going to lose the shop!' Tears came to his eyes and Katherine stared at him, feeling embarrassed, disbelieving and scared. 'I'm sorry but that's not my fault.' She heaved the struggling dog up in her arms and sank a few more inches. She bit hard on her lip before saying, 'Could you take him? He hasn't done you any harm.'

Andy did not move. 'Perhaps it *is* meant for you to die here. Not a nice death!' He added in staccato tones, 'There's someone coming this way. Perhaps they'll help you but you might be under by then.' He turned and marched away.

Katherine screamed as she sank a few more inches but the next moment Mick was there accompanied by a limping Patrick with his face still bruised. 'I wish I had my camera with me,' he said in a joky voice. 'But I suppose we'd better get you out of there.'

'Please!' Now was not the time to ask how he had got here.

'Throw Nelson to me,' said Mick, kneeling and stretching out his arms.

It was not an easy order to comply with because the dog's claws were now caught up in her scarf but somehow she managed to free him and propel him towards those straining fingers and to push so hard he flew through the air the necessary foot. In the process she sank several more inches and scared herself silly.

'Your scarf,' rasped Patrick as Mick dropped Nelson unceremoniously on to the sand before turning his attention once more to his daughter.

They watched as Katherine unwound the scarf. She thanked God for the fashion which had dictated Mrs Evans should knit it at least six feet long and in a drop stitch which stretched. She threw, not aiming straight along the surface where it might flop into the mud but up in the air. Patrick caught it and took it a turn about his arm and Mick gripped a handful of it too. Then they heaved with all their might. She was aware of an excruciating pain in her wrist, of sand and slime against her cheek. The stitches stretched and stretched as, slowly and inexorably, she was pulled free.

She lay on firm ground with her breasts heaving and her breath coming fast. She took fistfuls of sand and suddenly was crying. Then the two men were hoisting her to her feet and Patrick said with a tender smile on his face, 'I don't know what you're crying for?'

'I must look terrible,' she wailed.

'Awful!' And he took her in his arms and kissed her dirty face before hugging her while she half laughed, half sobbed on his shoulder.

'That's love for you,' said Mick dryly, standing with his hands on his hips and staring at them with a tolerant expression before turning and gazing after the marching figure of Andy Pritchard. 'What the hell was that bloke thinking of, leaving you here?'

'That's Mr Pritchard – the man Celia nearly married,' sniffed Katherine, lifting her head. 'I think he's gone loopy. He followed her around for a while but now he's started on me.'

'We'll soon put a stop to that,' said Mick, chin jutting aggressively.

'You and me both,' said Patrick, releasing Katherine.

'No, you don't! You're not safe to be allowed out on your own!' She caught hold of him and wrapped her arms round his waist.

'Look who's talking! You're a real mess!' He kissed her again.

'That's why we need each other,' she said, rubbing her wet eyes against his jacket.

'So you're definitely not going to Scotland?' His words were muffled against her hair.

'No. I don't know how I'm going to tell Ma but I'm staying here.'

'That's my girl,' said Patrick, kissing her again. 'I'd come to tell you I'd move up there but I'd rather stay in my own patch for now.'

'So you weren't cross with me for not visiting you in hospital?'

'Disappointed, but I guessed that you mightn't have known about it. Now, let's get you away from here and back to the house.'

It was an hour later. Katherine had bathed and washed her hair and now, wearing a pair of Mick's pyjamas and thick socks, was curled up in a corner of the sofa in front of the fire, dunking bread into a bowl of Heinz Scotch Broth. Patrick was sitting on a stool with her feet in his lap, drinking tea, and Mick and Rita sat close to each other at the other end of the sofa. A telephone call had come from Kitty a short while ago saying she would be with them in half an hour. Ben and Sarah were bringing her in the car and she hoped it was not inconvenient.

'What on earth does Ma mean by inconvenient?' said Mick, tapping his fingers on Rita's arm. 'I did ask her here last night . . .'

'Perhaps it's because she knows I'm here?' said Patrick.

'I can't understand that!' burst out Katherine. 'She actually told you where I was?'

'That's what I said,' he drawled. 'She even gave me Mick's number so I could telephone and tell him I was coming. I didn't want to arrive here and get the door slammed in my face.'

'Patrick was why we weren't in,' said Rita, smiling at Katherine. 'We thought you might both have been on the same train so we walked to meet you.'

'And I went and caught the bus! You must have only just missed me at the Arcadia, love,' said Katherine to Patrick.

'I wish I hadn't. You wouldn't have ended up in that horrible sinking sand because that terrible bloke was following you.'

'Well, that's the last you've seen of him, Katie,' said Mick. 'I told him I'd knock his block off if we saw hide or hair of him again.'

'You didn't hit him?' said Rita.

'I grabbed hold of him and he started crying!' There was a disgusted note in Mick's voice. 'I tell you, I couldn't believe it of a big bloke like that. But he told me the shop didn't belong to his sister as he'd thought but was only leased, and as he hadn't been paying any money over since she died they've told him to get out.'

'And all for the want of Celia,' murmured Katherine. 'Incredible!'

Mick and Rita smiled. 'You warm enough now?' she said to Katherine.

She was just about to say as warm as toast when the knocker went. The four exchanged glances and Mick got up and left the room.

Katherine made to sit up straight but Patrick put a hand over her feet and said, 'She knows we're a couple and there's nothing sinful about you resting your feet on me.'

'I know!' she whispered. 'But I've never taken up such a pose in Ma's company.' She glanced at Rita. 'What d'you think she's come for? It can't really be to talk about a party?'

'It's probably about the Arcadia,' said Rita in a low voice. 'I want to buy it but I want you to stay and work for me.'

Katherine felt a rush of pleasure. 'You want me?'

'Well, you're going to be my stepdaughter, aren't you?'

'So a wedding is in the wind?' said a voice from the doorway.

Katherine twisted her head and saw Kitty standing there, and despite what Patrick had said, she swung her feet on to the floor and stood up. So did Rita and Patrick.

'How cosy it looks in here,' said Kitty, her gaze passing serenely over them. 'I think I'd like a house like this.'

They stared at her in astonishment and Katherine noticed she did not have her stick. 'But –' she began.

Her grandmother did not let her finish. 'John and I have decided the house in Scotland is much too big for us. What do I want to carry on working for at my age? I did think that maybe Wendy could have helped me out but when Ben and Sarah told me they've started a baby, I thought, what are we doing going so far away from everyone? Even Jack's no longer up there in Scotland.'

'But – but what about Pops?' blurted out Katherine, keeping a hold on Mick's pyjama bottoms to stop them falling down. 'He likes walking the hills.'

'He's having trouble with his knees.' Kitty looked over her spectacles at her. 'What's them you're wearing? No, don't tell me! I suppose I should be glad you've found yourself a boy who'll come to your rescue and cares about old ladies. He tells me St Patrick is the patron saint of Protestants *and* Catholics in Ireland and he comes from a mixed marriage himself.'

'You asked him?' she said, bristling slightly.

'Of course I didn't! I hardly know the lad yet. Vicky told him it was something I was concerned about. But just because I've accepted him, there's no need to go rushing into marriage. You've still got some growing up to do, my girl!'

'Yes, Grandma,' said Katherine meekly.

'What about the Arcadia?' asked Rita.

Kitty's eyes twinkled. 'I presume you two will be working there? We're going to sell the Scottish house and buy a plot of land in Formby not far from Ben. He'll build us a bungalow, and if you ever find you can't cope, I can give you a hand.' She got no further because Katherine rushed over to her and began dancing her round, regardless of the drooping pyjamas.

Ben, Sarah and Mick were now able to enter the room and suddenly everybody seemed to be talking at once. Patrick watched with a smile on his face and reaching for his camera, focused and took his first family shot.

The flash caused everyone to freeze for a moment before resuming their conversations but Kitty took the opportunity to tell Katherine and Mick that although she was not ready yet to throw in the sponge, it had been a bit of a day and she would appreciate a sit in front of the fire and a stiff whisky.

Katherine led her over to the sofa and Patrick's camera flashed again. As he lowered it she caught his eye and they both smiled. Pure joy bubbled inside her because she knew now exactly where she belonged.

Also available from Ebury Press:

EMMA'S WAR

By Rosie Clarke

All she wanted was her husband to come home . . .

Newly married to the caring RAF pilot Jonathan
Reece, Emma thinks that life couldn't be better. But
her happiness is short-lived: within months, Jon's plane
is shot down over France and he is declared missing,
presumed dead.

Alone and with two children to care for, Emma's first
thought is how to support her family. But when she
makes a new friend in the American businessman Jack
Harvey, she is faced with a difficult decision. Should she
take a last chance at happiness?

EBURY
PRESS

Also available from Ebury Press:

THE FACTORY GIRL

By Maggie Ford

From rags to riches . . .

With the Armistice only a few months passed, times are hard for eighteen-year-old Geraldine Glover. A machinist at Rubins clothing factory in the East End, she dreams of a more glamorous life.

When she meets Tony Hanford, the young and handsome proprietor of a small jeweller's shop in Bond Street, Geraldine is propelled into a new world – but it comes at a heavy price . . .

EBURY
PRESS